Young Ted Smith, growing up in the smoke of the Potteries, has only one ambition, to sail in ships, like his brother Joseph. Beginning his nautical career at seventeen, he graduates from 'boy' to officer, from climbing the rigging on sailing-ships to manning the bridge of transatlantic liners. And then comes the climax of his career as he is put in command of the *Titanic*.

Told by the captain's great-great-niece, this biographical novel is seamlessly enhanced with imaginary characters and incidents – but nothing can detract from the ensuing reality: by the time Captain Smith says goodbye to his wife and daughter and sets off on his last voyage before retirement, we know and admire the man; we know what will happen on the *Titanic's* maiden voyage – we even know why. The result of years of research, this is a wonderful true story of travel and adventure, of romance and love, of a man who lives his life to the full – this is the story behind the greatest sea tragedy the world has ever known.

Pat Lacey is the great-great-niece of Captain E. J. Smith, Master of the *Titanic*, descended from his half-sister Thirza. She grew up in Abergavenny and took early retirement from the Civil Service to write. Now living with her husband and her border collie in rural Buckinghamshire, she is the author of eight previous novels and countless articles and short stories.

MASTER OF THE TITANIC

Pat Lacey

The Book Guild Ltd.
Sussex, England

The Book Guild Ltd.
25 High Street,
Lewes, Sussex

First published 1996
First published in paperback 1997
© Pat Lacey 1996

Set in Meridien

Typesetting by Wordset
Hassocks, West Sussex

Printed in Great Britain by
Antony Rowe Ltd.
Chippenham, Wiltshire.

A catalogue record for this book is
available from the British Library

ISBN 1 85776 221 5

This Book is Dedicated to my Mentor

Patricia Wendorff

1

Even though she'd read the letter countless times since its arrival by the morning post, Catherine Smith smiled in anticipation as she drew it from her apron pocket. To share it with Edward and Thirza would renew her pleasure.

In truth, it could hardly be called a letter. Six lines only, written in Joseph's careful copperplate.

'"Somewhere in the Indian Ocean"' she read aloud, then glanced up, her face alight with laughter. 'Do you mind how he used to give me latitude and longitude?' Accustomed to figures she might be, through practice at her accounts, but she was no navigator, and the jumble of symbols and numbers had sent her scurrying to the old map she'd pinned upon the wall. Not that she always wanted to know where he was. When he'd first come home, youthful pride had led him to tell of the dreadful winds and towering seas of the Horn, where even a barque of a thousand tons like his, could be tossed like a cockleshell from one gigantic wave to the next. Along with his mates, he'd boasted, he'd been sent aloft to the very top of the rigging, where his task had been to gather up the wet canvas of the sails and furl it to the yards. 'But what,' she'd asked, her voice faint with dread, 'if you were to slip and fall?'

She could still remember his reply, delivered with all the importance of his seventeen years. 'If I weren't dead *afore*, Ma, I would be when I hit the deck!'

'So what does he say, Ma?' Thirza was growing impatient. Bonnet and cloak already donned, she was waiting to run down Well Street to see her friend Anne Bebbington.

'"Dearest Mother, Father and Thirza,"' – Catherine

7

smiled briefly at her husband. It always pleased him when Joseph called him 'Father' instead of 'Step-father'. Joseph's real father, a potter like her present husband had died of consumption when the boy was no more than four and Thirza just a baby. She continued to read: " 'Today, we have seen dolphins and flying fish. We steer now for the Cape of Good Hope with a cargo of rice and grain. I say my prayers daily and think of you all often. Your affectionate son and brother, Joseph Hancock." '

The missive bore no date other than the year, 1854. Either Joseph had not considered it important or had not known it. So there was no way of telling how long the letter had taken and when he might be expected home. But not, clearly, for Christmas.

As Catherine returned the letter to her apron pocket and Thirza opened the kitchen door, there came the sound of a muffled sob. Thirza ran to the foot of the stairs.

'Teddy, whatever's the matter?' A moment later, she was back, a weeping child in her arms. 'There, there!' Quickly, she transferred him into his mother's outstretched arms. 'Ma, I must go. Anne will be waiting.'

'Don't be late home!'

'Am I ever?' And then she was gone, her cloak billowing behind her, her heels clacking through the shop, between the sacks of flour and sugar, the chests of tea and out into the wintry gloom of Well Street.

'What is it, son?' But already, comforted by the strength of his mother's arms and the sight of his father smiling at him from the depths of his old chair, his tears had dried.

'You didn't read *my* letter, Ma! The one Joseph wrote to *me*!'

'Because I had thought you already asleep, my pet, as little boys should be at this hour on Christmas Eve.'

'I'm sorry, Ma. I did try.'

'Let me have him, my love,' his Father offered, 'while you read him his letter.'

He went willingly, finding the warmth of his father's waistcoat preferable to the starched crispness of his mother's apron. And if luck was on his side, Pa would bounce him on his knee in his favourite game. 'This is the way the lady rides!' — smooth and quiet, Pa's knees hardly flexing. And 'This is the way the butcher boy rides!' — uneven, knees moving like pistons. 'And this is the way the farmer rides!' — clutching at Pa's beard for support, shrieking with mirth, he would be bounced higher and higher until Pa ran out of breath. But first, there was the letter.

' "My dear Teddy," ' his mother read, ' "I am writing this in the first dog watch." '

'That's four to six in the afternoon,' Teddy explained kindly to his father.

'Indeed? Thank you!'

' "It's a hot, sunny day and I am lying on the fo'castle deck." ' Teddy opened his mouth, then closed it. Joseph hadn't yet explained 'fo'castle' to him. ' "This morning, a schooner passed on our starboard bow." '

'That's to the right.'

' "At her masthead, she flew the skull and crossbones." '

'Pirates!' shrieked Teddy ecstatically, his heels drumming on his father's shins.

His father looked suitable impressed. 'Is that so?'

Catherine glanced up from the letter to frown at her husband. 'Not only is Joseph filling the child with nonsensical rubbish but you are compounding the falsehood!'

'Not a falsehood! It's not rubbish! It *was* a pirate!'

'Teddy that's enough! Pray, continue, my love. Perhaps it *was* a pirate in this case.'

Perhaps pigs could fly! She knew her son. However, she continued. After all, it was Christmas.

' "I pointed her out to the captain, who studied her through his glass." '

'That's not a real glass, that's a *'tellyscope.'*

' "Why, 'tis the ghost of Captain Kidd, himself!" said the captain.'

Catherine raised her eyes to heaven, but continued, ' "I looked more closely and found the captain was right. It was a ghost ship. Even as I watched, her sails floated away like

9

a silver cloud and her hull vanished in a puff of smoke."'

'I'll give him silver clouds and puffs of smoke,' Catherine muttered, for Teddy's eyes were like saucers, his thumb rigid in his mouth, his heels stilled. 'Heaven alone knows when we'll get the child off to sleep, now!'

'Is there no more?' her husband asked hopefully.

He was as bad as Joseph! 'Yes,' she said decisively, 'there's more!'

Fingers crossed inside the pocket of her apron, she called upon her own imagination. Two could play at this game.

'"I hope that you continue to be a good boy and perform diligently those tasks your mother sets you . . ."'

'I don't remember this bit, Ma! What's 'dillygently?' His mother, as his father put it, was the 'brains of the family'. It was she who read to him from the much-thumbed copy of *Pickwick Papers* that lived in the dresser cupboard. However, it was his father who answered him now.

'It means doing what your mother tells you, son. Tidying away your blocks. Washing behind your ears.'

Swiftly, he decided to ignore the delicate matter of his ears, which were much too available for inspection. 'I always put away my blocks, Pa,' he said virtuously. He could see them now, on the dresser, where he'd stacked them only that afternoon. Twenty-six of them, his mother said, although he could only count up to ten of them, as yet, and each with a letter painted on its sides, so that soon he would be able to read his own letters from Joseph. A sudden thought struck him.

'Pa, there are no post offices in the ocean, so how did my letter come?' Ma, although the 'brains', was not as knowledgeable as Pa about everything.

'A passing ship, perhaps? And taking a shorter route home than Joseph's.'

He nodded, then turned back to his mother. 'Anything else, Ma?' he asked hopefully.

Relenting, Catherine smiled at him. 'Just his love, Teddy. And he wishes you a happy Christmas.'

Christmas! He had almost forgotten Christmas! He snuggled

10

deeper into his father's waistcoat, wondering how best to postpone the moment when his mother would send him back upstairs. It certainly wasn't the time to suggest the horse game. Adult conversation might be the anwer. 'We've been very busy in the shop today, Pa,' he said innocently.

His father looked pleased. 'You've been helping your mother then, Teddy?'

'Yes, I counted out the oranges. And the eggs. And didn't drop a single one.'

'Good lad,' And then, as he'd hoped, his mother took up the story.'

'Folk have been asking for thread, Edward. And needles. I wondered if perhaps we should stock a small quantity?'

'If there seems the demand, my dear, and it doesn't put anyone else out of business. How did the extra tea go?'

'Surprisingly well! A Christmas treat, perhaps. And prices will grow cheaper, Joseph says, as the clipper ships compete one with another.'

They were talking about Thirza now; his pretty little half-sister who delighted in telling him, when his mother was not within earshot, about the pranks she and Joseph had played upon each other when they were young. Sometimes, he wished that he had a 'whole' brother or sister of his own, but soon he'd be going to school and it was good to have his mother to himself all day, to look forward to his father coming home from the potbank in the evening and Thirza from the Hanley dressmakers. Not that Thirza would be here much longer. Soon, she'd be marrying her Mr Harrington and setting up house on her own.

'Marrying well, is Thirza,' he'd heard his mother confiding to someone in the shop. 'William fits engines at the works.'

Drowsily, Teddy decided to abandon listening in favour of thinking – about Joseph, the gentle, golden-haired giant whom, he sometimes thought, he loved more than his parents. But 'honour thy father and thy mother', he was

11

taught in Sunday School and 'honour' certainly wasn't the word to describe how he felt about Joseph. Hugging him tightly, swinging him up 'aloft' to balance on his broad shoulders or describing life on the ocean wave, Joseph represented all that was exciting in life. It seemed to Teddy that to be at sea on a three-masted barque was the most wonderful thing that could happen to anyone. Fighting off sleep with all his might, he hoped fervently that Joseph would be home before he started school. He wouldn't want to miss a moment of his company.

Suddenly, it seemed as if he was already on the high seas, one moment wallowing deep in the trough of a wave, the next high on its crest.

But it was his father having one of his 'turns', shoulders hunched over his chest, his whole body racked with a fit of violent coughing.

'That old potbank!' he heard his mother mutter. 'Here, Edward, let me have him.'

He felt himself lifted from his father's lap. And this time, knew he'd be back in bed before he could say 'Jack Robinson'. Whoever Jack Robinson was. He must ask Joseph . . .

2

'Jack Robinson?' Joseph scratched his head. 'I don't rightly know, Teddy. Have you asked Ma?'

'She doesn't know, either. Nor Pa. Nor Thirza.'

'Well then, I reckon it's something you'll have to ask your teacher when you start school. Ma says you'll soon be going to the British.'

'Yes, behind the chapel. Will you take me on my first day, Joseph?'

'Captain won't be able to manage without me till then, Teddy. I'm only here now because of those perishing pirates.'

For Joseph, to his mother's quiet amusement once she had assured herself that he was unharmed, had been hoist with his own petard: attacked by pirates and all his possessions taken, even his second mate's certificate.

'Will you take me to Liverpool, Joseph?' Teddy was sitting on the rag rug and playing with the little wooden sailor Joseph had carved for him.

'Not this trip, Teddy. What would you do while I was talking to the Examiner?'

'I could talk to him, too. Tell about the pirates.'

'There'll be other things for me to do. Find a new uniform, for a start. Sign on again. But I'll take you one day, that's a promise.'

'Joseph, did the pirates really wear black patches over their eyes?'

'They certainly did. And the captain had a hook for a hand. It was early on the morning of the fourteenth of May when the corsairs came over the horizon. Becalmed off the

13

Barbary coast, we were. A sitting duck if ever there was one . . .'

Even Ma wasn't exactly sure what had happened on the morning of the fourteenth of May 1856, but certainly Joseph had come home with only the clothes he stood up in. And without his precious certificate. He had to compose a special letter about it, which he was doing now with Ma's help.

Off he went, then, to Liverpool and the Sailors' Home for a few days, and Teddy moped about the house – 'like a wet wakes week', his mother said. But when Joseph came back, he was smart in his new uniform, and brought presents to replace those stolen by the pirates: combs for Catherine and Thirza, a scarf for his father, and for Teddy, a tiny brass telescope that actually magnified when he held it to his eye. He scanned everything, from Joseph in bed in the morning to Mrs Marsh's cat cleaning its paws in the cake shop window.

'When are you off again?' His mother asked the inevitable question.

'A couple of weeks, Ma. The *Davy Fleming*, second mate.'

So – they must have given him another certificate. Secretly, Teddy was relieved. Even though *he* believed everything Joseph told him, he knew that others didn't, his mother for one. And he'd been just a little worried that the Examiner wouldn't either. But clearly he had.

'What shall we do today?' he asked, as he always did, whenever Joseph was home. It never occurred to him that Joseph might wish to spend time in other company.

'Joseph may want to see his friends, Teddy,' his mother intervened. 'He's twenty-four years old, after all, and not bad looking.' What did that signify? *He* was six and still, to his extreme annoyance, called a 'pretty little lad' by his mother's friends.

But Joseph seemed to know what his mother meant. 'The sea's no place for a wife, Ma. Not till you're a master and can have her with you. I thought Teddy and I might walk to the station at Etruria, watch the trains go by, and breathe some pure air on the high ground near the big house while we're about it. That suit you, Teddy?'

Would it not! The double pleasure of Joseph's company and the opportunity to stand on the station platform enveloped in a cloud of smutty, black steam!

The afternoon more than fulfilled its promise. Not only did they see a train arrive at Etruria from Stoke – three lucky passengers boarding, one dismounting – they also visited the wharf to gaze at the colliery barges fussing up and down the canal.

'I've heard there are many steamships at sea, now, Joseph,' he said knowledgeably, as they climbed the open ground towards Etruria Hall, where Mr Wedgwood had once lived. 'Pa was talking to the Minister about them the other day.'

Joseph snorted. 'Dirty, ugly things! Defiling God's pure air with their stinking black funnels. I tell you, Teddy, there's nothing can measure up to the glory of topsails billowing against a clear blue sky.'

'No, Joseph, course not!'

But doubts niggled. So far, the only topsails he'd seen were those on the little barque in the green glass bottle Joseph had brought home for Ma after his first voyage, before Teddy was even born, and which now lived on the topmost shelf of the kitchen dresser. Although he would have been hard put to find the words to describe how he felt, he knew that there was something about the might and power of steam that appealed to him, and unlike the winds, which, even Joseph admitted, could be wayward and unpredictable, man could control its power.

Each wrapped in his own thoughts, they walked in silence until Joseph paused and looked around him. 'Let's sit here for a while, Teddy, and admire the bottle kilns belching their foul smoke into the lungs of good Hanley folk.'

He'd made his point well. A shawl of smoke swathed the chimney-pots of the town. But here, the sun shone and larks carolled high above their heads. Joseph stretched out on the turf in the shade of a scrub oak and Teddy quickly joined him. Peace reigned, eyelids drooped. And then, suddenly Joseph sat bolt upright, a finger to his lips, and pointed towards a stand of hazel wands.

Something had moved. Joseph was sure of it. Muscles flexing inside his shirt – too hot for his new reefer, he'd decided, but he still wore his new trousers – he sat back on his heels and waited.

There was little that Second Mate Joseph Hancock wasn't ready for. In truth, he was eager for a fight. And although three o'clock of a summer afternoon seemed an unlikely time for a bout of fisticuffs, he wasn't altogether surprised. Some of the glances he'd intercepted on his way here had been mocking to say the least.

'Liverpool Limey!' one of the more daring of the youths hanging around the corner of Well Street had sniggered as he and Teddy passed. If it hadn't been for the proximity of his mother in the shop, he'd have had it out with them then and there. He glanced down at Teddy; fists clenched, the lad was gazing across at the hazel wands, then peeping up at Joseph, clearly waiting for him to make the first move.

Rising to his full height – six foot two if he was an inch – he ambled aimlessly towards the trees, even bending to pluck a daisy head or two as he went. Let them think him a complete ninny, fit only to make daisy chains for the child!

As he drew near, a profound stillness settled upon the leaves. With a sudden, abrupt movement, he pulled back the branches, at the same time snapping out, 'Up with you, varmints!'

The next moment, he was standing there with his mouth open, his eyes wide with astonishment and, perhaps for the first time in his life, deprived of speech.

Crouched in front of him was a girl. How old she might be was difficult to determine. There were none of the signs that would normally have guided him. Her hair – of a rich, chestnut hue – was neither hanging loose nor arranged in the tortured ringlets inflicted by some mothers upon their young daughters; but neither was it coiled around her head as Thirza wore hers. Instead, it was strained back behind

16

her ears into a single braid which hung almost to her waist. He was reminded of the pigtails worn by the Chinamen on the wharfs of Fuchow, except that theirs had been short and skinny and glistening with oil. Hers was thick as his wrist with, here and there, strands escaping into clusters of tiny curls – like a piece of frayed rigging, he thought fancifully before his eyes moved to her face. There, it was the expression that intrigued him the most: defiance – the chin raised, the dark eyes giving him stare for stare – and eagerness, satisfaction almost, as if to be discovered crouched behind a hazel bush on a summer's day was part of some deliberate plan.

Slowly, gracefully, she rose to her feet, and he saw that her gown, of some soft, sprigged material that clung to her small breasts, was neither as full nor as long as those Thirza wore, but gave her freedom of movement. Now the girl was brushing leaves and twigs from her skirt, and he saw that she wore a pair of men's boots, thick-soled, with sensible lace-up fronts. Her brother's perhaps? And yet these were no cast-offs, worn and scuffed by their previous owner. These were new and shiny and well cared for.

While he stared, the girl suddenly hitched up her skirt to show a shapely and white-stockinged ankle, and extended it for closer inspection, 'Shin up your sails like a monkey, you could, in a pair of these, sailor! But you're not having them!'

Astonishment that she should know of his calling fought with an urgent desire to correct her faulty knowledge of seamanship. The latter won. 'You don't shin up sails,' he reprimanded sternly. 'If you shin up anything, it's the masts or the ratlines.'

'Suit yourself!' She shrugged. 'You're still not having my boots for the purpose.'

'Joseph has his own boots, thank you,' piped up a clear if slightly wobbly voice behind them.

Teddy! He'd quite forgotten him! He turned quickly. The lad was standing, arms akimbo, staring at the girl, his eyes hostile. 'I saw you in the shop yesterday,' he accused.

17

'Nothing wrong with my money, is there? Your ma didn't seem to find it so anyway.'

'You asked where Joseph was. If he'd gone back to sea again.'

That pulled her up short, but only for a moment. 'Just something to say, that was all, while your ma weighed the sugar.'

'*I* weighed the sugar!'

Suddenly she laughed, putting back her head and showing white, slightly irregular teeth. And Joseph found himself laughing with her. For there was something comical about Teddy's indignation.

But their combined mirth was too much for Teddy. His face puckered and his eyes filled with tears. 'I *did* weigh the sugar, Joseph! I *did*!'

The girl reached him even before Joseph. Down on her knees once more, she put her arms around him and held him tightly. 'There, there, my pet! Of course you weighed the sugar. And did it well. Real proud of you, your ma was. As proud,' she sat back on her heels now, mopping at Teddy's cheeks with the handkerchief she'd pulled from her sleeve, 'as she is of Joseph.'

Joseph, who knew full well that his mother, in spite of her occasional scolding, considered him to be a cross between Christopher Columbus and Sir Francis Drake, with perhaps a touch of Lord Nelson thrown in, maintained a modest silence.

'She's prouder of Joseph than me. He *does* things,' Teddy protested.

'So do you, my pet. And one day, you'll do even more.' She was sitting now on the grass, Teddy pulled down beside her.

Joseph coiled himself beside them. 'Why did you follow me?' he asked.

For a moment, such was her obvious displeasure that he thought she would leap to her feet and go; he actually put out a hand to restrain her. But then she began pulling at a tuft of grass with furious fingers. 'I did no such thing. I just

18

happened to be sitting here when you arrived.'

'What? Hiding behind a bush?' he mocked and then suddenly realised that she could, indeed, have been hiding behind the bush for a purpose that no gentleman would ever dream of mentioning to a lady, and felt the blood rise in his cheeks. 'I beg your − ' he began foolishly.

She interrupted him with a hoot of mirth, clearly guessing his thoughts. 'Well, all right,' she admitted. 'I heard you talking to your ma this morning when I came in to buy candles. But I didn't follow you. I got here first and hid. Not that I was afraid. I just didn't know how to start asking you what it was like.'

He was nonplussed. 'What *what* was like?'

'The sea, of course.' She gazed at him expectantly.

'It's − it's − all right,' he said at last and was immediately struck by the lameness of the phrase. 'All right' was how he usually summed up his state of health when people enquired. It certainly wasn't an adequate description of how he felt when they hit the open sea and he shouted commands to the tiny, monkey-like creatures aloft, knowing they would be obeyed but remembering, too, that a good officer never permitted a lust for power to affect his judgement and that a happy ship was a just ship. And in truth, on such a ship, 'all' was gloriously 'right', even when becalmed in the doldrums or enduring the hell of Cape Horn. But how to convey this rightness to the girl sitting beside him who, in the most flattering fashion, seemed willing to hang on to his every word? He decided to play for time.

'Why do you want to know?'

Her reply came without hesitation. 'Because I long to travel in a ship. To see the world, the places I've only heard or read about.'

'You've attended school, then?' The question was not impolite. Many of his shipmates hadn't, and were none the worse for it. His own education, in Penkhull, had been patchy; days at the dame school when his parents could afford them, and Sunday school, of course. At sea, he'd acquired his knowledge through grim experience.

19

But, 'Of course I've been to school!' replied his new acquaintance, although she didn't say which one.

'*I'm* going to go to the British,' Teddy put in. The girl already had him comfortably settled in the crook of her arm, and now she picked up the end of her braid and used it to swat a bluebottle that was buzzing around his head.

'Are you, love? I hear Mr Smith's a lovely man.'

'How old are you?' Joseph suddenly dared to ask.

She grinned cheekily. 'As old as my tongue and a bit older than my teeth, my ma always says.'

'Seventeen?' he hazarded.

'Eighteen, end of April.'

Six years younger than himself. Although he would have been hard put to say why, the knowledge pleased him.

Somewhere in the town a clock struck the half hour, and regretfully, Joseph rose to his feet. 'Teddy, we must go. I promised Ma we'd be home by four.'

'Oh, must we?' But he rose, too. Ma's word was law.

Clearly, the girl had no intention of accompanying them. Nor did Joseph expect her to. In Hanley, if two people of opposite sex were seen together in public, it implied, if not an actual understanding, that they were well on the way to one. And yet – he was loth to leave her.

Self-contained and able to look after herself, she might be, but there was still something oddly vulnerable about her. Teddy felt it too.

'Will you be all right?' he asked.

'Yes, pet. I'll be all right. And Auntie's looking after the kids.'

Kids? Panic took him by the throat. 'You have children?'

She put back her head and roared with laughter. 'Eighteen, I said, not a *hundred* and eighteen. Ma's a paintress. In charge of others. Earns more than I would if I were to go out, so I stay home and look after the kids. And my pa – he's poorly with his chest.'

Joseph nodded. His stepfather, too, was 'poorly with his chest', causing his mother grave concern. And he knew that a paintress could earn good money with her delicate

20

brush strokes on the fine bone china 'I've yet to tell you about the sea,' he heard himself say.

She nodded but said nothing.

'Tomorrow?' he suggested. 'Same time.'

She nodded again and this time, she smiled. 'Same time.'

Five minutes later, as they came down to the railway line, he stopped dead. 'Teddy, we don't know her name.'

'I do,' said Teddy. 'It's Anna.'

'Anna what?'

'Just Anna.'

Fifteen minutes later, they turned into Well Street.

'Teddy?'

'Yes, Joseph?'

'I think we'll keep Anna to ourselves, for the moment, don't you? Just man to man.'

The temptation to share a secret with Joseph fought with the anticipation of telling his mother all about it; and won.

3

'Are you all right, Joseph?' asked his mother that evening. She was sitting behind the counter, checking her takings at the end of the day. Joseph, perched on a sack of flour, was whittling aimlessly at a piece of wood. Teddy, she knew, was sitting quietly in the corner hoping bedtime had been forgotten.

'Why yes, Ma! Very well. Why do you ask?'

'Because this evening you refused a second helping of suet pudding and now I've asked you three times where Thirza is.'

'Down the street talking to Anne about some frippery or other.'

'And your father?'

'Reading the good book in the kitchen.'

Her questions answered, Catherine still continued to gaze long and hard at her son. Her daughter was visiting, her husband occupied with his devotions but Joseph – her tall, handsome Joseph – sat on a flour sack, whittling wood.

'It's good to have you home, Joseph. But you mustn't feel obliged, son, to stay in with me.'

'Took Teddy out, didn't I, this afternoon? And I'll do the same tomorrow.'

'And grateful I am for it. But it's time you found a nice girl to bring home to meet me.'

'Yes, Ma.'

She closed her ledger, picked up her money-bag and slid from her stool. She'd said enough. No point in nagging the boy. 'Come along Teddy! It's well past your bedtime.'

'Ma?'

'Yes, Joseph?' Bag in hand, she waited.

22

'What's she like, then, this nice girl you talk of?'

She climbed back on to the stool, a tiny, indomitable figure in the big white apron that threatened to engulf her – and thought carefully. 'Like your sister,' she said at last. 'Choose a girl like Thirza and you won't go far wrong.'

'You mean – modish, pretty, good with her needle?'

'Modish and pretty, fiddlesticks! I mean kind, God-fearing, gentle. Thirza will be all those things, once she's settled.'

'Takes time, does it, for a girl to – settle?'

'Depends on her man. If she loves him, she'll settle!'

Joseph resumed his whittling. 'Thanks, Ma. I'll bear it in mind next time the mermaids come up!'

On her way to the kitchen, she cuffed him – hard. Teddy, following close behind, could hardly believe his eyes.

Next morning, it was raining; a steady downpour that seemed set to last all day.

'A good morning for a bath?' Catherine suggested to Joseph. What had got into the boy? Eternally gazing out of the window or going to the door although the morning delivery had long since come and gone with nothing for him, anyway. Teddy had been just as bad but she'd put him to cleaning his boots in the back kitchen. It was never too young to start, even though he was getting himself blacker than his boots.

'*Now*?' Joseph was horrified at her suggestion. 'In the kitchen, with the shop full of people?'

'Unless she can see through two inches of solid wood, the Queen herself could be standing there and it would be of no consequence.'

'But it's only Friday!'

'*You* don't have to heat the copper every Saturday night, no matter how hot the weather may be. Truly, Joseph, it would be of the greatest help to me if you were to take your bath this morning. Or there's the new Eastwood baths in town. I'll give you some soap and a towel and you can have a swim while you're there.'

And there was the faint hope that he might bump into Anna on the way. Why, oh why, had he not considered

23

the possibility of it raining? In any case, in spite of his mother's assurances, he knew from experience that the kitchen door could sometimes fly open of its own accord. The thought of suddenly finding himself exposed to the gaze of the Etrurian housewives, as naked as the day he was born, was too dreadful to contemplate, especially if Anna were among them. 'I'll go to the baths,' he said.

'Good lad! And I'll have your dinner ready for you when you get back.'

Anxiety was gnawing so hard at the pit of his stomach, he doubted if he'd be able to eat a mouthful of it; but he thanked his mother politely and set off. An hour later, scrubbed and clean but even more worried, he was back.

If anything it was raining harder than ever.

'All right if Teddy and I pop out for a little while, Ma?'

'In this weather? Don't talk daft!' She banged one of the brass weights on the counter to show her disapproval.

'I could wear my new boots, Ma. And I promise to stay out of the puddles, and there's the new jacket Thirza's made for me . . .'

'Don't you talk daft either, Teddy! Your new boots and your jacket are to to be kept for school, as you well know. If you want something to do, you can tidy the string drawer.'

The string drawer was where all the oddments of cord and twine were thrust, and tidying it was a job Teddy hated. Each length had always become entangled with another and, since they were all of varying size and thickness, the consequent tangle was one that even the most agile of young fingers found difficult to unravel. He'd far rather get wet with Joseph. He glanced up at his brother but found little to comfort him there.

Joseph, chewing hard on his lip, had reached a decision. If he ran all the way, forty minutes should do it; twenty there and twenty back. Not that she'd be there, he was certain. Well, *almost* certain. That was the rub. With a girl like that, he knew instinctively, there was only one thing you could be really sure of: that her behaviour would always be unpredictable. And he wasn't going to risk not turning up.

24

He just hoped Teddy would understand. About to open his mouth to say that he was going out to post a letter and that he'd be back in two shakes of a lamb's tail to help Teddy with the string drawer, he was suddenly forestalled by his mother peering out of the shop window.

'Here comes that nice Anna – in her pa's hat and coat by the look of it.'

No sooner had she finished speaking than Joseph was beside her.

'If I'd said a herd of wild elephants was charging down Well Street,' she confided to her husband that evening, 'he couldn't have got down the steps quicker!'

In fact, Joseph had almost collided with Anna at the foot of them. Ma had been right about the coat, it was like a tent. And the hat was a pudding-basin of sodden felt, its rim beaded with raindrops.

She gazed at him sternly. 'I'm going to Marsh's for muffins. I'm not here hoping to meet you. I'm not that daft!'

'Of course not! I'm not that daft, either.'

They stood and glared at each other. 'I'll be on my way, then,' she said, and turned to go.

'No, wait!' Anything was better than letting her go like this. 'It's not true. I *was* going to see if you were there.'

'Then you are daft!' but her expression had softened.

'Anna . . .it's the Fair, day after tomorrow. Will you be going?'

'Dare say the kids'll want to.'

'So will Teddy. Shall we – shall I see you there?'

'Dare say!' she said. And was gone.

Above him, in the shop doorway, Teddy breathed a long sigh of satisfaction; then glanced behind him at his mother. But she seemed to be happy too, smiling to herself as if it was she who had a secret. He'd never understand grown-ups.

Normally, Teddy loved Fair Day, especially when Joseph was at home. His hand held firmly in his brother's, they would wander slowly from booth to booth; from fat lady

25

to fortune-teller, from bowling-for-a-pig to skittle alley, but ending always with the roundabout, where Joseph would sit on the haunches of a fiery-nosed steed while Teddy held fast to its reins.

Every time Joseph knocked a coconut from its stand or rang the bell with the hammer, Teddy would almost burst with pride. No one else had a brother as strong, handsome and as full of life as Joseph.

But today – perhaps the last Fair before he started school – it was altogether different. To begin with, Ma had asked a neighbour to mind the shop and had insisted upon coming too. And it wasn't that he didn't love his mother dearly but her presence gave an entirely different flavour to the day. For a start, *she* held him by the hand and – unlike Joseph – told him to take the other out of his pocket. She also – unheard of on Fair Day – controlled the number of sweets he ate and stopped him from stroking the monkey on the hurdy-gurdy, even though the man assured her it 'wouldn't hurt a fly, let along a nice little boy like yours'.

'And what about fleas?' she'd asked sharply, and Teddy thought he would die of shame.

Even Joseph was different; absent-minded, turning his head from side to side as if he were a puppet on a string, utterly hopeless on the coconut shy and not even bothering with the hammer.

Really, the only good thing to be said for the day so far was that they'd stayed on the roundabout for two goes, straight off. And it had been exciting to have Ma standing in the crowd, waving to them every time they came round. It had almost made up for Joseph's wriggling about behind him like 'butter on a hot plate' – one of Ma's favourite expressions when he was having his hair washed.

There wasn't a sign of Anna, either. He'd said as much to Joseph when he was being swung off the roundabout, and Joseph said he'd noticed too, and perhaps she hadn't come,after all.

But then, suddenly, when he was least expecting it, there she was by the bran-tub, with a small boy – much smaller than Teddy – clutching one hand and a girl – about the same size as himself – the other.

Strangely enough, it was Ma who greeted her, not Joseph; and who, to his fury, suggested that Joseph and Anna should go off on their own, without him. Short of starting to cry, which he knew would only earn him a smart smack, there was nothing he could do about it. To add to his annoyance, the girl actually put out her tongue at him behind Ma's back. For two pins, he'd have stamped on her foot, except that his father had taught him never, under any circumstances, to harm a girl.

After that, he wouldn't have expected the day to grow much worse, but he was proved wrong when his mother suggested they all go and look at the cows and sheep. He could see those any time at the cattle market.

He did cheer up a little when, on the way back, they stopped at the roundabout again, but it was only to watch Joseph and Anna whirling round above their heads. He waved, of course, but they were so busy talking, his head only inches from hers, they didn't even see him.

And then he was taken home. Just like that. Without even a chance to say goodbye to Anna, although his mother did say she'd invited her round to tea on Sunday. But that meant she wasn't a secret any more!

Joseph knew Ma meant well; knew, too, that he was lucky because some mothers tried to hang on to their sons, inventing all manner of excuses to keep them tied to their apron-strings. Some of his mates had even gone to sea for that very reason. All the same, glancing around the tea table on Sunday afternoon, he was conscious that events were overtaking him faster than he'd anticipated.

Left to himself, he'd be stretched out on the hillside with Anna, talking of this and that as the spirit moved him; telling her about activities at sea as he thought fit: perhaps explaining how the stars could be used in navigation, how a sextant worked: the names, if she was interested, of the different sails and rigging. He'd got it all worked out in his mind now.

Ted would have been there as well, of course, if he'd been excused Sunday school; sitting there, quiet as a mouse for the most part but taking it all in. Having Ted there would have made it easier, somehow, to talk to Anna; made him feel less shy, less worried about whether she was expecting him to slip his arm around her shoulders and kiss her cheek. Or would she slap him on the face if he tried? That was the drawback about life at sea; except for the houses of ill repute to be found in any dockside area and which he avoided like the plague, there was no way of learning about the whims and fancies of the female sex.

All he knew was that his fingers itched to unbraid her hair until it tumbled about her shoulders, trace the contours of that determined little jaw, the angular cheekbones, the small, straight nose, the white column of her throat.

'Joseph,' said his mother briskly, 'stop dreaming and pass Anna the jam.'

They *all* tried to pass Anna the jam; Teddy, sitting opposite, angelic in his sailor suit with its big white collar; his stepfather, sitting on Anna's other side, funereal in Sunday black, his beard dead centre of his waistcoat buttons; Thirza, pretty as a picture in yet another new gown, her cheeks flushed with excitement because her Mr Harrington had come to tea. William Harrington, in fact, was the only one, as a fellow guest, who did *not* try to pass Anna the jam. Instead, he smiled at Catherine and said, 'A delicious tea, if I may say so, Mrs Smith.'

'You may, indeed, Mr Harrington. Thirza, pass Mr Harrington's cup up, if you please.'

Joseph, wondering privately how long it would be before 'Mr Harrington' became 'William' —· perhaps not until the day he wed Thirza? — suddenly caught Teddy's eye and winked.

The effect was disastrous. His mouth full of seed cake, Teddy exploded into a fit of uncontrollable giggles. Thank God, thought Joseph as he watched Teddy try vainly to stem the exodus of crumbs, that he hadn't been drinking tea! As it was . . .

'Teddy,' his mother began warningly.

But his father was coming to Teddy's rescue. 'Went the wrong way, did it, lad?' He patted his son solicitously on the back. 'Happens to the best of us.'

Joseph smiled at his stepfather. Often, he would deflect maternal disapproval, however richly deserved, away from his small son. And his mother, even though she might purse her lips and shake her head, would stay silent. Teddy was fortunate to have such parents.

But it was left to Anna, *his* Anna, to smooth away any remaining tension. Leaning over the table towards Teddy, she said confidingly, 'Chew every mouthful at least ten times. That's what I always try to do.'

Whereupon Teddy had to experiment, his lips firmly clamped, his eyes wide as saucers, while everyone watched and counted. After that, they all relaxed, Thirza chattering to Anna about a new gown she was making, Teddy explaining to Mr Harrington how he could actually count up to a hundred, and Catherine asking if everyone was going to evening chapel. What about Anna?

Joseph held his breath. No mention had yet been made of Anna's activities once the meal was over. For her to appear with the family in chapel would indicate not only their acceptance of her as his approved 'lady friend' but also her agreement with the situation. Once again, he was conscious of being rushed. And Anna, he knew, had a mind of her own.

However, he needn't have worried. Thanking his mother politely, Anna explained that she was expected home to mind the younger children so that her own parents could attend evening service; in their case, in the parish church of St John.

So all was well; or as well as it could be under the circumstances. He was not to be exposed to the inquisitive gaze of fellow worshippers, nor even the embarrassment of introducing Anna to them afterwards – even those who knew her well, would pretend not to! – but it had also been made clear that Anna, too, came from a God-fearing family.

The only disappointment – and it was a harsh one – was that he would be deprived of her company far too soon. But at least he and Teddy could offer to walk her home.

He said as much.

'Oh, I don't think that Teddy – ' his mother began.

'Oh, please Ma!' Teddy broke in.

'Teddy, don't interrupt! I'm sure that Anna and Joseph . . .'

But Anna was smiling at his mother in the most beguiling manner. 'Oh, please Mrs Smith, do let him come.'

So here he was, walking decorously as befitted the Sabbath, listening avidly, but minding his mother's whispered reminder as she'd buttoned him into his jacket – which he was quite capable of buttoning himself into – 'Remember, Teddy, don't interrupt. And speak only when you're spoken to.'

At first, there was nothing *to* interrupt. And then,

'I enjoyed my tea, Joseph.'

'Having the shop means we can afford things other families less fortunate cannot.'

In view of her sick Pa, Anna's family, thought Teddy, was probably 'less fortunate'.

'I didn't mean that, Joseph. I meant talking to your mother – properly, not just asking for a half-pound of sugar in the shop.'

'She's all right, is Ma.'

'And Thirza. I've always been a mite scared of Thirza, so pretty and smart.'

'She's all right, is Thirza.'

And me? What did you think of me? Teddy wanted to ask. Am I all right, too? But, mindful of his mother's injunction, he held his tongue. Anyway, Joseph was still speaking.

'I can't imagine you being afraid of anyone, Anna.'

'Not afraid, exactly, just mindful that *I'm* not pretty or smart.'

Joseph stopped so suddenly they all three nearly fell over, 'Not *pretty*? *You* – not pretty? Why, you're . . .'

Even Teddy had noticed that today Anna was a different

person from the girl he and Joseph had met on the hillside. But that was only to be expected. Sunday did that to people. Even he was better-behaved on a Sunday, thought twice before he spoke, was careful not to scuff his shoes nor dirty his jacket. But Anna, he thought now, was especially different. Not only was she not wearing her boots, but her braid was coiled neatly around her head and topped, now, by a bonnet; not quite as fetching a bonnet as those Thirza wore but pretty enough, with dark green velvet ruching beneath its brim and ties to match. And it wasn't only her outward appearance. The way she was looking at Joseph now was quite different from the way she'd looked at him on the hill. Just like Thirza looks at Mr Harrington, he thought in surprise. So, did that mean . . .'

'You're – you're. . . .' Joseph still seeemed to be having difficulty finding the right words. So much so, Teddy forgot all about Ma's embargo.

' . . . beautiful!' said Teddy. They both looked at him. 'Like a queen!' It was a term Joseph often used to describe a ship, but he didn't mention that.

Joseph laughed, a little shakily. 'That's it exactly, Teddy. Like a queen!' And now he was gazing at Anna and she was gazing at him and Teddy had the strangest feeling that if he were suddenly to drop from sight down a hole in the ground, neither of them would even notice.

'I'll be going back to sea soon,' said Joseph, in a choked-up, hollow sort of way.

'When?'

'Any day now, I'll have a letter.'

'Where to, this time?'

'America, maybe.'

'America!' And now her voice was both envious and excited. 'I'd love to see America.'

'Our captain,' and now Joseph couldn't get the words out quickly enough, 'our captain brings his wife sometimes.'

'To America?'

'To anywhere. If there's room. The Line encourages it. Keeps . . . 'em happy. The wives, I mean.'

31

As if by mutual consent, they started to walk again. No one spoke for several minutes. Then Teddy could bear it no longer.'

'Anna!'

'Yes, Teddy?'

'Joseph's only a second mate, now. But he'll be a captain one day.'

'Well,' asked his mother as she was tucking him into bed, 'did you behave yourself?'

For some reason he couldn't put his finger on, he had the distinct impression she was really asking him something entirely different. He thought quickly. He knew he mustn't tell lies, but. . . . 'I had to sort of help things along a bit,' he admitted.

To his surprise, his mother smiled. 'He needs a bit of a push sometimes, does our Joseph! Goodnight, son. God bless.'

'Goodnight, Ma. God bless.'

All in all, it hadn't been a bad day.

4

The next day was dreadful. By the morning post came Joseph's summons to Liverpool; he was to leave Hanley on the following day. From then on, the pattern of the day was turned on its head.

At least it was wash day. And fortunately it was a fine one, so that before midday, Joseph's entire wardrobe was blowing in the yard. Joseph sat in the kitchen in reach-me-downs borrowed in his absence from his stepfather, and would himself be laundered as soon as the copper was free from the wash and could be used to fill the tin bath.

Teddy sat with him, dumb with misery. Even Joseph's promise that he could scrub his back when the moment came did nothing to console him.

'What about Anna?' he asked.

The last words Joseph had spoken to her as they'd left her outside her house on the previous evening had been, 'See you tomorrow?'

'I'll be there, if I can,' she'd replied.

They all knew that 'there' was the hillside above the station. But what if she couldn't be there, or if her auntie wasn't able to mind the children? Teddy didn't fancy the idea of sharing their hillside with the girl who'd put out her tongue at him. But Joseph, in Pa's shrunken old shirt and trousers, clearly couldn't venture out to tell her what had happened.

'Ma,' he suggested, 'shall I go round and tell Anna about Joseph going away? I promise I'll look each way before I cross the roads.'

But telling Anna, he was told, in the annoying habit

adults had of arranging things without telling you, had already been taken care of. Joseph had written a note and his mother had asked a customer who lived near Anna to deliver it.

But the crowning indignity was yet to come. He wasn't, he was informed, to be allowed to accompany Anna and Joseph that afternoon.

It was Ma who broke it to him, Joseph staring at his clasped hands the while. 'Sometimes, Teddy, grown-ups want to be on their own.'

'But, Ma, she's my friend as well as Joseph's. We found her together!' His lower lip began to tremble. He'd known Joseph would soon be going away; he knew, too, that he had to be a brave boy and not cry – sailors didn't – but he had confidently expected to spend every waiting minute, from now until he waved him away on the train, with his brother.

He gave an almighty sniff and gazed appealingly at Joseph. He knew he mustn't appeal to him directly, that once Ma had spoken, that was it, but all the same . . . he could look.

And Joseph didn't let him down. He took him on his lap – at six years old he was considered past such childish customs, but today, nobody seemed to be sticking to the rules – then glanced over at Ma and made a faint movement with his head in the direction of the back kitchen, where the boiler had begun to bubble.

'Back in a minute,' said Ma, as she bustled out.

On their own, Teddy felt it safe to say, 'Joseph, *can't* I come?'

'It's like this, Ted. There are times in a fellow's life when the fewer people there are around, the better. Just himself and the person he wants to talk to.'

'Like when Ma or Pa are telling me off about something?'

'Yes, but not always for a telling-off. It can be when you want to ask them something special.'

It was beginning to make sense now. 'You mean like when Mr Harrington asked Pa if he could marry Thirza?'

34

'That's it exactly, Teddy! The poor chap could never have managed it if we'd been sitting around gawping.'

'So are you going to marry Anna? Is it *her* Pa you're going to see this afternoon?'

'Hold hard, Teddy! I think I'd like to marry Anna very much indeed, one day. But I don't know how she feels about it. I've got to give her time. But what I *can* ask her this afternoon, if we're on our own, is if she'll think about it while I'm away . . .'

'But Joseph, will you manage it all right on your own? Even Ma says you need a bit of a push sometimes.'

'Does she indeed?' He raised his eyebrows in the direction of the wash-house, where Ma was now invisible in a cloud of steam. 'Teddy, I appreciate the offer, but there are some things a man has got to do on his own. You'll find that out for yourself one day, when you're master of a ship.'

The prospect of becoming a ship's master quite took Teddy's mind off even Joseph's approaching departure. 'Joseph, d'you really think I will be, one day?'

'Clap me in irons if you aren't! Especially if you learn your stars and memorise the rigging chart I've drawn you. Now' – he suddenly smote his knee with his hand – '*that's* an idea!'

'What is, Joseph?'

'Why, you can start teaching Anna for me, while I'm away. She's dead keen to learn about life at sea.'

'Yes, I could, couldn't I?' In his excitement, he bounced up and down on Joseph's knee. And then he had a sudden, even better, idea. 'Joseph, if she doesn't want to marry you, maybe she'll wait for me!'

'Now that's a thought and a half, young Ted! But let me have first crack, eh? Let me have her to myself, just for the afternoon?'

'All right, Joseph. As long as you tell me what she says.'

'Aye, aye, skipper!'

It was Joseph who put Teddy to bed that evening and knelt with him while he said his prayers. After the Lord's Prayer came the 'God Blesses'.

'God bless Pa and Ma, Thirza and Joseph, all my uncles and aunts and cousins' – Pa being one of seven, he was allowed this blanket coverage – 'Mr Harrington, the Queen, Mr and Mrs Marsh, Spot' – the dog who lived down the street – 'Mrs Thomasina Houghton' – who kept the Etrurian Post Office and gave him sweets – 'the muffin boy' – who wore no shoes, even in winter – 'and . . . ' Teddy paused, opened one eye and looked enquiringly at Joseph. 'Anna?'

Joseph nodded solemnly. 'And Anna.'

'Before the Queen?' Only family, or almost family, came before the Queen.

'I think so, Teddy.'

So he said the prayer once more, this time putting Anna in her rightful place.

Then came Ma's prayer, the one her mother had taught her: 'Oh Lord, on whom I shall depend, keep me safely till my end. I trust in thy redeeming power for comfort in my final hour.'

Then he scrambled into bed, pulled up the counterpane and gazed expectantly at his half-brother.

That the afternoon had been a success had been evident as soon as Joseph returned home. He'd winked at Teddy, seized Ma around the waist and lifted her high into the air, then produced one of Mrs Marsh's special lardy cakes for tea. But he hadn't actually said anything. And Teddy had waited patiently until now. He came straight to the point.

'What did she say?'

'That I was a gormless half-wit and she wouldn't touch me with a bargepole!'

'She didn't!'

Joseph perched on the edge of the bed. 'Well, I wouldn't have put it past her! But no, she didn't. She said the odds were, I'd find her waiting for me when I next came home.'

Teddy did a quick calculation. 'If you go to the east coast of America, that could be in three months.'

'Could be sooner. But there might be some more of that salted cod from up north.'

Teddy nodded. 'From Newfoundland.' His knowledge of which cargo could be expected from what country was already very thorough. 'But she didn't actually *promise*, Joseph?' He liked to have everything neatly cut and dried.

'I didn't think it wise to press her for a definite promise, Ted. That's hardly the way with a girl like Anna. Try to tie her down and she'll flee like the wind. A gentle touch on the tiller should be all that's necessary. Just enough for her to know you're there. Anyway, she'll be coming to see me off at the station in the morning.'

Panic struck. 'I'm coming, too, aren't I, Joseph?'

'Of course! But I thought you could look after her for me when the train's gone.'

'Won't Ma be there?'

'No, she'll be minding the shop.'

He liked the idea of looking after Anna by himself. The thought conjured up another in his mind. 'So I won't be marrying her, after all, then?'

'Hope you don't mind.'

'Just as long as one of us does.' he said sleepily, turning over and curling up into his customary ball.

'That's the way I look at it,' Joseph said.

As always, they were too early. So it was understandable that Anna wasn't there. Even so, Joseph's brow creased with anxiety. 'Now don't forget, Teddy. If she doesn't come before the train leaves, you are to stay here until Ma comes to fetch you. Understood?'

'Yes, Joseph.'

'You are not, under any circumstances, to start walking home on your own.'

'No, Joseph.'

He couldn't think what all the fuss was about. Anna was sure to be here in time. And even if something prevented her, he could quite easily find his own way home. 'Shall we take a couple of turns on the quarterdeck?' he suggested hopefully.

'Taking a turn on the quarterdeck' had been initiated by

Joseph as a means of passing the dragging minutes before the train came puffing in. Watched by an indulgent Ma, it consisted of the two of them clasping their hands behind their backs and pacing a certain distance up the platform and the same distance back, pointing out to each other any passing craft or phenomenon they liked to invent. Sometimes, they were still in harbour.

'Well, I do declare, Mr Smith, if that isn't my old friend, Captain Doldrum, on the quayside. And waving his arms like a semaphore. What ails him, d'you think?'

'Perhaps he wants to come aboard, sir.'

'For a glass of grog before we weigh anchor, no doubt. What think you, Mr Smith? Shall we put down the gangplank?'

And on it would go. Teddy preferred it if they were at sea.

'Take the helm for a minute, if you please, Mr Smith, while I tie up my bootlace.'

'Aye, aye, sir!'

'Course South twenty-nine degrees East, Mr Smith.'

'South twenty-nine degrees East it is, sir.'

And he would break off his 'pacing' to stand, feet well-braced to turn an imaginary wheel.

So involved would they become, the arrival of the train was almost an anticlimax. 'Why, shiver my timbers, Mr Smith! If that isn't an old steam kettle on the starboard bow.'

'So it is, sir.'

'Must go aboard and inspect, Mr Smith!'

And Joseph would clasp Ma in his arms, shake Teddy solemnly by the hand and climb aboard. 'Good day to you, Mr Smith. Keep an eye on Mrs Smith, if you please.'

'Aye aye, sir.' And his voice would squeak with the struggle to keep the tears in check. At least until Joseph's wildly waving arm was out of sight.

And then, carefully not looking at her, he'd take Ma's hand in his and they'd walk silently home.

'Never mind,' Ma would say as they turned into Well Street, 'he's got to go away, so he can come back.' Which was absolutely true.

Today, however, it was all different. Clearly, Joseph had no wish to pace the quarterdeck. He just wanted to stand there, staring in the direction from which Anna should come, jingling his money in his pocket and not wanting to say a word.

The minutes passed. Two more passengers arrived and a man started to pile crates and boxes on the edge of the platform. Joseph began to gnaw at his thumbnail and even Teddy grew worried.

But then, suddenly, gloriously, there she was, running down the road like a mad thing, her unbraided hair flying like a banner behind her. So fast was she running, Joseph's outstretched arms were like a buffer stop. Breathless, she held on to him, her head against his chest.

'Sorry! Sorry! Auntie – late! Couldn't – leave the kids! Didn't even have time – braid my hair!'

Joseph's arms closed round her as he buried his face in its glory. 'I had a notion I'd like to see it unbound, but I didn't expect to, this soon.'

And now she was laughing up at him. 'Shame on you, Joseph Hancock!'

But then the train really was there. And Joseph was kissing Anna as if he expected to sail to Australia and not just across the Atlantic. Then he turned to Teddy.

'Goodbye, Mr Smith. God speed you.'

So he hadn't forgotten the game! 'God speed you, too, sir.'

And then he was gone, and Teddy was sliding his hand into Anna's. 'He's got to go, Anna. Just so's he can come back. That's what Ma always says.'

Anna knuckled her eyes and uttered a sound that was not quite a sob, but not quite a laugh, either. 'A great one, is your Ma!'

'And on the way home, I'll start teaching you the sails. There's mainsails and forsails and jibs. And topsails and royals and. . . .' They were halfway home before he'd got through them all.

5

'I can easily get Martha Brigginshaw to mind the shop, and take you myself, Teddy. No trouble at all. But,' even though they were alone at the breakfast table, Ma lowered her voice confidentially, 'I'm sure Anna is pleased to take you. Makes her feel like one of the family.'

Since he and Anna had waved Joseph goodbye, they had each received a letter. Teddy had shared his with everyone – Ma, of course, and customers in the shop and the muffin boy and anyone else he could persuade to listen.

But Anna had kept hers to herself.

The first indication that perhaps all wasn't as it should be on that memorable morning came when he was given his porridge. He swirled the one small spoonful of sugar he was allowed around the bowl, then lifted the spoon to his mouth, prepared to swallow. And found that he couldn't. Not only was there some obstruction in his throat, he knew that his stomach would rebel – with disastrous consequences.

'Eat up!' said Ma. And then stopped weighing out raisins on the end of the kitchen table and gazed at him in silence. Teddy gazed back.

'It won't go down, Ma.'

'Don't worry,' said Ma easily. 'It's your first day at school. You're bound to be a bit scared.'

'But Joseph says I should never be scared of anything.'

'What Joseph says and what Joseph really believes,' said his mother tartly, 'are sometimes two quite different things. Being frightened is nothing to be ashamed of. It's if you let it get on top of you that matters. Now, see how you get on with a glass of milk.'

But he only managed half a glass before Anna was at the door.

They did him up in his new jacket and tied his laces on his new boots. He could have done it all himself, but this morning, Ma told him, his fingers were all thumbs. Not that hers seemed to be much better as she fumbled away. Then she gave him a great smacker of a kiss and a big hug and waved him goodbye from the shop door.

Reaching the corner they both turned and gave her a final wave and then she was out of sight and, to his enormous shame, a tear suddenly spilled out of his eye and ran down his cheek. Quickly, he used the hand Anna wasn't holding to send it away. But she'd noticed, of course. She stopped, then squatted on the doorstep of the house they happened to be passing and drew him close.

'What if I were to say you needn't go to school, after all; that you can turn round now and go straight back to Ma? Would you go back or would you go on?'

His reply was immediate. 'I'd go on of course.'

'So, there you are! You know what you want to do. You've prepared for it as much as you can.' That was true, Ma had been giving him her accounts to check for weeks now, and her orders to write out. 'And you know that you don't want to spend the rest of your life helping Ma in the shop.'

'Oh, no! I'm going to sea, like Joseph.' She gave him a quick hug then. 'But I don't like leaving Ma on her own, either. She'll miss me, you know, Anna. There'll be no one to count the oranges or tidy the string drawer.'

'I don't doubt she'll miss you, but she wouldn't be paying three shillings a month for your education if she didn't want you to learn.'

'Is that what it's costing?'

'They reckon it's money well spent.'

He began pulling Anna to her feet. 'Come on, then! I mustn't be late!'

They arrived in a rush, so that there was no time for more than a muttered 'See you later!' from Anna before she gave him a little push towards the waiting figure of Alfred Smith, who was standing outside the building that on Sundays housed the Sunday school but on weekdays became 'the British'.

'Is he a relation?' Teddy had asked Pa when he'd first heard about him.

'Not as far as I know. On the other hand,' his father had given Teddy one of his twinkling smiles – 'there are a lot of us about!'

It was Ma who had suggested it might be as well if he made it clear from the beginning that he was not a relation. 'We don't want them accusing him of favouritism.'

'What's favouritism?'

'Being teacher's pet.'

He certainly didn't want that. On the other hand, it wasn't in his nature to be anything other than friendly towards people. So now he compromised by lifting his cap a few inches from his head, as Ma had told him to, but not actually smiling at his namesake. By then he was inside, anyway.

It all looked very different from Sundays. To begin with, there were a lot more children of all ages and sizes milling about, and although the illuminated texts were still on the walls, the chairs and desks had been arranged differently. A lot them were in the centre of the room before the big desk where, on Sunday, the Superintendent sat, but today, once he had closed the outer door, it was taken by Mr Smith.

'Silence, please!' there wasn't much noise to silence, as several of the bigger boys had been keeping order, but now there was nothing but an occasional scrape of a hobnailed boot on the stone floor and a sniff or two from those who had no handkerchief, and were afraid to use their sleeves. They began with prayers, and a passage read from The Bible. Teddy heard hardly a word. He was far too occupied observing the boy standing next to him. He was shorter than Teddy and not as well dressed. His cord breeches were patched at the knee, although tidily so, and the darns in his stockings – above the worn but well-polished boots – were a miracle of neatness. His jacket was patched at the elbows and was a shade too small. Above its dark collar, his face was like a pale moon, with a button of a nose, a wide mouth and eyes of the deepest blue Teddy had ever seen. His hair was bright red and brushed in a heavy fringe on to his brow, although tufts of it stuck up at the crown; 'like palm trees' Joseph would have said.

As Teddy studied him, the boy looked up and gave him an uncertain half-smile. And at that precise moment, Teddy's stomach, protesting against its emptiness, let out the most enormous rumble that no amount of doubling up and other contortions could do anything to stop. Immediately, both he and his neighbour collapsed into giggles.

'Be quiet!' hissed the nearest big boy and, surprisingly, his stomach did as it was told.

'All new boys to stay here, in front of me,' said Mr Smith, coming to the end of the Bible-reading.

There were about twenty of them, Teddy's new friend among them. The other pupils separated into groups and marched in line to various points in the room, where they halted and were joined by one, sometimes two, of the big boys. Teddy wondered in which group he would eventually be placed.

For the next few hours, he worked harder than he ever had before. First, they were shown how to secure their caps to the backs of their chairs, then they were given pencils and pieces of paper and told to write their names.

'Bert Brown', wrote Teddy's new friend in uneven, printed capitals and with much licking of his pencil point. Teddy himself had written 'Edward John Smith', in the joined-up writing that Ma had shown him how to do.

'We will start,' said Mr Smith, 'with a little mental arithmetic. I shall call out a question and you will write the answer on your piece of paper. And no boy is to help another. Is that clearly understood?'

The first question was easy. Too easy. 'How many fingers have you on each hand?'

Long ago, Joseph had caught Teddy with that one. 'Four', he wrote, 'and one thumb.'

Out of the corner of his eye, he saw that Bert had written 'Five'. Without taking his eyes off Mr Smith, Teddy made a fist out of his left hand, with the thumb pointing upward, and laid it casually on the desk in front of him. It was all he could think of to do.

'I repeat, no boy will help another,' said Mr Smith, although not actually looking at the class.

Teddy, his cheeks scarlet, hastily unclenched his fist. All the same, he hoped Bert had seen and understood.

'Next question. I go into a shop to buy six packets of pins at a penny ha'penny a packet. How much will I have to give the shopkeeper?'

Teddy wrote '9d.' without hesitation, thinking that they were expensive pins. However, several boys, he noticed, seemed to have to think before writing. Bert he daren't even glance at, but he had a horrible feeling he hadn't written anything at all.

And so it went on.

Next came Dictation: a piece of poetry by Alfred, Lord Tennyson, whom, Mr Smith told them, the Queen had honoured by making him her Poet Laureate. The poem, especially the way Mr Smith read it, was most exciting. 'Half a league, half a league. Half a league onward. . . .' He pondered for at least two seconds over the spelling of 'league', before writing 'leage' and hurrying on.

Then came Reading. Each scholar had but a short passage to read before passing the book on to his neighbour. Sometimes it was so short Teddy wondered how Mr Smith could possibly decide upon a scholar's skill. But certainly, when a boy stumbled and hesitated over almost every word, it was a relief when his embarrassment was over. Teddy himself read without hesitation because, for a long time, he had been reading pieces from the newsheets to Pa.

The book from which they were reading was Mr Dickens' *Bleak House*, which Ma had often read to him when he was small, so he was familiar with both the story and the characters. But it was plain to see that most of the boys were not. Bert, in particular, stumbled over all but the

44

simplest of words. The boy on the other side of him, a burly lad, older than the rest, dared to snigger, and Teddy turned and glared at him.

'Right, Williams, we'll see if you can do better, shall we?' said Mr Smith sharply.

Unfortunately, Williams could, and did. Although not, Teddy considered, as well as himself. However, their papers were now being collected and slates handed out. While the papers were being marked, Mr Smith explained, they could draw whatever they liked on their slates: a bird, an animal, a house, a mountain – whatever they chose.

Drawing was Teddy's weak point. As Joseph said, he was all right on straight lines. So, hoping that this work would not be gazed upon by Mr Smith, he drew his customary house with four windows, a front door and two chimney-pots. For good measure, he was adding a little stick man and a little stick wife, when he glanced idly at his neighbours's slate. And nearly dropped his chalk in astonishment.

On Bert's slate had appeard the most amazing drawing of a castle. It had round towers and battlements and a drawbridge over a moat with a swan leaving a lifelike arrow of ripples behind it. As he watched, a second swan appeared, and a tree on the far bank of the moat. Bert was busy covering the tree with leaves and blossom when Mr Smith told them to put their chalks down. In front of him their papers had been assembled into four neat piles.

He glanced around the expectant faces. 'Before I tell you where you are all to go, does anyone feel inclined to show us their work of art?'

No one did. Several of them, Teddy included, shifted in their seats uncomfortably.

'So modest, all of a sudden? Williams. I feel sure you must have something to offer. Pray, hold up your slate.'

But all that Williams had to offer was a copybook cat with whiskers, pointed ears and a curling tail. 'M-m-m-m,' said Mr Smith. 'I doubt if *he'll* catch many mice. Now, Brown, let us see what you have done.' Shyly, Teddy's neighbour lifted his slate a few inches from the desk. 'Higher, Brown, if you please, and let us all see it.'

He knew it was going to be good, all the time, thought Teddy, enjoying the murmur of 'oohs' and 'aahs' that was now rippling through the class.

After that, Mr Smith picked up one of the piles of paper in front of him and read out several names, that of Williams among them; then called a monitor who must have been standing nearby for that sole purpose, and requested him to lead the boys to 'Wainwright's group'. Off they marched and the next group was called. Then the third, until all that remained were Teddy, Bert and three others whose performance had been, in all subjects except art, not much higher than Bert's.

'You,' said Mr Smith, glancing around with a smile, 'will have the good, or bad, fortune – whichever way you look at it – to remain with me.'

Teddy felt both resentful and puzzled. Often enough at home, he was told that pride came before a fall. Had not proud Lucifer been cast into hell for daring to challenge God? And, as Jospeh had put it, in a more down-to-earth sort of way, 'At sea, it never does to think you're better than the next man. Ten to one, it'll be he who fishes you out by the seat of your pants if you fall in!'

Even so, he knew he had at least read better than Williams. And he knew his arithmetic had been better than Bert's. But perhaps he'd been too quick, perhaps his answers had been wrong. He suddenly became aware that Mr Smith was speaking to him; had, in fact, already spoken because he was obviously waiting for an answer.

'I'm sorry, sir, I didn't quite hear . . .'

'You mean you weren't paying attention?'

Teddy nodded dumbly.

'I was observing to your classmates that I think we can all benefit from helping each other. You, Smith, can perhaps improve your drawing skills under Brown's tuition, while he can benefit from your greater experience at figures and reading. Thomas, here is poor at writing, although his

46

vocabulary appears to be excellent. Can you spell vocabulary, Thomas?'

Thomas could and did.

'And the meaning of the word, Thomas?'

But there, Thomas was beaten. 'Don't know, sir.'

'*I* don't know, Thomas. Remember that every verb requires a subject. Can any boy help Thomas out with the meaning of vocabulary? Don't be afraid to try.'

Teddy could never resist a challenge. His hand crept up.

'Yes, Smith?'

'It's – words, sir.'

'That's right. It's the words we know and understand and can use. So, you see – we shall all be able to help each other.'

Soon, classes were over and, after another short prayer, they were all marched outside. Teddy could see Anna waiting a little way up the street with her little brother, Sam. He turned to Bert. 'You being met?'

Bert shook his head. 'Ma's working.'

'Mine is too. But my friend Anna's here.'

A further exchange told them that, to begin with, they shared the same way home. So Anna was introduced and they set off.

They finally parted from Bert where there was a pump at the junction of three streets. 'Tomorrow, fifteen minutes to nine o'clock,' said Teddy. And Bert agreed.

'So it was all right, was it?' Anna asked, once they were on their own.

'Oh, Anna, it was wonderful!' Absent-mindedly, quite forgetting he'd once decided not to like him, he took Sam's free hand and helped him jump the cracks in the pavement.

'And Anna . . .'

'Yes, Ted?'

'It was very kind of you to take me to school this morning, and *very* kind of you to meet me out.'

'But you won't be requiring my services tomorrow,' said Anna dryly. 'Is that what you want to say?'

'Oh, Anna, I didn't mean . . .'

'It's all right, young Ted. I know what you mean. Half

expected it, in fact.'

'*I* half expected it . . .' he began, and then stopped. *Never correct your elders*. Ma always said. On the other hand, *no verb without a subject*, Mr Smith had said. Diplomacy won. 'Thank you, Anna!' he said politely.'

'Mind you, we'll have to check with your Ma,' Anna said. 'She'll have the last word.'

Teddy, now jumping the cracks with Sam in a sudden excess of high spirits, hoped he never had to choose between Ma's last word and Mr Smith's. And my goodness, but he was hungry!

6

A couple of weeks later, Bert and Teddy came out of school and began the long walk home. It wasn't really long but they always had so much to talk about, they frequently forgot to walk at all. On this particular day, Ma had sent Bert an invitation to tea on the following Saturday. He had accepted rapturously, but what should have been a simple matter had become a seemingly insoluble problem of timing.

Teddy had his Saturday jobs – shoe-cleaning, shopping for Ma now that he was able to manage the change, helping in the shop if it was busy, – but his jobs were as nothing compared with Bert's: chopping firewood, carrying coals, selling news-sheets, even, he told Teddy proudly, managing the week's wash if his ma was really busy. As for cooking – well, any fool could boil an egg or make porridge, couldn't they?

Any fool might, but Teddy certainly couldn't. Good at words and figures he might be, but his education had been woefully lacking in other areas.

The more he learned about Bert's home life, the more he doubted if Bert's ma paid three shillings a month for his schooling. From what he'd heard, he was probably a 'Wedgwood boy'.

Everyone in Hanley knew about the Wedgwoods, who owned the biggest pottery in the town. It was their family who had started the British and Mr Francis Wedgwood, so Mr Smith had told them, frequently visited the school; and not always by appointment, his pupils would do well to remember.

But none of this helped with the problem of how to get Bert to tea on Saturday.

'P'raps I could help sell your news-sheets,' Teddy suggested, although he wasn't at all hopeful that Ma would agree to this. News-sheet vendors, along with muffin boys and match sellers, were to be treated with the utmost politeness and consideration — for they were all God's creatures, were they not? — but joining their ranks, Teddy knew instinctively, would be quite another matter.

Bert, too, was doubtful; not because of parental opposition but because 'the big boys don't like kids muscling in on their pitches'.

Teddy sighed. Being small seemed to have no advantages whatsoever, except perhaps an ability to be overlooked at bedtime. It was at that moment that he became aware of Williams walking slowly behind them; not so much walking as lurking, for Bert and Teddy had now reached the pump, where their ways divided.

In class, Williams never bothered them; there was a lot to be said for being with Mr Smith. But sometimes, when they trooped out at the end of lessons, Teddy would notice him eyeing Bert up and down and then making some sniggering remark to his companions. Now, Williams was on his own, but still menacing.

'Bastard!' he said suddenly in a loud voice and looking straight at Bert. 'Bastard Bertie Brown!'

Although he didn't know its meaning, Teddy knew that 'bastard' was not, according to Ma, 'a nice word'. If he had ever used it in her hearing, he would most certainly have had his mouth washed out with soap. He had seldom actually heard it spoken, but here was Williams using it to Bert, with no provocation whatsoever.

Teddy glanced at Bert. His face was white, his fists tightly clenched. 'I'm *not* a bastard!'

'Oh yes you are! Everyone knows your ma wasn't married when she had you.' So *that* was a bastard! 'Proper whore, she was!'

'My ma was *not* a whore!'

50

'Oh yes, she was! Still is, most likely!' And he began to do a sort of little dance around Bert, his fists shooting out to land with a dull thud on various parts of Bert's body.

Bert was crying now. 'My ma's *not* a whore!'

The accusation was so obviously ridiculous – everyone knew a 'haw' was the fruit of the hawthorn that blossomed in ragged patches along the canal bank in spring – Teddy joined in. 'She's *not* a haw, she's a paintress! And stop hitting Bert!'

'And who's going to stop me? Teacher's pet?'

That finished it He threw himself at Williams' legs. Caught off balance, Williams went over like a ninepin. 'Come on, Bert! You sit on his head!'

But Bert wasn't quick enough. The bigger boy had scrambled to his feet and was now punching wildly. One blow hit Teddy squarely on the nose and he felt the blood begin to flow. Another landed on Bert's mouth.

Again, Teddy went for the only part of Williams' anatomy he was confident of reaching. And this time, he used his teeth. Williams' squeal of pain and outrage brought doors flying open.

'Well, look at that!'

'No better than dogs!'

'I know what'll settle their hash!'

And the next minute, a pail of cold water was flung indiscriminately over all three of them. What breath still remained in Teddy's body was driven from it. Bert, too, was gasping. Williams, rubbing his shin and shivering like a leaf was limping away.

Recovering himself, Teddy faced the woman with the bucket, who was now grinning broadly. 'I'm extremely sorry, ma'am, to have inconvenienced you!" Just so had he once heard Joseph apologise to a lady whom he had knocked into in the market.

His cap, crumpled and dirty, lay in the gutter. Picking it up, he put it on his head then doffed it politely. 'Good day to you, ma'am! Come on, Bert!'

But Bert was still deeply shocked. 'Where to?' he asked stupidly.

'Well Street,' said Teddy, making up his mind quickly. 'Your ma's still at work, isn't she?'

''Yes, but what'll your Ma say? With us like this?'

They were indeed a sorry sight, with Teddy's nose bleeding profusely and blood beginning to flow from the cut on Bert's lip.

'We'll go in the back way,' said Teddy resourcefully. 'If she's busy in the shop, she won't see us till we've cleaned up a bit.' Pa always cleaned up from the potbank in the back kitchen.

But so much for wishful thinking! Ma was actually in the back kitchen, scrubbing potatoes, when they lifted the latch and sidled in.

'Hello, Ma!' said Teddy conversationally, as if it was customary for him to come home with his face and jacket covered in blood. 'This is Bert!'

'Pa,' said Teddy that evening. 'Berts ma's a godly lady, isn't she?' Godliness, he'd always been taught, ranked with cleanliness on the scale of virtues.

They were walking home, having just returned Bert to his mother. That, Ma had decided, after they'd explained to her what had happened – well, more or less what had happened – was the best thing to do.

What with her having to pop in and out to see to customers, it had taken most of the afternoon to clean up the two boys. Teddy's jacket, she declared, would never be the same again. And, of course, they'd had to be fed and, with Bert's lip out like a balloon, that had been difficult. Soup was the only nourishment he could manage.

'Who started it?' she'd asked after Teddy's nose had at last stopped bleeding.

'The other boy.'

'What other boy?'

'Don't know his name, Ma.' Already, he'd learned that one didn't tell tales out of school.

'Why did he start it?'

Teddy thought for a moment. 'Don't exactly know, Ma. But, he called us rude names. He said I was teacher's pet.'

This was so much what Ma had expected all along, no further explanation seemed to be required. The only worrying thing was that Ma said she was going to see Mr Smith about it. 'He can't just pick on you like that.'

'I don't think he'll do it to us again, Ma.

'You mean, you hit him?'

'No, I bit him!'

This shook Ma so much, she had to sit down on the old Windsor chair that was kept in the back kitchen. 'You *bit* him? Like a *dog*?'

'That's what the lady said when she threw the water over us.'

At this point, Teddy thought he might have to go and fetch Ma her smelling-salts. It had been a mistake to mention the water. Ma had been so concerned about the blood, she'd hardly noticed how wet their clothes were. By now, the whole incident was assuming the aura of a heroic action, with himself in the leading role.

'It was only a drop, Ma. And I told her I was sorry.'

'So I should think!' To his great relief, the shop bell had pinged at that moment, and Ma had had to go. When she came back, she was too occupied deciding what to do about Bert to worry any more about the water.

'I think the best thing will be for Teddy and his pa to take you home when he gets in Bert, and then they can explain everything to your ma.'

Bert hadn't needed much persuasion. For the first time, Teddy realised how cheerless it must be to return to an empty house each day. However he felt better about it after he'd met Bert's ma. She wasn't very old – not much older than Anna – and pretty in a tired, wispy sort of way. Her eyes were her most striking feature; a deep blue like Bert's and fringed with sooty black lashes. Her black hair, dragged back into a knot, seemed to stretch taut the pale, freckled skin over the high cheek-bones, and Teddy was reminded of the picture in one of his early story-books of a captive princess waiting to be rescued by her prince.

Plainly, she adored Bert. Teddy felt almost envious of the concern she showed over his cut lip; Ma had seemed more worried about the state of his jacket than his nose.

She stood there, in her tiny kitchen, her arm around Bert, her eyes soft and moist. And when she had thanked them for taking care of her son and bringing him home, she looked at Pa and said, 'I'm afraid Bertie has a lot to put up with, one way and another, Mr Smith.' It was as if she knew what Williams had said, although Bertie couldn't possibly have told her.

'He's a fine lad, Mrs Brown. You can be proud of him.'

'Oh, I am!'

'And your home does you credit.' Indeed, the room they stood in was like an Aladdin's cave. There was little furniture – a table, a few upright chairs, one ancient armchair and a standing cupboard. But the curtains were of orange, lined with blue, and an orange cloth covered the table. Patchwork cushions turned the armchair into a nest of colour, but the crowning glory was the wall opposite the fireplace. Painted straight on to the plaster was a wonderful picture of trees and flowers and a river purling over a rocky bed. Birds perched on the branches of the trees or skimmed the water, and in the foreground a bushy-tailed squirrel cracked a nut. Teddy was entranced.

'Did you paint this?' he asked Bert.

'Me and Ma.'

Teddy imagined a giant tea clipper sailing across the kitchen wall in Well Street. 'Pa,' he began, 'could we . . .'

'We'll ask Ma,' said Pa quickly. 'Meantime, Mrs Brown, my wife wondered if both of you could come to tea on Sunday. We understand that Saturday might present difficulties. But my cousin Samuel will also be coming on Sunday, and I should like you to meet him and his wife. After tea, perhaps you would give us the pleasure of your company at chapel?'

Mrs Brown was gazing at Pa as if he'd suggested a trip

to the moon.

'Mr Smith, I haven't been to chapel since before Bertie was born.'

'Well, it's up to you entirely, Mrs Brown. But rest assured, Mrs Smith and I would be proud to have you with us. And Bertie too, of course.'

Privately, Teddy thought it would be a lot more fun if he and Bert were left at home; although there wasn't much they'd be allowed to play with on a Sunday. Saturday tea would have been a lot better. However, Pa seemed set on Sunday.

Soon after Mrs Brown had accepted Pa's invitation, he and Pa took their leave. On the way home, he walked quietly, deep in thought, and then suddenly asked Pa about the godliness of Mrs Brown.

At first, Pa had seemed a little taken aback by the question, but then his reply left Teddy in no doubt. 'A very godly lady indeed, Teddy. The sort of lady a man without principles might easily take advantage of.'

'Taking advantage of' sounded mysterious, but Teddy didn't pursue the matter, as things were beginning to fall into place. Obviously it was of little consequence if Bert was a bastard or not. And as for a 'haw'; well, Williams definitely had it wrong. Before coming out, he'd managed a quick check in Pa's dictionary and 'haw' was exactly what he'd thought – the berry of the hawthorn.

Next time he was home, he might ask Joseph about it. And – he began to skip with excitement at the prospect – he'd also get Joseph to teach him and Bert how to box. Williams' leg had tasted most unsavoury.

7

He was ten when he heard Mr Smith's famous lecture, delivered to the whole school, on the sinking of the steam frigate *Birkenhead*.

He'd heard of it, of course, but apart from knowing that the *Birkenhead* was, in fact, a paddle-steamer adapted to a troopship, and that she had foundered off the coast of South Africa, he still did not know a great deal about her. Neither Joseph, nor Ma and Pa, spoke much of the disasters that could befall a sailor, at least when he was around. However, Alfred Smith was of a different mind.

'It was early in January, in the year of Our Lord 1852, that the *Birkenhead*, under the command of Captain Robert Salmond, R.N., headed for Queenstown in the South of Ireland. Does any boy know which Irish city is served by the port of Queenstown? Yes, Smith?' For Ted's hand had shot up almost of its own volition.

'Cork, sir.'

'Correct. On board already, were the 12th Foot under the command of a Lieutenant Fairclough and a small detachment of the 12th Lancers under the command of two young cornets, John Rolt and Ralph Sheldon-Bond. Now, before we go any further, does anyone know *why* the SS *Birkenhead* was being sent to South Africa with troops on board?'

No boy did, although one hopeful lad suggested the Crimean war; a theory that was treated with mild surprise by his headmaster and the suggestion that he consult his map of the world and ask himself why, if *he* were a general, he would despatch troops to the Crimea via the Cape of

56

Good Hope when there was a much speedier route through, — the what, Smith?'

'Straits of Gibraltar, sir, and then the Mediterranean.'

'Correct! Would that Smith's knowledge of history were as good as that of his geography! Clearly, like the rest of you, he does not know that we were at that time engaged in the Kaffir War, subduing those natives who did not recognise the benefits of British rule, and that the purpose of the *Birkenhead*'s voyage was to convey British reinforcements to Port Elizabeth. Now, why was the *Birkenhead* proceeding to Cork to pick up the greater proportion of the soldiery?'

This time, it was Bert's hand that shot up. 'Because of the potato famine in Ireland, sir. It was considered safer to join the British Army and risk possible death than to stay in Ireland and face certain starvation.'

Ted shot a quick, admiring glance at his friend. Always aware of the plight of the underdog, was Bert. Clearly, Mr Smith was of a similar mind.

'Well said, Brown! And you're quite right, of course. Young Irish men were only too eager to receive their shilling a day, fighting for the Queen. There were four hundred and sixteen of them that embarked on that fateful voyage, along with several families of the regular soldiers. All were under the command of Alexander Seton of the 74th Highlanders, already at thirty-eight years of age, a lieutenant colonel.'

The boys began to relax. Smithy was now so well launched upon his epic tale that it was unlikely he would involve them further.

In absorbed silence, they heard how the soldiers, raw undisciplined recruits though most of them were, and in spite of initial stormy weather, had gradually been drilled and disciplined by Colonel Seton and his second-in-command, Captain Wright; how three of the women had died in childbirth, brought on prematurely by the storm, and another of the dreaded consumption; and how, after a passage lasting forty-seven days, the *Birkenhead* had finally

57

docked in Simon's Bay, near Cape Town, to take on fresh provisions, horses for the officers and coal, before proceeding on the final, two-day leg to Algoa Bay.

'It was six o'clock on the evening of the twenty-fifth of February,' said Mr Smith in solemn tones, 'that the last voyage of the SS *Birkenhead* was begun. Reinforcements were needed urgently at the front and Captain Salmond's instructions were to proceed as quickly as possible. To do this, he had decided to set a course that would follow the coastline at a distance of about three miles.

'The troops, the women and children and those sailors not on watch, retired early to their bunks or hammocks. Soon after one o'clock in the morning, the *Birkenhead* was entering the area off Danger Point, a particularly treacherous part of the coastline where hidden rocks and reefs extended beneath the ocean. Captain Salmond had gone below, but the duty officer, Mr Davies, was fully aware of the precautions that must be taken. Two men kept a sharp lookout from the bows and another took frequent soundings of the depth of the water; the helmsman kept faithfully to the course Captain Salmond had worked out with the aid of the navigational charts of the area. It was just before four bells . . .'

'Two o'clock,' breathed Ted to Bert.

'. . . that there came the terrible sound of metal rasping upon stone as the iron hull of the ship struck a submerged and uncharted rock and came to a grinding halt, with its paddles continuing to thrash helplessly.

'On the poop, all was confusion; the helmsman fought with the wheel, Mr Davies, flung backwards by the impact, struck his head upon a beam and Captain Salmond came rushing out from his quarters. Later, it was discovered that the rock had penetrated the hull just behind the foremast, allowing the sea to rush unchecked into the area where at least a hundred soldiers, oblivious of their fate, swung in their hammocks.'

Here, Mr Smith paused; the silence in the hall was absolute, broken only by heavy breathing and an occasional, surreptitious sniff. Ted found that his hands were clenched into white-knuckled fists.

'All,' continued Mr Smith with great deliberation, 'must have perished immediately and unaware, one hopes, of what was happening to them. And indeed,' he added portentously, 'in view of what was about to happen on deck, perhaps they were the fortunate ones.

'Up on the poop, Captain Salmond had assessed the situation as well as he could and was issuing commands to his officers; several were despatched to various parts of the ship with instructions to scrutinise the damage and report back immediately. The engines were ordered to be stopped and an anchor dropped in the hope that the vessel would thereby be prevented from slipping into deeper water.

'Meanwhile, on the upper deck, Colonel Seton was instructing *his* officers to bring up the remaining troops with all possible haste.'

Again, Mr Smith paused, allowing his eye to rove among his pupils, as if he were Lieutenant Colonel Seton and they his men. Some, indeed, were so caught up in the narrative that they did, in fact, appear to be awaiting his instructions. Ted found that he was breathing quickly, his mouth slightly ajar, his cheeks hot as if flushed with the exertion required to scramble up a narrow ladder on to the open deck. Beside him, Bert seemed to be similarly affected.

'Captain Salmond had ordered the women and children to be brought up and the ship's boats lowered, although he knew them to be hopelessly inadequate for the numbers on board. Clad only in their nightgowns, with here and there a hastily snatched shawl or blanket, the women and children were a pathetic sight as they gathered under the poop.

'For a brief moment, when it was discovered that only one compartment of the ship had been pierced, Captain Salmond allowed himself to hope and gave the order to reverse engines, trusting that this would result in the freeing of the vessel from the rock. But tragically, the manoeuvre only caused the vessel to be holed again, this time near the engine-room, which took in water immediately, dousing the fires, stopping the engines and . . ." Once again, Mr Smith paused and Ted could have sworn there was a tremor on his voice as he continued, '. . . drowning those who were not able to reach the ladders. On deck, some of the soldiers had been detailed to help launch the boats and others to work the pumps which were fighting a losing battle with the torrents of water rushing into the doomed vessel. Others had been given the unenviable task of putting the horses over the side; a difficult and heartbreaking task, since the poor beasts had to be blindfolded; even so, their abject terror can only be imagined.

'But at least, that particular mission was accomplished. Those trying to lower the boats were meeting with less success, the tackle on one breaking before it had even reached the sea, the davits of another so rusted that the bolts could not be withdrawn, and another crashing upside down into the water. However, three were successfully launched, two large and one small, and into one of the larger boats, the women and children were put. Again, we can but imagine the scene as those who were leaving their husbands behind them, cried out and, in some cases, tried to stay with them. But, in spite of the heavy rolling of the vessel, all were safely transferred. The boat was then cut loose and pulled away under the command of Rowland Richard, the young master's assistant, with Coxswain George Till at the oars.'

At this point, all eyes turned automatically towards one of Ted's classmates, sitting nearby.

'We do not *know*,' Mr Smith continued, 'if our pupil Spencer Till is related in anyway to this brave seaman but it is certainly an uncommon name. So. . . .' He paused significantly, while Spencer Till kept his head modestly bent, then continued his story.

'On board, the situation was now desperate as the bow of the ship broke away at the foremast, hurling those who had been standing near into the sea. It was then that a further dreadful threat was realised. Sharks!'

60

There was a concerted hiss as the entire school drew in its breath in horror.

'Within minutes,' Mr Smith continued, 'the air was rent with screams and the sea crimsoned with blood. Still calm in the face of such adversity, Colonel Seton ordered his remaining troops to the poop-deck, where, in spite of the injuries that several had experienced, and the fact that none were fully dressed and many without even their boots, they stood as if on the parade-ground.

'It was then that Captain Salmond intervened. "Jump overboard and make for the boats!" he cried.

'Immediately, Colonel Seton realised that if the troops were to follow the captain's advice, the boat containing the women and children would be swamped and they, too, would become food for the sharks. Turning to face his men, he implored them to stand fast and to await their fate like true soldiers of the Queen. And, to a man, they did so.'

Here, a definite tremble occurred in Mr Smith's delivery and, taking a handkerchief from his pocket, he blew his nose loudly. All over the schoolroom, boys were audibly sniffing. Ted could feel a large tear rolling down his cheek unchecked, until he shot out his tongue and licked it away. But then the single tear became a trickle and only his sleeve could stem the flow.

Mr Smith put away his handkerchief. 'Then the hull of the *Birkenhead* broke in two and the stern rose high into the air so that those soldiers who were not standing near the rails toppled helplessly into the shark-infested sea. Those who were left turned to shake the hand of whoever was standing next to them. Someone– was it the brave colonel? – called out a blessing, and then the *Birkenhead* plunged for ever beneath the waves.'

For several moments, Mr Smith faced his pupils with his head bowed, as if in prayer. And then he looked up and delivered the final words of his lecture.

'Of the four hundred and ninety-one soldiers who had steamed away from Queenstown, a total of three hundred and fifty-eight perished. But every woman and child was saved. Truly, it can be said that those who died that day were British until the very end.'

After a moment, Mr Smith added, 'I have here the names of those who died, and those who survived to tell the world of the courage of their friends. If any boy wishes to consult them, he is welcome to do so.'

Immediately, there was a general surge of movement towards Mr Smith's desk while he obligingly stood back. All were of a mind to actually see the name of 'George Till' for themselves.

'Look!' said Ted suddenly, Here's a "John Smith", underneath George Till's name!'

A brief silence greeted this statement until one boy, peering over his shoulder, said, 'Yes, but . . . Smith! Well, I mean to say – *Smith*!'

'Ten a penny,' said another.

'More like a hundred a penny,' murmured a wag called Carpenter, but quietly, for Mr Smith was still standing nearby.

Perhaps it was the emotional tension created by the lecture that caused Ted to hiss back, 'Smith's as good a name as Carpenter, any day! And I'll prove it in Hall Fields – when school's finished!'

Hall Fields was where the school played – and fought. Ted, even before Joseph had taught him the rudiments of boxing, had often hurled himself into the fray on whichever side he saw fit to support. But this would be, so to speak, his first solo appearance.

'You'll be my second, Bert?' he asked, once school was dismissed.

'Of course! But Ted, why are you fighting, exactly?' Of the two, Bert was the peacemaker.

'To show that Smith's as good a name as Carpenter, even if there *are* a lot of us.'

'Well, there must be quite a lot of Browns, too. But I'm not going to fight about it.'

But by then, they had arrived at the fields and a sizeable collection of boys had grouped themselves around the two assailants.

'Fists or swordsticks?' enquired the seconds. There being no sticks immediately available, fists were decided upon.

'Begin!' shouted Bert, raising his right arm; then he retired smartly to the corner where Ted's jacket had been neatly folded.

The fight was brief but bloody. After five minutes, Carpenter's front teeth were loosened, and Bert was running out of the handkerchiefs generously donated by Ted's supporters as he tried to stem the flow of blood from his nose. It was at this point that one of the monitors intervened.

'What's all this about?' he asked Bert.

'To show that Smith's as good a name as Carpenter, any day,' said Bert stoutly.

'That's silly,' said the older boy. 'Without Smiths, horses wouldn't be shod, and without Carpenters, the carts they draw wouldn't be made. So one's just as important as the other.'

The logic of this, once passed on to the participants, brought the fight to a speedy conclusion.

'Shake hands,' ordered the monitor.

Not sorry to have the fight ended, for his shirt was now soaked with blood and, besides, he was beginning to feel extremely hungry, Ted extended his hand. 'Friends, Carpenter.'

'Friends, Smith.'

At the pump, where their ways divided, Ted paused, gave his jacket to Bert to hold and stripped off his shirt. 'Are you *sure* cold water brings blood out, Bert?'

'Certain sure! My ma always says so.'

'Well, I hope *my* ma agrees.'

Bert operated the handle while Ted swilled the shirt.

'Told you!' said Bert triumphantly. 'I should put your jacket on,' he added solicitously, 'or you'll catch your death. Want me to come home with you?'

But the suggestion smacked of cowardice. 'No, I'll be all right, thanks, Bert.'

'Well, good luck! And – be British!'

Sadly, it was a phrase that didn't cut any ice with Ma. 'Ted, whatever have you been up to? You look like a drowned rat with its throat cut!'

'I was just – being British, Ma.' And,' he added hastily as Ma still continued to advance upon him, 'defending the good name of Smith.'

Ma paused. In spite of herself, a smile crept over her face. 'In that case, lad, I'm surprised you're still in one piece!'

8

By the time he was fourteen, Ted's immediate future had been decided. William, now married to Thirza and the proud father of James and little Annie, had suggested employment at the ironworks and Ted thought he might as well go along with the idea – at least until Joseph came home and sorted things out for him. For Joseph now had his master's certificate and was presently at sea on the *Regent*; and with him was Anna.

This had only been possible because Ma had offered to look after their children, George and little Frank. 'At least,' Anna had confided to Ted, 'I know they'll be safe with Ma, especially with Thirza and William now living next door. And perhaps it will take her mind off your pa.'

For Pa – dear, kind, patient Pa – had succumbed to the consumption that was the scourge of so many men who had worked in the Potteries and been subjected, from an early age, to the alternate fierce heat of the furnaces and the damp cold of the sheds.

Ted would never forget the day when he'd come home from school to be told that he'd passed away. And with his grief had come the realisation that he must now shoulder some of the responsibilities of the household although Ma, with Thirza's help, still ran the shop.

Leaving the British had been a wrench, especially as Bert, having decided to teach, was staying on as a monitor; but he'd still be able to see him when his shifts allowed. Bert's mother had now married and his home circumstances were consequently greatly improved.

Just before Joseph and Anna were due to come home,

Ted was given the responsibility of operating the giant steam hammer; a task that gave him a heady sense of power. But now, at seventeen, he was ready for a change.

Ted was never sure if it was her own persistence that had persuaded Joseph to take Anna on his — Ted's — maiden voyage, or if it was Ma, wanting the reassurance of a feminine eye kept upon her youngest chick. But whatever the circumstances, here they were on the *Senator Weber*, on this cold February day, soon after his seventeenth birthday, warped away from the dockside and moving now on the tide, with a general cargo of pots and pans, cartwheels and cement, even a couple of pianos, done up like mummies in sheets and sacking. His arms still ached from the effort of helping to stow it all with the other two apprentices, James Grieve and Thomas Forster. Thomas, he knew already because he, too, came from Hanley, but James was still an unknown quantity.

The groups of stevedores scattered along the wharf sent up a ragged cheer as Joseph gave the command, 'Loose all sails!' The moment he had dreamed of, for as long as he could remember, was suddenly upon him.

It was a pity he hadn't more time to savour it. As it was, he was more than occupied in helping to man the halyards while the great sails came billowing out above their heads, cracking like gunfire as the wind took them. He hadn't been sent up among them — yet; but any minute now, he knew that he would be. Almost before the command 'Stop mainsail buntlines!' had left Joseph's lips, he'd caught the third mate's eye and, seizing the bundle of twine, was heading for the ratlines.

'Buntlines,' he'd once explained to a long-suffering Bert during one of his dissertations upon the sea, 'are ropes for hauling up the sails. When the sails are unfurled, then the ropes must be made secure or they will chafe against the sails and wear holes in them.' Bert, he seemed to remember, had been singularly unimpressed by this nugget of information.

In itself, it was not a difficult task and he'd been joined

by a big, burly seaman with a mop of tousled black hair and eyes bluer than Ted's own. What made it important to him was that it was the first time he'd been sent aloft.

The buntlines secured, he was in no hurry to descend but stood there on the foot-ropes, gazing down. Far below, but not as far as if he were up among the royals, was the deck; around it the cold, grey sea, not rough, as yet, but turning choppy and with storm clouds piling up on the horizon.

Two female figures, he noticed, were standing gazing up into the rigging – Anna and the young lady she was chaperoning to Hong Kong. As he watched, Anna raised an arm and pointed straight at him and he frowned; clearly, she was making no secret of her relationship to 'one of the boys'. And he wasn't sure that he wanted Miss Thingummybob to know. Joseph didn't encourage fraternisation between crew and passengers. Thinking along these lines, it was a few moments before he realized he'd been gazing downwards for at least a minute, with no feeling of vertigo. Which must mean that he was going to be, as Joseph put it, 'all right up top'. He found himself grinning with relief and for a moment was tempted to wave at Anna. But then he caught the eye of his companion and hastily turned his gaze shoreward to where Liverpool was becoming a rapidly receding jumble of masts and rigging, pierced by the spire of St Nicholas's and the high tower of St Luke's.

'Goodbye, Bert!' he murmured under his breath, for somewhere in that waste of mean streets and courts, among the hovels that were even more insanitary than those in the Black Country, was Bert; strong in his determination that some at least of the children living there should learn to read and write.

And then, like the bellowing of an angry bull, came the voice of the third mate, clearly audible in spite of the wind whistling about his ears. 'Afraid to come down, are we? Want me to come up and help you?'

Ted and his companion grinned at each other. 'A kick up the arse, that's all the help he'd give us,' said the seaman, beginning to inch his way back along the yard. 'And I'm James, by the way. James Hyslop.' There was a strong Irish lilt to his voice.

'I'm Ted. Ted Smith.' For the first time, he was grateful that Joseph was his half-brother. With a name like Smith, there'd be no questions asked.

As it happened, it might have been better if he and James had been left up in the rigging, for they were back within the hour. The clouds Ted had noticed were now directly overhead, the wind tearing through the rigging like a banshee as the *Senator Weber* dipped beneath the waves, her scuppers awash. Anna and Miss Thingummybob had long since disappeared.

Topsails only, Joseph had decreed, and securing bunt-lines, Ted soon discovered, was child's play compared with clawing in the wet canvas of the mainsail. Every time he heaved, the wind heaved harder. But this time the third mate was alongside him and managing in some miraculous fashion to ignore the maxim 'one hand for the Company and one for yourself' and to haul with both hands while still maintaining his balance on the foot-rope. It was, Ted decided, all a question of gravity, and did his best to follow suit. The next moment, he was being grabbed ignominiously by the slack of his pants.

'Don't want to lose you on the first day, boy!' said Henry Tate, and astonished Ted by suddenly giving him an enormous grin.'

Bark's worse than his bite, thought Ted; but he took pains, even so, to heave even harder.

9

When at sea, it was Joseph's practice, weather permitting, to hold a short service amidships on Sunday morning: a reading from the Bible, a few prayers and a hymn or two. The *Senator Weber* was fortunate in having a carpenter aboard, Robert Redfern, who could play the banjo, and on Sunday mornings he came into his own.

It was Anna, bonnet-ties flying in the breeze, wayward tendrils of hair blowing across her face, who stood beside Joseph on the poop-deck on that first Sunday morning and read from the Psalms:

' "If I climb into heaven, thou art there: if I go down to hell, thou art there also. If I take the wings of the morning: and remain in the uttermost parts of the sea, even there also shall thy hand lead me, and thy right hand shall hold me." '

The breeze in the rigging was no more than a gentle thrum and her voice, sweet but clear, rang across the deck. Her gaze, when she lifted it from her bible, seemed to embrace the entire company, and Ted noticed how the eyes of even the most hard-bitten seamen softened as they looked at her. It isn't only Joseph, he thought, who benefits from her presence.

He was proud of them both. At thirty-five, Joseph was in his prime. Like a lion, Ted thought, admiring the full, flowing beard of golden hair and wondering if his own tender chin would ever sprout so magnificent a growth; or his shoulders threaten, as Joseph's did, to split the seams of his jacket.

Miss Thingummybob, just behind Anna, stood through

69

the greater part of the service with her eyes fixed decorously upon the deck. Small hands, neatly gloved, clasped her prayer-book and a pair of shining black toecaps peeped from beneath her pale blue skirts. Little Miss Milksop! thought Ted disparagingly, and was considerably put out when, during the singing of the second hymn, she suddenly raised her head and, gazing straight at him, lowered one eyelid. It was little more than a twitch, a barely perceptible flutter of her lashes, but it was enough to send the blood rushing up into his cheeks. Hastily, he averted his own gaze, hoping that no one else had seen her. Otherwise, his life would be unbearable. Little baggage! he amended his first opinion.

When the last notes of *Bread of Heaven* had died away, the ship's company, except for the three apprentices, were dismissed. Anna, followed by Miss Thingummybob, disappeared into the captain's quarters and Joseph, descending from the poop, came to lean casually against the rail, there to survey the youngest members of his crew. Ted, for all the attention he was given, could have been a total stranger.

'Now, lads,' Joseph began conversationally, 'Sunday mornings, the weather being on our side, I like to have a little chat with you. At the moment, you have the advantage of me – you know who I am. But I shall learn your names, before long. Until then, if I shout "Boy!" and you're within hailing distance, jump to it! Most of the time, though, you'll have the third mate to contend with. You'll find Mr Tate a hard taskmaster – but a fair one. He'll never ask you to do anything that he hasn't, at some time in his career, done himself. And still does, when needed.'

At this point, almost absent-mindedly, Joseph reached out a hand towards Ted and tapped the top button of his jacket. 'Done up, if you please – er – Smith, did someone say your name was?'

'Er – yes, sir! Smith, sir! Sorry, sir!' Hastily, he pushed the offending button back through its hole, although he could have sworn it had never left it.

'Thank you. A ship can only be as smart as its crew. Now, back to business. Your navigation you will learn from Mr

Tate. Your seamanship you will learn from those around you. Some of the men have served with me before and, on the whole they're a good bunch. Treat them with respect. However, much can be learned from the sea itself. Sometimes, when you take the helm, you'll have to fight for control. The sea will be pulling the wheel one way and you the other and, now and then, the sea will win. Then it will be a matter of hanging on and riding it out; no point in trying to pit your puny strength against the might of the ocean. But remember two very important things: you have a brain and the sea has not, a ship has a soul, and the sea has not. So together, you and the ship can survive the mightiest of storms.

'Salt air's gone to his head, you may be thinking, but remember my words when you're perched high up in the rigging and the waves are washing the decks better than a thousand mopheads. If you've got sea sense, you'll survive.

'So there you are, lads. Work hard, be patient with each other and write home whenever you have time. I promise you I'll hail a passing ship with your letters. Tell your mothers you're not on some crack, record-breaking tea clipper, but a steady, reliable, three-master whose captain aims to get her home in one piece. Good luck!'

And then he was gone, leaving not just an empty space in front of them but, as far as Ted was concerned, a positive feeling of deprivation. For several seconds, all three stood in silence and then Tom Forster said, 'So, ships have souls, have they?'

Tom was two years younger than Ted and while also from Hanley, and an ex-pupil of the British, they'd never been friendly. He could only hope that Tom didn't know of his relationship to Joseph. Certainly, he had given no indication of it.

'No more unlikely than you having a brain, Tom!' They were getting to know each other now and Jim Grieve had obviously decided he could indulge in a good-humoured leg-pull. A tall, sandy-haired Scot, he had a dry sense of humour that appealed to Ted but also, he suspected, a quick temper. He, too, was only fifteen but could easily have passed for seventeen, at least. 'He's got it in for *you*, Ted,' he added.

'Looks like it!' In fact he'd welcomed Joseph's reprimand, which made it clear from the beginning that he must expect no favours. All the same, he guessed that Joseph, tongue in cheek, would have savoured the situation to the full.

'There's a lot in what he said, mind you,' said Tom.

'You mean Ted being a scruff? You're no tailor's dummy yourself, Thomas.'

'No, you fool! Us having sea sense.'

'*Non*sense in your case, Tom!'

'It may be Sunday,' the voice of the third mate crackled like gunfire behind them, 'but there's plenty of bright work needs polishing. So, off with those fancy jackets and jump to it!'

Greatly daring but, after all, it *was* Sunday, they groaned in unison.

For a split second, Henry Tate's face creased into a grin. Then, 'Right! I'm counting up to three. If you're still here when I've finished – you're cleaning out the heads. One . . . two . . . three. . . . Smith!'

First Joseph, now the third mate. It must be a conspiracy!

He was about to stand his first watch at the helm. One more hurdle would either be surmounted or prove his downfall. Already, he knew that he could climb aloft and stay there, as nimble as any monkey. He'd learned, too, that it was safer to climb on the side from whence the wind blew, otherwise the tilt of the vessel would be against him. Now, his concern was to remember that it needed only one moment's lack of concentration to send him tumbling to almost certain death, or maiming for life, which would be worse.

The other matter that Ted was now easy about was his stomach. During the roughest weather, it had shown no desire to throw up.

And even when Joseph, admittedly choosing a calm day,

had insisted that each boy climb out in turn along the bowsprit, edge his way to its very end and remain there, far out over the water, for several minutes, Ted had felt only an enormous exhilaration. Had felt, indeed, as if he were part of the ship, riding each wave as she dipped and soared like a bird. Or – and he had grinned hugely to himself – as if he were on the roundabout at Hanley Fair. Only now, he was swooping down towards an ocean deeper than he could ever imagine, so close he could feel the spray spattering his cheeks before he was swept skyward once again. And his stomach never budged an inch!

When he got back to the others – he had been the first to go – he hadn't been able to resist a quick, direct glance at Joseph, something he rarely permitted himself to do, for fear that eye contact would cause him to smile in too friendly a fashion. But then, to his great delight, he'd found that Joseph was also gazing at him directly.

'Well, Smith? How was it?'

'Mag-magnificent, sir! I – truly magnificent!' He'd even stuttered in his excitement.

And Joseph had beamed with satisfaction, before turning to Jim. 'Right, Grieve, your turn!'

But taking the helm had remained a challenge that he was by no means sure he would meet. What if his muscle power was inadequate, if all those hours he'd spent in the gym with Bert proved insufficient? Or his hands should slip on the wheel, his movements be jerky and spasmodic instead of the steady pull Joseph had once tried to demonstrate on an old cartwheel, in the backyard of Well Street? What if he were to let Joseph down? That was his greatest fear of all.

'Easy does it,' advised Henry Tate at his side. 'Sea's calm as a millpond, so just keep her steady. South-south-east.'

'South-south-east, sir,' repeated Ted, dry-mouthed, as he grasped the wheel. Calm as a millpond it might be, but the rudder still had a mind of its own; he could feel it resisting as he tried to keep the wheel absolutely still.

'Give a little, take a little,' advised the third mate. 'Don't

73

fight it. Relax.'

He did, allowing the wheel a little play, first to port, then to starboard. Suddenly he felt as if his arms were an extension of the spokes. His face threatening to crack in two with the enormity of his grin, he had an almost irresistible urge to sing at the top of his voice. He could do it!

The next minute, the wheel seemed suddenly to turn of its own accord as the rudder took it. He heard the canvas above his head crack in protest and knew a second of sheer panic.

'Ooops!' said the third mate, reaching out a steadying hand to bring them back on course. 'Relaxed just a litle too much there, we did. And this lady has a mind of her own. It's my belief she doesn't care for being named after a man.'

It was nearly midnight, just before eight bells, and any minute now the port watch would stagger up from below. But for the moment, Ted and Henry Tate were isolated in the pool of light cast by the lantern swinging above the wheel. Ted dared to risk a question.'

'All different, are they, sir, the ships you've sailed on?'

'All ships have a character of their own, Smith. I'm sure your brother would be the first to agree.'

The helm veered fractionally to starboard as Ted reacted to this information, but was instantly righted. 'Don't worry, lad.' Henry gazed innocently up at the stars. 'The secret's safe with me. And don't mind if I pick on you more than most. Captain's very keen that you should be treated just like everyone else, no favours given.'

'And none expected,' said Ted stoutly, somehow oddly delighted with the news that he was to be picked on. It was almost as if he'd been paid a compliment.

'Anyway, there's one thing you can be sure of,' said Henry, 'you've found your sea legs quicker than some. Keep her steady, boy!' he suddenly bawled. 'You're steering a ship, not a bloody baby carriage!'

For a moment Ted froze. He could have sworn he *was* keeping her steady. But then he saw the second mate walking towards them, yawning prodigiously. The calm was over.

74

10

The *Senator Weber* soon came under the influence of the north-east trade winds. Now, the starboard watch hoped and prayed, there would be no more reefing or setting of sails as they tacked to whatever wind prevailed; now, sails would be set in the reasonable expectancy that there they could remain while the ship scudded steadily southward. And to an extent they were right. But first, every shred of canvas had to be changed, from the tough, storm-proof sailcloth under with they'd left Liverpool to a worn, patched, fair-weather set which, nevertheless, should be sufficiently strong for the pressure of the trade winds.

'To think,' grumbled Jim, 'that we shall have to change the whole bleeding lot back again when we get into rougher weather!'

They were on deck, folding the heavy cloth for the sail-maker's attention, when Henry, as usual, appeared without warning. 'Right, Smith! Captain wants you in his cabin.'

Tom and Jim ceased their folding and gazed at Ted in stunned silence. What mischief had he been up to that could result in a summons to the Presence?

'A flogging, d'you think?' Jim was the first to recover his poise.

'Or stringing to the yard-arm?' Tom suggested helpfully.

'Stow it!' advised the third mate briskly. 'Whatever the reason, button your jacket, Smith, and be on your way. And you two,' he glowered at Tom and Jim, 'look lively! The deck's crying out for holystoning when you've finished with that sail.'

'And there was I thinking it was Henry's stomach,' Ted

heard Jim mutter under his breath.

He grinned to himself. Now for Anna and Miss Thing-ummybob!

He'd been right in his supposition. All three were gazing expectantly at the door as he walked through it. Carefully, he shut it behind him then, studiously ignoring the other two, addressed himself to Joseph.

'Sir?' A 'boy' on his first voyage didn't presume anything, even if the captain were his half-brother.

Joseph grinned broadly. 'At ease, Smith.'

'Smith, indeed! Darling Ted, how are you?' And the next moment, Anna's arms were around his neck and he was being hugged and kissed until his cap fell over his eyes. But even then, she didn't stop but merely pulled it off his head altogether and sent it skimming across the cabin.

Over her head, Ted caught Miss Thingummybob's eye and grinned shamefacedly.

'Come, my dear,' said Joseph, 'remember our guest.'

Guest, indeed! Someone, no doubt, would be paying the line handsomely for having her aboard. But certainly, they were treating her as one.

'Emma, forgive me! This is my own dear brother-in-law, Edward Smith. And this, Ted, is Miss Emma Dalrymple.' She released him sufficiently to allow him to extend a hand towards the girl, who rose from the small sofa and gave a tiny curtsey before putting her hand in his. Surprisingly, for he had expected it to be limp and languid, it was firm and warm – and remained in his for several moments before withdrawing.

'How do you do, Miss Dalrymple?'

'I do very well indeed, Mr Smith, thank you.'

Her eyes, like his, were blue but whereas his, he knew, inclined to seriousness unless provoked into mirth, hers gave the impression of permanent, twinkling liveliness. Her nose was small and straight, her mouth lusciously curving, the lower lip almost pouting in its fulness. Like Anna's, her dress was simple, the skirts manageable in the close confines of the cabin, but made of some pretty sprigged material, with a white lace fichu at the neck.

'You are not,' Anna pointed out in her direct fashion, 'at some grand function in England. You are in the middle of the ocean, miles from anywhere . . .'

'Latitude 23 degrees north, longitude 19 degrees west, to be precise,' murmured Joseph, *sotto voce*, and with a broad wink at Ted.

'. . . so there is no need to stand on ceremony.' His wife swept on regardless. "Miss Dalrymple and Mr Smith, indeed!"'

'My dear, in the fulness of time . . .' Joseph began reprovingly, but again he was waved down.

'Now, Joseph, you know quite well that there is no such thing as the fulness of time on board a vessel such as this. It is all bustle and activity from dawn until dusk.'

'And right through the night, my dear, only you are not always aware of it.'

'Is that true, Mr Smith? I mean,' Emma fluttered her eyelashes, 'Ted? You work right through the night?'

'Well, not *right* through it – er – Emma. The watches change at midnight and again at four.'

'Indeed? I must try and remain awake one night to observe it. A great ceremony is there, like the changing of the guard at Windsor Castle?'

He'd never been to Windsor Castle but the memory of himself and Tom and Jim being shaken awake fifteen minutes before the watch changed, then shambling up on deck, rubbing the sleep from their eyes, was enough to make him smile. 'Hardly that, Emma! In fact,' he caught Joseph's eye again and grinned, 'not at all worth the while of anyone to stay awake for. Even,' and he widened his eyes at her, 'young ladies who do *not* require any beauty sleep.'

The neatness of this last remark, which he would dearly have loved to be able to convey to Tom and Jim, was somewhat marred by a hoot of mirth from his sister-in-law.

Emma, Joseph explained to Ted, was journeying to Hong Kong to be with her parents. Her father was the Far Eastern representative of a Staffordshire manufactory which, besides making its own fine china, specialised in the importing of porcelain.

'So you see,' said Anna cheerfully, 'Emma and I have much in common. Our origins are both in the Potteries, even if Emma's are on a much grander scale than mine.'

It transpired, however, that Emma had spent very little time there, having lived with an aunt and uncle in London, where she had attended a select seminary for young ladies. She would stay in Hong Kong, she informed Ted, for as long as she found it interesting.

Would Ted, she enquired, be staying long in Hong Kong? She would so like him to meet her parents.

'How long I stay will be entirely up to the captain,' he explained, carefully not looking at Joseph, 'and I fear I shall have little control over my activities while I am there. The third mate – '

'Oh, poof to the third mate!' said Emma Dalrymple, which so exactly echoed the opinion of the starboard watch, at least when it was off duty, that Ted could do nothing else but smile broadly. 'Well, we shall have to see, won't we!' she continued, and now the bright blue eyes were twinkling merrily at Joseph. 'I'm sure the captain could be persuaded.'

'He has the reputation,' said Ted, tongue in cheek, 'of being a very hard taskmaster.' And you, Emma Dalrymple, he thought to himself, as laughter rippled around the cabin, doubtless have the reputation of getting your own way in most things. So, it will be interesting to see exactly what *does* happen in Hong Kong.

Anna spent the next few minutes in checking upon his welfare. Was he getting enough to eat?

She offered him a box of marzipan dainties, but three, he told her, would be ample.

'I think I should be getting back – sir.'

'I think you're right – before your sister-in-law makes a complete ninny of you.'

So he now had to endure yet more hugs and kisses and admonitions to 'take care on that dreadful rigging' and even to his surprise, a brisk 'now remember, Ted, one hand for the Company, one for yourself,' from Joseph.

Emma Dalrymple contented herself with a brief pressure of her hand on his but would, he felt sure, have offered more had they been – perish the thought! – alone.

'By the way, Smith,' said Joseph, just before he opened the cabin door, 'your knowledge of the stars is excellent and you've remembered the names of the various parts of the rigging with no difficulty. Pray tell your shipmates that they will be called upon to demonstrate their prowess in due course.'

'Aye, aye, sir!' And he touched the peak of the cap that he'd now retrieved from the corner where Anna had thrown it.

'Well?' they asked once he'd found them, hard at work polishing the brass of the signal gun. 'What did he want?'

'Oh, just a general chat,' said Ted airily. 'Did I think he was running a good ship, setting the right course, handling the crew fairly? And, by the way, he sent you these! And he produced the dainties from his pocket.

'So, what really happened?' asked Jim, munching steadily.

'He only asked me questions about navigation, positions of the stars, that sort of thing. ' "Your turn would come, he said." '

'And do you really get dainties,' Tom asked, licking his fingers appreciatively, 'if you know the answers?'

'Only if Mrs Hancock likes the look of you. I doubt if you two will stand a chance!'

11

For some days, the sky had been like a great metallic lid, pressing down upon their heads and seeming to stultify their brains. On this particular day, the seasoned sailors had sniffed the air and prophesied a storm before nightfall. At twelve noon, the boys of the starboard watch were late relieving the port watch; Tom's boots had mysteriously disappeared and then been found, after frantic searching, at the back of a sail locker.

'What time d'you call this?' Edward Smith was a seaman on the port watch; an aggressive man, as unlike his namesake as it was possible to be.

'If people's boots were left where they're put, instead of being planted in sail lockers,' Tom snarled, still seething with annoyance and confident that the port watch had been responsible, 'we wouldn't be late.'

'Getting too big for them, aren't we?' taunted Smith. 'Little runt!'

That did it. Although the seaman was almost twice his size, Tom sprang, going for the throat. Not expecting such belligerence, the man was caught off balance. But the boots which had been the cause of the trouble in the first place were Tom's downfall yet again. Urged on by Ted and Jim to hurry, he hadn't bothered to tie their laces and now, catching his foot, he fell heavily, hitting the deck like a felled tree.

'That's right!' jeered Edward Smith. 'On your knees!' And he raised a foot and kicked Tom hard in the ribs.

Jim had already gone to stand his watch at the helm but Ted was still there. It was Williams and his taunts all over again. Without a second thought, he launched himself at Smith. This time, however, he didn't go for the legs. This time, he knew just what he was doing. All the power of his right arm, strengthened by weeks of heaving wet canvas on to the yards, of fighting with a helm determined to take its own course, was behind the fist that connected neatly, sweetly, with Smith's jaw. He went down like a ninepin, on top of Tom, who was still spreadeagled on the deck.

Ted paused. What now? Did he leave Smith there, help Tom to his feet, then go about his duties? Or pull Smith up too, and offer to shake hands?

But the rules of the British weren't those of the *Senator Weber* and, in any case, he wasn't at all sure he wanted to shake Edward Smith's hand; kicking a man when he was down was something he abominated. However, the next moment the problem was taken out of his hands.

'Right!' said the third mate, coming cat-footed upon the scene and glancing quickly in the direction of the poopdeck. 'Down below, both of you! We'll settle this in a proper manner.'

'But, sir,' Tom began to protest as he staggered to his feet.

'About your duties!' snapped the third mate.

He's not interested in the whys and wherefores of the matter, Ted thought. All he cares about is having a good fight. Well, I'll show 'em, even if Joseph does clap me in irons for it!

The fight was brief but bloody. Edward Smith was a couple of inches taller but Ted was quicker on his feet and had learned from months of sparring with Bert in the gymnasium.

Even so, first blood was to Smith. A vicious left hook on the mouth sent Ted reeling back against the bunks that lined the walls of the half-deck. Dimly, he was aware of being helped to his feet by James Hyslop, the Irishman who'd spoken kindly to him on his first day and who had, ever since, greeted him with a cheerful 'Top o' the morning, young sir!' whenever they met.

Smith was now prancing about in front of him like a

puppet on a string and grinning like one, too.

'Go for his belly,' Hyslop growled in Ted's ear.

And Ted did, catching Smith fair and square in the middle of the solar plexus and causing him to double up with the pain of it.

The next minute, Smith was rushing at Ted like a maddened bull. Good! Ted side-stepped neatly so that Smith crashed straight into Hyslop, who bounced him back into the 'ring' like an indiarubber ball.

What would have happened next, if there hadn't been an enormous, reverberating crash above their heads as of several cannon firing simultaneously, would always be open to conjecture.

'All hands on deck and look smart about it!' The first mate's frantic bellow had them all rushing up.

The anticipated storm had arrived with a vengeance. The noise they'd heard was the splitting of the sails hoisted to catch the scant breeze that had been wafting them slowly southward since dawn, and which had now suddenly changed into a terrifying, easterly crosswind. With it, came a volume of rain such as Ted had never experienced before. Through driving sheets of it – like a steel curtain lashing his swollen mouth with slivers of sharp metal – he could dimly make out Joseph at the helm; with him stood Jim and one of the seamen. He hoped Tom was all right, but there wasn't time to worry before he was aloft, clewing up what remained of the canvas.

None of them were wearing oilskins, and within seconds, they were soaked to the skin, their feet slipping on the foot-ropes, their hands clawing frantically at the sodden canvas. Oh, that he were an octopus, and preferably a deaf one, for up here, the crack of the sails, the hiss of the rain and the shriek of the wind through the rigging had increased to a pitch that threatened the safety of his eardrums. Certainly, it would have been impossible to hear a command from below. Not that they needed any. They all knew they had to haul in the royals, the *Senator Weber*'s topmost sails, or what remained of them. Below them, working on the top gallants would be almost child's play, not that those doing it would have agreed.

Ted was on the inside of the yard, nearest the mast, and next to him – as luck would have it – was Edward Smith. Further along, he could see James Hyslop. Clewing up, especially in such a storm, required precise teamwork to be effective, or as precise as you could make it, bending and hauling in unison. Used to working together, the starboard watch had it down to a fine art, but now, with all hands mingled, Edward Smith was an unknown quantity.

So it could have been simply a lack of co-ordination that caused a sudden break in the rhythm, a release of strain where Ted had been poised to receive it. Whatever the reason, it was sufficient for him to lose his balance on the foot-rope and his grip on the sail and to clutch wildly at the air before hurtling downwards.

For what felt like eternity, but could only have been seconds, the wind seemed to rush right through his head, in at one ear and out, the other. And then he hit some hard, unyielding object. It wasn't the deck, because he was still travelling, but the object – it was the third mate, he later discovered, balanced on the yard of the gallants below – had deflected his passage outward into the shrouds. Frantically, he grabbed at the ropes. Leading from the ship's masthead to her sides, they were of little support, but his purchase, even so, was sufficient to help him swing his way inboard like a monkey.

There wasn't time to dwell on it; later, perhaps, but now he had to climb back up there, although every muscle in his body was shrieking its protest. Somehow, he managed it – to find the others securing the gaskets around the sails as if his sudden disappearance had never been noticed.

But it had, of course; by Smith and Hyslop, at least. And by the third mate. 'In a hurry, weren't we?' he asked when they were all back on deck.

Ted managed a feeble grin; reaction had set in now and a paroxysm of violent shivering was threatening to take over his whole body. 'S-sorry, sir! F-forgot my handkerchief.'

A weak joke, but it was the best he could manage.

'Well, next time let me know and I'll fetch it for you. You nearly had me off as well.'

'Thought you were a gonner,' said James Hyslop when the third mate had left them.

'So did I!'

'What happened?'

'Just lost my balance.'

'I doubt it,' said Hyslop. But left it at that.

It was next day, when the storm had become history, that Ted came up on deck and saw Hyslop in close conversation with Smith; although conversation, he decided was hardly the word for whatever was passing between them. Altercation, more like, and Hyslop was delivering most of it. Ted saw him raise his fist and Smith shrink back against the rail. The fist stayed in mid-air, just a couple of inches away from the other's jaw, and the threat was plain to see.

Ted turned smartly on his heel and went aft. He could guess what that little scene had been all about. In more ways than one, he was a lucky lad.

12

In the event, in spite of Henry's threats to the contrary, the South China Seas treated the *Senator Weber* in much the same fashion as a doting parent its favourite child: only occasionally goaded into a show of impatience and for the most part smiling benevolently.

'Don't know what all the fuss was about,' said Jim laconically as they dropped anchor in Hong Kong's Victoria Harbour on the seventeenth day of July after over five months at sea. It was oppressively hot and he was fanning himself languidly with his cap.

'They say July and August are the worst months for the typhoons,' said Ted almost absent-mindedly as he gazed about him, 'so it's as well we're at anchor.'

There was almost too much to take in. The deep, natural harbour, with Victoria Peak rising behind and Kowloon clearly visible on the mainland, was crammed with vessels of every description. He could make out the raked masts and sharp bows of several clippers towering above a mass of small, native craft: sampans, with their distinctive central sail that Joseph had described to him, sturdy fishing-junks, and so many primitve bamboo rafts and little boats it was a wonder there was water enough to keep them afloat. And why they didn't all sink under the weight of their gesticulating, chattering occupants and their cargoes of fruit and vegetables, fish and chickens, many of them still alive, was a minor miracle. A fragrance that he couldn't identify, sweet and somewhat sickly, vied with the familiar dank harbour smell.

'And all this is part of the British Empire?' Tom's voice

expressed not pride but amazement, tinged with disaproval.

'Since the treaty of 1841,' said Jim knowledgeably. He was always telling them how vastly superior Scottish education was to English.

'A pimple on China's arse, is how some describe it,' contributed Henry Tate, coming to peer over their shoulders, 'and caps, may I remind you, boy, should be worn on the head, not fluttered about like a cow's tail. Think yourself already in a whore-house, no doubt,' he added, to Ted's somewhat shocked surprise.

'Chance,' murmured the worldly Jim, as he placed his cap where it belonged, 'would be a fine thing!' But he kept his voice low. Henry had been a lot friendlier of late, but even so, it didn't do to presume.

Suddenly there was a great commotion below them on the quayside as a procession of rickshaws, pulled by coolies in white conical hats and loose cotton shifts above their bare legs, drew up on the cobbles. A stout grey-haired gentleman, sporting a magnificent set of Dundreary whiskers, sprang out from the first and, moving swiftly to the second, handed out a middle-aged lady clad in elegant, dove-grey silk whose angular features were framed, somewhat incongruously, by the pale pink ruching of an elaborately trimmed bonnet. Once on the ground, they stood for a moment gazing expectantly upward at the deck of the *Senator Weber*. And then —

'Mama! Papa!' came a shrill, female cry, and down the gangway flew Emma Dalrymple, skirts flying, hatless, her slippered feet seeming hardly to touch the boards.

Fascinated, the watchers gazed down on the little group as hugs and kisses were exchanged, and questions asked to which no answers, apparently, were expected. And then Emma was leading them back up the gangway and Anna and Joseph were welcoming them aboard.

It took Ted several seconds before he was sure that it *was* Joseph, for he was now magnificently clad in a new reefer suit and sporting a tall pot-hat. The little party all disappeared in the direction of Joseph's cabin.

'Lucky devil!' said Jim.

He was immediately rounded upon by the third mate.

'Hard work and determination, boy. That's what's put Captain Hancock into a position of authority, and don't you forget it.'

And Ma, thought Ted, thinking how proud she would have been to see Joseph now.

In the more relaxed atmosphere prevailing on board, now that they were in harbour, the boys remained leaning over the rail until, about ten minutes later, Emma, her parents, Anna and Joseph emerged and walked down the gangway to the waiting rickshaws. Before she climbed into hers, Emma, as if aware of their gaze, turned with one foot on its step and looked straight up at them; then waved one tiny, white-gloved hand in farewell. As one man, they waved back.

'Attractive lass,' said Jim.

'Bit skinny,' Tom qualified.

'Plump or skinny, I doubt if we'll see Miss Dalrymple again,' Ted said, a shade regretfully. And then the third mate was behind them again.

'Just because we're in harbour and Captain Hancock's gone ashore doesn't mean there's no work to be done. Decks need holystoning and brightwork's crying out for a rub. Not to mention the heads. They stink to high heaven.'

13

Ted was mistaken in thinking they'd never see Emma Dalrymple again. Next day, he was summoned to Joseph's cabin.

'Captain wants to see you urgent,' said the third mate, dropping the eyelid furthest away from Tom and Jim as all three looked up from the letters they were writing, ready for despatch on one of the clippers sailing directly home. The *Senator Weber*, they'd been told, would sail eventually for San Francisco with a cargo of tea and silk.

'Something to do with going ashore, I understand,' the third mate added.

Ted walked aft to Joseph's cabin in some trepidation. Surely he wasn't to be singled out to accompany his relatives ashore?

But after Anna's fervent hugs and kisses and Joseph's firm hand-clasp and the brief comment, 'You're doing all right, lad, I hear,' his half-brother explained that Mr and Mrs Dalrymple had extended an invitation to Anna and himself to dine at their house – ' "With a few of your crew, including, if at all possible, the lad Emma seems to have taken such a fancy to. The tall, fair-headed one with the charming smile," ' said Joseph with a grin, thoroughly enjoying Ted's obvious discomfiture.

'Anyway,' continued Joseph, 'I thought it would be quite proper to suggest I not only brought you but your two friends as well. That way, there should be no suggestion of favouritism. And I shall, of course,' he added, 'instruct our host to make no reference to our relationship. I trust that my dear wife,' with a meaningful glance at Anna, 'will observe similar care.'

'I'll ignore him the whole evening,' Anna promised.

Dinner at the Dalrymples' was all that he expected; and more, much more.

Perhaps because of the contrast between the Spartan rigours of the voyage and the graciousness of the household in which they now found themselves, the starboard watch seemed to sparkle with wit and intelligence. Even Tom and Jim, at first overawed in the company of their captain and his lady, relaxed and, under the influence of the excellent wine that Mr Dalrymple provided, chattered freely. The seating at table was so arranged that Emma sat between Ted and Jim at one end, with Tom opposite, while their elders occupied the other.

It was left to Joseph to apologise for the absorbed silence that descended upon the junior members of his party immediately the first dish was put before them.

'And are you finding Hong Kong to your liking, Miss Dalrymple?' Ted enquired at last and in as sophisticated a voice as he could manage with his mouth full.

'I like it well enough, thank you, Mr Smith,' she replied prettily, arching her eyebrows at him, 'but will like it even more, my parents tell me, when the weather is cooler.'

'At least, up here on the Peak you catch what breeze there is,' Jim contributed. 'Down below, it's hot as . . .' He paused. Did one mention hell in the company of a young lady of breeding? He glanced at his shipmates for guidance.

'. . . as a furnace?' offered Ted, recalling his days at the works.

'. . . as Henry's curry?' suggested Tom, remembering the disastrous occasion when Henry Goff, the ship's cook, had been moved to add curry powder to the salt beef.

Both suggestions, however, paled by comparison with Miss Dalrymple's own contribution – '. . as Hades!' she said. Whereupon they all dissolved into laughter and any inhibitions still remaining vanished completely.

'What I *do* lack,' confided Emma, surveying all three but

allowing her gaze to rest particularly upon Ted, 'is company. Young company, that is.'

'Surely,' said Jim, 'there must be other young ladies in Hong Kong whose fathers – '

'Oh, there are young *ladies* a'plenty,' Miss Dalrymple interrupted scornfully, as if she were referring to the cockroaches that abounded on the island. Glancing down the table to where her mother was trying to pump Anna about the latest English fashions – a fruitless endeavour! thought Ted fondly, noticing his sister-in-law's glazed expression – and her father was having rather more success with Joseph and the Australian gold rush, she whispered,

'I mean young *men*. Spotty clerks and clergymen, that's all my parents seem to know.'

'Soldiers?' suggested Jim.'

Miss Dalrymple conceded that there might, indeed, be some among the garrison who would meet with her approval. 'But my parents do not appear to have an entrée there.'

'Sailors, then,' said Tom. 'There's no shortage of those. *And* without spots,' he added complacently, caressing his as yet unshaven chin.

'Exactly!' said Emma. 'Sailors. And what better example than the crew of the *Senator Weber*?'

'What indeed!' Ted took up the challenge, as he raised his glass for a quick, steadying gulp. 'We can offer Germans, Norwegians, the odd Greek and Italian . . .'

Jim joined in the fun. 'Even a Dane or two.'

It was left to the guileless Tom to say, 'But what about *us*, Miss Dalrymple. Wouldn't *we* do?'

'You certainly would, Tom,' said Emma, but with her eyes fixed firmly upon Ted.

It was Jim, to his great relief, who settled the matter. 'We'll discuss it with the third mate,' he promised. 'If Henry agrees, then we're at your disposal.'

Masterly! thought Ted, knowing full well what Henry's reaction would be.

'On the other hand,' Jim continued, 'Henry might like

to come too. He could show you the sampler he's working on, Miss Dalrymple. "Thou shalt not shout at thy shipmates", it says, in rainbow-coloured silk.'

At this preposterous flight of fancy, their laughter became impossible to control.

'You're teasing me, sir!' said Emma indignantly.

At once, they were all contrition. 'I'm afraid,' Ted tried to appease her, 'we're unused to the company of young ladies.'

'And likely to remain so,' she said tartly, 'if you behave like this.'

But she cheered up considerably when, the meal finished, her mother suggested that she take them out on to the verandah.

It was a place of light and shade, with coloured lanterns set romantically among cascades of foliage and strange, exotic blooms. Although there was no moon, the sky was encrusted with stars. Stars, moreover, of which Ted knew the names. So absorbed did he become in pointing them out that it came as a shock to turn from the railing and suddenly discover that they were alone; Tom and Jim must be attending to the call of nature elsewere in the house.

'Come and sit here,' Emma coaxed, patting the cushion beside her on the bamboo sofa.

He ignored the invitation and made for a nearby chair clearly designed to accommodate one person only. But Emma's hand left the cushion to manacle his wrist. 'Beside me, I meant.'

He was almost sitting on her; so close, the almond fragrance of her hair was thick in his nostrils and he could hear the soft rustle of her skirts as she moved even closer. Dear God! Where were the others?

And then a most extraordinary thing happened. Little as he truly cared for Emma Dalrymple, knowing full well her nature was too shallow and selfish for his liking, he suddenly discovered that the arm nearest to her had crept around her shoulders and that his lips were searching urgently for hers – and finding them.

91

They were soft yet firm, yielding but demanding. And then his mouth was invaded by her tongue as it prised open his lips, pushing and probing with relentless vigour. At the same time, her body turned into his, her skirts flattening like so many layers of gossamer as she pressed closer and closer and his own body responded.

The next moment, he had torn himself away from her and was on his feet, staring down at her.

'What's the matter, Ted? Don't you like kissing me?' Her hands reached up to pull him back.

'Matter' was hardly the word to describe the sudden knowledge that the physical union of one body with another could be the most exciting and pleasurable act known to man – and woman. But equally as strong was the realisation, even though his body now cried out for fulfilment, that Emma Dalrymple was not the one to give it.

Vaguely, he was aware of footsteps, the murmur of Jim's voice and Tom's reply, and suddenly he felt very old and wise – and even just a little sorry for Emma that he could not oblige her.

14

They had thought that to be at anchor would mean a time of comparative tranquillity, while hands became softer, ligaments less strained and brains idled pleasantly.

'We may even have whole days to ourselves,' Jim had suggested , while they were still far out at sea.

'And there'll be shops to buy things from,' Tom had said, 'and money to buy them with.'

For there was one good thing, at least, about life at sea: you saved your money. Apart from the stock of basic necessities kept by Joseph, from which purchases could be made, there was nothing to spend it on.

To an extent, their hopes had been justified. The day after their visit to the Dalrymples, Henry Tate had actually ordered them ashore – in his company. Joseph, Ted suspected, had been behind it.

'Right,' said Henry, soon after breakfast. 'Hats on! Boots polished! We're going ashore.'

There was no disobeying him and, indeed, on this occasion, they had no desire to. In line astern, they followed him along the Playa, into dark poky shops, little more than holes in the wall, where they bought ornaments of wood and ivory to take home – yet another for Ma's collection, thought Ted, choosing a bird whose delicately carved wings seemed poised for flight – past their company's offices and those of the other ships berthed beside them or anchored out in the Roads, and past the many bars, already crowded with sailors of every nationality. 'Plenty of time for that later,' said Henry ambiguously.

Several houses, behind whose beaded curtains tiny Chinese

ladies could be seen sipping tea and chattering among themselves, he passed without comment, beyond a muttered, 'You needn't bother with them – not *this* trip, anyway!'

'D'you think he'll be back later, on his own?' Jim whispered to Ted.

'I doubt it,' said Ted, whose opinion of Henry Tate's character had been steadily growing.

They moved on to what Henry, who'd once worked the French ports, knowledgeably referred to as the 'piece of resistance' – a fleeting visit to an opium den.

'Here you are then, lads! But don't ever let me catch you inside one!'

They peered through the curtain which Henry had unceremoniously dragged aside, but after the bright sunlight their eyes could see nothing although the heavy, cloying smell left no doubt of what was offered there. And then, as their eyes adjusted, they made out hunched figures leaning against the walls, the long bamboo pipes in their hands or lying abandoned beside them; some lay on the earthen floor, their eyes closed, oblivious to everything except their dreams.

'I wonder . . .' said Jim, as Henry let fall the curtain and they moved away. Immediately, Henry rounded on him.

'Just you leave it at that, boy! Many a good seaman's been left behind because he's forgotten his own name, let alone that of his ship.'

But he did allow them to have their fortunes told – by an old man with a thin, straggling beard who seemed hardly able to focus his rheumy eyes on their palms let alone see into the future. Most of his pronouncements were to be expected.

'Vellee happy marriage,' he said to all three, and, 'Long life. Plentee children. Travel far.' But with Ted, he lingered. 'Travel far,' he repeated, but then rubbed his own palm across the other, as if to make clearer what he saw – or else erase it.

'Going to be an admiral, is he?' Henry asked facetiously. And they all laughed, Ted most of all. He'd never go over to the navy, let alone achieve such a rank.

But the old Chinaman shook his head. 'Not admiral. But

vellee big man. *Vellee* big.' And although he continued to brood for at least a minute, all he would add was, 'Vellee, vellee big.'

After that, they all made a great joke of it. 'Make way for vellee big man!' they said when Henry eventually found an eating-house he deemed worthy of their custom. And 'vellee big appetite', they added, when the rice was dished out, with, to Tom's horror, chopsticks.

It was soon after their return from this expedition that Ted's namesake, Edward Smith, began to cause trouble. Since the day they'd fought and Ted had fallen from the rigging, an uneasy truce had existed between the two Edward Smiths, although Ted never went out of his way to exchange more words than were necessary. He was aware also, and took comfort from it, that James Hyslop clung to him like a leach whenever 'all hands' was called and the watches mingled. And certainly, if it had ever come to a case of the crew taking sides, then the odds would have been heavily weighted in Ted's favour. For, although Edward Smith had his particular cronies, he was not popular among the majority of his shipmates.

A troublemaker, James Teevens, the first mate, had called him when Smith tried to incite the men to protest after *Senator Weber* had suffered damage in a heavy storm and extra duties were called for. Admittedly, as James Teevens was generally considered a reasonable sort of man, provided you did your duty, Smith hadn't met with much success. Only Mathew Mudd and Francis Gallichan – both tarred with the same brush, said the first mate – had supported him. And the discovery of a half-drunk bottle of rum in Mathew Mudd's locker hadn't improved matters, grog on board being strictly forbidden by the Company.

Drink, it was suspected was at the root of the trouble, it being a comparatively easy matter to smuggle a bottle on board or even to purchase one on the quayside without leaving the ship. Whatever the reason, Edward Smith flatly refused to carry out a simple command to holystone the decks; that he would have been joined at the task by a seaman, Robert Davies, and the three 'boys', probably influenced his decision. He'd not signed on, he informed the first mate, to do the work of boys and ordinary seamen. An able-bodied seaman did not holystone the decks.

'While at sea,' said James Teevens, tight-lipped, '*all* seamen obey orders.'

'But we're not at sea,' the other pointed out belligerently. 'We're in bloody harbour and I'm entitled to go ashore with my mates.' Mudd and Gallichan, having been given permission to go ashore, were, in fact, lingering on the quayside.

'I'm not arguing with you,' said the first mate, fists clenched. 'You'll do as you're told, or suffer the consequences.'

'And who's going to make me?' sneered Edward Smith, squaring his shoulders. 'You and whose grandmother?'

'Grieve,' the first mate inclined his head in Jim's direction, 'kindly inform the captain he's required on deck urgently.'

'Aye, aye, sir!'

'And while you're about it,' Edward Smith called after him, 'kindly inform the captain I'm not holystoning no bloody decks.'

'Silence!' the first mate roared.

Ted held his breath. What if he defied Joseph, too?

But he needn't have worried. Joseph was awe-inspiring. Gone was the gentle giant up whose legs the young Ted had climbed in Well Street, whose golden beard he'd tweeked and whose stories he'd listened to, enthralled. I doubt Ma would recognise him now, he thought, gazing at the frowning brow, the ice-cold eyes, the determined chin.

'What seems to be the trouble, Mr Teevens?'

'Begging your pardon, sir, but we have an insubordinate seaman on our hands. Smith, here, has refused to carry out my orders.'

'Which are, Mr Teevens?'

'That he assist in the holystoning of the deck, sir. As you know, while in harbour, all hands are expected – '

'I am well aware of the rules of my own ship, Mr Teevens.

96

You, Smith' – for the first time, he looked directly at the seaman, who was gazing open-mouthed and slightly pop-eyed, at his captain – 'will come before the magistrate forthwith, for refusal to obey an order. You, Davies, will act as escort. Mr Teevens, kindly hand over to Mr Brewer, if you please, and accompany me ashore. The rest of you will continue to work upon the deck.'

He doesn't waste any time, thought Ted admiringly. And all without raising his voice more than a fraction.

'Why doesn't he just go?' Tom asked as, the excitement over, they collected pails and brushes, and the large, bible-shaped stones. 'Smith, I mean. If he doesn't want to work, why not just leave the ship?'

'For one thing,' said Henry Tate, coming to help them, or at least see that they did the job properly, 'he'll still have some pay owing. For another, if he deserted, he'd be on British soil – Hong Kong, as you may remember, being a British possession – and therefore liable to be arrested and thirdly. . . .' He paused, glancing towards the mainland, where the mountains rose high above Kowloon. 'He wouldn't get far in this God-forsaken country. Now, America – that'll be a different matter altogether. You could disappear over there with no difficulty – and make your fortune, if you're one of the lucky ones. They'll all be jumping ship in 'Frisco, you mark my words.'

'Really?' Jim Grieve was clearly impressed at his forecast.

'Like fleas,' confirmed Henry Tate. 'And you've left a bit over there, young Jim, by that bulkhead.'

'So I have,' said Jim, scrubbing diligently, but with a thoughtful look on his face.

He wouldn't dare! thought Ted, noticing it. He's only fifteen, when all's said and done. On the other hand . . . his heart isn't in seafaring and he has a lively and inquisitive nature. Well, time would tell.

The saga of Edward Smith continued. 'He didn't seem to care,' reported Robert Davies, returning from escort duty. 'Even when the beak gave him three days in gaol, he just tossed his head and glared right back at him. If looks could kill. . . . Well, I reckon the captain'll need to watch out if Smith ever comes back on board.'

But come back he did; under escort from the gaol – only to vanish completely a few hours later. That, they decided, and in spite of Henry's views to the contrary, must surely be the end of him.

But perhaps the going was rougher than he'd expected, perhaps he'd spent all his money, perhaps he felt the need of company; whatever the reason, towards the end of August, he came slinking back. By then, Joseph had his hands full with his cronies, Mudd and Gallichan. They too had jumped ship but had been apprehended and taken before the magistrate. As a result four days' pay had been stopped.

Immediately afterwards, Henry Goff, the cook, sought an interview with Joseph, the result of which was his leaving the ship 'by mutual consent'.

'We get more like a railway station every day,' said Jim, after they'd helped carry Henry Goff's possessions down to the quay. 'Where's Henry off to, d'you suppose?'

'Australia,' said Henry Tate, who, as usual, knew all the answers. 'Got a brother out there who's found gold. So Henry'll sign on with the next clipper going that way that needs a cook.'

The same day that Henry Goff left, Francis Gallichan pleaded illness and refused to work.

'Says he did himself an injury last week, heaving cargo,' reported Henry. 'Anyway, Doc Freeland's coming out to see him.' Doc Freeland was the Company doctor.

'Hernia,' Henry passed on the diagnosis. 'Only thing is – it's so small, it wouldn't hurt a fly. Doc says he must have had it years. Anyway, he's given him a truss and told him to report for duty.'

But Francis Gallichan didn't report back for duty. He knew his rights, he said, and demanded a second opinion.

'Very well,' said Joseph – who also knew *his* rights – and sent him ashore via the magistrate, who redirected him to the civil hospital. But again, the diagnosis was the same.

Stubborness, however, was Gallichan's strong point. He wasn't, he told the magistrate, going back to the *Senator Weber* – and that was final.

'So, *he's* got a month in gaol,' Henry passed back the word, 'and with a bit of luck, we'll sail while he's still inside.'

They might have done, too, if it hadn't been for the typhoon.'

For days, it had been growing steadily hotter. On Joseph's instructions, makeshift awnings of old sailcloth had been erected over the decks, but even so, the heat was almost unbearable.

The storm finally broke one night in early September –· and raged without ceasing until morning. Those who had been sleeping on deck were soaked to the skin even before 'batten down hatches' was shouted. After that, sleep was impossible. Besides the incessant growl of the storm and the relentless drumming of rain on the hatches, there was the far more ominous sound of the hull grinding against the quayside and the crash of falling spars on the deck overhead. But worst of all were the heavy reverberating thuds of one vessel striking another in the closely packed harbour.

When they staggered on deck at first light, the devastation was dreadful to behold. Several ships, *Senator Weber* among them, were jammed together into a mass of tangled masts and rigging, their hulls leaning drunkenly one against the other. One ship, the *Minerva*, they learned later, had been driven right across the bows of an American vessel and foundered immediately; with what loss of life it was not yet known.

'Siamese twins, that's what we are,' said Henry, as they ducked beneath the festoons of ropes and spars to stand at the rail and gaze down on to the decks of the *Regina*, which had dropped anchor at a respectable distance on the previous day but now appeared to be welded firmly to the *Senator Weber*'s hull. 'It's a mercy we weren't holed. At least our rigging's fallen *on* us and not into the sea. Like yon *Linten*, bare as a baby's bottom!'

But there wasn't time to stand and compare; it was a case of all hands on deck. Or, in Ted's case, below it. A new cook had not yet been found and he was despatched to the galley to brew tea and whatever else he could rustle up for breakfast.

'Just my luck,' he grumbled, 'missing all the fun!'

'Fun,' said Henry, 'is not what you signed on for. An army marches on its stomach, someone said, and a ship's the same. Except that this ship won't be marching anywhere for quite a while.'

He had managed to light the galley stove and filled the giant kettles when he heard a familiar voice behind him. 'Move over, Ted! This is woman's work.'

'Anna! Am I pleased to see you!'

'Thought you might be, though Joseph needed a bit of persuading.' Her sleeves were rolled up and she wore a makeshift sacking apron. 'I've been idle for too long.'

After that, tea-making ceased to be a chore. Almost, he expected Ma to come bustling in. Anna must have read his thought. 'All we need now is your ma reminding us to warm the pot.'

A cold breakfast it would have to be, Anna decided, and set him to smearing jam on the doorstep slices of bread she cut.

After breakfast had been given out to the lines of hungry seamen and Ted had helped Anna with the washing-up, he was summoned to Joseph's cabin. The damage to *Senator Weber* had now been assessed and the information must be taken to the Company's office, for telegraphing to Liverpool

'My own opinion,' said Joseph, 'and I've said as much, is that most of the work we shall be able to do ourselves. Robert Redfern is an experienced carpenter – and the men will work well for him. At least,' he added wryly, 'most of them will. And those that don't. . . .' He shrugged expressively. 'Your namesake, for one, may decide that carpentering is beneath his professional dignity. However, much will depend upon the condition of the other damaged vessels. Even with the new Hope Dock, there are still only two graving docks on the island – and there'll be a long wait for one of those.'

As he went on his way, carefully skirting the debris scattered over the quayside, shaking his head over the number of dismasted yachts in the harbour, Ted reflected upon the subtle change that had crept into Joseph's attitude towards him. Just now, he had spoken almost as if he were a contemporary, someone to be kept fully informed of what was happening. Which must mean, thought Ted with a feeling of some small satisfaction, that he was doing all right, or at least not letting the family down. For the first time, he reflected upon the loneliness of a captain's life at sea, where discipline and order were of the highest importance.

Joseph was right. The Company would be most grateful, the clerk told him, if Captain Hancock could undertake the repair of the *Senator Weber* himself. Accordingly, they would arrange for a supply of timber to be delivered as soon as possible.

Also, as Joseph had anticipated, Edward Smith objected strongly to doing work to which he was not accustomed and for which he was receiving no extra pay.

Robert Redfern was a pleasant, easygoing man who hailed from the Isle of Man. But there was one thing he could not bear – to see the ill-treatment of wood. Edward Smith, it soon became clear, had no such scruples. Time and again he either ruined the wood he was working on or misjudged the measurements he'd been given, so that the whole operation had to be repeated; a time-wasting and expensive mistake. Besides this, Smith seemed to have a deep-seated antipathy towards Manxmen.

It was towards the end of the month, when the weather was fractionally cooler and work was well under way that the matter came – or rather, boiled up – to a head.

Until then, Smith, although he had grumbled, had not refused to work, albeit badly. But on this day – it was a Saturday – he had refused point-blank.

Robert Redfern, even though he had been given authority

101

by the captain, was reluctant to use it. Had Edward Smith not told him to his face that he was going to fashion no more spars or cross-trees for a 'bloody Manxman', he might have simply turned away and left him to his own devices. But this was too much. He sent for the first mate.

By now, James Teevens was deeply resentful of Smith. If *he'd* been Captain Hancock, he'd have been discharged long since. When the seaman still refused to do as he'd been told, he sent for the captain. The captain came. And those crew members detailed for the working party found themselves lingering in the vicinity, the 'boys' among them.

It took Joseph only seconds to size up the situation. Ted, watching him, thought how tired he looked. They'd all had extra duty these last few weeks but at least the crew had had some time away from the ship – one day, he, Henry, Jim and Tom had even walked some distance up into the hills – but Joseph, except for visits to the Company office, had rarely been ashore.

'I understand that you are refusing to do your duty, Smith.'

'It's not my duty. I'm not a bleeding chippy.'

'Watch your language, man!' That was the first mate.

'And I'm no lawyer nor ship surveyor, bleeding or otherwise,' said Joseph crisply, 'but I've had to be both these last days. This is a time of emergency, Smith.'

'Not at a week's end, it ain't.'

'Except for the Sabbath, one day's like another at sea.'

'We're not *at* sea, are we? That's dry land out there,' he waved an arm inland, 'or hadn't you noticed?'

'Silence!' And now Joseph's voice was the roar of an angry bull. And Smith *was* silent. But still defiant.

Joseph turned to the first mate. 'Mr Teevens, detail two men to tie Smith to the shrouds and remove his shirt, if you please. Mr Brewer' – the Second Mate was close at hand – 'kindly bring me a thick, strong rope.'

The sharp hiss of indrawn breath from the watching seamen – and they'd given up all pretence of work, long since – was clearly audible. Flogging, under Captain Hancock's command, was a rare occurrence. No matter that few among them liked the man, no one was eager to come forward and seize Edward Smith. They shrank back. Some began to sidle away unobtrusively.

'Jackson, Johnson, take the prisoner to the shrouds. Hyslop, fetch cord to tie him. And look lively!' The sooner this unsavoury business was concluded, the first mate seemed to be indicating, the better for them all.

Ted, on the outskirts of the little crowd, found that he was leaning heavily against the side of the midship house as if his legs were no longer able to support him. His mouth was slightly open and seemed suddenly dry as a bone. Out of the corner of his eye, he saw Jim and Tom, their faces white as sheets, their eyes popping, and guessed he looked the same.

It was when Joseph, feet braced, swung the rope-end for the first time and Ted saw the scarlet weal on the naked flesh and heard Smith's shriek of agony that he knew he could stand it no longer. He turned and almost fell around the back of the midship house, then sank to his knees, his head between them, fighting the nausea that threatened to engulf him.

Not only was he witnessing the flogging of one man by another – and that man unable to defend himself – but the one inflicting the pain was his brother Joseph: the gentle, genial companion of his childhood. His world lay shattered around him.

15

Afterwards, Ted could remember little of that Saturday morning duty, except that an almost tangible pall of gloom lay, like a shroud, over the entire ship.

Once Edward Smith had been removed to gaol, still mouthing insults, the working party had finished the jobs in hand, then gone about their various pursuits, some remaining on board as anchor watch, others seeking permission to go ashore. The boys had intended passing a quiet few hours in studying and letter-writing but Ted knew he could no longer face such passive occupations; he had to get away by himself.

'I think I'll take a walk,' he told the other two; and they let him go without demur. They, too, he reflected, might need time to themselves.

When he asked Henry Tate for permission to leave the ship, the third mate shot him a strange look. 'All right, are you, youngster?'

'Yes, I'm fine thank you, sir,' he said and went on his way.

He followed the same path, that all four of them had trodden only a few days previously on a walk, and soon the Playa lay below and he was climbing up between the houses and gardens of the Peak. Briefly, he thought of Emma Dalrymple and her parents. Repairing the damage caused by the typhoon had meant that no further meetings could be arranged, and for this he'd been supremely grateful.

The air was cooler now and heavy with the fragrance of the gardens and of the wild pink bauhinias that, so Mrs Dalrymple had told him, gave the island its exotic smell and indeed, its name, for Hong Kong meant 'fragrant harbour'. Not, he thought grimly, that there'd been anything remotely fragrant about the drama that had been played out there that morning.

After the houses came rough grassland dotted with trees and eventually he reached the river. A few days ago, it had been a rushing torrent, still swollen by the heavy rains of the typhoon, but now, it was no more than a wide stream, gurgling peacefully over its rocky bed. Tired and dejected, he sat beside it, leaned heavily against a stony outcrop and closed his eyes.

But not to sleep; deliberately, he forced himself to relive the scene he'd witnessed that morning, before nausea had made him turn away. Again he saw Joseph, feet braced, rope coiled over his left arm, right swinging back and down towards the naked back of the man spread-eagled across the shrouds; saw again the crimson weal on the white flesh and heard the cry of pain. How many times the arm had raised and fallen, he didn't know, because the man's cries had merged into one continous howl of agony.

All right, he had known about flogging from an early age. Hadn't Ma, in fact, often threatened him with a 'good one' if he didn't do as he was told? But he'd always known that she never would; any more than she would ever have made him go hungry for his sins. By the same token – if he'd ever given serious thought to the matter – he'd assumed that Joseph would never have gone to such lengths either. Hadn't he, on one occasion when Henry had caught them fooling about in the rigging, assured Tom that Joseph would never flog him because his wife was on board?

Anna! Where had she been when the flogging had been administered? Not watching it, surely, from the shelter of Joseph's cabin? Such a possibility was not to be considered.

His head sunk into his hands, he groaned aloud. And had the shock of his life when a hand suddenly descended upon his shoulder.

'There, lad,' said Henry Tate, in a voice quite unlike any that Ted had heard him use before, don't take on so!'

'Henry!' Had Joseph himself materialised beside him, Ted couldn't have been more surprised. And then he blushed. 'Sorry − sir!'

For a moment, Henry allowed his hand to rest lightly upon Ted's shoulder. 'Don't worry, lad. In fact, "Henry" suits me fine.' He sat himself down by Ted and gazed about him. 'I guessed you'd be up here. It's a peaceful spot.'

Ted said nothing, but waited. 'The sort of place, would you say, for a man to sort himself out? If, that is,' Henry contemplated a minute insect that was climbing the toecap of his boot, 'he needed to sort himself out.'

Again, Ted said nothing. He had the dreadful feeling that if he were to open his mouth, he would burst into tears.

'If, perhaps,' Henry flicked at the insect with his forefinger, 'circumstances had caused him to look differently upon a person, a close relative, maybe?'

'I know,' he admitted after a moment or two, during which he appeared to be waiting should Ted wish to reply, 'because much the same thing happened to a friend of mine. Only he was younger than you.'

He suddenly lay back with his arms crossed behind his head, his eyes closed against the sun. In his case, it was his mother. The kindest, sweetest woman alive − and he worshipped her. His family were poor as church mice − on account of the father having died, you see. My friend was the eldest, then two sisters and then a little brother. The mother did cleaning jobs in some of the big houses in Liverpool. Then one day, his little brother was taken ill and he had to go and look for his mother. He had a job finding the house − it was one kept by a widower, on his own and my friend was in a right sweat when he got there. So he didn't hang about knocking on any doors. He ran straight in to the kitchen.' Henry stopped abruptly, and Ted gazed down at him, his own troubles forgotten. Unable to imagine what dreadful thing had happened next and was obviously causing Henry such pain to relate, he waited. Had the child died?

'Perhaps,' Henry continued after a moment but with a

voice now thickened by emotion, 'you can guess what he found. Or perhaps you can't, a well-brought up lad like you. His mother wasn't in the kitchen, scrubbing the master's pots. Nor in the parlour, polishing his furniture. But she *was* in his bedroom. And so was he. And it certainly wasn't the bed they were making!'

Ted lay back beside Henry, so that he could no longer see his face; and did his best to imagine finding Ma in such a situation. And for a moment knew revulsion, anger and shock. But then, Ma never would. . . . But clearly, Henry's friend had considered it just as unlikely that *his* mother would.

'What happened to the little boy?' he asked after a moment.

'Died,' said Henry briefly.

'And your friend?'

'Ran away to sea. But not before he'd had a thing or two told him by his aunt Lizzie – just like I'm trying to explain things to you now. She said his ma didn't have any choice. If she didn't oblige, in *every* way, she was out on her ear, with plenty of women ready to fill her shoes. Aunt Lizzie had a husband, even though he did drink most of his money away on a Friday night. Otherwise, she reckoned, she'd have been doing it, too.'

'But your friend still went to sea?'

'Signed on, by then, he had. But,' Henry rubbed his nose reflectively, 'he hasn't done too badly. And he still loves his ma and makes sure she's never short of a bob or two, so she doesn't have to. . . .' His voice trailed away. 'Anyway, young Ted,' – he suddenly shot up to a sitting position – 'the moral of the story is – judge not, that ye be not judged. I think someone else said that before me – but it's still true. Today, Captain Hancock did what he had to do. And knowing him, didn't like doing it any more than we liked looking at it. It's a tough life you've chosen, lad; no quarter given and none expected. And we work as a crew. If Edward Smith is allowed to cheek the captain in harbour, he's going to be a damned sight worse at sea. And then we'll all be at

107

risk. He's a brave man is your brother, and don't you ever forget it.'

He didn't forget it. Later that day, after he and Henry, walking in companionable silence, had come back on board, he almost bumped into Joseph on the after deck.

Usually, when this happened, Joseph would pass him with hardly a nod, but this time he stopped. 'All right, Teddy?'

He couldn't remember when Joseph had last used his childhood name. 'Yes, thank you, Joseph,' And then, noticing how lined and anxious his brother's face had become, added impulsively, 'Are you?'

'Yes, lad, I thank you.'

'And Anna?'

There was the briefest of pauses before Joseph said, 'Yes, she's all right − now. Dressing up to go out, in fact. Dr Freeland has invited us to dinner.'

'That's good! You − could both do with going ashore for a while.' He would have saluted then, and passed on, but Joseph still lingered.

'Ted, no need to mention *everything* to Ma, when you write home. Just − the good things.'

Did he, Ted wondered, remember the last occasion he'd proposed caution where Ma was concerned − on that day when they'd first met Anna above Etruria Station? But all he said now was, 'No, of course not, Joseph.' And then couldn't resist adding, using the very words that Joseph had used then, 'Man to man, Joseph?'

He was rewarded by a broad grin, smoothing away at least some of the lines. 'Just so, Teddy. Man to man!'

Soon afterwards, Ted leaned over the rail and watched the two of them descend the gangway to the waiting rickshaws. Joseph resplendent in his best uniform and tall pot-hat, Anna in a gown of creamy silk, her neat bun persuaded into a golden snood.

'All right then, Ted?' Henry was beside him at the rail.

'All right, Henry.' And then, as the rickshaw runners pattered away across the quay, 'Thank you.'

Next day, they heard that Edward Smith had been given six weeks' hard labour. 'Now, we really will go without him,' said Henry with grim satisfaction.

And they did, sailing eastwards for San Francisco at the end of October.

Up in the rigging, Ted spared a swift glance for the receding shore line. Strange how he'd learned more about life in the last three months that in twice as long at sea!

16

When San Francisco was just over the horizon, Henry, just as he'd warned them of the dangers of Hong Kong, did his best to disillusion them about their next port of call. By comparison, they gathered, Hong Kong had been a bed of roses.

'Crimps,' said Henry. 'That's what you've got to watch out for. Some skippers ain't as good as they should be and have trouble finding a crew. And crimps, you might say, are the middlemen. To put it another way, if you get bashed on the head down some dark alley, or drink too much grog, and wake up on some ship you've never even heard of, under a captain you don't much like the look of, ten to one it'll be the crimps. But by then you'll be out on the ocean blue and not able to do a thing about it. It happens in a lot of ports, but 'Frisco's probably the worst.'

'But you'll be there to protect us, won't you,' Jim asked innocenty. Too innocently.

'Don't bank on it,' said Henry.

'No crimp's getting me!' Tom flexed his muscles.

'Well, watch it,' said Henry. 'That's all I'm saying.'

San Francisco might be a den of iniquity, but it certainly didn't look it on that bright January day, just a week before Ted's eighteenth birthday, when they sailed through the narrow straits, aptly named the Golden Gate, into the largest land-locked natural harbour in the world. Forty hills it was built on, Henry told them, but, even up in the rigging, they gave up after twenty-five.

'Walking up Nob Hill,' said Henry, 'you have to bend over backwards, just to stay on it!'

Dusk was falling when they tied up, considering themselves fortunate they were on the quayside and not anchored out in the bay; even though it did mean they were vulnerable to any of the shadowy figures lurking along the waterfront.

Next morning, for the first time in many weeks, the half-deck was allowed to sleep in. When he awoke, Ted glanced across at Jim's bunk, fully expecting to see it empty. But he was still there – and snoring heavily.

But he was no fool. That morning, Joseph paid out precious dollars to the crew and Jim was one of the first to stand in line. Tom joined him.

'Coming, Ted?'

One thing was certain, he couldn't let Tom wander off on his own. Ted, too, joined the line.

When they reached Joseph, he glanced up. 'Watch out ashore, lads, and stay together.'

'Aye, aye, sir!' And indeed, all three made a brief foray along the quayside in the light of day. It was, they decided, much like Hong Kong. Except that, as Tom observed, there was a lot more of everything.

Chinatown was there, with the familiar Chinese lettering on the laundries and eating-houses, but cheek by jowl with areas adopted by other nationalities: Spaniards and Italians with dapper little beards and moustaches, enormous Negroes, skin glistening in the sun, coffee-coloured Malays and hand-some Greeks, all jabbering in their own tongues.

'This,' said Jim, standing in the middle of the Embarcadero – and *that* took some tongue-twisting to get right – the wide street running parallel to the shore, and gazing about him, 'is America!'

He could be Christopher Columbus in person, thought Ted, noticing the dazed, almost drugged, look on his face. After this, the *Senator Weber* would be like a prison to him. At the same time, he thought how much he was going to miss the quick-witted Scots lad, even though – perhaps, because – he was so different from himself. True, *he* found San Francisco a fascinating place too, but he knew that he would be quite happy to leave it when the time came. The pull of home would be too great. So why, he wondered idly, become a sailor in the first place? And thought perhaps the answer lay in his parting message to Ma; that was more a promise than a farewell. If one didn't go away in the first place, the pleasure of home-coming was lost.

That night, they all went ashore again. And Henry, on anchor watch himself, let them go with only the briefest of admonitions to stay together. But to Ted, he murmured, 'Keep an eye on Forster.'

And Ted did, sticking to him like a limpet, even when they went into one of the many bars scattered along the wharves. Even so, it was here that they lost Jim. Ted, turning from trying to persuade Tom, unsuccessfully, that the liquor he'd already consumed was more than sufficient, found he was no longer by his side. The call of nature, perhaps?

He gave him ten minutes, then turned to Tom. 'I think we should get back to the ship.'

'Must wait for Jim.' Tom's speech was already slurred. 'Can't leave old Jim on his own.'

'Tom,' he had raised his voice to make himself heard above the din in the bar, 'I don't think Jim *is* coming back. I think he's jumped ship.'

The suggestion seemed to sober Tom – momentarily. 'Nonsense! Stay together, Henry said. Jim always obeys orders. Well,' he added, even his fuddled mind admitting this was not always the case, 'almost always.'

'And this isn't one of 'em,' said Ted grimly. 'Come on, Tom! You don't want the crimps to get you.'

'Wouldn't get *me*!' cried Tom, flexing the muscles of the arm that wasn't holding his glass.

'That's the spirit!' said the man standing next to him at the counter. 'Not that any crimp'd stand a chance against a fine, upstanding feller like yourself! Here, have a drink on it!'

And before Ted realised what he was doing, he'd poured a goodly measure from the bottle at his elbow into Tom's glass. And Tom, grinning like an idiot, had downed it in a single gulp.

'You, too sailor?' said the man, now waving the bottle towards Ted's glass. Ted didn't bother to answer.

'Come on, Tom! We're leaving.' And slamming his glass on to the counter, he seized Tom by the arm and manhandled him to the door.

Out on the wharf, he gulped in a great, satisfying breath of fresh air. Now to get Tom back on board!

They'd gone only a few steps before he heard a rush of feet behind them. ''ere they be, lads!' It was the voice of the man at the bar. The next moment, Ted was fighting for his life as, caught off balance, he and Tom were shoved into a dark alleyway leading off the wharf. Rough hands pulled back his arms until he could have howled in agony. Gritting his teeth, he tried to yank himself away and then, realising the futility of that manoeuvre, suddenly went slack in the man's grip, shoving his buttocks hard into the other's stomach.

Now, it was the man's turn to be caught off balance, though taking Ted with him as he crashed to the ground. But his grip was loosened. Twisting like an eel, Ted managed to tear himself free and stagger to his feet. And then, aiming for the groin with his metal-tipped boot, he kicked the man as hard as he could. Again and again. No time, this, for the Queensberry Rules! Judging by the shrieks and groans the man was letting out, he'd found his mark.

'And that,' he put all his strength behind the final kick, 'is for Tom!' For there were no other sounds coming now from the alleyway; his friend had gone.

'I couldn't do a thing about it,' he told Henry. 'Not a bloody thing!' It was an indication of his anguish that he swore without realising it. 'By the time I was rid of the man on my own back, Tom just wasn't there any more.'

'That drink,' muttered Henry darkly, 'would have been drugged.'

Next morning, it was discovered that not only Tom and Jim were missing, but over a dozen of their shipmates as well.

'The crimps may have got some of 'em,' said Henry, 'but

113

most will have jumped ship – and I'm not surprised. The Golden Gate to a new life is how a lot of them see 'Frisco. Poor fools! By the time they've found out their mistake, most of them will be on their uppers.'

'Jim will be all right,' said Ted. 'I'm sure of that. It's Tom I'm still worried about.'

Henry shrugged. 'He's probably at sea by now. And wondering what hit him. You did all you could, lad. He's got to learn the hard way.'

Henry was right, of course. No point in dwelling on it.

17

Dearest Ma,

Thank you for your most welcome letter, awaiting me upon our arrival here, courtesy of the American stagecoach.

I thought of you all at Christmas and hope that you managed to enjoy it. You will be pleased to hear that my birthday was a great event – I dined with the captain and his lady wife! An unprecedented event in the annals of the *Senator Weber* even, perhaps, in those of merchant shipping.

In fact, it was easy enough to arrange as, only a few days previously, sixty-six and two-thirds per cent of the half-deck had jumped ship! My good friends, Tom Forster and Jim Grieve had disappeard into the San Francisco night; voluntarily, I am sure on the part of Jim, he had an uncle somewhere in California, to whom he would go. However, with young Tom, his fate is not so certain. Henry thinks he is probably already at sea on some other vessel. Should you meet his mother, it would perhaps be best not to mention this, since she would undoubtedly worry.

Anyway – to return to my birthday – there was yours truly siting down to dine, not only with the captain and his wife, but with the first, second and third mates!

At that point, Ted ceased his writing and, sucking the end of his quill, brought back to mind that evening in Joseph's cabin. In view of the occasion, he had been given a seat of honour at one end of the table with Joseph, of course, at the other. On his left was James Teevens and on his right Richard Brewer. Next to Richard was Henry.

It was, as Joseph had decreed, a festive occasion. Not only were they remembering his young brother's birthday – all present knew of their relationship – but they had also completed the first half of their voyage. From now on, they would be homeward bound.

However, in spite of this double cause for celebration, Ted noticed that Joseph's glass held only a minute quantity of wine. The bo'sun, Ludwig Teddersen, who had sailed with Joseph on previous voyages, had been promoted officer of the watch for the evening, but a captain must, he knew, at all times have a clear and sober head.

When everyone's glass but his own had been recharged, Joseph rose to his feet and thumped the table.

'Gentlemen and' – with a courteous bow to Anna, at his side – 'lady!' A discreet burst of cheering here, for Anna was high in everyone's esteem. 'May I propose a toast to our youngest officer, Third Mate Edward John Smith!' And they had all, Anna included, risen to their feet, glasses raised and repeated,

'To Third Mate Edward John Smith!'

And he, flabbergasted, totally shocked and speechless, had sat there, his mouth as wide as a barrel, Henry told him later, and stared at them all as if they'd taken leave of their senses. Or had *he*, perhaps, taken leave of his, picked up some strange Yankee sickness which caused delirium and hallucinations?

'Pinch him, someone!' said Anna. 'Joseph, you really should have warned him.'

'So I should,' said Joseph, but looking not at all contrite.

'But – but. . . . ' Ted had at last found his voice, if not the ability to form a sentence. In the end, he simply pointed a finger at Henry Tate.

'No, Mr Tate's not leaving us.' Cries of 'Shame!' and 'No such luck!' from Henry's superiors. 'But, in view of the fact

116

that certain members of our crew have seen fit to leave us, Mr Tate will have his work cut out educating their replacements. So I have decided that he should have some assistance. And what better person to give it than young Ted Smith?' He didn't wait for an answer to what was clearly a rhetorical question but swept on.

'Nepotism, you may say,' – they didn't; none, by then, looking capable of understanding the meaning of the word, let alone uttering it – 'but I have taken the decision only after due consultation, especially with Mr Tate himself. This doesn't mean, of course,' he smiled benevolently upon Ted, 'that any preferential treatment will be offered him.'

It was Henry who, after the meal was over, explained it to him in rather more basic terms. 'Think about it, Ted. You're the only boy left on board now, and if you were to remain so, your life wouldn't be worth living. You'd have the heads to scrub out every day, the bright work to shine, the decks to swab and, quite honestly, young Ted, you're worth more than that.'

'Why not make me an AB, then?' Ted asked.

'Well, it may sound a funny thing to say, but you're not quite up to it yet,' was the surprising answer. 'You're not tough enough. But you will be, by the time you reach home.'

'But what about you, Henry? Won't you resent it?'

'Bless you no, lad! I'll be glad of the company. As long as they pay me my two pounds ten a month, I don't mind what I do. And it's no bed of roses you've landed in, young Ted. Well, if it is, there's plenty of thorns to be found. It's the third mate who does all the jobs the first and second don't want. And don't think, just because you're the captain's brother, you'll be let off lightly, because you won't. He'll see to that.'

Good old Henry! He was sitting opposite him now writing to *his* mother. Ted dipped his quill into the ink-pot and went back to Ma.

'And the long and short of it is, that I have been promoted to third mate and will serve alongside Henry

117

Tate, as good a messmate as you could hope to meet. Whether I get paid for it – two pounds ten a month, which is a sight more than my solitary pound! – will depend on the Company. Mind you, I don't expect for a minute that it would have happened with any other captain but Joseph. But at least everyone else seems to approve, including Henry. I just hope I'll manage it.

All my love to you. Before this year is over, I hope that you will be seeing again – Your devoted son,

Edward J. Smith.

It was not as difficult as he'd expected. From his old shipmates, the men who knew that, until now, he'd been a mere 'boy', his promotion caused little reaction other than congratulations.

James Hyslop clapped him hard on the back and said, 'Couldn't have happened to a nicer feller! We all think so.'

But it was Henry, as usual, who put it into a nutshell.

'People treat you like you treat them, Ted. And you've shown yourself to be a likeable enough lad. No side to you and helpful with it. And another thing,' Henry continued, 'you don't have to holler and shout to get things done. Not like me!' And indeed, Henry's bellow would have done credit to a sea cow.

But hollering and shouting, especially in a storm, could come in useful and he was proud of the way he was learning to project his voice. On the whole, though, he found that a quiet approach, the assumption that, once given, an order would be obeyed, was sufficient. He did his best to look the part, too.

'Forgotten to shave then, have we?' enquired Henry, tongue in cheek, 'or is that a beard we're sprouting?' Henry was clean-shaven.

Self-consciously, Ted massaged the incipient growth. 'Thought I'd just try it out.'

Slowly, he began to relax, even to enjoy the privileges of his new status; not, as Henry had warned him, that there were many. More often than not, they were up in the rigging or heaving on the capstan bars with the rest of the crew. But now he was allowed to stand watch at the helm alone, and that, even though they were now in the doldrums as they slowly approached the equator, gave him the biggest thrill of all. And there was still the Horn to come!

But before the Horn, came one of the most sobering experiences of Ted's career to date, reminding him that the way of life he had chosen was indeed a tough one.

Sailing steadily southwards from 'Frisco, en route for Callao, he drew Henry's attention, one day, to another square-rigger on their starboard bow. Within a safe sailing distance, they were still near enough to see that its crew were congregated in two groups, one aft and the other for'ard; all except for one man who, it appeared, was being bound hand and foot.

'What's going on, Henry? A flogging?' He had no wish to witness another of those.

Henry looked, then drew in his breath sharply. 'Not a flogging, young Ted. Much worse! It's a keelhauling.'

A keelhauling! He had heard, of course, of the dreadul punishment for an insubordinate seaman of tying a long rope around his neck and ankles, then throwing him into the sea at the bows and dragging him along the keel of the vessel until he resurfaced at the stern, where he would be hauled back on board, more often dead than alive. But he'd thought the barbaric act no longer practised.

He said no more. In fact, he would have been hard put to find words to express his horror. And then he became aware that behind him, those hands on duty on the *Senator Weber*, had ceased their work and were gazing, too.

Across the water, there floated the sound of a command. Immediately, the man, powerless to resist, was thrown into the water and the men standing aft began to haul.

'They'll haul as quick as they can,' said Henry. 'No matter what the bugger's done, no one likes a keelhauling.'

But it looked to Ted as if the tempo was being set by the figure on the poop-deck and it seemed an eternity before the man suddenly shot up in the wake of the vessel. What

119

it had seemed like to him, Ted could hardly bring himself to imagine, the frantic holding of his breath against the force of the water, the pounding of his heart as his lungs stretched to bursting point, the agony of contact with the barnacle-encrusted keel as his body was dragged along its length.

They watched while he was hauled on board and a seaman bent to cut the ropes. But he still lay there, inert. Was he dead? Had his lungs finally burst under that terrible pressure, or his head been crushed against an unyielding hull? They would never know. The figure on the poop gestured, shouted a further command and the body was dragged below.

Back on the *Senator Weber*, the crew let out its breath in an audible gasp, but still nobody spoke. And then Joseph's voice rang out from their own poop-deck, where he, too, must have been watching the spectacle. 'Right, lads! Back to work!'

'And remember, all of you,' added Henry Tate, but softly so that Joseph would not hear, 'that there, but for the grace of God. . . .' He left the sentence unfinished.

And Ted, resolutely swallowing the nausea rising in his gorge, thought that now he had seen everything.

120

18

Their stay in Callao was short. Just long enough to exchange their cargo of grain for one of guano.

'Bird-shit!' said Henry briefly. 'that's all it is. And stinks to high heaven. But after a few days, you won't even notice.'

Richard Brewer was more informative, although just as explicit. 'Remember how your ma used to send you out with a bucket and shovel after the horses?'

Ma – not being given to cultivating the tiny patch behind the house in Well Street – hadn't, but he knew plenty of children whose mothers had, and others who'd sold the pails of droppings to wealthier Hanley citizens. So he nodded, to show that he knew what Richard Brewer was talking about.

'Well, the guano bird spends its summer on the Lobos Islands, doing its business out on the rocks, and when it leaves, men come over from the mainland and shovel it up. Better than any animal dung, they say.'

Better, it might be, but they all went round with their neckerchiefs masking the lower half of their faces for the next few days. And then, as Henry had predicted, they ceased to notice.

The forests of Peru gave way to those of Chile, and for the first time, Ted knew the magic of the South Pacific.

'Make the most of it,' said Henry. 'The Horn's coming up!'

They were leaning over the rails, with little to do aloft, and enjoying the sun's warmth. Enjoying, too, as far as Ted was concerned, the pleasant sensation that while much holystoning of decks and polishing of bright work was going on around them, he was not involved, apart from an occasional urging to scrub or polish with even greater vigour.

Gazing down at the sea gushing past, he saw that dolphins were now keeping the ship company; but these were no ordinary dolphins, like those they had seen in the Atlantic, but of exotic blue and green, the colours of the sea itself, and above, a shoal of flying fish danced over the waves as though connected by invisible cords to the creatures below.

'Soon,' Henry continued, 'the days will grow shorter and darker, the seas more mountainous.'

'And the prevailing winds will be from west to east,' intoned Ted, as if reading from a manual, 'and a following wind will make for a rough voyage. In latitude 62 degrees south, there may be vast icebergs. . . .'

As he paused to draw breath, Henry said sourly, 'I was forgetting for the moment that Captain Hancock is your brother.'

'I am sure,' said Ted quickly, for to discomfit Henry was the last thing he wanted, 'that no amount of copybook knowledge on my part would prepare me for the actual experience.'

'You couldn't speak a truer word,' said Henry, a shade mollified. And, as always, he was right.

Joseph had chosen the longer but safer route around Staten Island. The cold was intense and, as Henry had predicted, the days grew shorter. When the sun did manage to appear from behind the wracks of cloud, its heat was insufficient to even begin to thaw out the frost that now coated the shrouds and rigging like a coarse grey fur.

Having sailed far enough southward to give the Cape a wide berth, Joseph steered east. With her topsails set to catch the following wind, even when in the trough of the deepest wave – and they were becoming steadily more and more mountainous – the *Senator Weber* seemed certain to round the Horn in a couple of days at most. But then the wind changed, coming strongly from the east and laced with stinging flurries of snow and sleet. It was a case of all hands reef tops'ls before they were all in tatters, and all hands meant everyone on board, including the third mates – and excluding only the captain.

Not that Ted would have wished it otherwise. In fact, if his first rounding of the Horn had been – as he'd once heard Joseph describe it to Ma, 'nothing worse than crossing the Mersey in a row-boat on a winter's day' – he would have been sorely disappointed.

Now, heaving on the sodden canvas until his hands, already horny and hardened, were raw and bleeding, he was hardly conscious of the pain. More, he was filled with a sense of awe and wonder as, perched like a gull in the rigging, he saw the ship plunge downwards into waves so deep that only her poop and deck houses were visible above the ocean. Then, her timbers groaning in protest, she rose again, and hung poised at the crest of the next dreadful wave, before plunging back into the abyss.

Not that there was time to stand and stare, only to bend and heave and heave again, until the topsails were close-reefed and they could tumble down to the deck and try to introduce some semblance of warmth into their frozen fingers.

Then, even the most hard-bitten of seamen exchanged wry grins, grateful that, for the moment at least, their ship was as secure as she could be; but always with the knowledge that at any moment, the wind might change once more and they'd be back up there to release the tops'ls.

But on this occasion, they were allowed two days of dubious relief as they lay to, close-reefed, and rode out the storm. Then, with one of those unpredictable changes which made the Horn one of the most hazardous of shipping routes, the wind dropped, taking the temperature down with it. Suddenly, the sea was dead calm.

'Don't like it!' said Henry. 'Ain't natural!' And indeed, a strange, almost supernatural, hush had fallen over the entire ship.

'What's come over Meyer?' asked Ted. Andrew Meyer was a Norwegian, older than many and more experienced

123

in the ways of the sea. He was now standing at the rail amidships, staring intently southwards into the heavy mist that surrounded them. His head was tilted back and Ted was reminded of a dog raising its nose to sniff the air.

'What is it, Meyer?' Henry called. 'Seen a ghost?'

'Ice.' he said. 'There's big ice out there.'

A murmur of apprehension ran though the men. 'Best tell the captain,' Henry murmured into Ted's ear. 'There's not much these Norwegians don't know about ice.'

But when Ted arrived on the poop-deck, he found Joseph, like Meyer, already gazing into the bank of cloud. Gesturing Ted to silence, he continued to do so for what seemed like an eternity while the ship drifted on a sea grown smooth as glass. And then, as if the curtains of some celestial theatre were opening on a performance destined for their eyes alone, the clouds suddenly parted and shafts of sunlight, poured down on to an iceberg of such dimension, Ted could only gasp in wonder and, forgetting his position, stand shoulder to shoulder with Joseph, his hands gripping the rail until the knuckles shone white.

It could be likened to a cathedral, its spires and pinnacles wreathed in cloud, glittering in the bright sunlight, a huge opening at its base like an immense door leading into a nave where the spirits of mariners long gone, might kneel.

It was not, as Ted would have expected, of a pure whiteness, but of a clear translucent blue, the indigo at its centre fading to violet at its edge. Only where the water frilled at its base was it truly white.

At his side, he heard Joseph audibly thanking God for its position, several miles distant, although Ted could see no guarantee that it would remain there. Even so, there seemed no reason to panic. In fact a strange sense of calm came over him.

'It's beautiful!' he said. 'The most beautiful thing I've ever seen.'

'Lets hope,' said Joseph dryly, 'that you always think that way. For myself, I am constantly reminded by such sights of what a puny creature man is. And how presumptous.'

Then, straightening his shoulders, he called, 'Your helm hard up, if you please, Mr Teevens!' And then glancing at Ted with a comic lift of an eyebrow, 'Just enough breeze to catch those tops'ls, I think, Mr Smith?'

So it was back into the rigging for him while Henry put others to bracing the yards. Slowly, slowly, with infinite caution, they moved westward and the iceberg fell astern.

Next day, the wind freshened and they were off. Two days later, a respectful distance to the south, they passed Cape Horn. At least, so Henry said. Much to Ted's annoyance, the island was totally invisible. But a few days later, they sighted the Falkands and knew, without a shadow of doubt, that they were heading homeward at last.

19

It was wonderful to be home, to feel Ma's arms around him and to hear her voice exclaiming at how he'd grown and broadened, tears of joy coursing, all the while, down her cheeks. And then to put up his head and sniff the appetising smell that had assailed his nostrils the moment he'd opened the door.

'Ma, it isn't! It can't be!'

'It *is*,' said Ma.

'Rabbit stew! Ma, you're a marvel.'

And then he had to give way to Anna and Joseph behind him, their arms already full with Georgie and Frank. Later, after Thirza and her brood had come in from next door and everyone had been given their presents, he sauntered slowly down Well Street, trying not to swagger in his uniform but hoping that at least a few doors would open as he passed. And nor was he disappointed, for several people came out of their houses to shake his hand and enquire how he was. He wished that Bert were not in Liverpool, but at least – if Joseph allowed him to – he would see him before the *Senator Weber* sailed again.

That night, as he prepared to leave – for, accommodation being limited, he'd been given a bed at Thirza's – Ma held him close then drew back her head to gaze at him closely, laughter in her eyes. 'That beard's a miracle and no mistake!'

'And I thought you hadn't even noticed.'

'How could I help but notice when it tickles my cheek like a feather?'

'I'll have you know it's made of best-quality human hair.'

'Don't worry, lad! Joseph's was the same when he was

126

your age. Bum fluff, Pa used to call it, though never in his hearing. I was always afraid your little fingers would pull it out when they tugged.'

Well, one thing was for sure, he thought, as he bade them all goodnight and let himself out, he'd never grow too big for his boots as long as Ma was alive!

They hadn't long at home; at least, Joseph and Ted hadn't.

'I'm contracted for another year,' Joseph told Ma. 'But then I shall have a rest. The Company will be quite agreeable.'

'And they'll have you back when you want to go?' Ma asked anxiously.

'So they've said. And I've no reason to disbelieve them. Unless, of course,' he grinned across at Ted, 'the rising generation has taken over by then!'

The rising generation threw a well-aimed orange at his brother, which was immediately caught and returned. 'No fear of that!' he said, and thought how good it was that they'd fallen back so easily into their old relationship.

And this time, when they left home, it would not be for long, for their next voyage would be to the ports of the Mediterranean.

He was lucky. Once the cargo was safely stowed – a mixed bag of coal and Staffordshire pots, cotton goods and salt – Joseph was agreeable to his going ashore to see Bert; provided he was back in good time, for they were sailing on the morning tide.

As he left the ship, the early dusk of a February evening was creeping over the waterfront. Fortunately, he knew where to find Bert; had even made a tentative arrangement by letter to meet outside the new Exchange buildings. He had left himself plenty of time to mooch along the wharfs in case a steamship was berthed there, but he was out of luck; there was nothing of any size. However, he decided as he went on his way, it couldn't be long now before steam came into its own.

In any case, to gain his master's certificate, he must serve his apprenticeship under sail. And, of course, he reminded himself with an inward grin, there were such trivial matters as his mates' certificates to acquire first; but in the fulness of time, he should manage those. But not *too* much time, he hoped. They said the Suez Canal would be opened later this year, and then steamships would have it all their own way.

Rumour had it along the wharfs that Thomas Ismay had just purchased, for the sum of a thousand pounds, the name of the ailing White Star Line, with the object of operating his own fleet of steamers in the North Atlantic, and everyone knew that when Ismay put his mind to something, it usually happened. He'd always admired that red burgee with its neat white star in the centre.

Shoulders hunched against the bitter wind blowing off the Mersey — it would be cold up top tomorrow! — he continued on his way to meet Bert. Would he have changed beyond all recognition?

He needn't have worried. Bert's red head shone out like a beacon under the light still flowing from the Exchange, especially as he seemed to be at least two feet taller than everyone else. They stood for a moment, hands on each other's shoulders, broad grins on their faces while they studied each other critically.

'*Formidable!*' said Bert at last, giving the word its French pronunciation. '*Un jeune homme très formidable!*' And then, when Ted stared at him in astonishment, added, 'I've been rehearsing that for days.'

'Well, it's certainly impressive. What else can you say?'

'So far, that the postillion of my aunt has jaundice, that thunder is expected within the hour and that my digestion does not permit me to eat snails. Gilly,' he added shyly, 'is teaching me.'

'Gilly? Who's Gilly?'

Bert blushed scarlet. 'My — er — young lady. I'd hoped she might come with me to meet you but she had to get back to Aigburth. Some sort of concert her mother's putting on for the local church. But she sent her best wishes and hopes to meet you on some future occasion.'

'So, you expect there to be a future occasion?'

'Oh, yes! God willing, we shall marry one day. We plan, in fact, to set up our own school. She will teach needlework and other practical domestic skills and I will offer the three Rs, plus, of course, Art.'

'How wonderful to be so sure,' Ted marvelled. 'I envy you.'

By now, they were walking briskly and without consultation into a nearby bar. Pints of ale in hand, they found a secluded corner.

'But surely,' said Bert, once they were settled, 'you too have planned your future?'

'Yes, indeed.' And Ted told told him about his thoughts as he'd walked up from the docks. 'But as far as the opposite sex in concerned, you're way ahead of me. It's the only aspect of a sailor's life, in my opinion, that leaves something to be desired.'

'Well, you know what they say, a girl in every port.'

Ted wrinkled his nose. 'That may be so for some, but not for me. However, I wish you and your Gilly every happiness.'

A most satisfactory evening was spent. When Ted returned to the *Senator Weber* – a little unsteady on his feet for long abstinence had left him unprepared for any form of alcohol – Bert went with him as far as the gangway.

'Well, so long, Bert. Look after yourself – and be British!'

'Cheerio, Ted. Safe voyage – and be British yourself!'

Smithy's maxim was now their own private joke – and yet, not quite a joke. Although they would have died rather than admit it, both attached great value to the qualities Smithy had implied in being 'British': integrity, resourcefulness, doing one's duty, no matter how humdrum that might sometimes be, and above all, courage in the face of adversity.

There were to be many more meetings with Bert over the years; and many more tales to tell.

*

He was fortunate that the Company left him under Joseph for most of that year of 1870. But then, in September, it was goodbye to the *Senator Weber*. And indeed, Joseph himself bade her a temporary farewell, as he kept his promise to Ma and went back to Hanley for a year or two. Ted's new ship was the *Amoy* and – under a new captain – he was no longer a third mate but an able-bodied seaman. Not that he cared, as long as he was at sea.

After the *Amoy* had come *Madge Wildfire* and then, in July of '71, he put up at the Sailors' Home, paid his one pound examination fee, and sat for his second mate.

He was twenty-one but looked, he fondly hoped, considerably older. Not that an appearance of maturity was likely to impress the examiners. They wished only to be satisfied of his competency in Navigation, Seamanship and Commercial Code Signals.

'Well, of course you passed,' said Joseph, when the certificate, beautifully embellished, arrived in Well Street. 'Look who taught you!'

'I wish Pa could have seen it,' said Ma, admiring the curlicues of the script that proclaimed Edward John Smith 'qualified to fulfil the duties of Second Mate in the Merchant Service.'

Next time he was home, Ted noticed that the certificate had been not only framed, but hung – in the shop, where everyone could admire it.

Not quite two years later, Ted's second mate certificate was joined by his first. He was twenty-three, tall and broad-shouldered and with a most respectable pair of mustachios. They curled about a mouth whose lips when not parted in a smile, showed firmness and determination. He was a good officer – and knew it.

'I think I'm a better officer than I was a seaman,' he told Alfred Smith, when he paid a visit to his old headmaster.

Smithy nodded his understanding. 'As you were a better monitor than an ordinary pupil. Some of us are made that way, but not all of us are blessed with as happy a disposition as you have, Ted. I must confess, when you first entered the Merchant Service, I had doubts about its suitability as a career for you – in spite of that wonderful brother of yours – but I can see now that I was wrong. You have the appearance of a man who has chosen wisely and well.'

'Thank you, sir,' Smithy's approval still had the power to swell his chest with pride.

'And what now?' Alfred Smith asked. 'You're still with the Andrew Gibson Line, I take it?'

'Yes. Just off the old *Mosher* and I think it will be the *Arzilla* next.'

'Still under sail, then?'

'Yes, sir. But I'm keeping an eye on the White Star Line.'

'I'm sure they appreciate your concern! I thought of you when I read that the *Oceanic* sailed for New York in March.' He said no more but continued to gaze at his former pupil, with a tell-tale twinkle in his eye.

Ted grinned. 'I know! Developed engine trouble soon after leaving port and was delayed for two weeks. But steam'll come, sir, it'll come.'

'And you, I'm sure, will be there when it does.'

20

'Of course you'll pass, E.J.! If I was a betting man, I'd put my life-savings on it – although precious little that would be.'

It was May of 1875 and Joseph, living at home during one of his periods away from the sea, had come up to Liverpool for a couple of days and was staying with Ted in his Hanover Street lodgings. The following day, Ted was to sit for his master's certificate.

'It's time I visited the Andrew Gibson offices anyway,' Joseph had told Anna. 'Out of sight, out of mind, they say, and I don't want them to forget me.'

'As if they could!' she'd said fondly. But she'd let him go, all the same. That he cared for her with all the love and devotion of his generous nature was beyond doubt, but she also knew that it was as essential for him to breathe a whiff of sea air from time to time as it was for a bird to stretch its wings and fly.

So, 'Give Ted my love,' she'd said and packed a bag with clean shirts, socks and handkerchiefs – enough for a day or two, but no longer.

Ma, of course, had sent her love too. Now that she'd given up the shop Joseph had wondered if she'd like to come with him, but she'd said no. 'Just as long as one of us is there. You know how Teddy can get into a state sometimes when he's thinking too much about what's ahead. Magnificent when things *are* happening – as cool a head as you could wish for. But I always remember the day he started school. It was Anna who took him in the end. . . .'

Ma, Joseph had noticed, was living in the past quite a

bit, these days. When she didn't have grandchildren crawling over her, he'd quite often find her just sitting gazing into the fire or out of the window, but not really seeing what she was looking at.

'Come on, E.J.,' he suggested now. 'We'll go for a stroll.'

Calling Ted, 'E.J.' was a legacy from his first voyage on the *Senator Weber* and the confusion of having two Edward Smiths on board. Joseph always made a point of using the abbreviation if he thought his brother's confidence needed boosting. It sounded, he thought, both businesslike and important. And in all honesty, there were enough Smiths about to make any form of identification useful.

They strolled – automatically and without conferring – towards the docks. 'Thought we might take a look at that new *Germanic*,' Joseph said.

'Capital idea!' Good old Joseph, Ted thought, doing his best to take my mind off the morrow. A steamship must be the last thing he really wants to look at. *He*, of course, had already studied the *Germanic* in great detail, but that didn't mean he wasn't eager to look at her again, and again.

She was, in fact, almost identical to her sister ship, *Britannic*.

'Still has four masts, I see,' said Joseph with satisfaction. 'Can't trust those ridiculous twin cigars to do the job unaided.'

Ted grinned. 'Averages fifteen knots, they say.'

Joseph sniffed. 'The old *Senator* could do that with just her tops'ls set.'

'But this one's five thousand tons.'

'And with a crew to match, no doubt.'

'Over a hundred and thirty.'

Joseph thought of his forty-odd on the *Senator*. 'Like a floating hotel! How can one man be expected to look after all those?'

'Well, there's the usual chain of command. And engineers, of course, for the technical side. And stewards to take care of the passengers. Nearly two thousand of those, I'm told.'

'I'll wager she cost a small fortune to build.'

'Two hundred thousand pounds.'

'I've heard these Cunarders take a bit of beating,' Joseph said.

'Oh, indeed! But White Star hold the record for the transatlantic crossing. Have done since '72. Just under eight days! It's small wonder they have the mail contract.'

His enthusiasm was contagious. In spite of himself, Joseph grinned. 'Properly sold on the White Star Line, aren't you, lad?'

Ted grinned back. 'You could say so! But there'll never be anything to beat a sailing-vessel for sheer beauty, I'll give you that.'

He'd passed! The Lords of the Committee of Privy Council for Trade were satisfied that one Edward J. Smith was competent in the handling of sail, in navigation, mathematics, mercantile law, 'flag-wagging' etc., etc.

A third certificate for his collection!

Sadly, though, he couldn't take it back to Ma himself. Inwardly bursting with pride, although trying hard to appear unimpressed by his success, he knew there wouldn't be time before he was off again on the *Arzilla* – still as first mate, but that was only what he'd expected. By next May, the elderly clerk at the office had assured him the three-masted *Lizzie Fennell* – just over a thousand tons and therefore smaller than the old *Senator*, but a lovely vessel, all the same – could be his.

'Well, young Ted, you've made it! And I'm proud of you!' And Joseph raised his tumbler. Whiskies, they'd decided, were in order on this very special occasion.

'I owe it all to you, Joseph. D'you remember how you showed me my way among the stars, out in the backyard with Ma shouting at us to put our coats on?'

'You were always an apt pupil, Ted. A pleasure to teach.'

Even so, at this auspicious moment in his life, Ted felt he must place on record his appreciation of Joseph's kindness; his patience and tolerance of a small boy's inevitable shortcomings, no matter how hard he tried. 'All the same, Joseph, I must thank you. I won't mention it again, I promise you, because I know it embarrasses you, but I feel happier now I've put it into words.'

As he had expected, Joseph shrugged dismissively. 'Believe me, Ted, I wouldn't have had it otherwise. And now, would Captain Smith care for a cigar?'

Would he not! Until now, it has seemed presumptuous for a mere mate to indulge in such a symbol of affluence and anyway, the evil-smelling cheroots that many sailors favoured were not to his taste. But this was different: a plump gold-banded cylinder of rich Havanna tobacco.

Solemnly, Joseph produced his clippers and with the dedicated care of a high priest engaged in some ancient ritual, cut off the end. Then brought out a box of vestas.

Ted closed his lips around the smooth brown leaf as Joseph extended the burning vesta.

'Inhale, Ted. But not too strongly.'

Slowly, carefully, he did as he was told and his nostrils filled with the heady, nerve-tingling aroma.

'Gently, does it! I'd let it go now if I were you.'

The smoke hung above his head like a cloud of incense. It was fitting, he thought, that Joseph should be the one to initiate him.

'Good,' said Joseph, well-pleased. 'Now, a few more puffs and then I should put it aside. We don't want Captain Smith retching over the side like a cabin-boy on his first voyage!'

21

After the *Arzilla*, he served again, for a few months, on the old *Senator*, and wallowed for a while in memories, some pleasant, some less so. Just there, at the rail, he had stood with young Tom and Jim, gazing enthralled at the busy harbour of Hong Kong. And just there, Edward Smith had been lashed to the shrouds while Joseph flogged him. And there, Emma Dalrymple and Anna had stood at Sunday morning service, their bonnet ties streaming in the breeze. And finally, there were the heads that Henry Tate had set him to clean so often. Dear Henry!

Once again, he spent Christmas on the *Senator Weber* and this time dined legitimately, if a shade stuffily, with the officers. And if, now and then, he wished himself back on the half-deck, there would be other occasions, he assured himself, when he could indulge his enjoyment of a good laugh and a joke. *His* ship, he devoutly hoped, would be a cheerful one.

At home, he missed the arrival of Edward Joseph Harrington, but Joseph stood as godparent for the two of them.

In the event, it was April '76 when he left Liverpool in the *Lizzie Fennell*; she was bound for Antwerp to pick up her cargo and crew, and Captain Robinson was still aboard from her previous voyage, on his way to take command of another vessel.

Ted didn't mind; he knew Robinson well, in fact, and was more than willing to listen to any suggestions he might make.

'Good luck, Captain Smith!' the little clerk in Liverpool

had said, handing him his papers, and Ted had thanked him most civilly for his good wishes. He'd been grateful, too, for the forethought – Company policy though it might be – in giving him such a reliable first mate as William Sinclair. He was just off Joseph's ship the *Mohur*, and his brother must have regretted his transfer, for a good Scotsman took a lot of beating. And William Ross, born of a Danish mother, still had a Scottish father and, at thirty-five years of age, should be a sensible and reliable second.

Ted, in fact, was the youngest officer on board, being two years junior to Sinclair, but he had no intention of advertising this minor detail; anyway, his beard was now developing most satisfactorily. Even Ma said so.

As always, the crew were a motley collection, but with a goodly proportion of Scandinavians, he was pleased to see, and with a bo'sun, Charles Rivers, who'd served on the old *Senator* with him. But the circumstance he was most pleased about was that *Mohur* and *Lizzie Fennell* were bound for the same destination: Callao and the Lobos Islands, for a cargo of guano.

Joseph had warned him how it would be. 'It's the isolation, Ted, more than the loneliness; the knowledge that yours is the ultimate responsibility. No longer can you say it wasn't my fault, I was only doing what I was told. Oh, I know,' as Ted's eyebrows had shot up in protest, 'you're not given to saying any such thing, but even so, the Company certainly would.'

Now, safely cleared from Antwerp, they were sailing briskly westward, all plain sail set, into the path of the setting sun. Either of his officers, Ted reflected, and probably several of his crew, could have achieved as much. But would they wish for the responsibility? William Sinclair, he felt sure, would welcome it, but William Ross, he felt equally sure, would remain content to be the middleman, simply obeying orders, and thereby playing as vital a part in the smooth running of the ship as anyone. He remembered Alfred Smith's words on the subject: some are born to be leaders and others are not, and happy the man who recognises not his limitations but his proper place in the scheme of things.

Gazing down from the poop, Captain Edward J. Smith was pleased to observe that all was as it should be; buntlines secured, ropes neatly coiled, those sails not yet unfurled snugged down on the yards. Already the familiar smell of boiling beef came from the galley, and at this stage of their journey there was a plentiful supply of onions. He hoped that his steward – a Frenchman with the exotic name of Chatillon Nicolas ('Old Nick' his shipmates were already calling him!) was on good terms with the cook. But *he* was a German, so anything could happen!

In a little while, he'd make a tour of the ship; not ostentatiously but quietly, methodically, nodding his approval when appropriate but careful not to frown in annoyance when it was not, merely making a mental note to mention it later to William Sinclair.

That was another thing Joseph had impressed upon him: delegation. 'Know your officers, Ted – and trust them to the limit of their capabilities. Be available at all times if they need you, but otherwise leave them to it. Some skippers are as possessive of their ships as of their wives – more so, sometimes, and in neither case does it work.'

'A fair prospect, sir,' said William Sinclair, appearing at his elbow. 'Will you be taking the helm tonight, sir? Or shall Mr Ross and I take turn and turn about?'

For a moment, he was tempted by the prospect of a whole night undisturbed in his bunk, but with only the three of them and the crew still an unknown quantity. . . . 'I'll take the midnight watch, Mr Sinclair.'

'Aye, aye, sir! Thank you, sir.'

He had chosen wisely.

He should have realised, long before he did, that Joseph Paulo was sick. He, like Charles Rivers, had come with him from the *Senator Weber*, so he was a familiar face. Perhaps that was the trouble; he'd grown so accustomed to the

Italian seaman's olive skin, dark eyes and thin, wiry frame that he hadn't noticed until too late that his eyes had sunk even deeper into their sockets, his cheeks grown pale when others' had darkened under the sun's rays and that his mouth wore a perpetual grimace, not of discontent, as he'd thought at first, but of pain.

For Joseph Paulo had the clap, the disease picked up by so many seamen coming into a foreign port at the end of a long voyage. Once again, he remembered Henry Tate's words – 'abstinence makes the heart grow fonder. And not only the heart!'

When William Ross had come to him that morning and reported the seaman still abed – and writhing in agony – they'd both known he was beyond human help. It was August now and they were well out into the Atlantic, heading south; far distant from any port where he could have been put ashore. All he could do was detail a seaman to sit beside him to lay cold compresses upon his forehead and administer sips of precious water whenever needed.

It was a relief to everyone when he breathed his last. They hove to, and for the first time, Ted spoke the words of the committal. It was soon over and Joseph Paulo was consigned to the deep. And then, as tradition demanded, a sale was held of his effects.

It was a macabre practice but sensible; far better that Paulo's sparse wardrobe be put to good use than allowed to grow musty in his locker. So Ted told himself, but he still felt a nagging sense of guilt that it had been necessary at all.

Over the years, he'd seen more men die of the clap than he cared to remember. But this had happened on *his* ship, under *his* command. He hoped it wasn't an omen.

The roughest ocean in the world, they called the Atlantic; but it was the Pacific that was responsible for the next disaster.

The Horn safely rounded – and, to Ted's relief, without drama or incident (extraordinary, that he had once wanted

139

both!) – they were making good time up the coast of Chile. Journey's end, if not exactly in sight, was no more than a couple of weeks away.

It was close to midday and several members of the starboard watch, waiting to be relieved, had sighted a school of whales blowing vigorously out on the port bow. Carl Johanissan, an enterprising Swede, immediately began to take bets – so many glasses of grog when they reached port – upon which blow would reach the highest. With two of his mates, Nielson and Carl Olson, he mounted the rigging to view 'the field' more clearly.

At the same time, William Ross, up on the poop-deck, observed a heavy squall coming hard at them on the starboard bow. Just as he gave the command, 'All hands on deck! Reef tops'ls!' one of the whales sent up a spout of such marathon proportions the seamen at the rail raised a triumphant cheer.

It was this, perhaps, that caused the helmsman to lose concentration momentarily, allowing the wheel to spin as the *Lizzie Fennell's* topsails caught the full blast of the wind and she keeled over. The seamen in the rigging were taken completely by surprise and tumbled from their perches like overripe fruit from an orchard bough.

As Ted, alerted by the sudden violent movement, came out on to the poop-deck, closely followed by William Sinclair, who was preparing to take over the watch, he saw a scene of the utmost confusion: canvas in danger of tearing to shreds, men clinging to anything they could lay hands on, the decks awash and the helmsman struggling frantically with the wheel. At the same time came the cry 'men overboard!' from a seaman who had narrowly escaped being knocked into the sea himself by his falling shipmates.

'Assist at the helm, Mr Ross, and hove to! Mr Sinclair, see to the boat!' And then, in an enormous bellow that would have done credit to Henry Tate, he reinforced the call for all hands.

For over two hours, they sculled around in mountainous seas as the *Lizzie Fennel* rode out the storm. It was a sodden, downcast and silent crew who pulled the boat back on board and then stood, heads bowed, while Ted, yet again, spoke the words of the burial service. By common consent, the sale of the dead seamen's effects was postponed until the next day; they had been good shipmates and would be sorely missed.

That evening, Ted held an informal court of enquiry.

'It was a combination of circustances, E.J.,' said Joseph, 'that could have happened to anyone. And certainly could not be anticipated. It isn't your fault if men are foolish enough to lark about in the rigging when the officer of the watch is occupied elsewhere.'

'They weren't exactly larking,' said Ted. 'They were all good men whom I was sorry to lose.'

'Even so,' said Joseph firmly, 'you cannot be expected to hold their hands every minute of every day.'

'That,' said Ted, 'was more or less what we decided.'

'We?'

'William Sinclair, Charles Rivers and myself. I thought it politic,' he explained, 'to include them in my enquiries.'

'Very wise!'

The *Mohur* and the *Lizzie Fennel* were anchored near each other in the harbour at Callao, and Ted had invited Joseph to dine on board. They had eaten in the company of the first and second mates but now the two masters – wreathed in cigar smoke – were alone in Ted's cabin.

As his host rose to pour coffee from the tray brought in by Chatillon Nicolas, Joseph pondered upon Ted's future. A couple more years as skipper under his belt and he'd be off to try his luck in the black-funnelled monsters that Joseph could not bear to look upon without wincing. And good luck to him! His own personal animosity didn't come into the matter.

'That *Germanic*,' he observed politely, as he took his cup from Ted, 'was in dock when I left Liverpool. She and the *Britannic* seem to be having it all their own way across the Atlantic.'

141

Ted grinned to himself. Joseph, he'd noticed, invariably prefixed a disparaging 'that' to the name of any steamships he could bring himself to mention 'That *Germanic*,' he seemed to be saying, 'no better than she should be!'

'Yes,' he said easily, 'they're a good pair.' But left it at that. Courtesy deserved courtesy. And Joseph was clearly trying to be an obliging guest. 'I'm hoping for the east coast, next trip,' he continued, 'Canada, maybe. And the Southern States, if I'm lucky.'

'Now, there you're talking,' said Joseph. 'Give me a lovely little port like Savannah, any day of the week! I'd like to see that *Germanic* trying to push her nose in there. Wouldn't get further than the Tybee Roads before she grounded.' And then, remembering his resolution, added kindly, 'Manages all right in New York, no doubt?'

Ted nodded gravely. 'But the Savannah river and the Hudson bear no comparison.'

'If you do go to Savannah,' said Joseph, 'You must look up a gentleman by the name of Walker. A Mr George Walker. As kind a man as you'd find anywhere. He'll make you welcome.'

'I'll remember that,' Ted promised. It was a prerequisite of having your own ship that hospitality was often extended by port officials or local merchants, especially in the Southern States.

22

Less than a year later, in the American fall, as the *Lizzie Fennell* sailed from the Atlantic swell into the calm of the Tybee Roads and hove to, to await her tug, Ted remembered the conversation he'd had with Joseph in Callao.

His hopes had been fully justified; after disposing of that odorous cargo of guana, he'd been given the eastern coast of North America, with short voyages and more attractive prospects at the end of them. First, Miramichi in New Brunswick and now Savannah.

John Henderson, his first mate, stood beside him on the poop; he was an old friend whose last berth had been on *Mohur* with Joseph. 'Stealing all my best men!' Joseph had grumbled, although Ted guessed he was secretly pleased.

As they moved slowly up-river between rice fields yellowing for harvest groups of black men and women waved as they passed.

'They seem happy enough,' Ted observed.

'Enjoying their freedom, no doubt,' said John Henderson.

Nearing Savannah, Ted felt his customary pleasure at viewing a township from the sea. Even Liverpool had a mystical quality when seen from the Mersey, and Savannah viewed from its river was purest magic.

The sunlit wharfs were alive with activity. Sailors called down to stevedores from the prows of their ships, stevedores shouted back; crates and barrels and sacks were being piled into carts and drays or hoisted aloft into the gaping maws of the warehouses. Behind the warehouses, the ground rose steeply to a row of solid stone buildings, some curlicued with balconies but all gracefully proportioned. Above rose

143

the tower and clockface of what Ted knew to be the City Exchange, and all about, so that the city seemed to nestle in a cradle of greenery, were sweet-smelling forests of pine.

John Henderson sniffed appreciatively. 'A change from that old guano!'

Ted, suddenly filled with an inexplicable sense of well-being, grinned back. 'It certainly is!'

He had promised to write a descriptive letter to Bert whenever he dropped anchor at a point of particular geographical interest.

'It might keep my young ruffians quiet for a few minutes!' Bert had explained. Not the most effusive of compliments, although he knew what Bert meant. Bert and Gilly were still teaching in the city slums but were living now in Seaforth.

Savannah, Georgia, was born, if you like, in the year 1733, when an Englishman named James Oglethorpe sailed eighteen miles up the Savannah river and decided that here was the perfect place to found a settlement. Fortunately for him, the native Indians, who had been of that opinion for many years, were co-operative and actually welcomed the new arrivals.

However, this city was not allowed to grow in the higgledy-piggledy fashion that so many cities do.

At this point, Ted looked up from his writing while he thought for a moment of the jumble of streets and alleyways in Hanley, twisting downhill to the Market Square, then rushing on again to Hope Street and the bottle kilns beyond. In truth, he wouldn't change a brick of it, no matter how grimed with smoke it was. However, the youth of Liverpool must make its own comparisons!

He resumed his writing; a pleasant enough occupation while John Henderson supervised the rearranging of the general cargo they were to take on to Texas.

It is as if the city fathers had decided that in no way was the work to be rushed and that beauty must always take precedence over convenience. And, indeed, the result more than justifies this theory; a city of wide thoroughfares connecting leafy squares of gracious, well-proportioned houses with the occasional spire of a church pointing to a sky that seems perpetually blue. As delightful a prospect for the passer-by – and this includes a gawping, awestruck sea captain – as for those who dwell within the houses or worship in the churches.

He finished off with a few geographical facts about the rice and cotton plantations around the city, the tobacco and lumber industries that made it such a thriving seaport, and then leaned back in his chair. He could allow himself a few minutes before showing his face on deck.

A few minutes to remember the evening he'd spent as a guest in one of those gracious houses, with the Templeton family. George Walker had been as kind as Joseph had promised, introducing him to friends who had actually vied with each other for the privilege of entertaining a British sea captain.

It was a smaller house than many of its neighbours. The wooden framework of its construction was incorporated into its interior with little benefit of plaster, so that exposed beams ran the length of the long, narrow room in which they sat, and curved gracefully within its walls. The floor was of wood also, its polished surface scattered with gaily patterned rugs. The fireplace crackled with the flames of scented apple logs. At his elbow, a crystal bowl of deep pink roses stood on a small table, one of which scattered its petals when his hand brushed against it.

'I'm sorry, ma'am, that was careless of me,' he apologised to his hostess.

'My dear Captain, think nothing of it! They would have dropped before long, in any case.' He loved their voices; the soft, sensuous drawl was so different from the clipped vowels he was accustomed to.

'Miss Eliza,' said his host, 'was fortunate to find so many,

145

so late in the fall. You love your roses, don't you, my dear?'

Miss Eliza? He could have sworn the remark had been addressed to the lady of the house, but clearly he was mistaken. This dark-haired young girl, her eyes demurely downcast, who had risen from her chair to scoop up the offending petals must be Eliza. Why had he not listened more carefully to their introductions?

'Thank you, Miss Eliza,' he said when the petals had been removed.

To his astonishment, the eyes flashed open — they were the exact colour of the wood violets he'd once bought for Ma on her birthday — and she laughed; a delicious sound, like the cool splash of water.

'Miss Eliza is my mother, sir! I am Miss Julia.'

They'd all laughed then, her mother and father and her two older sisters, Selina and Mattie, while they all explained at once that the courtesy title of 'Miss' was given to all ladies, no matter how old.

'We reckon it's more polite that way,' his host explained. 'Even an elderly lady likes to think she has some vestige of youth about her.'

'Thank you, my dear,' said his wife, a comely middle-aged matron.

Ted had joined in the laughter and then explained that in England, it was the other way round; a cook, for instance, in one of the big houses was given the courtesy title of 'Mrs', irrespective of her marital status.

From then on, they'd assumed he was an authority not only on the English upper classes, but on royalty too, and had plied him with questions. Had Queen Victoria recovered yet from the death of Prince Albert? Was she still in mourning? Did people really bow or curtsey when she passed? And did she wear a crown at all times? Even for breakfast?

He answered their questions as best he could, and then dared to pose one or two of his own: why did they call their gardens, 'yards' and pavements, 'sidewalks'?

Once, when her mother asked her to pass him a cup of

146

coffee, Miss Julia's hand brushed against his, and it was as if he had suffered a minor heart attack, so exciting a sensation did he feel.

They spoke to each other hardly at all. 'And what does Miss Julia think?' he was once emboldened to ask; although he could not, for the life of him remember afterwards what they had been speaking of. Whatever it was, she had blushed in the most delightful manner and explained prettily that she was not sufficiently long out of the schoolroom to have formed views upon such matters. However, her eyes had indicated, there were *other* matters upon which she had thought long and deeply and would, if given the opportunity, be happy to discuss with him.

The Exchange clock was striking midnight when, whistling like a schoolboy, he'd clattered over one of the iron bridges down into River Street, before striding up the gangway of the *Lizzie Fennell*. Sixteen, would she be? Even seventeen, perhaps? Ten years was nothing between a man and his wife; a desirable interval, in fact.

'Be sure to come and see us when next you're in Savannah,' her parents had said as he left. Wild horses wouldn't keep him away!

23

Nearly a year passed before he saw her again.

Fuming at the contrariness of Fate, he'd had to lie to in Galveston for nearly two months after leaving Savannah, while he waited for a cargo back to Liverpool. Admittedly the Texans had proved as hospitable as the Georgians and his Christmas had been as enjoyable as any he'd spent at sea, but why could the delay not have occurred in Savannah?

It was something, he supposed, that after his return from Texas, the *Lizzie Fennell* had been kept on the Atlantic crossing. So he had, at least, been able to 'practise his American' as Joseph put it. But Maryland wasn't Georgia. And when the ship sprang a leak just out of Baltimore and he had to put back for recaulking, again he wondered why the delay could not have occurred in Savannah.

But at last his prayers were answered. Back in Liverpool, the little clerk, full of the most profuse apologies, told him that the *Lizzie Fennell* would have to turn around and go back again.

'What? To Baltimore?'

'No, Captain, to that heathen hole, Savannah.'

'That heathen hole, Savannah?' What possessed the fellow? Did he not know that Savannah was the most beautiful city in America, possibly in the whole world? But at the same time, he could have kissed the bald, pink pate, swept the kind little man off his high stool and hugged him to death. Instead, he asked mildly, 'Heathen? Savannah?'

'Those heathen blacks, Captain! They're still there, you know, in spite of having their freedom.'

He thought of Maria, the black maid in the 'wooden

148

house', whose face was perpetually wreathed in smiles. 'What else could they do? Take ship back to Africa? Who would be willing to pay their passage? And they're certainly not heathens!' And he took great delight in telling the clerk about the Baptist Church in Savannah where the Negroes worshipped with great vigour and enthusiasm. 'The Gospel choirs are wonderful to listen to. And they even think,' he added solemnly, 'that God is a black man!' And then, because the little clerk was clearly shocked at such a remark, relented and assured him that the population of Savannah, whatever their colour, were as Christian as those of Liverpool. More so, perhaps.

And then, because his heart was bursting with joy and goodwill to all men, he pressed a note into the clerk's hand before going on to complete the formalities of discharge. After that, it was off to Hanover Street, to his usual Liverpool lodgings for a night or two. No time, even, for Hanley.

It was late September when he anchored once more in the Roads and saw the dunes of Tybee Island gleaming golden in the sunlight; and knew that the eighteen miles that now lay between him and Savannah would seem an eternity. If only the *Lizzie Fennell* could sprout a funnel for the next couple of hours!

But in truth, he would not have altered her appearance by one iota. Every inch of her brasswork glistened in the early morning sun and a meal could have been safely eaten from the scoured surface of her decks. For there was always the possibility that Julia might be allowed to visit him aboard; although not, of course, unchaperoned.

The captain of the steam-tug was the same that he'd had in the previous year. 'Captain Smith, isn't it? Mighty pleased to see you again, sir!'

There was one advantage, he'd discovered, about his name. People rarely forgot it. He introduced his first mate on this voyage, a Liverpool Irishman named Patrick Eagan. He was the same age as Ted, black-haired and blue-eyed, and with a pleasant easy-going disposition. As there'd been

149

no second mate available at the time of departure from Liverpool, he and Ted had shared the watches and an easy friendship had grown up between them.

'And how long are you staying for this time?' the captain asked.

'A couple of weeks, I think.' Not long enough, but sufficient, he hoped, to form some sort of a bond between himself and Julia. Too soon, of course, to speak for her but enough time to at least establish himself as suitor.

At last, Hutchinson Island looming behind her, the *Lizzie Fennell* nudged the Savannah wharf, her prow high above River Street. Not long, now! But no matter how hard he tried to expedite the formalities, to hand in his articles to the vice-consul with the greatest possible speed, to report to the agents, consult with factors and visit chandlers, pleasantries must be exchanged and refreshments taken and it was dusk before they were finished.

Suddenly indecisive, he deliberated upon what he should do. Impatient though he was to go ashore, would it not be more politic to arrive at the wooden house spruce and fresh, in daylight, rather than try to find his way through the darkening streets and squares and perhaps discover some entertainment in progress?

Wryly, he reflected that 'the other woman' in his life must not be neglected and anchor watches for the *Lizzie Fennell* had not yet been arranged.

So, he decided, he'd go early to his bed; just as he'd done as a child on Christmas Eve, to make the morrow come more quickly. But would he sleep? Would it not be sensible first to smoke a cigar or two, while he took a stroll along the quayside?

In the end, he pulled himself together, reminded himself that he was twenty-eight years of age, not eighteen, and should behave accordingly. Which meant that he played cards with Patrick Eagan, retired at midnight – and overslept.

The sun was already high in the heavens when he walked down the gangway. It had taken so long to trim his beard,

150

to get the balance exactly right between one side and the other. A careless snip could mean the whole business begun again, with a good half-inch lost in the process.

But he was now reasonably satisfied with the result. His cap set at a jaunty angle, he strode down Bull Street, counting the squares as he went: Johnson, White, Chippewa. Before Maddison, he must turn to the right. Or was it left? Panic threatened until he recognised a house with a particularly ornate balcony and knew he was on the right route.

Part of his mind – that part trained to notice the slightest shift in the wind, the increased density of the clouds, or swell in the ocean – was aware that some of the trees in the squares and along the streets were changing colour to russet brown and palest gold, that the glossy green of the magnolia leaves shone as if newly washed, that the swags and streamers of Spanish moss hung, like ghostly fingers, from the evergreen live oaks.

He turned, crossed a broad thoroughfare, turned again – and there it was; its pink-washed walls still hung with the ripening fruit of the peach trees. And there, polishing the already glistening door-knocker to a peak of perfection, was Maria.

It was with difficulty that he stopped himself leaping over the wooden palings of the fence and taking the steps in a single bound. Instead, he opened the gate and stood there looking up at her.

'Good morning, Maria.'

Startled, she turned and almost dropped her cloth. 'Well, if it ain't Cap'n Ted!'

Her instant, delighted recognition pleased him beyond measure. An omen, he hoped, for the future. 'Anyone . . .' his voice croaked slightly, '. . . at home?'

'Well, Miss 'Liza's gone calling. And Mr George, he's in his office. But the girls are here. And right pleased they'll be to see you!' She pushed open the door and bustled inside, calling as she went, 'Miss Selina! Miss Mattie! Miss Julia! Look who's here!'

151

It was fortunate that he was tall and well-built, for the next moment he was almost swept off his feet by what seemed like a bevy of brightly hued butterflies, seizing his hands, his arms, the lapels of his jacket and dragging him up the steps and into the house. And the most beautiful, the most colourful of them all, was Julia.

She wore a gown of blue, sprigged with white, her long dark ringlets held back by a broad band of the same cloth. And she was a little taller, a little plumper in the face. All this he observed later. Now, all he was capable of taking in was the flash of her smile, the unmistakeable delight in her eyes and the sound of her voice, although they all spoke at once.

'Captain Ted! Come in! Come in!'

'Mama is out . . '

'. . . so you must stay at least until she returns.'

'You must stay all day!'

'For how long will you be in Savannah?'

'Maria! Some tea, if you please, for the captain.'

But Maria had already gone through to the kitchen to see to it, and he was being pulled into the living-room, where they all stood back and gazed at him as if he were something extraordinary they'd found washed up by the sea – which, in a manner of speaking, he was.

'We thought you were our brother William.' He hadn't known there was a brother.

'Home from West Point.'

'And refusing, in the most ungentlemanly manner, to take us about.'

'Unless we promise to hold our tongues.'

'And that, for some reason, we find impossible to do!'

Then the tea came and soon afterwards, the brother they'd mentioned: a pleasant, well set-up young man with a mop of auburn curls and a markedly cheerful disposition whom Ted warmed to straight away. Plainly, in spite of their teasing, his sisters adored him.

'Have you ever seen such an undisciplined lot, Captain?' he asked as they fluttered around him, relieving him of his cane, pouring his tea, enquiring if he would like more cream or sugar. 'I doubt they'd last a minute on your ship, no more than they would in any regiment I commanded.'

'That will be the day, brother, when you command a company, let alone a regiment!'

It was the perfect cue for him to suggest a visit to the *Lizzie Fennell*. He hadn't envisaged such a large party, but the more he tried to assess the situation, the less likely it seemed that he would ever be able to separate Julia from her sisters and brother. It was almost like a conspiracy; and it increased when their mother came home and seemed, on the surface at least, to be as pleased to see him again as her children had been.

'Of course you must stay to lunch, Captain. A simple repast but one we would be honoured to have you share.'

He was secretly amused to find that the 'simple repast' consisted of pork – one of the staple constituents of his diet over the last months – but prepared in such a way, with the addition of strange spices and herbs, that it was almost unrecognisable.

By the end of the meal, it had been arranged that, although he must now return on board, 'the young people' as their Mama fondly called her offspring, would present themselves on the quayside next day for a guided tour of the *Lizzie Fennell*.

'Could I, perhaps, bring a friend?' Selina, the eldest, enquired tentatively and was the immediate recipient of knowing glances from the rest of her family.

So the 'friend' must be both male and eligible, Ted deduced, and therefore doubly welcome. If he could pair them *all* off, then he and Julia. . . . He grew quite light-headed at the thought.

It was a shock to discover Patrick Eagan so practised in the entertainment of women. From the moment the party had come aboard, shepherded up the gangway by Ted, he'd cast off his normal role of mate – restricting communication to what was needed for the smooth running of the ship – and emerged as what Ted could only describe as a ladies' man.

153

Admittedly, he was only carrying out Ted's explicit instructions 'to act in whatever capacity seems expedient to make the visit a success'. But so immersed did he become in his new role, bowing low over the hands of the girls, saluting the young men, he almost extended the same courtesies to Ted himself, bringing up the rear of the little procession like a faithful sheepdog.

And while it was obviously desirable, in view of the narrow confines of the ship, to divide the party into two groups, why did it have to be Julia and Mattie who went with Patrick, while he was left with William and Selina and Selina's friend Henry? A quiet, unassuming young man, Henry had been allowed out from his factor's office in order to broaden his knowledge of a sailing vessel. However, since he appeared to have eyes only for Selina, it was doubtful, Ted thought sourly, if the visit was of any benefit at all; except perhaps in the furthering of their relationship.

But young William was a responsive audience and it was to him that Ted addressed most of his remarks and explanations.

'In truth,' he felt obliged to comment after the young ensign had shown an immediate and intelligent grasp of the principles of navigation and asked the most astute questions concerning the purpose of the various sails, 'if you had not chosen the army as a career, you would have made an excellent seaman.'

'Why, thank you, Ted. I value that comment greatly. And had it not been for a stomach that objects strongly to any motion more violent than a rocking chair, I might have chosen differently. But tell me, why is an enterprising fellow like yourself content to remain under sail? Are you not more interested in steam as a means of locomotion?' And he pointed to a paddle-steamer that was making a steady, undeviating course up-river, leaving an arrowhead of ripples in her wake.

So then he had to explain how he must first serve his time as master under canvas, but that it was his intention to move over to steam eventually, although it would mean starting at the bottom of the ladder again.

Then William began to tell him all about the SS *Savannah*, the sailing-vessel with auxiliary steam power that had made the crossing to Liverpool in under thirty days, and that way back in 1819.

These Americans, he found himself thinking at one point, they know it all! And then, glancing amidships and seeing Julia balanced on the lower rungs of the ratlines, steadied there by the strong arms of Patrick Eagan, he reminded himself that his dearest love was an American, born and bred.

Altogether, it was a most unsatisfactory afternoon, with even his bo'sun, Samuel Pollock, catching everyone's attention with his quick Welsh wit.

The only crumb of consolation came as they left, when Julia, placing her hand in his, thanked him for a delightful afternoon and reminded him that they were all meeting next day for a walk in Forsyth Park. At least, Patrick Eagan hadn't been invited to accompany them!

'Went off very well, I thought, sir,' said Patrick as they stood at the rail gazing at the backs of the retreating party. And added, as Julia turned suddenly to wave – at whom, he wondered? – 'A remarkably pretty young lady, that!'

'Passable,' Ted heard himself say.

The expedition to Forsyth Park was more successful than the visit to the *Lizzie Fennell*.

At first, it had seemed as if he might even be allowed to escort Julia alone. As a result of 'all that walking about on the cobblestones yesterday', Selina had a blister 'the size of a dollar piece', while Mattie pleaded a headache and William was frankly scornful of 'paradin' about, gawpin' at a load of plants'; if Ted was botanically inclined, then why not sit on the back porch and study the roses that climbed all over it? Only Julia appeared to be looking forward to the outing.

It was at this point that Miss Eliza took over, quickly providing Selina with ointment and a roll of lint, briskly informing Mattie that fresh air was just the thing for a headache and assuring William that if he didn't mind being at the eye of the hurricane that was shortly to be set up by brush and broom, then he was welcome to stay – even, if he was of a mind, to join in.

Five minutes later, they were all strolling down Bull Street towards the park.

It *is* a conspiracy, thought Ted, and not my imagination. Miss Eliza doesn't want me to be alone with Julia, even though it would have been perfectly proper for me to have escorted her to a public place in broad daylight. Half of him was flattered – at least he was being taken seriously as a suitor, even if unwelcome – but the other half was deeply hurt. And yet, Miss Eliza appeared to like him well enough. For the first time, he considered the implications of an American girl marrying an Englishman: long periods away from her family and friends, the bringing up of children without benefit of grandparents, the coming to terms with a culture different from her own.

And yet – he glanced down at Julia, walking at his side, her face hidden by the brim of her bonnet, her hair a cascade of dark curls against the apple-green of her gown, her gloved hands folded demurely across her small, pointed breasts, her tiny, slippered feet showing just a glimpse of a white-stocking'd ankle – and ached with longing for her. Surely, if two people cared sufficiently for each other, any number of sacrifices could be contemplated?

As if to prove his point, Julia suddenly lifted her head and gave him the most meaningful of glances, her eyes like limpid violet pools, her lips slightly parted to show the pearly lustre of her teeth. It was fortunate indeed that they were not alone, otherwise he could have done none other but put his arms around her, in full view of whoever was passing. As it was, when she slid a hand into the crook of his arm and gave it an almost imperceptible squeeze, he had the greatest difficulty in continuing to walk in a straight line.

If Miss Eliza was dubious about encouraging their friend-ship, then her daughters, it soon became abundantly clear,

156

were not. Soon after they'd reached the park, Mattie and Selina each took one of William's arms and propelled him rapidly down a side path.

'Look!' he heard Mattie exclaim. 'Isn't that your old school friend, Sam Bullen? He's simply dying to hear all about West Point.'

William's reply — that Sammy Bullen was an idiot and no friend of his — was barely audible, so fast was he now travelling.

Within Ted, elation fought with panic; elation because surely this united front must have been decided upon in advance and with Julia's consent, and panic because now that he was actually alone with her, an unaccustomed shyness was rendering him speechless. Where were the adroit speeches, the neat turns of phrase he'd rehearsed so diligently on the poop of the *Lizzie Fennell*?

Fortunately, Julia had no such inhibitions. 'No wonder,' she said with an infectious giggle, 'that William is so indignant. Sam Bullen is a most loathsome individual.'

'Poor Sam Bullen!' said Ted, recovering slightly.

'Why *poor* Sam Bullen?'

'Why, because anyone who does not have your complete approval must deserve pity.'

Her silvery laugh rang out. 'And Englishmen,' she observed, apparently to an azalea growing beside the path, its leaves like freshly minted golden coins, 'are supposed to be grim and silent. Not given to fine words nor pretty speeches!'

He saw that beyond the azalea was an iron bench, shielded from the view of passers-by. 'Shall we sit for a while?'

'I think not,' said Julia judiciously. 'Not here, at any rate. I must show you our magnificent fountain. And besides, that is where I have arranged to meet my sisters. And, of course, my brother, only he does not know it!'

He was amazed at her frankness. 'So, it *was* arranged? Sam Bullen was a figment of your sisters' imagination?'

She chuckled. 'There's no way Sam Bullen can be described as the figment of anyone's imagination! He is

157

large, hairy and has the most revolting spots.'

He fingered his own smooth chin between the silky strands of his beard. 'Spots,' he said magnanimously, 'are but a sign of youth. *Callow* youth,' he added hurriedly, lest she think him old as Methuselah.

'Spots or no,' she said, 'I prefer older men.'

'You do?' He would not have thought her *that* experienced.

By now, they had reached what was indeed a magnificent fountain, and after a few moments while he dutifully admired the crystal jets and the graceful arc of their descent into the basin, Julia sat herself down on a nearby bench and motioned him to join her.

'Well,' she continued their conversation, 'let us say that I find my brother's friends distinctly gauche and uninteresting and not to be compared with the older men I have met so far.'

He wasn't sure that he cared overmuch for that 'so far'. However, 'For a permanent relationship,' he ventured to suggest, 'I think a gap of a few years – around ten, perhaps? – is eminently suitable.'

'You really think so, Captain Ted?' Her eyes flirted outrageously.

'Undoubtedly so, Miss Julia!'

'Now, tell me,' she said, 'about your life in England. About the place where you live.'

For the first time in his life, he wished that he lived elsewhere but Hanley, with its bottle kilns, its pall of smoke, its perpetually grimy buildings. And then he remembered the people of Hanley, their kindness and generosity, their sharing of what little they might have with their neighbours, their courage in times of adversity; as if the darker and dirtier their surroundings, the brighter and purer, their souls.

Suddenly, he had a picture of Ma, scrubbing away at her front step in the early morning, even though she knew full well it would be filthy again within minutes once she opened the shop, and calling out a greeting to the other women doing the same, all down Well Street. He saw Pa, too, setting off briskly enough for the potbank but coming back, stooped and coughing, though still finding the energy to take him on his knee. Whatever happened to him in the future, he must always remember the stock from which he'd sprung.

'Ted?' said Julia tentatively, summoning him back to the beauty of his present surroundings. For a moment, the park was too perfect, the air too bland, the sky too clear and the girl beside him almost too pretty.

'Eh, Hanley folk are grand folk,' he heard himself say, using the clipped, forthright speech of Staffordshire. 'The best in the world.'

She looked puzzled. 'I didn't mean the people, Ted. I meant the place.'

'But places make people,' he insisted. 'A person's character can be formed by the place they live in. Because *you've* been brought up in a beautiful city like Savannah, that beauty will probably influence you for ever. It could be, 'his voice faltered for a moment, as he realised where this train of thought was leading him, 'that you'll want to live among such beauty for the rest of your life. That your spirit will crave it.'

But she wasn't interested in her spirit only her body. She dimpled provocatively. 'You mean you find me beautiful, too, Ted? Just like Savannah?'

'Oh, *very* beautiful!' he agreed. Impulsively, he caught her hand. 'But Hanley isn't like Savannah, Julia. It's dirty and smelly, with crooked streets and little houses built back to back, with just a yard between. But the people who live in them are the salt of the earth.'

'But *you* don't have to live in them, do you, Ted?' Still she wasn't comprehending what he was trying to say. Still she was viewing everything from a personal viewpoint. But at seventeen, he decided, feeling very wise and mature all of a sudden, how could it be otherwise?

'No – that's true,' he said patiently. 'One day, I'll probably move to Liverpool, although that's just as dirty. But part

159

of me will always belong to Hanley, where I was born.'

But she was wrinkling her nose. 'Did you say Liverpool? Papa has been to Liverpool. He said it never stopped raining. Every day and all day!'

'Just as it does in Hanley. And not just rain. It pours — cats and dogs.'

'Cats *and* dogs?' she exclaimed, as if one animal was possible but certainly not two.

And now she was laughing and he with her. And he wondered why he had exaggerated so; because not all of Hanley was dirty, any more than the weather was always dreadful. There were days in early summer when he and Bert had walked out into the countryside, heard larks, picked bluebells, watched sheep and cattle graze. Had he been deliberately trying to discourage her? He was spared further conjecture by the sudden appearance of Selina, Mattie and an indignant William.

'Sam Bullen, indeed! That was no more Sam Bullen than I'm George Washington! Now Julia — and you, too, Ted — do you not agree that it's time we went home? That hurricane must surely have blown itself out by now.'

'Well, Ted,' Mattie whispered into his ear as they moved away, 'I hope you made the most of your opportunity.'

'D'you know,' he said, 'I think I did.'

24

There was no way that Mattie could be considered as pretty as Julia. Where Julia's face was plump and rounded, Mattie's was sharp and pointed, a shade too long in the jaw, which she had a habit of thrusting out in a most determined manner when wishing to make a point. As she was doing now.

'It's no good, Ted. You won't convince me!'

'But all men should be *born* equal,' he protested. 'What happens afterwards is another matter. Circumstances may force them into a life of abject poverty, but at least they should be born their own master. In England, no one comes into the world with shackles about their ankles.'

'Nor do they in America, now, as you know full well. All I am saying, if you would only listen and not jump to conclusions, is that it all happened too quickly. Emancipation of the slaves should have been a gradual process. As it was, the poor things had no idea what to do with the freedom they were suddenly given. They could not have been more confused when they were brought from Africa in the first place! No wonder that some of them banded together and tried to terrorise the whites.'

'Is that what happened?' Uncomfortable aware that this slip of a girl knew far more about slavery than he did, Ted rested on his oars and tried to ease his aching back.

He had returned from Forsyth Park in a state of euphoria. His realisation that he was not so much enamoured of Julia as of his mental picture of her, had been both a relief and a renewal. He had felt as an unblinkered horse must feel, suddenly exposed again to the sight of its fellow creatures:

able to let his gaze range freely, to see life with a fresh eye, almost as if for the first time.

The suggestion of a river picnic had sounded positively idyllic.

'I'll bring Patrick Eagan,' he'd said without a second thought.

So here he was, with Mattie, Selina and Selina's Henry in one rowing-boat and Patrick Eagan, William and Julia in another, heading up-river for what had once been a thriving cotton plantation before the turbulent years of the Civil War. Now, much of it had been divided up into parcels of land, Mattie explained, each planted by different families of Negroes. They paid their rent with part of their crops — which was all right as long as the crops were good.

'What delayed you?' William called as, still discussing the sharecropping system, they arrived at last at the wooden landing-stage, where the other boat must long since have tied up. He rose from the little group that sat in the shade of a tall pine above the river.

Patrick Eagan, Ted noticed with amusement, was just a fraction later in rising to his feet. He couldn't blame him; Julia looked more enchanting than ever, her bonnet removed, wisps of hair curling about her forehead. It was Patrick's jacket, Ted saw, that she sat upon.

Mattie noticed the little black faces of some piccaninnies peering out from the bushes and gestured the others to silence while she beckoned them to join the party.

They needed little persuasion. Soon, they were sitting around the picnic cloth and tucking in to the appetising contents of the basket.

'They look well enough,' Ted observed quietly to Mattie.

'Oh, yes! They're fed adequately. The negroes work hard in the fields and grow their own corn as well as cotton. Rice is cheap enough, too, and there's always fish in the river. It's the variety they lack.'

'Now what?' William enquired, as the girls began to pack away the debris. 'A game of cricket, perhaps, Ted? It's all the rage in England, I understand.'

162

Was it? A sailor had little time for cricket or, indeed, any other game. He raised his eyebrows at Patrick, who immediately shook his head; there were certain lengths, he implied, to which even a first mate should not be asked to go by his captain!

'I was wondering, sir, if I might take a stroll in the woods for a while? I have a young sister who is dedicated to the study of flowers and plants, and always demands that I bring back some specimens from the countries I visit.'

That was the first Ted had heard of a sister, let alone one with aspirations towards the science of botany, but he was happy to give his blessing to the expedition, especially when Julia rose with Patrick.

'Perhaps I could help you identify your specimens, Patrick?'

William watched them go, Patrick's hand placed solicitously under Julia's elbow. 'Holly leaves,' he called after them, 'will require little identification!'

'Don't tease so, William,' Mattie rebuked him. 'Now,' she turned to Ted, 'my knowledge of cricket is non-existent. So, instructions please, dear Ted!'

No one, he reflected afterwards, could say he didn't try. There were, he remembered, eleven players on each side. That being impossible, he divided up the piccaninnies and the adults into two groups with five on one side and six on the other. As he was deemed to know what he was doing, he was elected captain of the smaller side and William of the larger.

'All we need now,' said Ted confidently, but wishing he'd paid more attention when Bert had tried to instruct him in the game, 'are three pieces of wood – the wicket, you know – a ball and a bat.'

Three pieces of wood of roughly the same size were chosen from the pile brought to them by the children, a piece of sawn-off planking found as bat, and a sweet potato of suitable proportions dug up as ball. Then Ted, in order to demonstrate how it was done, selected himself to bat first and William, once he'd been instructed to arrange his

163

team about the clearing at strategic intervals, to bowl.

However, as the piccaninnies seemed to find Ted's voice excessively amusing and doubled up with mirth every time he opened his mouth, strategic planning was difficult to maintain; the 'field' tending to huddle together and giggle among itself. But eventually, a pattern was established.

'Play!' shouted William, getting that part right, at least, and beginning to gallop down the pitch like a demented warhorse, releasing the sweet potato at Ted's head from a distance of about ten feet.

Ted ducked; and so, fortunately, did Mattie, standing behind the wicket. The sweet potato, hotly pursued by the entire force of piccaninnies, disappeared into the woods.

'I am not,' Ted said indignantly to William, 'a military target. The object of the exercise is to allow me to hit the ball.'

'*I* thought,' said William truculently, 'that the object of the exercise was for me to *prevent* you from hitting the ball.'

'The object of this particular exercise,' Mattie intervened, 'is to enjoy ourselves! Just try it Ted's way, William. Please.'

So the next sweet potato came as a gentle lob, high in the air. Ted squared his shoulders, screwed up his eyes against the dazzle of the sun, swung back the plank and took a mighty swipe at the point where the 'ball' should have been – and fell flat on his back.

There was a moment of stunned silence before pandemonium broke out. Selina and Mattie shrieked in alarm, the piccaninnies shrieked with mirth and William gave what sounded suspiciously like an Indian war cry. Then, as Ted remained perfectly still, his eyes closed, silence fell again.

'Ted, are you all right?' He opened one eyelid a fraction. Mattie's face peered down at him, to be immediately joined by those of William, Selina and Henry, the piccaninnies forming a black fringe behind.

He groaned realistically, opened his mouth to speak but then raised a hand to beckon them closer. Mesmerised, they came. As if about to express a last, dying wish, he motioned them even closer – then suddenly shot out his hand to seize

William's ankle and pull as hard as he could.

'I think,' said William, a minute or two later, and still rubbing the back of his head, 'that cricket is a vastly overrated pastime, suitable only for mad Englishmen – certainly not for sane, sensible Americans.'

'How about some races, then?' Ted suggested, happy to abandon cricket.

'Brilliant idea!'

Even the piccaninnies understood the meaning of races, especially when they were allowed to ride piggyback on the shoulders of their elders. Fleetingly, as his own rider thumped him hard on the back, kicked him painfully in the ribs and treated his beard like a pair of reins, Ted remembered the little clerk back in the Company offices in far-off Liverpool and wished that he could be there.

After the piggybacks came wheelbarrow races, ending with a marathon struggle between William, steered by Selina, and Ted, steered by Mattie, each with a load of piccaninnies in the 'barrow'.

Soon, Julia and Patrick emerged from the trees, Patrick studiously avoiding his captain's eye and clutching a sheaf of twigs and leaves which looked suspiciously as if they had been gathered in haste from a single bush. Julia, he thought, looked like the cat who had swallowed the cream; and was anticipating several saucers more.

Then the party took to their boats once more and were pushed off by the picaninnies, who stood waving on the bank until they were out of sight.

'Enjoyed yourself, Ted?' Mattie asked as they rowed down-river.

'Very much, Mattie. It's been a memorable day.'

'Well, Mr Eagan,' Ted asked, as they were leaving the shelter of Tybee Island for the open sea, 'how do you feel about leaving Savannah?'

'Mixed feelings, Captain. I have never had a more agreeable stay in any port, and I am grateful to you for introducing me to the Templetons. But I am looking forward

165

to Christmas at home.'

'You are one of a large family, Mr Eagan? Besides your – er – botanically minded sister?'

The colour rose slightly in Patrick Eagan's cheeks. 'My sister Louise has a considerable collection of pressed flowers, sir,' he said stiffly.

'As my niece, Annie Harrington has, also,' Ted said easily, 'although, selfishly, it has never occurred to me to add to her collection. . . .'

He would have liked to pursue the conversation since he thought highly of Patrick Eagan and was interested in his background, but a sudden heavy squall and a consequent reefing of sail kept them both busy for the next hour or so, and afterwards, to have returned to the same topic might have seemed like prying.

Ted did not refer again to Savannah and the Templetons. But he noticed no sign of lovesick longing on the part of his first mate; no staring up at the night sky for longer than was needed to check their course, nor any other absent-minded behaviour.

Indeed, if anything, Patrick showed an increasing cheerfulness as they sailed steadily eastwards. A sensible, level-headed fellow, Ted decided. He would do well to follow his example.

25

But Patrick Eagan was destined not to have his Christmas at home. News of another rapid turn-around awaited them in Liverpool.

'And it's back to Savannah again, I'm afraid, sir,' said the little clerk. Since last they'd seen him, he'd acquired a pair of spectacles and now he squinted over them anxiously. 'But Captain Hancock may also be there this time, sir. In *Mohur.*'

That was good news, indeed! He'd miss a thousand Christmases, for the pleasure of seeing Joseph again.

And Patrick, too, after an initial sigh, showed no wish to remain in Liverpool for the festive season, then seek another ship. Neither did Samuel Pollock, his bo'sun, nor Matts Santander, his carpenter. Ted was pleased. When responsible seamen elected to stay with him, he could feel reasonably sure he ran a happy ship.

There was just time to make a lightning trip to Hanley, to Ma and Thirza to deliver the presents he'd brought from Savannah. Joseph and Anna now lived in Liverpool; comfortably ensconced in the suburb of Fairfield between two other master mariners, so that wives could keep each other company when husbands were at sea. It was an arrangement which Ted thoroughly approved of, since not only could Anna now indulge her new-found passion for gardening, but Bert and Gilly had started their own boarding-school for waifs and strays in a big old house not far from the Hancocks, so that his visits to both establishments could now be combined. He had yet to meet Caroline, the new

167

addition to the Brown family, but Hanley, on this occasion, must be his first priority. There, he was astonished to discover that his nephew, James, had signed up with a Russian line as an ordinary seaman, and was now on the high seas – much to Thirza's distress.

'I'll keep an eye open for him,' Ted promised. 'If I can possibly get him on the *Lizzie Fennell* later in the year, I will.'

'Oh, Ted, thank you! That's a great weight off my mind.'

The short break was soon over, but it had been good to see them all again. Especially Ma, now showing her years but still as valiant as ever.

Together, he and Patrick watched *Mohur* come slowly down the Tybee river, noticing that her topsails, as they caught the breeze, were torn and tattered.

'She's had a rough passage,' said Ted. 'Even so,' he added, 'she's a lovely sight!'

'That, she is,' Patrick agreed.

Again, Ted felt the now familiar conflict within himself: sail or steam? Beauty or the Beast? Often, tossing like a cork in mid-ocean, at the mercy of a howling gale, or lying becalmed in the doldrums, the sight of a steamship, black smoke belching from her funnels but still maintaining course, had filled him with envy. But today, with the sun shining down from a mild blue sky and sparkling on the gentle ripples of *Mohur*'s wake, he was lost in admiration. In the very nature of things, the days of the sailing-vessel must be numbered, and yet. . . .

' "A thing of beauty",' Patrick Eagan suddenly quoted at his side and then, catching his superior's astonished eye, blushed furiously but still finished ' ". . . is a joy for ever". I'm very fond of poetry,' he added, almost defiantly.

'I, too,' said Ted, thinking that no matter how well you thought you knew a man, he could always surprise you. 'But beauty lies also "in the eye of the beholder",' he contributed.

The *Mohur* came sufficiently close for them to recognise Joseph on the poop, so, discreet waves were exchanged, and Ted was suddenly reminded of expeditions to the railway line at Etruria when he had waved, rather more exuberantly, from his vantage point on Joseph's broad shoulders. He'd like to see Joseph take his weight now!

And then, continuing to gaze at his brother across the diminishing stretch of water, he noticed with a sudden sense of alarm that amounted almost to panic, that those same shoulders were now, very slightly, stooped.

How old was Joseph? Nearing fifty, if he was a day. But good, he would have thought, for many years to come. And yet, for someone as conscientious as Joseph, who would never stay snugly in his quarters, whatever the weather, seafaring could be a demanding life. Especially in sailing-ships.

They watched *Mohur* warp in and drop anchor about fifty yards up-river from the *Lizzie Fennell*, and then went about their own duties. Joseph would have plenty to attend to for the next few hours, particularly with that canvas.

'It's no good, lass,' said Joseph, 'I just don't understand why you want to leave all this,' he gestured widely to include the entire Gothic façade of the Cathedral of St John the Baptist, in front of which he, Mattie and Ted were standing. 'It's as good as Lichfield, any day.'

The three of them were on a tour of the Savannah churches – principally for Joseph's benefit – and had already visited Christ Church, the Episcopal church where John Wesley had once been rector. Here, Joseph himself, resplendent in frock-coat and tall stove-pipe hat, had delivered a short lecture on the foundation of Sunday school classes by the famous Methodist preacher; a lecture listened to with considerable interest, not only by Mattie but by several passing residents of the town.

'Now, tell me again, my dear, why you wish to leave this beautiful city for the slums and tenements of New York?'

'I'll answer that question with another,' said Mattie, taking Joseph's arm. 'Why did you want to leave Hanley, which, I understand from Ted,' she glanced up at him,

169

walking somewhat disconsolately on her other side, 'is some distance inland from the sea?'

'Two reasons,' said Joseph. 'The first that I was taken to Liverpool by my father at a tender age and shown this wonderful white bird sailing before the wind – and I never forgot it. And the second, that I had no intention of spending my life in the grimy smoke-infested air of the Potteries.'

'There you are, then,' said Mattie. 'That proves it! All young people have this urge to leave the place where they were born and brought up.'

Joseph considered. 'But that wasn't the reason in my case. If Hanley had been clean and beautiful, like Savannah, then I might have stayed there.'

'Anyway,' Ted murmured, 'you were born in Penkhull.' He knew the remark made not the slightest difference to Joseph's argument but he was feeling more than a little neglected. Naturally, he'd wanted them to get on, but not to the exclusion of himself. However, the interruption went unnoticed. Mattie's eyes were flashing.

'But *if*,' she persisted, '*if* you had been born into a more affluent world. *If.* . . .'

Joseph stopped abruptly, bringing Mattie, also, to a halt. ' "If ifs and ands were pots and pans, there'd be no work for tinkers"! That's what my Ma used to say – remember, Ted? – and never spoke a truer word. Don't try to alter the world too much, lass.'

'Oh, so you and Ted are just going to sail bigger and bigger ships across the Atlantic, no doubt full of wealthy people who don't know what else to do with their money.' There was more than a touch of scorn in her voice and Ted felt himself bridle.

'Thats where you *are* wrong,' said Joseph decisively. 'Most westward-bound passengers, these days, come steerage ready to put up with all manner of hardships for the privilege of entering this brave new world of yours. And who do you suppose,' he was warming to his theme, 'is responsible for bringing in that China tea you all love to drink?'

'Not to mention the delicate china you sip it from!' Ted

170

pointed out, beginning to enjoy himself.

'Fashioned no doubt, in the Pottery towns you were telling me of,' Mattie retorted swiftly, 'where all is dirt and smoke. And those who make it toil in terrible conditions, no doubt, with little pay and victimised by owners who —'

'Now, just a minute!' Joseph interrupted her. 'Have you never heard of those great philanthropists, the Wedgwoods? Why, Ted wouldn't be here today if it wasn't for their influence on education, alone.'

Still wrangling happily, they went back to the wooden house, to drink their China tea from porcelain cups which — to Miss Eliza's astonishment — they all insisted upon turning over, once the tea was drunk, to examine the base.

'Look, Mama!' said Mattie. 'Made in Hanley, Staffordshire!'

'Well, isn't that something!' said her mother, as if Ted and Joseph were personally responsible.

During the next few days, Joseph gave Ted little cause for worry over his health. Indeed, it was he who suggested they climb aboard a paddle-boat and chug up river to Tybee Island. 'I've seen it so often from on board ship, I've often wondered what lay behind the dunes.'

'But, Joseph, you do realise that a paddle-boat is powered by *steam*?'

'And there was I, thinking it propelled by elastic fibres!' said Joseph dryly. 'On the same principle as the catapult I took away from you when you were six!'

Mattie came with them to Tybee. Selina and Julia had been invited but had declined; Selina because she was shopping for her trousseau and Julia because she wasn't 'walking over all that sand, even for the pleasure of *your* company, sir!' And batted her eyelashes at Joseph as she did to all men, no matter what their age.

'Flighty little miss, that one,' Joseph had commented to Ted when he'd first met her, and from then on paid her only the minimum attention that courtesy demanded. Ted had breathed a secret sigh of relief that he was safely over

171

his infatuation; for Joseph's criticism would surely have dented it severely.

He wasn't sorry, for another reason, that the Tybee party was a small one; the picnic hamper, on this occasion, could be carried conveniently on his shoulder.

They inspected the remains of the Fort from whose walls the Yankees had successfully bombarded those of Fort Pulaski during the Civil War.

'But it took some doing!' said Mattie stoutly. 'We held out for several days.'

'You're still a little Southerner at heart,' Joseph teased her.

'And I suspect always will be in spite of my determination to go to the North. However, William insists it's only a matter of time before we feel and act like true united Americans. And he should know. He and Selina remember the war quite clearly. It's just a blur to me, I'm afraid, and Julia can't remember it at all.'

'Thank God,' said Joseph devoutly, 'that Savannah was spared the worst of it.'

Mattie nodded. 'Amen to that! I'll say that much for General Sherman: he knew when to stop. Just think,' she continued, grinning hugely at Ted and Joseph 'a hundred years ago and we wouldn't have been talking together like this. *We* would have been at war. A war, may I remind you, that you lost!'

'More a tactical withdrawal, I should say,' Joseph said glibly. 'Anyway, we were the pioneers. We turned the first sods for you.'

'The Indians were here before you came,' Mattie reminded him tartly, 'You know, I suppose, that Tybee is the Indian word for "salt"?'

''No, I didn't know,' Joseph admitted.

'And I'll tell you something else you may not have known. John Wesley knelt here, on Tybee, and declared his faith, not only in God but in the country of America.'

Whether Joseph had known but was tactfully keeping quiet about it, Ted couldn't decide, but he certainly allowed

172

himself to be led to the open ground where Mattie claimed that Wesley had first stood on American soil. And insisted that they stand for a moment in reverent silence.

Soon, for a brisk breeze had begun to blow in from the sea, they gave the recently completed Fort Screven a cursory inspection, then found a sheltered spot among the dunes to eat their lunch. And then it was back to Savannah, sitting in the lee of the funnel until Ted was drawn to the side to stare down at the churning water. When he came back, he had a thoughtful expression on his face.

'Now, he's going to extol the virtues of steam power,' Joseph told Mattie. 'You see if he don't!' But he was wrong.

'Joseph,' Ted resumed his seat between his brother and Mattie. 'You remember the wreck of the *Birkenhead*?'

'Of course! Another paddle-steamer but rather larger than this. Nearly two thousand tons, if I remember correctly. Why do you ask?'

'Smithy gave us a lecture on it when I was at the British. And I've never fogotten it.'

'Nor should you! One of the finest examples of courage the world has ever seen.'

There came a pause while Mattie looked interested, Ted furrowed his brow and Joseph waited patiently. In his own good time, Ted would say what was on his mind. But Mattie was not so patient.

'What was so special about this *Birkenhead*?'

Briefly, Joseph explained how the troopship had struck a rock off the coast of South Africa and sunk with the loss of over four hundred men, but the saving of every woman and child on board. 'They stood on deck, firm as the rock of Gibraltar while the ship went down. No panic, no mad rush for the boats that could have endangered the lives of the women and children. And to make it worse, they knew that there were man-eating sharks circling the ship.'

Mattie shuddered, was silent for a moment and then said quietly. 'Thank you, Joseph.'

'It was Captain Salmond I was thinking of,' Ted said. 'And the criticism directed at him for his conduct in steering too

173

close to the shore. And of not being on the bridge at the time of the impact. Valid comments, and yet he was deemed to be a man of the highest integrity and of wide experience, who acted with great courage once the ship had struck.'

'And why are you concerned now, particularly?' Joseph enquired.

'It was watching the paddle at work. But I've never forgotten Smithy's lecture. At ten years old, I was particularly impressionable, I suppose. But as I've grown older, I've sometimes wondered how I would have acted had I been in a similar situation.'

'I, too,' said Joseph thoughtfully, 'have wondered. I was only twenty when the disaster occurred, with no qualifications, but I already knew enough of a seaman's life to realise that we take risks every moment we are at sea – but without always thinking about them. We grow accustomed to not knowing what is ahead, what trick the elements may suddenly play upon us. True, we take what precautions we can, but are never sure that they will be enough. And we grow used to this state of affairs, so that our senses are perhaps dulled a little. We are the victims of our own knowledge and experience and of those who have gone before us. We think we know all there is to know about a certain situation.'

Mattie shivered suddenly. 'You're cold,' said Ted. 'Let's go below. We old salts become so hardened, we forget that others may not be so tough.'

Even so, he, himself, had to repress a shiver as they descended the companion-way; as though – how did Ma describe it? – a goose had walked over his grave.

'Landlubbers,' said Joseph scornfully, once they were comfortably seated in the saloon, and quite forgetting that Mattie belonged in that category, 'should keep their mouths shut about matters of which they know nothing. But it's always the same. Hindsight is such an easy thing to have, especially by those who were not present at the actual event. *The Times*, I seem to remember, had a field day. But it's a grave fault of human nature, that a whipping-boy must always be found when disaster strikes and in this case, it was Captain Salmond, who, sadly, was no longer there to defend himself. But no master mariner came forward to maintain that he would have acted differently, if he'd been in Captain Salmond's shoes.'

'At least,' Ted reflected, 'some good came of it. Lifeboats are now inspected regularly.'

'And were they not before?' Mattie asked in some surprise.

'Alas, no! Davits were rusted on the *Birkenhead*, tackle rotten; one boat crashed into the sea quite empty.'

'But there's still not enough of them,' Joseph pointed out sadly. 'Certainly not for the ships you hope to serve on, Ted. There'll have to be another disaster, I fear, before the powers-that-be decide to do something about *that*.'

'Heaven forbid!' said Ted and wondered, for a moment, if it was his fate to be buried in the middle of a farmyard, for yet another goose appeared to have sauntered across his grave. Suddenly needing to be cheered, he turned towards Mattie.

'At least, the *Birkenhead* established the principle of women and children first!' he said brightly.

But Mattie seemed singularly unimpressed. 'Why should women always be treated as fragile little flowers, incapable of helping themselves? If I had been there, I would have insisted upon taking up the oars in one of the boats.'

'I believe you would, too,' said Ted admiringly. She was a plucky little creature, was Mattie, and no mistake!

Not until the middle of March, did the *Lizzie Fennell* leave Savannah; the *Mohur* and Joseph long gone. By then, there was hardly a man on board who had not formed some sort of liaison with a Savannahian resident.

Mattie had been Ted's constant companion, strolling with him in Forsyth Park, sitting with him by the river, taking him on tours of the city so that soon he knew it almost as well as she did herself; including the plans for the new sewers!

But now, his goodbyes said, he had other things on his

mind; like the safe crossing of the Atlantic with his cargo of raw cotton, bound not for Liverpool but for Tallinn, capital of Estonia. The white cliffs of Dover, as they beat up the Channel, would be the nearest to home he would manage. A pity in more ways than one; not only would he not see family and friends but his promise to take his nephew James would remain unfulfilled. Also, he had hoped to call in at the White Star offices, have a word with the marine superintendent there and discover what his chances might be. Still, he could hardly expect the Andrew Gibson Line to make it too easy for him.

26

He needn't have worried. 'James Harrington, Ordinary Seaman, earning £1 15s per month', was on his crew list when he left Gravesend in the middle of August, along with several of his Finnish mates, all off the same Russian ship.

'I told them you were a good bet as a skipper, Uncle Ted,' James said jubilantly when Ted, as soon as he could make an excuse for doing so called him to his cabin. 'And when I knew you were bound for Savannah, that clinched it. You and Uncle Joseph have gone on about it for so long, I knew I had to see it for myself.'

'But we'll only be there for a few days,' Ted cautioned. 'Then we're off to Virginia.'

'That suits me fine,' said his nephew. 'Just as long as it's not to Ruskyland. I've had enough snow to last me a lifetime!'

Ted considered him carefully. You could never tell with James. A cheerful exterior could sometimes hide all manner of fears and uncertainties.

'Are you enjoying life at sea, James? Is it all you thought it would be?'

'Well, it is – and it isn't,' said James. 'I knew it would be hard. You and Uncle Josh had never made any bones about that. But I didn't expect it to be quite as hard as it is. If I'd been on a British ship in the first place, it might have been better. At least I would have known what they were shouting at me!'

'Well, you'll still get shouted at on the *Lizzie Fennell*,' his uncle promised, with a grin'Mr Eagan has quite a way with words. But, if he knew you were my nephew, he'd no doubt shout even louder! So, we'll keep that little secret to ourselves, for the time being.'

It was early October when they dropped anchor off Tybee, to await their tug.

'Good to be back, sir?' suggested Patrick Eagan.

'*Very* good! A pity it's only a few days.' But even a few days should be enough for what he had in mind.

During the last month, he'd thought a great deal about Mattie. Not in the besotted, almost feverish manner in which Julia had been perpetually on his mind, but steadily and contentedly, as he often thought about his family and friends.

There would be problems, of course, if they were to marry, and there could be oposition from her parents; but nothing, he felt confident, that they could not overcome – if they set their minds to it. And there, of course, was the rub. *Would* Mattie set her mind to it? Or was she already too dedicated to an independent life to be diverted on to another tack?

This, he had decided, on what was possibly his last visit to Savannah for some while, was the time to find out. If he were fortunate enough to be accepted by White Star and if Mattie still wanted to live in New York, surely a compromise could be reached. In fact, the more he thought about it, the more delightful the prospect became. A wife in New York and Joseph and Anna in Liverpool – the best of both worlds! He could hardly wait to put it to her.

'James, do hurry up!' He was reminded of the expeditions he'd taken his nephew on as a child; always, he'd lagged behind, studying with great intensity whatever appealed to his infant gaze. Now, it was the squares and thoroughfares of Savannah.

At long last, he led him into the familiar square, almost dragged him across it to the wooden house in the far corner and propelled him up the steps. As he lifted the knocker, he had a sudden, heart-stopping fear that the family might be away. Anything, he thought, panic-stricken, could have happened since he'd been here last.

But the panic only lasted a moment before he heard the familiar shuffle of Maria's footsteps down the hallway.

'Praise the Lord, if it ain't Cap'n Ted!'

'Dear Maria!' He shook her exuberantly by the hand. 'This is my nephew, James.' He paused only briefly to allow them to greet each other, then swept on. 'Miss Eliza? The girls?'

But there was no need for Maria to answer. Miss Eliza came gliding out of the living-room, Julia came scampering down the stairs and Selina bustled out from the kitchen quarters.

After James had been embraced almost as rapturously as himself, they were led into the living-room.

'Mattie?' he enquired as soon as he could get a word in edgeways.

Miss Eliza's face fell. 'You haven't heard?'

Once again, fear gripped him, but this time its fingers were like a vice. Surely, Mattie hadn't. . . ?

'She wrote to you, Ted. That was the last thing she did before she left.'

'Left?' he echoed stupidly.

'For New York. You know Mattie! Once she was twenty-one, she was off.'

'And you – you allowed it?'

'There was little we could do to stop it. There was a legacy – her great-aunt Mathilda, after whom she was named – not a great deal, but sufficient. At least we were able to arrange for her to stay with an old friend of mine who lives up there. And, of course, William is not too far away at West Point.'

He was so flabbergasted, he found he was sitting down without having been invited to do so. Dimly, he was aware that Julia, at the far end of the room, was engaging James in animated conversation – really, he should have warned the lad! – and that Selina had disappeared, presumably to the kitchen to arrange refreshment.

'I'm so sorry, Ted. But I know she hopes to see you again.'

'And I her,' he said automatically as he fought a terrible

179

wave of depression.

It was, he felt, a good omen. As they came into Liverpool they saw the *Britannic*, westward bound for New York. Like the *Lizzie Fennell*, she was square-rigged, but there the similarity ended. Not a shred of canvas fluttered from her four tall masts and from her two cream-painted, jet-rimmed funnels, smoke belched as black as . . .

'. . . the ace of spades,' said the pilot, beside him on the poop, disapprovingly. 'I'm a sailing-ship man, myself.'

'I know,' said Ted. 'I know. But think of it, man! Over five thousand tons and she'll be docking in New York in just a week.'

'Who wants to be docking in New York in a year, let alone a week?' asked the pilot sourly.

'Oh, *I* would,' said Ted devoutly. '*I* would!'

27

Ted had always known that Joseph would want to see him board the *Celtic*, his ferocious scorn of steam power tempered by a mariner's natural curiosity about any seagoing vessel. And young Frank – well, wild horses wouldn't have kept *him* away. Only the urgent pleas of his mother were preventing him from emigrating to the United States of America at this very moment.

But Anna! Now that, he hadn't expected. And much as he loved her, Ted could have done without his sister-in-law's company on this bleak March morning in 1880 with a chill breeze blowing straight off the Mersey. Even though they were standing in as unobtrusive a spot as he had been able to steer them, in the lee of a wooden shed on the wharfside, it was still uncomfortably cold. Ostentatiously, he turned up the collar of his new jacket with the White Star insignia on its shining brass buttons and stamped his feet as if delaying the onset of frostbite only by seconds. Any moment now, Joseph would cease his careful inspection of the great ship anchored there in front of them, and pass scornful judgement. But when it came, Ted was surprised by its mildness.

'You could do worse, E.J.!'

And that, from Joseph, a dyed-in-the-wool champion of sail, was almost tantamount to approval. Ted allowed his own gaze to wander fondly over the sleek lines of the black, yellow-banded hull. From it, rose four graceful masts, their slender height easily dwarfing the single funnel. Although her sails were still neatly stowed in their white canvas covers, her yards proclaimed her to be square-rigged on her fore and mainsails and fore-and-aft on her mizzen and jigger. Had Ted not known of the power of her engine and the existence of the twelve boilers and twenty-four furnaces deep within her bowels, he might have thought sail to be her principal method of propulsion.

'I'm glad to see they haven't lost *all* sense,' Joseph observed.

'Sail can still be extremely useful as an auxiliary means of power,' Ted admitted, a shade stiffly.

'The *only* method, if that single screw should fail!' said Joseph, and grinned broadly when he saw Ted's obvious surprise at the technicality of his remark. 'Didn't know I was so knowledgeable, did you, young Ted?'

'It was I who explained it all to him, Uncle Ted,' said Frank, but was promptly shushed by his mother.

'And I well remember,' Joseph pursued, 'back in '74, how this very same ship had to be towed into Queenstown by the *Garlic* because her propeller had snapped.'

'*Gaelic*, if you please!' Ted said tersely and then, catching the twinkle in his half-brother's eye, grinned wryly. Trust Joseph to pull his leg, and trust *him* to swallow the bait! But it was time to stop mixing his metaphors and get aboard.

Anna thought so, too. 'Now, you two, stop arguing and let's see Ted safely settled.'

This was the moment he had dreaded. First impressions, he knew were important and he wasn't likely to make a good one with a sister-in-law clucking at his elbow, no doubt demanding to see his quarters so that she could personally test the softness of his mattress!

Fortunately, Joseph shared his misgivings. 'Ted's only a fourth mate on the *Celtic*, my love. Not master, as he was of the *Lizzie Fennell*.'

'D'you think I don't know that?' asked his exasperated spouse. And she pulled her shawl more closely about her shoulders in a most determined fashion.

However, Joseph firmly, albeit tactfully, proposed that he go aboard with Ted to give him a hand with his chest. Then he would have a word with the captain, whom he'd met a couple of times, and say that, if convenient, he'd like to show his wife and son around.

The suggestion found favour with everyone, and they said their farewells briefly and without undue emotion upon the quayside.

But as he took one handle of his sea-chest and Joseph the other, Anna had the last word. 'We'll come to see you off, Ted!'

Well, he thought philosophically, that needn't worry him unduly. There'd be enough people on the quayside, waving and shouting; three more wouldn't make that much difference. As long as they didn't expect him to wave back!

'I didn't know you'd met Captain Gleadell,' he said to Joseph as they mounted the gangway.

'Made it my business to,' said Joseph briefly, 'once I knew you were on *Celtic*.'

Dear Joseph! Even though Ted was now thirty years old, he would never be anything but his baby brother.

Some of the differences, he had expected; his cabin, for instance, was tiny compared with that on the *Lizzie Fennell*, but neat and clean and perfectly adequate for his needs.

And the change in 'cargo'. But no doubt he'd soon grow accustomed to the passengers, who would be coming aboard tomorrow; around fifty first-class, he'd heard, and well over seven hundred steerage.

Of the rest, it was all so different, he might as well put the *Lizzie Fennell* out of his mind completely and start afresh.

'Acclimatise yourself for an hour or two, Mr Smith,' Captain Gleadell had suggested courteously when he'd come aboard with Joseph. 'My other officers are about their business — we sail tomorrow, as you know — but they are expecting you and will do all they can to help.'

So he'd made the most of the little time at his disposal before being given his own duties. The feeling of space was perhaps his major discovery; at least in the passenger area, where deck housing had been joined up to create covered, and consequently sheltered, promenade decks. The exposed poop-deck was something he could forget about now, for when he was on duty in the wheelhouse, he would be protected from the elements and able to focus on compass and helm without fear of sea and rainwater blinding his vision.

He noted the watertight bulkheads and the number of lifeboats; well above legal requirements but still – and here he spared a thought for Joseph's strongly expressed views upon the matter – based upon the ship's tonnage rather than the number of souls on board. As if it were for the ship's safety that they were slung from their davits and not for human beings at all!

He saw, and thoroughly approved of, the open railings that replaced the solidity of bulwarks. No doubt, in high seas the *Celtic* would ship water like any other vessel, but at least it would go as quickly as it came.

For several minutes, he stared, suitably impressed, at the luxury of the first-class accommodation amidships; the velvet upholstery, the fresh running water in the cabins, the enormous portholes. Steerage accommodation, of course, was less palatial but still spacious and – at around £6 for the single crossing – very good value, he considered.

He was as proud as a peacock to be an officer, albeit a very junior one, with the prestigious White Star Line. If young Bruce Ismay, soon to be brought into the Company by his father, Thomas, a major share-holder, was feeling half as contented with his lot, then he had nothing to complain of either. 'You'll be new boys together,' Joseph had remarked when they'd heard rumours of his appointment.

'Now won't that be nice!' Ma had observed cosily, as if they'd be sharing their lunch-boxes and tripping over each other's bootlaces in the rush and tumble of the playground.

'I don't suppose,' Ted had observed, 'that I shall ever clap eyes on him, except from afar.'

'You never know!' Ma was the eternal optimist.

It was Ted who was entrusted with the operation of the engine-room telegraph on the auspicious day when he 'sailed' out of Liverpool under the red and white burgee of the White Star Line for the first time. The moorings had been cast off and the tugs attached. 'Slow ahead!' ordered the pilot. Carefully, Ted moved the handle to the correct point on the dial, a bell clanged and was answered somewhere deep within the ship, and then he felt the vibration under his feet as the screw began to turn. Simultaneously came a quick warning blast on the whistle and a mighty cheer from the people crowding the wharf. Among them would be Anna and Joseph and Frank, Anna and Frank no doubt waving their handkerchiefs like mad but Joseph, arms folded, giving only his usual quiet smile. It was more than Ted's life was worth to turn his head by a fraction, but he hoped they were standing far back enough to see him. Unexpectedly, a lump came into his throat. In spite of all his protestations to the contrary, he was glad that they were there.

The tugs towed them to midstream and were then cast off. But it was still slow ahead, with the engine doing little more than grumble to itself. But then they were over the bar, and the pilot, mission accomplished, was climbing down the ladder.

Then, suddenly, without thinking, he caught himself glancing aloft, for a moment expecting to see a mighty billow of canvas cracking out above his head. But there was nothing except one solitary plume of oily smoke streaming from the black-topped funnel. And, for the first time, he knew exactly how Joseph felt.

He surprised himself at the speed with which he adapted to the new routine. There were some hiccoughs, of course, and the first officer, to whom he was immediately responsible, seemed to believe in allowing him to commit errors then correcting them. Why, for instance, wasn't he told that all orders must be relayed to the bo'sun through the quartermaster? However, both men had been discretion itself in their tactful handling of the situation.

Oddly, the biggest difficulty he had, was in adjusting to

having so little to do. Once the course was set, the compass needed only an occasional check; the steering was always in capable hands and the wind could change direction a thousand times without his caring a toss. Most of his watch was spent in staring knowledgeably at the horizon; unless, of course, there were other craft to gaze at. And if these happened to be under sail, then the tongue of the first officer, who had also served before the mast, would be miraculously loosened and they would reminisce like any pair of old salts puffing at pipes on a tavern settle.

Once they were in the open sea, the engine telegraph stood always at full ahead, for speed on an Atlantic mailboat, Ted soon discovered, was of the greatest importance. Three years ago, White Star had shared the mail contract with the Cunard Line, and since then, competition between the two companies had been intense. Besides, many transatlantic passengers were businessmen who wanted a fast crossing.

'Don't we ever decrease speed?' he once dared to ask the first officer during a particularly ferocious storm. 'Not,' he added hastily, in case it might be thought he was concerned for his own safety, 'that I'm suggesting that we should.'

'Just as well, Mr Smith,' said the first officer dryly, 'because I doubt if the captain would listen.' And then, presumably taking pity on Ted's inexperience, added, 'Maybe if you or I were at death's door, he might. But certainly not if he were himself. Even at heaven's gate, his first words would be, "Full speed ahead, St Peter, if you please"!'

'Fog?' Ted queried. He knew that could be a hazard off the coast of Newfoundland.

'Per*haps*.' But the stress on the second syllable made it sound extremely unlikely.

'Ice?' Because that, too, could be a problem off the Grand Banks, particularly at that time of year, when the ice-fields would be breaking up.

'Well, now,' conceded the first officer, 'that *might* make a difference. But only if visibility was poor. Usually, it's enough to take a more southerly course and crack on, regardless. And then, we'd probably fire up another boiler to make up the time we'd lost.'

There was one particular aspect of his duties which surprised Ted greatly. Mattie – awaiting him, even now, in New York, he hoped – had once remarked that he was 'good with all manner of people.' And now Captain Gleadell seemed to hold a similar view.

'Mr Smith, kindly use your inimitable charm to persuade those passengers foolhardy enough still to be on deck that they'd be far better off below,' he said one day, when a storm was threatening.

'*Me*, sir?'

Captain Gleadell grinned. 'Yes, you, Mr Smith! You seem to have the happy knack of making a hurricane sound like a Sunday school outing.'

So off he went, not at all sure he liked to be known for his diplomacy, rather than his seamanship, but aware that passenger safety was of paramount importance, particularly if the old man was going to crack on at his usual pace.

It was surprisingly easy. 'Just a squall, ma'am! But that charming hat won't be improved by a splash of sea water.'

Or, 'Best take your wife and child below, sir. Nothing to worry about, you understand, but it may get a little damp up here.'

'A smile,' Ma always said, 'will get you further than a scowl, any day.' And he was certainly proving her right now.

There came the day, well before they reached the busy waters near the American coast, that he stood his first watch alone. Two hours being considered long enough to maintain concentration at the helm, the quartermasters changed watch halfway through his own. So, after exchanging a few pleasantries with the new arrival, checking unobtrusively that the correct course was still being maintained, glancing briefly up into the cloudless sky, he continued his measured pacing, wondering when it would be seemly to check yet again on the course. Surreptitiously, he checked his watch. He'd give himself five more minutes before strolling back to the binnacle, meanwhile he would continue to gaze about him and allow his mind the freedom to wander. It was a fair-weather trick Joseph had taught him.

'Keep your weather eye open, Ted, but let your brain idle. It is a great source of mental refreshment.'

So he allowed his thoughts to dwell upon Mattie, to whom it was his firm intention to propose marriage at the earliest opportunity. But how would she take it?

Not for the first time, he wondered if she would even consider for a moment exchanging her present free and independent life for that of a sailor's wife. True, their friendship had grown swiftly and surely during the days he had spent in Savannah awaiting his orders, but it had been based not so much upon shared interests – for *he* would have been no good at caring for snotty-nosed youngsters nor ladling out nourishment in a soup kitchen – but upon a shared sense of humour, a mutual delight in the absurdities of human nature and the ability to discuss and argue and still remain friends.

But was his the sort of life to ask a woman to share? Hers would be the passive, waiting role, for there'd be no going with him as Anna had with Joseph – and if there was one thing he was sure of about Mattie it was her lack of passivity. He remembered the piquant, eager little face, the dark eyes flashing approval or disapproval as the spirit moved her, and smiled ruefully. Perhaps he was hoping for the impossible. Perhaps his quest for a perfect love must still remain unsatisfied.

This time, his station was at the bows, his reponsibility – along with the third officer – to see to the anchor and the ropes, whether thrown aboard from tugs or tenders or cast from their own decks as they moored. It was an ideal position for someone approaching New York harbour for the first time.

They were still some miles off shore when the third officer had pointed out the steep bluff rising from the flat stretches of the New Jersey coastline. 'There's the old *Neversink*!'

Ted had grinned politely, knowing full well from studying the charts that its correct title was the *Highlands of Navesink*. Now, as they neared the bluff, he could make out the fish-hook shape of Sandy Hook, which meant that they were about seventeen miles from the tip of Manhattan Island. Soon a pilot would be taken aboard, for beneath the waters of the Lower Bay was a broad sand bar, dangerously near the surface at several points.

'South-West Spit, Flynn's Knoll, Dry Romer,' the third officer ticked off the hazards as they left them safely to starboard. And now, it was slow ahead as Coney Island fell astern and they steamed in to the narrows between Staten Island and Brooklyn. But then, like a cork popping from the neck of a bottle, they were out into the Upper Bay and he was gazing for the first time across the expanse of grey water to Manhattan.

It was like no other port he'd visited; a huge spur running out into the water, fringed, as far as the eye could see, with piers and jetties where the funnels of steamships seemed far outnumbered by the masts and rigging of sailing-ships. Behind, the tall buildings he could see must be the warehouses and chandlers', the machine shops and stores that he would have expected at any great port, but soaring up amongst them were several even taller structures.

'The sky's the limit,' said the third officer. 'They have to build high because there's no room to go sideways – a silly place, in a way, to build a city. That's the Western Union Telegraph Office on Broadway.' He pointed out the tallest and largest building. 'And there's the new Post Office on Park Row and the Tribune building with its spire – more like a church than a newspaper office.'

'They're certainly using every available inch of space,' said Ted admiringly. 'And all built upon solid rock, I understand.'

Now, he transferred his gaze back to the Bay itself, where craft of all shapes and sizes, under sail and steam, were moving at various speeds and angles from one shore to the other, or straight ahead to Manhattan. Many of them, he noticed, were 'side-wheelers' as the Americans called the paddle-steamers, and he thought briefly of the last journey he'd made on one, up the Savannah river to Tybee Island with Joseph and Mattie. Very soon, now, he'd be seeing her again.

They dropped anchor off Quarantine Point and the health officers came aboard to check their bill of health. No cases of yellow fever, cholera, typhus or smallpox were allowed to enter this new, virgin territory.

'Actually,' said the third officer darkly, 'they have quite enough disease of their own, without our adding to it.'

But the *Celtic* was cleared without incident and they steamed slowly, majestically – a mammoth among midgets – across the Bay towards Battery Point and Castle Gardens. Here were the long sheds where the passengers would disembark to be scrutinised by the immigration officers, and those staying in New York and seeking employment might, if they were lucky, find jobs immediately at the Labour Exchange.

'One hundred and eighty thousand immigrants there were, last year,' said the third officer soberly, as they watched the long line snaking its way into the sheds, anxiety writ large upon many of the pale faces.

'Where will they all go?' Ted wondered.

'West to Minnesota, maybe, or Wisconsin or Missouri. And most will have a hard time of it, but some will soon be sending for their families. It's the land of opportunity, all right, whether you be farmer, butcher, baker or plain labourer. Especially labourer, when you think of the roads to be made and the trees to be felled.'

Then the tugs were easing the *Celtic* away from Battery Point and up-river, to be nudged into her berth at the end of West Tenth Street.

'Well, that's your first Atlantic crossing safely over, Mr Smith,' said the third officer, extending his hand. 'May the others be just as safe and trouble-free.'

'Amen to that!' said Ted devoutly.

28

It was typical of Mattie to suggest a meeting on the Lower East Side. The secluded ways of Central Park or even the Battery, where he could have discoursed knowledgeably about the craft on the Hudson, would have been much more to his taste.

But no, it had to be the city's slums, where stinking alleyways led into courts of decaying tenements and pathetic rags hung limply from a maze of washing-lines. It was something, Ted supposed, that their owners tried to maintain at least some degree of cleanliness.

Reconnoitring early in the day, he'd lingered in the area only long enough to locate the cheap eating-house where Mattie, in the message she'd sent to the ship, had suggested they meet. Not only the smell – a sickening stench of unwashed bodies, human excreta and rotting vegetables – had persuaded him to move on. Although he was big and brawny enough to take on any one, or even two, of the ill-nourished specimens of manhood idling on sidewalk or stoop, they had a tendency, he noticed, to congregate in ethnic groups: Chinese, Italians, Jews, Negroes and whites, many of the last speaking with the unmistakable brogue of Ireland.

How a slip of a girl like Mattie managed to survive in such surroundings, he couldn't imagine. At least the eating-house she'd suggested was on the fringe of the area, nearer to Broadway than the notorious Mulberry Street, and not that distant from City Hall Park. With luck he'd persuade her into that rather more salubrious district after they'd eaten their evening meal.

'Now look after yourself, Ted,' the third officer had cautioned as he went ashore that morning. 'And keep to the West Side. Take your young lady shopping at Macy's, I should.'

Impossible to explain that if Mattie was anything like the girl he'd last seen in Savannah, the only satisfaction she'd derive from visiting a big store would be to hurl a brick through its windows in protest at the opulence of its customers.

He gazed, greatly impressed in spite of his determination not to be, at the height of the Brooklyn Tower, with the bridge beyond still under construction. Now he was on familiar ground, for sailing-ships crammed the wharfs of the East River, their battered figureheads gazing blankly over the confusion of barrels and boxes, shouting men and patient horses at the façades of warehouses, sail-makers', chandlers' and stores.

Then he boarded a streetcar for a cursory inspection of Fifth Avenue opulence and the new St Patrick's Cathedral, with its spires still to be added.

After such a surfeit of architecture, it was a relief to plunge into the depths of Central Park, with its leafy, winding pathways. But he still found a moment for the Oyster Market, floating off West Tenth. One day, he'd visit Long Island where the oysters came from — perhaps, he and Mattie could take a picnic there, like the ones they'd had in those carefree Savannah days? — but meanwhile he watched for a while as the oysters were shucked; some, no doubt, destined for the expensive restaurants he'd seen 'downtown', but many for the oyster bars scattered along the quaysides, cheek by jowl with the coffee booths. Provided he had a cent or two, there seemed no reason for a New Yorker to starve.

She hadn't changed! That was his first thought as Mattie came swiftly towards him, her long skirts brushing the cobblestones as she dodged between the carts and drays in her haste to reach him.

'Dear, *dear* Ted! How good to see you!'

Still the same eager little face, upturned to his, the same wide smile as she took his hands in hers and stood on tiptoe to kiss his cheek.

'And to see you!' So overwhelmed was he, in fact, he had a sudden urge to put his arms around her and sweep her high into the air, as if she were a child. And why not? This was America, after all, not staid old England! Hands around her waist, he held her aloft for several seconds while she laughed down at him.

And then, back on the sidewalk, she turned, still in the circle of Ted's arms and, for the first time, he saw the young man standing behind her.

'I'd like you two to be friends. Seth Harrison, Ted Smith. Seth comes from Virginia, Ted – but I don't hold that against him! – and studying to be a doctor. Seth knows all about *you*, for I've talked of no one else these past weeks!'

So they must see each other regularly, his dazed mind registered, as he allowed his hand to be pumped up and down and heard himself reply automatically to the other's friendly greeting. For there was no doubt – and this, perhaps, was the unkindest cut of all – that Seth Harrison was a pleasant fellow. Steady grey eyes gazed out from beneath a thatch of unruly black hair and his lips were parted in a smile of unexpected sweetness as he assured Ted that any friend of Mattie's must indeed consider himself a friend of his.

Biting back a temptation to point out that he was more than a little particular to whom he gave his friendship, Ted forced himself to bow courteously and trust that Mr Harrison was in good health. Mattie, linking an arm through his, grinned up at him.

'Oh, I do love your perfect English manners, Ted!'

But not, presumably, himself. For she was now linking her other arm in Seth's and urging them both towards the door of the eating-house, where a chalked notice informed them that a plate of beef hash would set them back no more than twelve cents apiece.

193

And it was surprisingly good hash. They ate in silence, for whatever Mattie and Seth had been busy at during the day, it had obviously left them ravenously hungry. As she swallowed an enormous forkful Mattie caught Ted's eye and grinned apologetically, but said nothing until their plates had been polished clean with crusts of bread and they were sipping at cups of piping-hot coffee.

'Sorry, Ted, I'm afraid I eat like a horse these days. No Southern elegance about me any more.'

He looked at her trim costume of dark blue serge, the neck of her shirt-waister a neat white circle above the closely fitting jacket and said gallantly, 'You'll always look elegant, Mattie, no matter how you spend your day.' And then paused, willing her to tell him what she had been up to. As he had feared, she grinned at Seth.

'Today, I have been at Seth's disposal.'

'By which,' explained Seth, 'she means that she has been slaving from dawn until a short while ago on the wards of my hospital.'

'Doing what?' Ted asked. But then knew it to be a stupid question. For what else would Mattie be doing but the most unmentionable tasks she could discover? And he was right.

'Things, my dear Ted, that my mama would faint at the thought of.'

Her mama. Dear, kind, *normal* Mrs Templeton and her equally normal husband. Soon he would ask after them, but first, he must hear how Mattie spent her days.

'Sometimes,' she continued, 'they permit me to help with quite important things. Sometimes, I am allowed to change dressings and even to be present at an operation, where I serve in a most menial capacity although, of course, keeping my eyes and ears open. That may be the direction I shall eventually take, for there is a medical college for *women*, here in New York, Ted. Is that not wonderful?'

Marriage, it was becoming abundantly clear, did not appear to play a central part in Mattie Templeton's plans for the future.

'But I must be quite sure,' she continued solemnly, 'that

194

that is the right path for me. For there are many alternatives, Ted. The new Society for the Prevention of Cruelty to Children, the soup kitchens, the reform of the sweatshops – you cannot imagine, Ted, the low wages they take home. If, indeed, they have a home to go to. For some sleep rough over the hot-steam gratings in winter and on the roofs of the tenements in summer.'

She paused for breath. She mentions these alternatives as other women would talk of garden parties or balls, Ted thought admiringly. 'I can see,' he said, 'that you are quite spoiled for choice!'

And now it was the old familiar Mattie, her eyes snapping with fury. 'Ted, are you patronising me?'

So then, in spite of Seth's presence, he must take her hand and assure her that of course he was not patronising her; that he admired her crusading zeal as much as he always had. And if there was a touch of sadness in his voice, lamenting a future that only he had dreamed of, he doubted if she even noticed. However, Seth Harrison did choose that moment to apologise for his presence.

'I do assure you, Ted, that it was only concern for Mattie's well-being that prompted me to intrude upon a meeting between such old friends. It's probably more than my life is worth to say it, but I don't like her walking these streets alone, if I can help it.'

So, while Mattie frowned at such a low opinion of her ability to take care of herself, Ted assured Seth that it was a pleasure to meet a real, live New Yorker, even if he did hail from Virginia! From there, it was a simple matter to enquire after Mattie's family in Savanah.

All, he was told, were in good health, and the preparations for Selina's wedding later that year to her Henry were well in hand.

'And you, of course,' he teased, 'will act as her bridesmaid, dressed overall in all manner of frills and furbelows!' He had only the vaguest notion of what a furbelow was, but knew, instinctively, that mentioning it to Mattie would be like waving a red rag at a bull.

195

Nor was he disappointed. 'Perish the thought! Though I hope to be present at the ceremony, of course, *if* my return railroad fare is provided. And you, Ted? Will you be there? I have no doubt that Selina and Henry would be delighted to have you.'

The White Star Line, he explained, did not sail to Savannah. 'I doubt that I shall ever sail up the Savannah river again. But Joseph probably will.'

So then he spoke of Joseph's health and present circumstances. Mattie had the fondest memories of him.

'He's a great person,' she told Seth. 'Forthright, honest, down-to-earth, but with his own bluff charm and a splendid sense of humour. And how he loved Savannah! I think, had it not been for his family, he would have considered living there. Wouldn't you agree, Ted?'

So that was his cue to tell her of Frank's ambition to see the city his father had spoken of so fondly and probably to live there. 'Now tell me, how is your brother, William?'

'Still at West Point, from where he descends upon my aunt Hester as often as he is able. You know, don't you, Ted, that I live for the moment with this friend of Mama's, whom I have always called aunt?'

'And what does *she* think of your. . . .' He had been about to say 'goings-on' but hastily changed it to 'activities?'

'As long as I don't embarrass her by storming into her drawing-room in front of her fashionable friends and complaining bitterly about some fresh social injustice I've discovered, she is happy to let me do as I wish.'

'And do you ever,' he dared to enquire, 'allow yourself a little relaxation?'

'Sometimes!' she assured him. 'When summer comes, and the city grows unbearably hot, Seth and I will no doubt take a steamboat ride some evenings over to the Jersey shore or even to Coney Island.'

'I was thinking more in terms of concerts or the theatre. Or an exhibition of pictures. I understand that New York has much to offer in that way.'

'*If* you have the money!' But just for a moment, she

sounded almost wistful; and he thought, perhaps, that is something we could do together. Perhaps, with luck, Seth has no artistic appreciation.

Their meal over, they emerged into darkness. Although the shabbiness of the neighbourhood was now hidden, the light spilling from the saloons and cafés lent a sinister quality to the people still shuffling along the sidewalks or congregating in little groups to gaze hungrily in at the windows of the eating-houses. In the dark alleyways, unmentionable acts of violence and depravity could be taking place, unheeded by those in the main thoroughfare. Ted glanced down at Mattie.

'What do you usually do after you've eaten?'

It was Seth who answered. 'Usually, I walk Mattie home if the night is fine or take a streetcar if it isn't, but I'm more than happy, Ted, to delegate that responsibility to you tonight.'

'One might think,' observed Mattie caustically, 'that I was no more than a package to be transported from one depot to the next.'

'And so you are, my honeychile!' Seth put his hand over his heart in a dramatic gesture. 'But a package more precious than a king's ransom, eh, Ted?'

It was a pretty speech, especially when delivered in that sultry Southern drawl. By comparison, Ted's acceptance of Seth's offer sounded almost surly. But at least he was to be alone with Mattie for the next hour or so.

They stolled up Broadway towards Madison Square, through crowds more fashionably clad by far than those they had just left, and between buildings of an imposing size and grandeur.

'Look!' Ted pointed out proudly. 'That's the head office of the White Star Line.' But Mattie was too busy complaining bitterly against the iniquities of a social structure that could allow families like the Astors and the Vanderbilts to live in luxury while others existed in total squalor, to pay it much attention.

Ted, while agreeing in principle with all that she said,

197

thought privately that there would always be such injustices. And anyway, at that moment, there were other, more pressing matters on his mind.

'Seth Harrison,' he observed suddenly, 'appears to be a good man.'

'Seth?' Mattie paused. 'Yes, Seth's a good, kind person. I like him very much.'

'Only – *like*?'

'Why, Ted!' She stared up at him, a half-smile on her lips. 'I do believe you're jealous!'

'Of course, I'm not jealous!' But why deny it? Wasn't this just what he wanted to talk to her about? He grinned wryly. 'Oh, well, perhaps – just a little.'

'Oh, Ted, you are ridiculous! You have no reason to be jealous. Don't you know that Cap'n Ted, as Maria used to call you, holds a very special place in the heart of all the Templetons?'

'It's one particular Templeton I'm concerned with at the moment.'

'And I hope you always will be. Even when you're a respectable married man with a horde of children, I trust you'll still think of me with affection. And that your wife,' she added with a broad grin, 'will not object to our friendship.'

'Mattie.' He stared down at her. It was now or never. 'There's one way of making sure that she wouldn't.'

'What's that, Ted?'

'Why, by becoming that wife yourself.'

And now, for the first time since he had met her that evening, she was lost for words, gazing up at him with softening eyes, her lips parted in a tender smile, so that, for a moment, he thought that she was about to accept his bizarre proposal. But then, slowly, regretfully, she shook her head.

'Dear Ted! You do me the greatest honour, but the answer must be no. We have so little in common.'

'And therefore would find each other's company constantly stimulating. Answer me truthfully, Mattie. Have you

198

ever been bored by me?'

'Never, Ted! But that's no basis for a lifetime together. Before long, you would grow irritated by my perpetual grouch against the wealthy and my championship of the poor.'

'There will always be those who have and those who have not,' he said. 'That's the way life is.'

'I'm afraid I can't accept that. What is that dreadful hymn you sing in England? "The rich man in his castle, the poor man at his gate. God made them, high or lowly. And ordered their estate".'

'Mattie,' he said firmly when she had finished. 'I do *not* wish to discuss the unequal distribution of wealth in London, New York, San Francisco, Timbuctoo or any other city. I wish to discuss *our* future.'

'For pity's sake, miss, give the gentleman his answer! And then perhaps I can get on with my work.'

The interruption came from a big, burly man in the braided uniform of a doorman.

'And if I were you, miss,' he continued, 'I'd give the offer my serious consideration. He's a well-set-up young fellow, even if he is a Limey.'

Now they were all laughing as Ted took Mattie's arm and began to urge her along the sidewalk. But their pace was slower, as Mattie put her case.

'Ted, I've no intention of marrying anyone for years. Not Seth Harrison – even if he asked me – nor Ted Smith, nor anyone. Marriage just isn't part of my plans.'

'Even if you care deeply for someone? As I care for you.' He hesitated to use the word 'love'. But Mattie had no such scruples.

'And I'm honoured to hear you say so, Ted. But you don't *love* me – not as you will someone else, one day.'

'How do you know?'

'Oh, feminine intuition,' she said infuriatingly. 'Call it what you will. I *know*!'

So deep were they in their argument, they crossed Madison Square with hardly a glance for its magnificent mansions, and came at last to the house where Mattie's aunt Hester lived. Less pretentious than many, it still had a well-to-do air about it.

'And I know what you're thinking,' said Mattie as they mounted the steps. 'But it was part of the bargain I struck with Mama and Papa that I should stay here for at least a year. When that's up, nothing will keep me here, much as I love Aunt Hester. You'll come in and meet her, won't you, Ted?'

But he declined the invitation. 'Another time,' he assured her. 'Now I should be thinking about getting back on board.'

Gently, he took Mattie's face between his cupped hands and brought his lips down upon her forehead. It wasn't the passionate embrace he'd envisaged, but, deep within himself, he knew that she was right. They wouldn't have suited. Like most sailors, especially those who'd served their time before the mast, he gave little thought to the class structure against which Mattie railed so vehemently. At sea, you took your orders from the man above you, be he belted earl or potter's son, and the system seemed to him to be eminently sensible.

Thus ruminating, Fourth Officer Edward J. Smith of the White Star Line straightened his shoulders and walked back to his ship, giving a wink and a grin to his friend the doorman as he passed him yet again.

'Any luck?' he asked. And when Ted shook his head, the man said, 'That's tough. But plenty more fish in the sea! Yes, *sir*!'

When an American said 'Yes, sir', Ted reflected, it was to emphasise a statement and not, as the English would use it, to express subservience. And a forelock was a tuft of hair between a horse's ears, not something to be tugged in deference! Raw and uncivilised it might be, but this melting-pot of creed and culture that was America had the right idea about a lot of things.

29

It took several crossings for him to become accustomed to the vagaries of the route they followed across the Atlantic, west-south-west from Queenstown in a gentle curve to Sandy Hook. In spring and early summer, the curve would be deeper to clear the ice that drifted down, dislodged by the spring thaw, from the Arctic glaciers, although it was never totally avoided. But he came to recognise its varying shapes: the enormous bergs, sometimes over two hundred feet in height and double that in width, and then only showing one-eighth of their total size above the water; the growlers, pieces broken off as the bergs 'calved' in the warmer water of the Gulf Stream and treated with equal respect, for the parent berg could still be in the vicinity; and the pack ice, sea-water that froze over into a continuous, solid sheet.

On a clear day, ice could be spotted many miles away and the rails would be crowded with passengers eager to see such shining examples of nature's artistry. To view a berg by moonlight was pure, breathtaking magic, with the sea frothing silver around its base; but even on a dark night, provided there was no cloud, one could be seen from a good half-mile away, and a quick turn to port or starboard be sufficient to avoid it.

Only when there was fog, or the sky overcast, was the *Celtic's* speed reduced because of ice. At all other times, it was a matter of steaming on at the maximum permissible revolutions of the screw, the crew ever mindful of the great Cunarders snapping at their heels and just as eager as they to cut even an hour or two from the eight-day passage.

201

Ted worked hard and his devotion to duty eventually resulted in his promotion to third officer. 'I'm on my way! Yes *sir!*' he boasted to Mattie.

She, in her several spheres, was working as hard as he, but could on occasion be persuaded to spend a few hours in his company. Sometimes Seth Harrison came too, but usually several young people, eager to meet Mattie's English friend, would turn up at their meeting-place in the City Hall Park. In summer, there'd be excursions to Coney Island or Rockaway, or strolls along the shady walks of Central Park, and on one occasion he was taught, after several tumbles, to ride a newfangled velocipede along Riverside Drive. In winter, it was skating in Central Park, his cheeks tingling, his beard rimed with frost as, arms encircling each other's waists, he and Mattie swooped and swayed in perfect unison.

But most of all he enjoyed the concerts to which he was sometimes permitted to escort her, provided the tickets could be acquired cheaply enough. For she never allowed him to be extravagant, to buy her flowers or chocolates, and always insisted upon 'paying her way'.

All in all, he'd thoroughly enjoyed New York but was ripe for change.

Similar in many ways to the *Celtic, Coptic* also boasted a two-cylinder, single-screw engine and four masts. Two voyages to New York having disposed of any teething problems, in March 1882 she was bound for Yokohama, via Suez and Hong Kong, with Captain William Henry Ridley on her bridge and newly promoted, Second Officer Edward John Smith stationed aft.

Thus placed, ensuring the cast-off ropes stayed clear of the propeller, he was able to spare a quick glance for the cheering crowd on the wharf. And especially to note that Frank and Anna were standing in the position they'd agreed upon, slightly behind and to the left of the main mass so that they could easily be picked out. Joseph was sailing in Australian waters, but they were more than making up for his absence, Frank now waving with both arms. Ted put up his own hand and tugged thoughtfully at his beard, at the same time raising the other to straighten his cap; thus giving the prearranged signal that he had seen them. Next year, when Frank would be twenty and his apprenticeship completed, he would sail for Savannah. Already, the Templeton family had undertaken to see him safely settled.

Poor Anna! It would be sad for her to have both husband, son and brother-in-law so far away, but at least she was used to separation from her loved ones. And George, after all, was still in Liverpool and doing well in a solicitor's office.

For himself, promotion to second officer on *Coptic* had come faster then he'd dared hope. And Japan – they were to operate between Yokohama and San Francisco – was a country he'd long wished to visit. A couple of years in the North Pacific wasn't to be sniffed at. He'd miss his friends in New York, of course, but there would be compensations; sailing through the Suez Canal, for one thing, then writing to Joseph of the experience.

To most of the crew and, indeed, to much of the Western world, the country of Japan was still a closed book. Ted knew that the rule of the samurai had now ceased; but that the power of the Emperor, as the descendant of Japan's divine dynasty, still remained, although tempered now by a group of statesmen who effectively managed the country's affairs.

'And they are eager,' pronounced Captain Ridley, 'to learn from the West.'

'Great little imitators, the Japs,' asserted one of his officers who had sailed already in Eastern waters. 'But no good at working things out for themselves.'

'That's true,' Captain Ridley agreed, 'but once they've learned all they can from us – and the Americans – the Japanese could become a powerful nation, and one that Her Majesty's Government may well have to contend with in the future.'

They all nodded wisely, although Ted privately resented

the implication that the might of the British Empire could ever be challenged by a nation that consisted, after all, of only four small islands on the edge of the Pacific Ocean. But come to think of it, Great Britain was only *two* small islands on the edge of the Atlantic! And Will Ridley usually knew what he was talking about.

He wrote to Bert:

Yokohama is a thriving port on the south-east coast of Honshu, the largest island of Japan, twenty-six miles from Tokyo but with a rail link already established into the capital.

When Jock – the second engineer, with whom I have become friendly – and I are fortunate enough to have our time ashore together, we often sit outside one of Tokyo's many cafés, sipping our rice tea – and trying not to grimace unduly! – and gaze around us at the passers-by. What a contrast to those of the West! The men are dressed in a sort of wide-skirted coat – mostly black but sometimes striped with colour – that reaches a little below the knee and is tied at the waist with a braided cord. This garment is called a *haori*.

That is the men. But, the women! They are like exotic butterflies in their gaily coloured kimonos; again, a wide, loose-fitting coat with voluminous sleeves, sashed at the waist and worn over the *Hakama*, a long, loose trouser. They flutter like butterflies, too, for their feet have been bound up from childhood to prevent their natural growth, so that they are able to take only the smallest of steps. The practice, I assume, is dictated by fashion to make sure their feet are as tiny as the rest of them, but it struck me as a most barbaric custom. However, they seem happy enough, chattering away among themselves in a language I shall never begin to understand and, as the days grow warmer, twirling brightly hued sunshades. They are fascinating creatures to study, and study them we do, peering covertly over the rims of our teacups, while they, seeming absorbed in their own affairs, still contrive to flash us quick, curious glances. No doubt, if the language was not such a barrier, we might manage to know them better, for indeed they are most attractive with their almond-shaped eyes, pale skins and wings of jet-black hair held back by ornamental combs.

For the rest, the countryside around Yokohama is a fertile area, where rice, vegetables, tobacco and tea are cultivated. We are too late, alas, for the flowering cherry but have been told that in spring, the whole countryside becomes a sea of blossom.

My best wishes to Gilly and young Caroline. Gilly must be nearing her time and I hope that all will go as well as possible. Needless to say, I shall deem it a great honour to stand as godfather, whatever its sex.

Thirza and William are both well and Annie is now an attractive young lady of sixteen, although still not very strong. As for James, he has finally decided to give up the sea and is now married. He will soon be setting up in Hanley as a painter and decorator. Dear little Ned continues to astonish everyone with his prowess at school, although his health, too, causes concern. And Ma, as always, remains the central pivot of them all.

So there is my family brought up to date. Now that your parents have moved to Derbyshire, I realize that you have little cause to visit Hanley, but I know that they would be delighted to see you, if ever you are that way.

Your affectionate friend, *Edward J. Smith.*

30

After *Coptic* came *Britannia*, and he'd been on her for well over a year – with dynamic Captain Hamilton Perry, under whose command there was never a dull moment and many an exciting one – when Joseph wrote from Savannah.

My Dear Ted.

Today, one of Anna's most cherished ambitions was fulfilled. Our dear son Frank was united in holy matrimony with Annie Oakes Hatch, in Christ Episcopal Church, Savannah.

We are both greatly relieved that Frank has chosen so wisely, for Annie – our 'American Annie', we have decided to call her, to avoid confusion with our dear niece – is a most delightful girl and comes from a highly respectable and God-fearing family. Frank's future, we now feel, will be assured. He is still with Clarke and Co., timber merchants, and, by all accounts, doing very well.

We are staying – you will be most impressed to hear! – in the Pulaski House Hotel. But from tomorrow, we are the guests of our dear friends the Templetons. They are as delightful as ever, Ted, and send you their very best wishes. William is doing well in the army and Selina and Henry are now married and have an adorable little girl, Jane Vitoria. Julia is now engaged to some unfortunate young man!

I was out early this morning to roam the streets of my beloved city and found them hardly changed. Forsyth Park was a haven of peace, heavy with the scent of honeysuckle. We are most fortunate that Annie and

Frank chose the month of June for their wedding, for twilight in these Southern States seems to last for ever and we have many hours in which to explore.

Anna expresses herself as delighted as I am to be here, and has already made one – expensive! – foray into Broughton Street for presents to bring home.

We were all so sorry that sailing schedules did not permit your presence at the ceremony, but Frank and Annie are looking forward to a visit from you before too long.

You have been much in my thoughts lately, as you can imagine, especially when I wander down to the riverfront. Anna has all but prevailed upon me to give up the sea after my next voyage and, in many ways, I shall not be sorry. But you, dear Ted, are going from strength to strength. I am delighted to hear that you may soon be promoted to first officer. Soon, perhaps, master? Ma will be so proud of you, not that she will tell you in so many words!

Ah, well, I must cease my meanderings and join Anna in our sumptuous bed. She is already sound asleep and snoring gently in the most contented fashion.

But I'm glad I've shared this auspicious day with you, Ted.

Your loving brother, *Joseph Hancock*

Ted smiled to himself. Wild horses wouldn't have persuaded Joseph to mention by what means he had travelled to Savannah, but the necessity to arrive on time must have forced him to go by steam!

The letter pleased him enormously. It was good to know that at least one member of the family had put down roots in the New World, particularly in Savannah. He was pleased, too, with his own progress, for there was no doubt that he *was* progressing. Not only was he thought to be a competent officer – although no more so, he considered, than most of his colleagues – but his face, as far as the Company was concerned, seemed to fit. As Captain Gleadell had observed on his first trip, 'E.J.' was known to be good with the passengers.

'I knew we'd be safe as long as *you* were on board,' an elderly American lady said to him after a particularly stormy crossing.

'Madam, I can't control the weather. I'm not God!'

'No, but you're a darned sight more comforting. I can *see* you and I can't see the Almighty.'

A steady income – for White Star paid their officers well – had a beneficial effect upon his way of life. He took lodgings out at Runcorn, away from the noise and dirt of the docks, and made new friends. One was Thomas Jones, the landlord of the public house where he went for a relaxing drink and a cigar. Soon, he was dropping in just to talk to Thomas, enjoying his lively Welsh wit, his shrewd assessment of people and his determination to advance in the world.

'I'm going to own this pub one day, Ted, not just run it. And maybe, if things go really well, I shall own the brewery that supplies the beer you're drinking.'

'In that case, Thomas, I'd better have the other half, before you put up the price!'

Only one thing marred his contentment; he could do with some regular exercise when he was ashore. Now that he had money to spare, could he perhaps afford the luxury of his own horse? He had long wanted to ride. He talked to Thomas about it; then, sailing next day, promptly forgot all about the conversation. But Thomas didn't.

'It's all laid on,' he said, handing Ted a pint pot when he next appeared in the bar. It was a warm June day and he was very thirsty.

'Thanks, Tom. I've been dreaming of this ever since I left New York.'

'I don't mean your beer, numskull! I mean your horse.'

Next morning, they travelled out on the train to Newton-le-Willows and were met by a pony and trap. Thomas taking the reins, they drove up a long, gentle hill between fields where marguerites starred the summer grass and poppies glowed in the hedgerow corners. At the top of the hill stood a public house called the Bull's Head, its doors invitingly open.

'Not now, later!' said Thomas firmly, before Ted could even open his mouth, and turned the pony sharp right. About a mile on, he turned up a short avenue of chestnut trees to where a big white farmhouse stood back from a tiled barn, and a yard held a clutter of implements.

'Here's John Pennington,' said Thomas as a young man came out from the rear of the house.

But Ted wasn't listening. He was gazing fearfully at three equine heads peering down at him over a nearby hedge; all wore expressions of extreme benevolence but all were so tall he cricked his neck gazing up at them. 'Thomas,' he whispered. 'What d'you take me for? I could never ride one of those!'

Thomas burst out laughing. 'Those are the shires, numskull! John breeds them here, at Woodhead.' He turned to greet the young man, then introduced Ted. 'I was just telling my friend about your shires, John. There's still call for them, is there, in spite of all this newfangled machinery?'

'There's many still prefer the old ways, Thomas. And there's the brewers, as you know. Those fellows there will probably go to the railway companies, meeting the trains and collecting the heavy goods.'

John Pennington offered the visitors refreshment, which they declined, then paused at the open door of the barn. 'Are you there, Kennedy?'

'Comin', yer honour!' And out of the barn came a little, old man with stooped shoulders and a face so wrinkled, the black boot-button eyes would have been invisible but for their twinkling brightness. 'Is it Midnight you'll be wantin', yer honour?' He spoke with the unmistakable brogue of Ireland.

'Please, Kennedy!'

'I'll fetch young John, then.' And the old man turned and went back into the barn, emerging a moment later carrying a head collar and followed by a man who, clearly,

209

was even older than he. 'Won't be two shakes of a lamb's tail, yer honour!'

And with astonishing agility, both men shinned over a nearby gate and started walking across what appeared to be an empty field.

A confusion of commands, counter-commands, whistles, whinnies and not a few choice swear-words soon came floating up from the bottom of the field. Ted's hands, thrust deep into his pockets, grew hot and sticky. And then, up the field, plodded a jet-black horse so broad and round young John's legs, perched as he was upon its back, were practically at right angles to his body.

'We've got him, yer honour!' It might have been a man-eating tiger Kennedy was leading, so triumphant did he sound.

'Now, Mr Smith,' said John Pennington 'as you can see, he's a good solid, sturdy animal, well up to your weight and sound as a bell. Run him up and down a bit, Kennedy.'

And Kennedy, with young John apparently glued to the animal's back, demonstrated the horse's easy, rhythmic movement.

'Why doesn't Mr Smith try Midnight for himself, John?' suggested a high-pitched, girlish voice behind him. 'Wouldn't that be best?'

What a dreadful idea! Ted turned sharply, to behold not one but two young girls – of about Annie's age, he thought – and dressed alike in brown holland smocks with sun-bonnets tied demurely beneath their chins. The only visible difference between them was that one had clusters of auburn ringlets escaping from beneath her bonnet and the other, brown.

'What a good idea!' said Brown Ringlets. So! Auburn Ringlets must be the one who had made the preposterous suggestion. He vowed vengeance.

'It would be as well, Mr Smith. I'll give you a leg-up, shall I?'

Too late, Ted realised that Thomas could not have told John Pennington of his inexperience. There seemed to be

210

no turning back, especially with those two young misses grinning away like – two Cheshire Cats! Thank heavens Annie wasn't here, to add her mirth to theirs. He couldn't even plead the unsuitability of his attire for, not wishing to appear out of place, he'd chosen to wear a pair of fawn breeches with matching gaiters, a smart, checked jacket and a dashing, curly-brimmed brown bowler. All he could hope for was that Kennedy would continue to hold on to the head collar, now young John was back on the ground.

John Pennington moved forward and made a convenient step with his knee, at the same time cupping his hands for Ted to insert his foot. The next moment he was aloft, his fingers thrusting deep in to the long coarse hair of Midnight's mane.

No one ever agreed as to precisely what happened next; Kennedy maintained that one of the shire colts down in the Marl field had called to Midnight; young John that Midnight objected to the sudden extra weight on his back; and John Pennington that Ted must have unconsciously tightened his thigh muscles, thus giving Midnight the command to set off at speed, downhill. Whatever the reasons, the result, as Ted later described it to Captain Perry, was that the 'beast was somehow given full-speed-ahead on his engine-room telegraph and shot off at a good twenty knots'.

Dimly aware that Kennedy, after dangling from the end of the rope for a few perilous seconds, had finally let go, Ted clung on with every available part of his lower limbs. At the same time he felt himself slipping irrevocably sideways. Wordlessly, he prayed that the end, when it came, would be swift and painless. But it was to be neither.

At the bottom of the field, Midnight suddenly swerved to port through an open gate and stopped abruptly. For several seconds, Ted seemed poised in mid-air and then, losing all control, slid slowly down over the horse's withers – to land, head-first, in a pool of brackish water.

Winded, gasping for breath, he bent forward, clutching his stomach, the beautiful brown bowler floating at his feet.

And then he heard yet another female voice, but this time deeper, softer and husky with anxiety.

'Are you hurt, sir? Oh, whatever could John have been thinking of to let this happen?'

Still clutching his stomach, still unable to catch his breath, he was dimly aware of a faint, elusive perfume – violets, was it? – of gentle hands trying to lift up his head.

'Don't try to speak. You'll get your breath back in a moment or two, and then we'll get you inside and clean you up.'

His head still held by those soft fingers, he found himself gazing into eyes of a deep, velvety brown – pansies? he wondered dreamily, or a bumble-bee's furry body?

It was really of little consequence. All that mattered was that Second Officer Edward J. Smith had, for the first time in his thirty-five years, fallen deeply and irrevocably in love.

Her name was Eleanor and she was a younger sister of John Pennington's.

Halfway up the field to the house, with her arm solicitously about him – and, indeed, his ankle really was more than a little painful – they were met by her brother.

'Mr Smith, please do forgive me! I had no idea you hadn't ridden before.'

'I cannot believe,' said Eleanor grimly, 'that the Marthas were not somehow concerned in this mishap.'

'The Marthas', he discovered were the two young girls who had first suggested he ride Midnight; Martha Pennington, 'the baby of the family', and Martha Hindley, who lived 'down at Monk House'. It was all very confusing.

'Marthas, apologise at once!' Eleanor commanded, once the circumstances of Ted's epic ride had been explained to her and the girls summoned to attend.

'We're truly sorry, Mr Smith,' they chorused obediently.

The sooner the subject was changed, the better, he decided. 'Which of you,' he enquired civilly, 'is Miss Martha Pennington?'

The auburn-haired one raised a hand. 'And I'm Martha

Hindley,' said the other.

'Don't ask me why our mothers were so unimaginative in their choice of names, Mr Smith,' said Eleanor.

'Not unimaginative at all!' said a stout, elderly lady bustling in at that moment from the yard, a basketful of eggs on her arm. 'We simply thought it appropriate that our first-born should be Mary and our last-born Martha.'

'But how did you know, Mama,' enquired Martha Pennington with, Ted suspected, deceptive innocence, 'that I *would* be the last-born? And anyway, the other Martha wasn't, was she? Ada came after her!'

'Never you mind about that,' said her mother sternly. 'And if Martha's staying for lunch, off with you both to wash your hands. And good morning to you, Mr Smith. I'm delighted to make your acquaintance. Thomas, here, is an old friend.'

The time had come, he decided, to dispense with formality. 'The name,' he said firmly, 'is Edward. Or Ted, to my friends.'

'Then Ted it must be! And I trust that you and Thomas will both stay to lunch?'

'As long as I'm back by evening opening time,' said Thomas comfortably, 'we'd be delighted to, eh, Ted? And we've yet to discuss Midnight.'

It was a cheerful meal. Kennedy and young John lived in, and were clearly considered to be part of the family; the young servant girl, once she had dished up the meal, also sat down with them. Mrs Pennington took her place, clearly as of right, at the head of the table so Mr Pennington, Ted surmised, could no longer be alive. Maria, a quiet, unobtrusive young woman, sat on one side of her mother, with John Pennington on the other. Ted, to his great delight, was placed next to Eleanor.

At first, the talk was of a fête to be held shortly in the grounds of Winwick Hall, the home of the rector and his wife, with which they all seemed to be greatly involved.

'Perhaps you'd like to come over for it, Thomas?' Mrs Pennington suggested. 'And Ted too, of course.'

213

'And their wives also, Mama?' asked Martha Pennington, gazing at Ted with unashamed curiosity.

'That goes without saying,' said her mother crisply.

'I – er – have no wife,' stated Ted firmly. 'And I should be delighted to attend your fête and perhaps,' his glance flickered sideways to Eleanor, 'I might be allowed to assist in some way?'

'You can help Martha and me with the pony rides,' said the youngest Miss Pennington swiftly.

This wasn't at all what he'd had in mind. 'If, of course,' he added with equal swiftness, 'I am not at sea.'

The statement caused an immediate silence then they all spoke together.

'You didn't say your friend was a sailor, Thomas,' said John.

'No wonder he can't sit a horse!' That was Martha Pennington, but softly so that her mother wouldn't hear.

'It's a brave man ye are, yer honour!'

'And you lookin' every inch the country gennleman!' Young John was full of admiration.

'Have another potato.'

'And a slice of ham.' Maria and her mother had presumably decided to fortify him for the voyage!

But it was Eleanor's comment, or rather question, that he valued the most. 'How far will you be going, Ted?'

'Oh, just to New York. I shall only be away for three weeks or so.' But already it seemed an eternity.

'And Midnight?' enquired John, as they rose from the table.

'Oh, I should be delighted to have him, if I may. But would it be possible to leave him here, at livery, I mean? At least until I've mastered the art of remaining on his back for longer than a few seconds!'

They all thought that would be a capital idea. 'And I'll teach you,' Martha Pennington offered. 'For I can ride astride as well as any man. Is that not so, Eleanor?'

'I'm afraid it's only too true, Ted. I don't ride myself but I can tell that she is indeed a good little rider. Our dear father taught her.'

And trustworthy? he wondered.

'Don't worry,' said Eleanor softly, clearly guessing his thought. 'I'll see she doesn't play any tricks.'

The gods smiled on him that summer.

'I'm afraid,' said Captain Perry when he next boarded the *Britannic*, 'that this will be your last trip with me, Ted. The Company's moving you to *Republic*.'

'Oh, no!' For *Republic* was smaller, older and not as fast as *Britannic*. And anyway, he enjoyed serving under Hamilton Perry.

'Shall I tell them you don't want it, then?'

Ted stared at his superior officer in astonishment. He must know how preposterous such a suggestion was.

'Although personally,' Perry continued innocently, 'at your stage of the game, I'd be happy to go to a bath-tub if it meant getting my First.'

'You mean. . . ?'

A broad grin spread over Perry's handsome face. 'Yes, you'll be going as first officer, under Captain Irving. He's quite looking forward to having you, I understand. Can't think why!'

31

'Grip with your thigh muscles, Ted, not your calves!'

He grinned to himself. Surely Martha wasn't supposed to know he *had* calves, let alone thighs; and certainly not to mention them in this casual fashion!

It was his first lesson – in the field immediately below the house so that Eleanor could keep an eye on them – and he was finding it a novel experience to be told what to do by a mere chit of a girl. But Eleanor was right, Martha was a good little rider; as he could see when, wearing a pair of men's breeches pulled in tightly about her waist, she mounted Midnight herself for practical demonstrations.

'That will be enough for today, Ted,' she declared after he'd made a circuit of the makeshift track at a slow trot. 'Your backside will be sore enough tomorrow, as it is.'

Eleanor came out of the house. 'You're doing famously, Ted!' She wore a white dress, loose from the shoulders so that he could only guess at the soft curves of her body, and high to the neck, but with the two top buttons of the bodice undone, for it was a warm day. 'A drink first, and then I'll show you St Oswald's Well. All visitors to Woodhead must be shown our well.'

'A splendid idea!' And the well, with any luck, would be at the furthest point from the house.

'I'll come too,' Martha offered.

'Mama,' countered Eleanor swiftly, 'wishes to see you in the parlour.'

'Oh, fiddlesticks! What about?'

'I think,' said Eleanor judiciously, 'it may be something to do with the holes she discovered in some of your stockings when she was tidying your bedroom this morning.'

'Stockings!' fumed Martha. 'Why can't I wear breeches all the time?'

'Even then, you'd have to wear socks,' Ted pointed out. 'And they grow enormous holes, I can assure you! But thank you, Martha, for my lesson. I think you're an excellent instructor.'

'And you're not such a bad pupil,' she called over her shoulder as, a shade mollified, she went off to the parlour.

The well, disappointingly, was at the bottom of the field where he'd had his lesson.

'I'm afraid it's not much to look at,' said Eleanor as they gazed down at the bubbles of a small spring gushing out into a pool fringed with kingcups. 'But St Oswald himself is said to have caused it to appear when he died here, a martyr to his faith. Drinking its waters is supposed to restore you to health if you are sick.'

'I have no wish,' said Ted solemnly, 'to recover from the hopeless condition from which I am at present suffering.' He gazed down meaningfully at the crown of her head, noticing the tendrils of dark hair at the nape of her neck and the creamy whiteness of her skin, and had the satisfaction of seeing a blush creep up her throat.

During that afternoon at Winwick Fête, when he'd helped her on the produce stall, he'd been aware of a bond growing steadily between them as they sold their cakes and pots of jam and honey, their bunches of golden carrots and plump, pink beetroot. It had seemed as if every other customer was a relation, and Aunty This and Uncle That – not to mention all those Marys! – had gazed at him in the most pointed fashion until Eleanor introduced him.

'I think,' she'd said in the end, 'that I shall simply tie a label around your neck with your name on it!'

Already, on the drive up from Newton, he had told her about his family and his childhood in Hanley. About Ma and Pa, Joseph and Thirza; and that although he now had lodgings in Runcorn, he still went regularly to Hanley, thus paving the way, he hoped, for Eleanor to accompany him

217

there one day.

As he'd left her on the platform of Newton station that evening, with John waiting tactfully in the trap outside, he'd thanked her for a wonderful day.

'I, too,' she'd told him, letting her hand stay in his just a fraction longer than was necessary, 'have enjoyed it.' And he'd gone away the happiest of men.

But even so, he cautioned himself now, he mustn't rush his fences – already he was acquiring the idioms of the horseman! – but must court her with as much patience and forbearance as he could muster. 'It's such a lovely day,' he said, 'could we not walk a little further?'

'By all means.' And she directed their steps away from the well – and the house – explaining the peculiarities and preferences of the land over which they walked. Ted expressed the deepest of interest, although not caring in the least whether the Marl field produced oats or oysters.

They came at last – via the Nine Acre, where mares, heavy with foal, dozed in the shade – to the Far Field. 'For hay, as you see,' said Eleanor. 'Most of it will be sent to Liverpool for the carriage horses. And in return, we take their muck – manure, I should say.'

'How – how sensible!'

'Good husbandry, father used to call it.'

But today, the grass was as yet uncut, sweet with clover and drowsy with bees. 'Could we,' he suggested, 'rest awhile?' And taking her silence to mean consent, took off his jacket and spread it in a shady corner, at the same time offering his hand to assist her down to it.

Eleanor sank into the gossamer pool of her outspread skirts and gazed about her. And suddenly started to shake with laughter.

At first, he was affronted. The situation wasn't in the least comic. And then, seeing his discomfiture, she impetuously took his hand.

'Ted, I'm so sorry! It's just that I've scrambled about these fields since I was a child and here I am, allowing myself to be handed down to sit like a high-born lady in a corner that I know better than the palm of my own hand. I've pushed through those hedges more times than I can remember because I was too lazy to go round by the gate, and crawled into the ditch again and again when I was hiding from John or Maria.'

By now, he was laughing too. 'You must find me more than a little tedious.'

'Oh no, Ted! It is I who am tedious with all this talk of muck and manure!' Her hand tightened on his. 'I would not like you at all if you were too smooth and urbane, too practised in the art of pretty speeches that mean nothing at all.'

'Have you known many such?' he found himself asking, and regretted it immediately as the hand was removed.

She looked down at her lap. 'Well, one or two, perhaps.' And then her eyes came up to meet his and once again, she was laughing. 'Ted, I refuse to spend such a lovely day talking about what is past. *Now* is what matters.' She bent to pluck a buttercup that was curling itself around the edge of his jacket. 'So let us play the buttercup game.' And she leaned forward to place the golden cup beneath his chin, stopping abruptly and pulling a comic face when she realised it was hidden by his beard. And now it was his turn to laugh.

'Even Hanley children know how to play this game.' And taking the flower from her, he held it under her own chin; she tilting it slightly so that the delicate column of her throat was exposed. The buttercup forgotten, his eye moved downwards to where the unbuttoned neck of her bodice showed the first, faint swell of her breasts.

'Well, Ted! Do I like butter or do I not?' He forced his gaze upwards to where the petals cast a pale golden reflection beneath her chin.

'Yes, Eleanor, you like butter.' His voice was low and husky with emotion and she lowered her chin to look at him. There was nothing he could do to hide his longing. 'Dear Eleanor. . . !'

She leaned towards him, her lips parted. 'Ted . . .'

219

And then, like a genie summoned from the sky, Martha suddenly crashed through the hedge, no doubt through one of those same holes Eleanor had made long ago.

'Oh, here you are! Sorry, Nellie, did I kick you? Mama says to tell you tea's ready.'

That night, when he said goodbye, he bent to kiss her. But she drew back.

'I mustn't keep John waiting, Ted. Enjoy yourself in Hanley tomorrow.' And then she was gone.

Alone in his compartment, he worried like a dog over a bone at his dismissal. What was it she'd said when speaking of the men she'd known? 'One or two, perhaps!' Looking as she did, there must have been many more – and still were?

'Welcome aboard, Mr Smith.'

'Thank you, sir.'

It was good to have a new ship to take his mind off the persistent, nagging worry about Eleanor. Finding his way about *Republic*, meeting the other officers, several of whom were already known to him, learning – or relearning – their ways but at the same time assessing their worth, gave him plenty to occupy his mind.

There was his family to think about too, particularly Thirza and William who had also decided to move to Runcorn. A suitable house had already been found in Greenway Road, not far from his own lodgings.

'And what will happen to Ma?' he'd enquired of Thirza, for she was nearing eighty now and would surely not welcome a change.

'That's all been taken care of, Ted. She'll live with James and Pattie in Hanley for the time being but come to me as often as she wishes. And when Joseph and Anna are settled, she'll go to them from time to time.'

For Anna, determined that Joseph should soon retire, was of a mind to move to the far side of the Mersey, where a retired mariner could sniff the ocean breeze and still imagine himself at sea.

Ted could help, Thirza had suggested, in finding William suitable employment; in one of the big engineering works perhaps, where ships' engines were constantly being overhauled and repaired. With William's record, that should present no problems.

As yet, he'd said nothing to any of them about Eleanor, other than that he now kept a horse at Winwick.

His spirits lifting, as they always did when he was at sea, he began to look forward to meeting Mattie again. Not that he would mention Eleanor to her. Not yet.

But, he did, of course! Mattie, after speaking to him three times before he answered her, asked bluntly, 'Ted, are you in love or something?'

'No, of course not!' But his expression gave him away and, before he knew it, he was telling her everything, his worries included.

'Come on, Ted! Where's that British backbone you're always telling me about? Even if there is someone else, you're as good as they are, any day of the week!'

He hoped she was right. But by the time they docked in Liverpool, he was convinced he hadn't a chance. Even Thomas couldn't persuade him otherwise.

'It's very kind of you to meet me, Maria. But, Eleanor. . . ?

'She told me to tell you how sorry she was, and that she'd be back as soon as she could. But our aunt Margaret, at Delf House, has been taken poorly. Mama was quite worried, so she and Nellie have walked over there with a few comforts – quince jelly, beef tea, a bottle of Mama's blackcurrant cordial, that sort of thing.'

'Walked? But if you had not been meeting me with the trap . . .'

'Ted, don't worry! It's a pleasant day, the lanes will not be muddy and they would probably have walked anyway.'

His initial deep disappointment at not finding Eleanor waiting for him in the station yard faded slightly. 'All the same, I do hope I'm not being a nuisance.'

'A nuisance, Ted? How could you ever be that? Now –

tell me what you've been up to since we saw you last. How is your mother? Has your sister moved yet? And how was the *Republic*?' It was gratifying to have such an interest shown in his affairs.

Her questions answered, he enquired in return, 'And what has been happening at Woodhead?'

She seemed to know that it was really Eleanor he wanted to hear about. 'Oh, the usual routine. The curate called to ask Nellie to do the flowers. She always takes her turn, of course, but this time was an extra because Mrs Hopwood – she's the rector's wife, as you may know – had to go to London.'

He had never known Maria to be so talkative but then, he had never been alone with her before.

'However,' she continued, 'Nellie was going to a concert in Warrington that particular Saturday, so I –'

'Who with?' He hadn't meant to ask the question so sharply – nor so ungrammatically! 'With whom?' he amended in a softer voice.

Maria seemed not at all put out. 'Oh, just the Hindleys from Monk House. They are a very musical family. Nellie loves music, you know. Her performance on the pianoforte is quite remarkable.'

That was good to hear! He had lapsed into a delightful daydream in which he and Eleanor sat, hand in hand, in a darkened concert hall, occasionally turning their heads to gaze fondly into each other's eyes – when he became aware that Maria had turned her head and was gazing at him expectantly, her normally serious face alight with laughter.

'I'm sorry, Maria. My thoughts were elsewhere. Please forgive me!'

'You should forgive *me*, Ted, for clearly, your thoughts were most pleasant and should not have been interrupted! I was only enquiring if you, too, enjoyed music?'

'Oh, very much! I should dearly love to hear Eleanor perform. Does she also sing?'

'Oh, we all sing, even Martha! Mama has a truly lovely voice and Papa sang in the choir for many years. You should hear us when the nights draw in and we gather round the parlour piano.'

Oh, that he should be allowed such a privilege!

In such enjoyable conversation was the journey passed. As they drew up in the Woodhead yard and young John, his face creased in a broad smile, came out of the barn to take the pony from the shafts, Martha appeared from the house.

'Hello, Ted. I'm all ready.'

'Give the poor man a chance,' Maria remonstrated. 'He may care for some refreshment before his lesson.'

'Well, I just thought, as it's such a lovely day, we could go for a ride out.'

'So soon? Ted's only had one lesson.'

'But he shows exceptional promise,' Martha insisted. 'And we'll go somewhere quiet. Out towards Parkside Farm, I thought. The horses are all ready.'

And indeed, Ted saw that Midnight, already saddled and bridled, was hitched to a post at the far side of the yard, and beside him was a piebald horse.

Five minutes later, they were tittupping down the drive. 'Pressure on the left rein and the right knee,' Martha directed as they approached the end of it.

Obediently, Ted did as he was instructed and Midnight swung obligingly to the left. But probably, Ted mused, he would have done so anyway since he seems permanently glued to his stable-mate Badger's rump. Eager to see if he did indeed have some control, he applied a firm and steady pressure to Midnight's flanks, and to his great delight the animal responded immediately, moving up at a shambling trot to edge alongside Martha.

'Well done!' she said. 'Now we can talk.'

Tentatively, Ted enquired if they might trot for a little.

Martha deliberated, but decided they should keep to a walk for the moment.

It was just as well, for the next moment, a governess cart, drawn by a mettlesome high-stepping bay pony, came smartly round the bend ahead and headed straight for them.

223

'Whoa, there! Steady, girl!' The driver stood up in his seat to apply additional pressure upon the reins and the cart drew up with only a few feet to spare. Taking the least line of resistance, Midnight promptly sidled into the ditch, but Badger, as befitted a veteran, gave only a token buck, although rolling his eyes fiercely at the intruder.

'Miss Martha, pray forgive me! And Mr Smith, isn't it? Do forgive me, sir!' The driver of the cart was profuse in his apologies.

'Think nothing of it, sir,' replied Ted courteously, emerging from the ditch. The driver, he now realised, was the Winwick curate, James Carson, whom he had met at the fête.

After he was assured Ted was unscathed, the curate prepared to drive away.

'Please inform Miss Eleanor that I shall be calling upon her before too long. *She* will know the purpose of my visit.' And with that enigmatic remark, he vanished in a cloud of dust.'

'Now what did he mean by that?' Ted mused as they resumed their walk, his curiosity getting the better of his manners; for indeed, he had no right to enquire.

Martha gazed at him shrewdly then, looking straight ahead between her horse's ears, said innocently, 'Why, to fix the date, no doubt.'

'What date?'

'Well, I'm not *sure* about what I am going to tell you, Ted, so please do not repeat it to anyone. But I should be surprised if there is not some cause for celebration at Woodhead before long.'

His mouth was suddenly dry as a bone, his limbs weak, his concentration non-existent. Had Midnight chosen that moment to gallop away across the fields, he would have been unseated within seconds. 'You mean. . . ?

'Well, Nellie *is* quite an attractive young lady, Ted, you must admit. Quite the catch of the county! The only question is – which of her young men will she finally choose?'

So there *was* more than one! His worst fears confirmed, he nodded dully. 'Who, for instance?' Not that their names would mean anything to him.

'Well. . . .' Martha screwed up her face in concentration. 'There's Ernest Mather, for one. He's the son at Parkside Farm, where we're heading for now. Not as many acres as Woodhead, but she'd be doing quite well for herself.'

Better even than a first officer with the White Star Line? 'Who else?' he forced himself to ask, like a tongue probing at a sore tooth.

Martha shot him a quick glance. 'Give Midnight a longer rein, Ted, while we're walking. Now, who else? I suppose you could say Richard Athy was one of her favourites, and then there's George Moister of Red Bank – they both live close at hand in the village.' While he was thousands of miles away in America, or some other distant country.

'That's Parkside Farm, by the way, although I don't see Ernest.' Martha pointed ahead to a huddle of farm buildings dominated by a house of rose-red brick. 'But we'll turn off here down Barrow Lane and have a little trot.'

'Having a little trot' took all his energy and concentration if he were not to be unseated.

'Well done!' Martha slowed at last. 'We'll go home by Back Lane, then take the path across the fields.'

They could have ridden through the Sahara Desert for all he cared. But taking the path meant they had to go in single file, so he was spared further conversation.

'Now, don't forget,' Martha cautioned him as they rode up the Woodhead drive, 'not a word about you-know-what!'

Eleanor was back; that, at least, was some comfort. And pleased, it seemed, to see him.

'Ive left Mama at Delf House. But I wanted to get back to apologise for not meeting you at the station, Ted.'

'Maria,' he said gallantly, 'was a splendid substitute. And Martha has been looking after me too.' They were all, including little Ada, the servant girl, drinking tea around the big kitchen table.

'Weren't you going to show Ted the view from the attics,

Nellie?' Maria asked. 'That is, if Ada doesn't mind. The best view of the Mersey,' she explained to Ted, 'is from Ada's bedroom.'

'I'll come too,' said Martha, as Ada assured Eleanor that no, of course she wouldn't mind.

'There's ginger cake in the tin, Martha,' said Maria quickly. 'And those scones,' she pointed to the tray of freshly baked scones cooling on the window-ledge, 'should be ready to eat now.'

'I'll take some with me.'

'You'll do no such thing! You know Mama doesn't approve of food in the bedrooms.'

'Nor would she approve of Nellie taking Ted into one of them alone,' asserted Martha virtuously.

Ted had a sneaking suspicion she was probably right, but he certainly wasn't going to argue the point. There was too much at stake.

'Come along, Ted.' And Eleanor ran lightly up the wide stairway ahead of him.

Ada's room, compared with some of the maids' rooms he'd heard about, was most adequately, if simply, furnished, and the window of a reasonable size. They knelt at its broad sill, and suddenly into Ted's mind came a picture of another situation in which he and Eleanor might be kneeling side by side, and with the Reverend Carson facing them. The thought, heightened by emotion and his recent conversation with Martha, was both too wonderful and too unlikely to consider for long. But it had the effect of rendering him almost speechless.

'Look, Ted! You can see the masts quite clearly! Now which, d'you suppose, are the *Republic's*?'

It was, of course, a nonsensical question and he was sure that Eleanor, in normal circumstances, would never have posed it, for the masts and rigging of the ships anchored in the Mersey were no more than a fretwork forest against the deep blue sky. So was she, perhaps, seeking a suitable opening to tell him that she was going to marry Ernest, Richard or George?

226

He did his best to keep the conversational ball afloat, replying to her somewhat incoherent enquiries about life on shipboard as best he could.

And then, through the trees, they saw Mrs Pennington rounding the corner by Monk House. In a few more minutes, she would be home.

'We'd better go down,' said Eleanor reluctantly.

They came out on to the landing and walked towards the head of the stairs, Ted just behind Eleanor. Gazing down at the beribboned knot of her hair, bitterly regretting the waste of his lost oportunity, he suddenly found himself seeking for a stair that, inexplicably, simply wasn't there. The next moment, he was sprawling in a most ungainly fashion upon the stairs and Eleanor was crouched beside him.

'Ted, are you all right? I should have warned you about that stair. The top tread, for some reason, is much deeper than the others. You don't notice it on the way up but on the way down . . .'

Her words died away, for Ted, overcome by her nearness, so close that her hair brushed his cheek and the scent of it filled his nostrils, put his arms around her and drew her close.

'Oh, Eleanor, I do love you so!' And now his lips were seeking hers and she, if not actually responding as passionately, was certainly not drawing back. The ecstasy of it! The bliss! It was like suffering a seizure, yet with no pain but only acute breathlessness; this, in the end, caused him to draw back — a fraction.

'Eleanor, my love, my darling girl!'

'Ted. . . .' For a second he feared a rebuff, but then saw that her eyes were bright and shining. And then Maria's voice came floating up the stairwell — very loud and clear.

'Come and sit down, Mama. I'll pour you a cup of tea.'

Hand in hand, they ran, sure-footed now, down the stairs.

'We'll talk later, Ted,' Eleanor promised before pushing open the kitchen door.

'I'm sure, my love, as sure as I'll ever be.'

'Ted, this is only the fourth time we have met.'

'But I knew the moment I clapped eyes on you.'

'You were half-concussed at the time!'

'And doubly so, after I'd looked at you!'

It was late afternoon and they were on top of the Tump, a solid sand-stone construction, not quite as high as the barn, that stood in the field below the house. A good five foot across at the top, it was just the right size for one person to stand and gaze out across the surrounding fields; for which purpose, Eleanor had informed him, it would probably have been built long ago, perhaps by her grandfather.

It was also, Ted had pointed out, just the right size for two people not averse to each other's company to sit and 'repel boarders'; for it could only be reached by the steps cut into one side of it.

'But if we stay quiet, no one will even know we're here,' he'd said jubilantly. Gone now were all his fears and inhibitions, and not even Eleanor's apparent lack of belief in the strength of his feelings could upset him now that he had actually declared himself.

'Surely,' he said, 'you felt something for me, too? Surely it was not completely one-sided?'

'I was far too concerned about your injuries to think of anything else.'

'But afterwards, when we sat together at lunch, you felt – something?'

'Oh, I admit I found you a most personable young man. And quite unlike any I had met before.'

'Quite unlike Ernest Mather or Richard What's-his-name or George Thingummybob?' he couldn't resist asking, quite forgetting Martha's embargo.

Eleanor wrinkled her brow in obvious puzzlement. 'Ernest Mather? Why, Ted, what on earth has he got to do with anything?'

It was too late now to retract. And in any case, he was beginning to think it would be no more than Martha's just deserts that Eleanor should know of her revelations. He gave her the gist of them.

'The little monkey! Just wait until I get my hands on her!' And then she began to laugh, so hard that Ted, whipping out his handkerchief, leaned forward to wipe the tears from her cheeks. And then, while he was about it, kissed her lightly upon the mouth. At least, he meant it to be only lightly, but only a fool would have drawn back voluntarily from such an exquisite experience.

'Ted, we shall fall off, if we're not careful.'

That was true. 'Tell me about Ernest Mather, then.'

'Let me see. . . .' She calculated quickly on her fingers. 'He must be all of ten years old by now and in my Sunday School class for the last two of them. And yes indeed, we do get on exceedingly well together.'

'And this Richard and this George of − Red Bank, was it?'

'Ah!' And now Eleanor's voice grew soft and dreamy. 'Now that is quite a different kettle of fish! Martha must have meant George Moister, a most presentable, upright young man of about my own age and with an excellent position as carpenter at the reformatory. Unfortunately. . . .' She paused, shaking her head sadly.

'Unfortunately?' Ted prompted.

'Jane Moister found him first!' Her laughter rang out again. 'They are a devoted couple and I doubt if George has ever looked at another woman, nor ever will. And this Richard − she must mean Mr Athy, who is superintendent of the reformatory − *he* is kept well in hand by his wife Emily, and anyway is old enough to be my father. Poor Ted − you were indeed taken for a ride, in more ways than one!'

'Nothing matters now, except to hear you say you love me − just a little − and that one day, will marry me.'

But Eleanor would not be rushed. 'Let us say, for the moment, that I have the warmest regard for you, Ted. Anyway, can you imagine what Mama would say if we were to tell her we wished to marry after such a short acquaintance?'

'*My* mother would be delighted.'

'*Your* mother, from what you have told me, is a quite exceptional lady on every count. But I think even she might understand that I do not want everything to happen at once, that I wish to savour every precious moment of your courtship.'

'By the way,' Ted asked when, a moment or two later, they were obeying Maria's call to tea, 'what did the Reverend Carson want to talk to you about? If . . .' he added hastily, 'I may ask.' At this delicate stage of their relationship, presumption must be avoided at all costs.

Eleanor chuckled. 'He wishes to discuss Martha's suitability as a Sunday school teacher. It *could* be the making of her!'

32

Eleanor was right, he decided, to insist that their 'under-standing' remain secret, for it served only to strengthen the bond that grew steadily between them during the remainder of that year of 1885. When in company, he was careful to show her no more attention than courtesy demanded. Only occasionally did he allow his gaze to linger upon her; as she leaned, perhaps, over the keyboard of the parlour piano, while Martha, watch in hand, timed her rendering of Chopin's *Minute Waltz* to the last second, or in the hayfield, when even he was pressed into service and he would look up from stook or stubble to see her with Maria at the edge of the field, carrying the baskets in which their lunch was packed. Such pictures he stored away in his mind, to be taken out and gloated over during those long, often un-eventful watches while he paced the bridge of *Republic*.

Dog-roses gave way to meadowsweet and the giant purple thistles beloved by butterflies and then, overnight it seemed, the hedges were bright with the scarlet and crimson of hips and haws and the purple bloom of sloes. Expeditions were made to gather elderberries for wine and blackberries for preserves; and sometimes, when Martha was persuaded to accompany her mother on a round of calls, and Maria, suddenly busy with the household accounts, declared that she 'had not a moment to spare', he and Eleanor would be despatched alone.

Those were precious times, when he could allow his eyes to feast upon her for as long as she would permit it. Sometimes, she would delight him by coming, unbidden, into his arms and he would hold her, gently at first and then closer and closer – until he could feel the steady beat of her heart through the material of her dress and it took all his willpower to explore no further; for there must be no surreptitious fumbling behind a hedgerow, no guilty aftermath of regret. When, God willing, he claimed her, it must be a sweet and total surrender, unsullied by haste and furtiveness.

He still visited Hanley frequently but perhaps not quite as regularly, and Ma began to gaze at him with shrewd, discerning eyes.

'Everything all right, son?'

'Everything's fine, Ma.'

'Thirza tells me they see little more of you in Runcorn than when they lived here. Still busy with that horse, are you?'

And he, although so proficient now that he and Martha often acted as outriders to Eleanor in the trap, would say, 'Still learning, Ma. Still a long way to go!'

And she would hum and ha, clearly not believing a word of it – for had he not always been quick to learn, whether it be at marbles or mathematics? – until one day he relented and admitted that soon, he hoped, he would bring 'a young lady' to visit her.

'Well, don't leave it too long, lad. I'm not as young as I was.'

'You're as young as you feel, Ma. So that must make you all of seventeen!'

But even so, he hoped it wouldn't be too long. Ma must dance at his wedding, that was for sure.

Thomas was lucky if he saw him at all that summer and autumn, although he always made a point of calling in for a quick pint after docking.

'I should think Midnight is worn down to his fetlocks by now,' Thomas observed on one occasion. 'And your friend Bert called in the other day and remarked that you must be the most accomplished rider in all Cheshire.'

'All right is he? Bert?'

'Right as ninepence. Told me to tell you your godchild's

being brought up in a God-fearing manner, no thanks to you!'

'Good old Bert. He'll understand how it is.'

'So do I, numskull! So do I!'

They were good friends – none better.

It was at New Year that their 'understanding' became an official engagement. Christmas Day, he'd spent at sea – just as well, perhaps, for he would have been grievously torn between Winwick and Hanley – but New Year's Eve found him at Woodhead, caught up in the preparations for the party the Penningtons were giving.

'Eleanor all right?' Ted asked Maria once he'd been hugged and kissed by everyone, except Eleanor. She was busy stirring some spicy concoction on the stove and had barely acknowledged his arrival, except to turn her head and call, 'Hello, Ted,' as if he was just back from a ride with Martha.

'Yes, I think so. But she's been a little strange of late. Last week, I caught her with a calendar marking off the days until you were due in at Liverpool, but now, I must admit, she does seem a little pre-occupied. But don't worry, Ted. I'm sure she's as delighted to see you as the rest of us.'

In spite of Maria's reassurance, Ted was still feeling decidedly worried. However, he asked her mother if there was anything he could do.

'Yes, Ted,' Mrs Pennington responded. 'You can pop down to Piper's Hole for me, if you would, for some crystallised ginger.'

'Of course.' Pleased to be occupied, he donned his ulster and went out into the gathering dusk. Piper's Hole, according to John Pennington, had once been the place where they made pipes from the white clay that was dug in the area, but it was now Mr and Mrs Winstanley's grocer's shop.

Soon after he'd started coming to Woodhead, he'd met the Winstanleys and told them about Ma having also been in the trade. Ever since, they'd been punctilious in their enquiries after her health and had frequently sent her little

233

presents: a tin of Huntley and Palmer's biscuits, perhaps, or a bag of the toffee that Mrs Winstanley made to sell in the shop. To offer payment would have been ungracious, but now, with the arrival of their first-born – a daughter – Ted had seen an opportunity to reciprocate. In his pocket, he had not one but a whole family of plush velvet rabbits, bought last week in Macy's, with Mattie's help.

Mrs Pennington's requirements seen to, he was invited into the cosy living-room behind the shop to inspect baby Lydia. Naturally, he expressed deep admiration, although he could see little of her inside the swathes of pink shawl in which she nestled. 'A present from Woodhead,' Mrs Winstanley said proudly.

'And I have a small gift, too, Mrs Winstanley, if you would be kind enough to accept it. From Ma and me.' And he produced his rabbits.

Mrs Winstanley was profuse in her gratitude. 'All the way from New York, too! Thank you, Captain Smith – and your dear mother, of course.' He'd been 'Captain Smith' to the Winstanleys ever since the day he'd gone into the shop in his uniform, and no amount of explanation had made the slightest difference. What they would call him when he did qualify, he could only guess. Commodore, no doubt!

Their good wishes for the New Year ringing in his ears, he walked slowly back up the Woodhead drive, hoping that the other gift he'd brought all the way from New York – which Mattie had *not* helped him to choose – would be as acceptable to its recipient. A light snow had begun to fall and he quickened his pace, thinking gratefully of the warm house that awaited him and of the party ahead. If only Eleanor . . .

'P-s-s-t! Ted!' A figure in a long dark cloak came through the gate of the garden at the side of the house.

'Eleanor, my love!'

She came immediately into his arms and there was no doubt now of the warmth of her welcome. The hood of her cloak fell back and a snowflake landed squarely on the end of her nose. Quickly, he bent to kiss it away.

234

'My darling girl, you mustn't get cold.'

'I know! But Mama sent me to unlock the front door, ready for the first-footing, and I couldn't resist waiting for you. I wanted to tell you something.'

His heart leaped. Was his patience to be rewarded at last?

'I've made you wait long enough, Ted. I'm ready, if you are, to announce our engagement.'

'Ready? Oh, my dearest girl, you know that I've been ready since the moment I first saw you!' And now he was feeling in his pocket for that little box bearing the name of the Fifth Avenue jeweller.

'Eleanor, please do not think that I was taking your acceptance for granted, but when I was shopping for gifts in New York, I couldn't resist choosing something for you. And I saw this in a window. But the young lady assured me that they would be happy to exchange it for something else if it was not to your liking.'

He opened the box to reveal a ring that, even in that half-light, flashed with points of green fire. It was an emerald, set in a circle of tiny seed pearls, the whole clasped between two minute golden hands.

'Oh, Ted! It is *very* much to my liking!'

He took her left hand and slid the ring carefully on to her finger – it was a perfect fit.

'Ted, how did you know the size so accurately?'

'D'you remember one afternoon in the summer, when I wound a piece of grass around your finger? Well, it wasn't just a passing whim.'

'You are so clever!' Eleanor peered down at her hand. 'The simplest of rings would have sufficed, but this is beautiful. Thank you, my dearest. I, too, have a gift for you, but I am afraid you must wait for it. Mama will be sending out a search party if I do not go back soon.'

She took off the ring and gave it back to him. 'I thought, if we were to announce it as soon as John has first-footed, that it would be a double cause for celebration.'

'Trouble with the bolts?' Mrs Pennington enquired, not bothering to turn round from the table and the cake she

235

was icing as Eleanor led the way into the kitchen. The front door at Woodhead was rarely used except on ceremonial occasions, most people finding it far more convenient to step inside from the yard.

'I think perhaps a little oil would be beneficial,' Ted observed. 'We had the greatest difficulty, had we not, Eleanor, in persuading them to move.'

'The greatest,' she agreed solemnly.

The room grew suddenly silent; everyone stopped whatever they were doing and looked up in surprise. But it was left to Martha to put it into words.

'Well, I know you're a clever one, Ted. But I don't see how even you could pull back the bolts from the *outside*!'

He glanced quickly at Eleanor. Should they try to bluff it out? But her eyes were like stars, her cheeks flushed and, most incriminating of all, her hair was white with snow.

So there was nothing for it, then, but to tell them everything, to show them the ring and succumb to the kisses and hugs and handshakes.

'Mama and I were hoping you would not wait too long,' said Maria.

'And I,' said Martha jubilantly, 'will now win my wager with Martha Hindley. A whole sixpence, she bet me, that you'd announce it next year. But I insisted you could never wait so long and it would be this year.'

So much for secrecy!

'I'd begun to think Ted had left it too late.' Ma, twinkling benevolently over the spectacles she now wore, held Eleanor's hand in hers. 'But now – well, I can see that you were well worth waiting for, my dear! That's all I can say.'

But it was enough. Eleanor, as pretty as a picture in a gown of pale lilac wool with a matching jacket, dimpled and smiled and assured her mother-in-law to be that she would do her very best to care for her son in the manner to which he had been accustomed.

'And when is the wedding to be?' Ma asked.

'No date has been agreed,' Eleanor told her, 'but we

236

thought perhaps the late summer, after harvest. If that is a convenient time for you and the rest of Ted's family.'

'Any time would suit me,' said Ma, 'for I am a lady of leisure these days, drat it! But we shall have to consult Thirza and William, of course. James, working as he does for himself, would no doubt be able to manage any day you choose. And there are so many Smiths, it would probably be safer to invite none at all. But,' she wrinkled her nose at Ted, 'what about Joseph? Anna tells me he's not expected home until the beginning of next year.'

'Well, in that case, we will wait until next year,' said Eleanor firmly, 'for from what Ted has been telling me, it would not be a proper wedding without Joseph.'

And Ted, although greatly disappointed at having to wait so long for his bride, knew that he would not have it otherwise.

Later in the year, Ben Gleadell took over command of the *Republic* for a short while, and Ted found their relationship had changed subtly since his 'maiden' crossing on *Celtic*. Now, he was treated, if not as an equal, certainly as one who would be so before long; and Captain Gleadell seemed to feel an almost proprietorial interest in his future with White Star.

'It's as good a Line to work for as any, E.J.' he said one evening, when they were lingering over an after-dinner cigar. 'Scratch their back and they'll scratch yours.'

'In what way, sir?'

'Well, have you ever read the booklet the Company presents to the passengers, along with their tickets?'

'Scanned it fairly thoroughly, sir.'

'Then you'll be aware of the emphasis they place upon safety, telling them all about watertight, fireproof bulkheads and how we follow Maury's Shipping Lanes in order to avoid fog and ice – and other ships, of course. In short, they promise that no risk will be taken, that safety is paramount. Agreed?'

'Agreed.'

237

'But turn the pages,' Ben Gleadell continued, 'and what do you find? Paragraphs devoted to the White Star's reputation for *speed*. Chapters about the records we've broken. For they know full well that many of their first-class passengers are businessmen to whom time means money. But how can the poor, benighted Commander promise both speed and safety at one and the same time? But if his performance does not equal Company expect-ations, if he does not, at it were bring home the goods, then he's for it. Before you can say "knife" he'll be walking his own plank.'

'I seem to remember, sir,' said Ted slyly, 'that in that same booklet, *you* are held up as an example of another of the Company's virtues – its record for saving life at sea. I gather that *you* did not hesitate, back in '75, to steer the *Baltic* off course to effect the rescue of the crew of the *Oriental*, when the wreck was sighted.'

'But what the account does *not* mention,' Captain Gleadell pointed out,' is my subsequent worry about what would happen to me when I reached Liverpool considerably later than scheduled. But even there, you see, the crafty monkeys turned it to their own advantage, making me sound like St Christopher himself.'

He pulled deeply upon the butt of his cigar. 'Believe me, E.J., they've got you by the short and curlies every time. They'll never say, get your ship to New York or Liverpool or wherever on time, or else! But you know damned well, that's what they mean. It's all right when you're a young man. *You'll* probably relish the challenge of it – con your own ship into New York, no doubt, just to take a minute or two off the record – but when you're getting on in life, you begin to wonder if you're not just an instrument for other folks' ambition. I probably shouldn't be talking to you like this, but you're a good sailor, E.J. One day, perhaps, you'll remember what I've said. But now, I must stir my stumps and check the bridge before I turn in. Goodnight, E.J.'

'Goodnight, sir.' It was good of the old boy to talk to him

like this. Must be getting on for sixty now, and thinking of retirement, but a brave, conscientious master, for all that. And he was right about one thing, at least. It *would* be a challenge!

At Woodhead, little seemed to be spoken of but preparations for the wedding; Eleanor often expressing astonishment that they'd ever contemplated holding it earlier than next year. The other great event of 1887, the Queen's Jubilee, was rarely mentioned.

There was much discussion about where they should live after they were married. Clearly, it must be within easy travelling distance of Liverpool but also, Ted insisted, within easy access of Woodhead, for it could be a lonely life for a mariner's wife unless she had the company of family and friends.

'I understand Spa Well Cottage will be empty next year,' Eleanor said tentatively.

Ted knew Spa Well Cottage; it stood by itself at the end of Delf Lane, not far from Delf House, where Eleanor's cousin Mary lived with her parents. He agreed it would be very suitable.

'And an easy drive from Woodhead,' Eleanor added.

'But not in January and February,' Ted pointed out. 'Then, I understand, the mud makes it almost impassable and whoever is living there must prepare themselves for a long siege.'

'Ted, don't exaggerate!' But Eleanor was blushing. He had already explained how, with luck, he would be granted at least two months' away from the sea after their wedding, 'Anyway,' she added, 'it would take more than mud to keep the Marthas away.'

'Not if I have anything to do with it!'

33

Across the table, he caught Ma's eye. She could relax now. Her elderly, decrepit son was married at last!

And to what a bride! He turned his head to gaze fondly at her, a vision in creamy silk and pearl-encrusted lace. When the triumphant burst of the *Wedding March* had rung out in St Oswald's that morning, and he had turned, Joseph at his side, to see her upon John's arm, pacing slowly, demurely and yet proudly up the long aisle towards him, he could hardly believe his eyes – nor his good fortune. Was this dream of loveliness really to be his? It had needed Joseph's nudge and whispered, 'Go on, lad!' to bring him to his senses and move forward to join her in front of the Reverend Carson.

But from then on, he had needed no bidding.

'I, Edward John, take thee, Sarah Eleanor. . . .'

Responses and vows had been clearly spoken, and the rings safely exchanged. Even the sudden sob, quickly stifled, from behind him had disturbed him hardly at all. For it had come from Ma, and she, looking quite magnificent under a toque of violets set atop the silver wings of her hair, must be allowed to show a little emotion upon this memorable day when her youngest son had come at last 'safely into port'.

Afterwards had come the procession into the vestry, with John and Maria witnessing for Eleanor, and Joseph and Thomas for himself, and the Reverend Carson addressing them, for the first time, as 'Mr and Mrs Smith'. Then it was back down the aisle, with the organ going full blast – Vivaldi, was it? – between pews of Penningtons and Hindleys to starboard and a hotchpotch of Hancocks and Harringtons, with a sprinkling of Smiths and Browns, to port.

Out into the crisp winter sunshine, then, with Eleanor's Sunday school pupils cheering their heads off and the clash of bells overhead; a moment's pause while Eleanor laid her posy of Christmas roses upon her father's grave, and then he'd seized her hand and they were running, laughing and breathless, between the handfuls of stinging rice to where Kennedy, resplendent in a new smock, stood beside an open carriage lined with evergreens, and with Midnight, a bow of scarlet ribbon upon his headband, between the shafts. There was more cheering and waving from the little knots of villagers at the roadside who had braved the cold to wish them well. They drove past Monk House – with a great placard tied to the gate   BEST WISHES TO THE HAPPY COUPLE – past Piper's Hole, with the Winstanleys in the doorway and little Lydia held high in the air, and then the comparative calm of the Woodhead drive and a few precious seconds alone before they reached the house.

The marquee, hired from Chester for the occasion, was already a-bustle with helpers pouring wine, arranging chairs, tending the charcoal braziers set about the wooden flooring. There was time only for Eleanor to adjust her wreath of camellias – sent by the rector from the hothouses of Winwick Hall – before the families arrived, then it was a matter of lining up quickly to welcome the guests: he and Eleanor, John and his mother, Ma – seated, of course – with Joseph at her side.

But now the formalities were over, the meal eaten – such a wealth of meats and vegetables, such a plethora of puddings and pies – the speeches made and toasts drunk, and everyone thanked for whatever part they had played to make the day such a success. Soon, very soon now, Eleanor would disappear into the house to change into her going-away costume and Kennedy would drive them to the station for the London train. But for a few precious minutes, he would sit here and enjoy the united presence of his family, for heaven alone knew when they

241

would all be together again.

Ma, he noticed, had withdrawn from the table and was sitting, the purple toque just a little tilted over one eye, with Ted's uncle George. Anna and Joseph, still at the table, were unashamedly gazing into each other's eyes with all the enjoyment of a loving couple who had been separated for many months. Even so, he was more than a little worried about Joseph.

About the same age as Ben Gleadell, he looked much older; both his beard and hair were now completely white, his face heavily lined. At least his seafaring days were now over; soon, they would be moving into the snug little house at Seacombe, on the Wirral, that Anna had found.

Thirza, he had no worries over at all, for Runcorn had brought the roses into her cheeks. Annie was keeping company with a young man, and little Ned – now no longer little, but towering above his father – was happily settled in his boarding-school at Chester. William, too, seemed content enough in the engineering works; and James was flourishing in his business at Hanley.

It occurred to him that it wasn't only Eleanor's status that had altered during the morning's ceremony. All his life, until now, 'home' had meant Ma. Throughout his schooldays and the long years before the mast, telling Ma about the things that had happened, be they good or bad, had been part of his life – and of hers. When under steam, he'd been obliged to take lodgings in Liverpool, but Hanley had been the place he'd made for as soon as he could, knowing that Ma would be waiting.

But now, although he'd still see Ma whenever circumstances allowed, Eleanor would be the most important woman in his life; the one to whom he would tell the innermost secrets of his mind and heart. It could not be otherwise, he knew but it seemed hard on Ma. If only there was some easy way he could convey his gratitude and appreciation, and, above all, his enduring love. . . .

But he needn't have worried; Ma, as always, took command of the situation. 'Thank you, son,' she said when he put out a gentle hand to straighten her toque. 'I didn't want to wear the dratted thing in the first place. But Thirza said I must do you credit today, of all days.'

'You've always done me credit, Ma, and I just wanted to say thank you – for all that you've done for me and all that you've meant to me.' And now, there was a tremor in his voice; only a slight one, but Ma noticed it. She put out a hand and stroked his cheek.

'I know, Ted, I know! And I thank *you* – for everything. But now you must go. Eleanor will be waiting.'

He took refuge in the magic formula. 'Must go away, Ma . . .'

'Just so you can come home!' Now Ma's voice broke too, and he saw that her hands were tightly clenched around the little beaded bag in her lap and knew that he must prolong her pain no further. Kissing her swiftly upon the cheek, he went to find his wife.

'We went to the pantomime for the Marthas' Christmas treat, Ted. Did they tell you? *Sinbad the Sailor* at the Alexander in Liverpool. Such storms on the stage as even you could never have seen! And what do you suppose our Martha whispered to me when the good ship *Nevergetthere* was wrecked?'

'I can't imagine, my dear. What did she whisper?' They were seated at dinner in the otherwise deserted dining-room of the quiet family hotel in Kensington. It had been after eight when they arrived, and now, as the hands of the ornate marble clock upon the mantelpiece moved steadily nearer the time when they must retire, Eleanor's tongue seemed to be gaining in impetus.

'Why,' she exclaimed, 'that Ted would never have allowed such a disaster to occur!'

'Eleanor, my love, I think that the waitresses may wish to clear.'

'Of course!' Instantly contrite, Eleanor rose to her feet. 'I'm so sorry if we have delayed you,' she told the waitresses, as they immediately sprang to attention.

243

Their room was all that he could have wished: red velvet curtains drawn against the winter's night – snow had been falling when they'd hurried from their cab – a bowl of tawny chrysanthemums upon a table in the window alcove, giving off their spicy scent, snowy bedlinen already turned back over an immaculate counterpane, rose-shaded lamps set about the room, and before the brightly burning fire, the luxuriant softness of a huge sheepskin rug.

Eleanor took one look at the bed and turned away – only to find herself imprisoned in the circle of Ted's arms. Gently he pushed her backwards until she was forced to sit upon the bed; he sat beside her.

'Eleanor, my dearest, I can guess how you are feeling. But I have been given to understand one's wedding night need not be a rude awakening.' He paused.

'You have been given to understand, Ted? You mean. . . ?'

He nodded. 'I mean that I am as inexperienced as you.'

He had never lied to her; even so, she could hardly believe him. 'But Ted, I had thought that all men . . . and particularly sailors. . . . Those foreign ports . . .'

'Ports where I have seen sights that convinced me I should remain celibate. You have no idea, my love, nor ever will, I trust, what a dreadful fate can await men who are promiscuous in their passions. And, even more dreadful, who may bring grievous harm to the women they may one day truly love. So, my dear one, we are both novices at the game, and so must help each other. But I promise you that I shall go as gently as you wish.'

'I know that you will, Ted.' There was complete trust as well as love in her eyes, and he prayed to God that he would have the patience and forbearance and the instinct to act as he wished to.

Slowly, painstakingly, making her laugh with him over the complexities of unfamiliar buttons and hooks and tapes, he undressed her until she stood naked upon the white rug, her hair unbound, the firelight flickering over the milky softness of her long, elegant limbs.

Quickly taking off his own clothes, he drew her down

244

on to the rug and then, with infinite gentleness, began to trace the exquisite curve of her breasts, lingering upon the rosy pinnacles of the nipples, until she began to moan softly and turn towards him. But his hands were moving downward now, over the dimpled smoothness of her belly, down into the warm, damp softness of that dark triangle, probing seeking, until there was no doubting her response, as she drew him into her with only the tiniest of gasps at the moment of penetration. There came then a climax of such sweetness, he fell across her, burying his face in the warm valley of her breasts.

'I love you, Eleanor.'

'I love you, Ted.'

Now he knew that they truly belonged to each other.

'I'm so glad,' said Eleanor next morning as they walked in Hyde Park, pausing occasionally to watch the skaters upon the Serpentine or gaze up into the frosted filigree of the trees, 'that we chose January for our wedding.' She wore a full-skirted coat of cherry-red velour with a matching scarf and a fur-trimmed hat, and Ted a heavy, caped ulster and brown bowler, a silver-topped cane clutched in his hand. They were, they considered, as fashionably dressed as any of the other men and women braving the elements on that wintry morning.

Returning to their hotel for luncheon, they found a little match girl on the corner of their street, shivering under the meagre covering of a garment apparently made entirely of sacking.

'Matches, kind sir?' Hopefully, she held out her tray with its few pathetic bundles of vespas.

'Just what I wanted!' And indeed, he did require some to light the cigar that Eleanor had agreed he might smoke in the gentleman's smoking-room after their meal, while she sat leafing through the journals or chatting to other residents in the ladies retiring-room.

'I'm sorry sir, I don't 'ave no change.' She stared, as if hypnotised, at the sovereign he had placed upon her tray.

'No, that is perfectly all right, my dear. I have no change either. Please keep it.'

''Onest, sir? You won't go tellin' the rozzers as 'ow I've pinched it?'

'No,' he assured her gravely, he would not be calling the rozzers. But he would like to ask, if he might, what she would do with the sovereign.

'Why, take it back to my ma, sir. Sharpish!'

'And what will she do with it?' he pressed.

'Coals, sir. Bread. Lump o' cheese. P'raps some scraps from the butcher, if we're lucky.'

Impulsively, Eleanor unwound the long red scarf from about her neck and gently wound it around that of the child, pulling it up as far as it would go over her head and crossing it at the back to tie around her skinny waist. 'There, that'll help to keep you warm.'

The waif, dazed by such munificence, still managed to stammer a breathless, 'Th-thank 'ee, ma'am!'

'I just hope,' Ted murmured as they moved away, 'that her ma doesn't sell it.'

But her ma didn't sell it. Next morning, when they came out of the hotel to take a hansom to Richmond – where, they had heard, the snow was so deep that the deer in the Park were being fed by hand – the waif was there at the corner swathed in scarlet.

'As bright as a pillar-box,' Ted murmured to Eleanor.

The waif's pinched little face cracked into a broad smile when she saw them. 'Ma said to say thank 'ee. And she's sent you this.'

And from the tray, she took a little bag of pale blue calico, tied at the neck with white ribbon. 'Smell,' she instructed Eleanor, holding it up to her nose.

'Why, it's lavender! How lovely!' Eleanor took the bag. 'Please thank your mother, my dear.'

'She makes 'em!' said the waif proudly. 'Gets the lavender cheap from a woman in the room next to ours 'oo 'as an auntie out Peckham way, and then buys material from a shop.'

'Then what does she do with them?' Eleanor asked.

'I takes 'em instead o' matches when she's done enough.'

'They're just the thing to take home for presents,' declared Eleanor. 'We shall be here for another ten days at least. Is that not so, Ted? So I should be greatly obliged if your mother could make me a dozen or so before we leave.'

'I'll tell 'er, ma'am. And thank 'ee!'

'What is your name?' Ted asked as he purchased his matches. 'And I'm afraid I still have no change.'

'Addie, sir. Short for Adelaide.'

'Well, Addie, we shall look forward to seeing you to-morrow.'

And so Addie became part of the pattern of their days. No matter how early they were each morning, she would be there. And often with a little gift: a bunch of violets, drooping somewhat but still sweetly-smelling, or a carnation in a maidenhair spray, its petals only a little brown at the edges. And each night, Ted would set out a gold sovereign upon the chest of drawers, along with his pocket watch and his cuff-links and two fresh white handkerchiefs – one for display and one for use.

It was, they were told, the coldest winter London had seen for many years. 'I'm just so grateful,' Eleanor told him once, 'that Addie's no longer on the corner when we come back at night, 'for I don't think I could bear to leave her there.'

'At least,' Ted said comfortingly, 'she will have a fire to go home to, now.'

The days passed swiftly, for there were many places to visit: the Tower of London, St Paul's, Westminster Abbey, Hampton Court.

'If we're lucky,' Eleanor said, 'we may even see the Queen.'

But the Queen, they read, was at Osborne, preparing, no doubt for the celebrations that lay ahead. Already, there was plenty of evidence in the shops that this year was to be *her* year – as well as the Smiths'. Pyramids of gaily-coloured mugs – most of which, Ted was pleased to see, bore the stamp of the Potteries – rows of enamelled tea caddies and biscuit tins, stacks of painted fans and trays, were all emblazoned with her picture. And there were tiny, revolving globes with the Empire picked out in bright pink, and dolls made in her image, too. 'It's a wonder,' said Ted wickedly, 'they don't put her on the chamber-pots!'

Shopping for presents to take home took up a great deal of their time when they were not sightseeing, attending the concerts at St James's Hall or viewing the exhibitions at Burlington House; although it was the theatres, perhaps, that they enjoyed the most. Indeed, their stay was extended by several days so that they might see Mr Beerbohm Tree in *Hard Hit*, his new comedy at the Haymarket. And along with half London, the catchy tune *Queen of my Heart* from *Dorothy*, the comic opera showing at the Gaiety, was rarely off their lips.

But perhaps the highlight of their stay was the new Gilbert and Sullivan production at the Savoy; so new, its title of *Ruddigore* was not even decided upon until the very first night of its performance. 'Imagine,' grumbled Ted, 'launching a ship without knowing its name!'

And running like a golden thread through the tapestry of their days was the knowledge that each night would bring them even greater delight; for now it was as if each strove to surpass the other in the giving of endless pleasure.

'I shall miss Addie,' Eleanor said at breakfast on the morning of their departure.

'And she us, I fear, but we shall pay her handsomely for the lavender bags,' Ted comforted her.

One morning, soon after their return, Ted was delighted when Eleanor, awakening him early with a kiss upon the end of his nose, reached under her pillow to bring out a jeweller's ring box. Inside, nestled a broad gold band set with one enormous agate, its dark, luminous surface veined by the finest threads of white chalcedony. She slid it on to his finger. 'Happy birthday, my darling!'

He was amazed that in the excitement of the wedding

and the honeymoon, she had even remembered the event, let alone found time to seek out such a handsome present. 'Thank you, sweetheart! It is a most glorious gift and one that I shall treasure for the rest of my life.'

Nearly three blissful months they had at Spa Well, before the letter came recalling him to *Republic*. But this time — and he could hardly believe his eyes — as her master.

34

He was in New York when Bruce Ismay was appointed owners' agent for the Line; the youngest, at twenty-five, to represent a leading shipping company although, as eldest son of a major share-holder, it was hardly surprising. So there were mutual congratulations when they met. Rumours were rife that Ismay might now live permanently in New York, for it was common knowledge that he was friendly with beautiful Florence Schieffelin, 'the Belle of New York' as the journalists called her.

At least, thought Ted, with some satisfaction, I'm ahead of him in the marriage stakes.

'Queen of my Heart,' he wrote to Eleanor from New York – for indeed, being away from her was causing a great loneliness of spirit – *'you are always in my thoughts and I long for the time when we shall be together again. Please keep on the tenancy of Spa Well, at least until the end of the summer. And threaten the Marthas with a flogging if they so much as set foot in Delf Lane while I am in residence!'*

In August, it was back to *Britannic* as first officer, but at least he could now be reasonably sure that the Line considered him suitable for promotion.

In February of the following year, in company with several of his colleagues, he sat and passed his extra master's certificate.

'This qualifies me to join the Royal Naval Reserve,' he told Eleanor.

Her face paled. 'You don't mean – to *fight* Ted?' There was always some skirmish or other going on in the vastness of the Empire.

'Don't worry, sweetheart! My task would only be to transport the troops to wherever the fighting was, then turn around in the most cowardly fashion and run for home. But it will mean that I shall have to go away on a course or two.'

Not that that would make much difference to Eleanor. They lived in Warrington now, and although this meant she was still within easy distance of Woodhead, it grieved him that she must spend so much time alone. One unexpected visitor she had was Annie's friend, Ted Meadowcroft, whose occupation as general merchant sometimes brought him to Warrington.

In April the Company again showed its approval by giving him the old *Baltic* to skipper on her final crossing; that same ship which Ben Gleadell had dared to steer from her scheduled route to pick up survivors from the *Oriental*.

Getting on in years she might be, but in her time she'd won the coveted Blue Riband for the Line, and so Ted treated her with the greatest respect and consideration. After all, he reasoned, it was almost as great an honour to bring a ship home on her final voyage as to take her out on her maiden. But he hoped, all the same, that he wouldn't wait too long for that particular privilege.

Surprisingly, it came much sooner than he'd dared anticipate – at the end of the year, on *Cufic*, White Star's first livestock carrier, still bound for New York.

Bruce Ismay, he discovered when he reached New York, had married his Florence in the Church of the Heavenly Rest; and in a quiet ceremony over on the East Side, without even telling her family, Mattie had become Mrs Seth Harrison.

'Honestly, Ted,' she pleaded when he protested that she had not let him know, '*no one* knew. Not even ourselves! We just suddenly upped and did it. No fuss! No bother! We just wore our usual working garb, although Seth did buy me a carnation. But that dropped off halfway through the ceremony. Carnations and me don't go together, somehow!'

Which was unlikely to be a sentiment expressed by the

new Mrs Bruce Ismay. She – so said the journal he bought to take home for Eleanor – had worn silver brocade with diamonds and pearls for her wedding, and carried a bouquet of white roses and lilies of the valley. Soon after the ceremony, they told him in the Company office, the couple had sailed for England on the *Adriatic*, to visit Ismay, Senior.

'But I'm afraid it's only beef cattle for you, Captain!'

'Suits me fine!' said Ted. Company officials were not his favourite cargo, with or without their wives.

Just after he and Eleanor had celebrated their second wedding anniversary, the Company gave him back *Republic* for her final crossing. But this time, disaster struck, and for a while he thought it might also be the final crossing for Edward John Smith.

'I tried to run before I could walk,' he confessed to Joseph when he finally got *Republic* back to Liverpool in one piece. 'I know the sailing directions for New York well enough. The pilot laws clearly state that masters of foreign vessels must either take on a pilot when entering harbour *or* pay the same pilotage. "Strangers", it goes on to say, "are strongly recommended to accept the earliest offer of a pilot". And that means at Sandy Hook.

'Well, I was no stranger, and ever since I first crossed on *Coptic*, I've itched to con my own ship right up the Narrows and into harbour. It was just one of those goals one sets oneself – like running a mile in six minutes or climbing to the top of the royals in one.'

Joseph nodded approvingly. It was such ambition, he considered, that divided men into those who were satisfied with their station in life and those who strove to rise above it; and Ted, even as a child, had always been a striver.

'This time,' Ted continued, 'I thought I'd try it, especially as it happened to be my birthday! Well, there's this rather tricky turn soon after Sandy Hook. Let me show you!' And he pulled from his pocket the rough chart he'd made. 'As you can see, you've got the South-West Spit, the first of the sandbanks, lying to starboard and the tip of Sandy Hook to port. The turn of the channel between them is about a hundred and ten degrees and the depth about six fathoms – plenty deep enough for *Republic*. There's nothing to obstruct the view, either. Had I not allowed my ambition to cloud my judgement, I should have managed it with ease. As it was, I took it too fast, went some considerable distance off track to where the depths began to shoal outwards from the turn – and grounded! Five hours we were stuck here, like a beached whale, the laughing-stock of every passing craft, before we were floated off.'

Joseph suppressed a smile. 'I shouldn't let it worry you too much, lad. I'll wager a box of Havanas to a quid of shag, you'll be trying the same manoeuvre again before long, but this time with a little more care.'

But Ted was not to be so easily consoled. 'I doubt,' he continued darkly, 'if any self-respecting pilot will condescend to board me again. I met one of them after we'd docked, and he said next time I wanted to con my own ship, would I please give due warning and they'd widen the channel!'

This time, Joseph laughed outright. 'I don't suppose the passengers were best pleased either,' he said, wiping his eyes.

'Nor the cooks! Having to conjure up an extra meal for well over a thousand people!'

'And what about the Company?'

'I'll know more about that tomorrow when I'm summoned to give an account of myself, but no doubt there'll be all hell to pay. Over in New York, it was treated lightly, compared with what happened next. In fact, Joseph, I'm a selfish bastard going on like this about something that was entirely my own fault and meant no more than a temporary inconvenience and loss of pride. What happened next was quite dreadful.'

He paused, his face suddenly that of a much older man. Joseph waited.

'It happened, thank God, after the passengers had landed – to find, incidentally, a streetcar strike in operation, which didn't improve their tempers! — and I was preparing to go ashore to make a clean breast of what had happened out on the Spit. Suddenly, there came a most tremendous bang somewhere in the bowels of the ship. It turned out that a furnace flue had fractured, killing three men outright and seriously injuring several others. You cannot imagine how terrible it all was.'

'At least,' Joseph dared to suggest, 'that was not your fault.'

'If it had been,' Ted said soberly. 'I doubt if I could have endured it. Fortunately, the doctor was still on board, but even so, there was little that could be done, except to call the city ambulances. And then to deal with the newspaper men who seem to have a nose for such disasters and appeared on the scene within minutes, like a swarm of angry bees. My first reaction was to buzz back at them, but then Company discipline asserted itself and I assured them that the damage to the ship had been slight, that she would be quickly repaired and that there was no reason to think, at the moment, that she would do other than leave for England on schedule.

'There was nothing I could say about the three poor fellows who had perished, except that their deaths would have been instantaneous. I did point out that some, at least, of those injured had been able to walk to the ambulances, but that was of little consolation.'

For a moment, he bowed his head. 'It's strange, Joseph. One expected these disasters in the old days under sail. A sudden storm, tempestuous seas, a fall from the rigging — there was little one could do in those circumstances, as you well know. But I don't expect it now, when man's inventive mind has made seafaring so much safer. So it's all the more shocking when disaster does strike.'

'Man proposes, God disposes,' said Joseph. 'We must always remember that, Ted. But now you must get home to Eleanor; she will be waiting for you.'

Ted brightened. 'Yes. How fortunate I am in that respect! But I'm glad I've seen you, Joseph.'

'So am I, lad. So am I.'

Ted need not have worried unduly. The Company seemed to have enough on its mind with the recent launching of the giant *Teutonic* – not a single sail, much to Joseph's chagrin! – to give him more than a routine caution, though they did rest him for a couple of blissful months before giving him *Celtic* in April.

And then, towards the end of the year, after one trip on *Adriatic*, came the news he had half expected. He was appointed to take *Coptic* on the South American – New Zealand run. A feather in his cap, of course, but he would have sacrificed even that for the privilege of serving in *Teutonic* – in any capacity whatsoever. For she had taken the Blue Riband for the Company, doing over *twenty* knots!

35

The public, the Line had decided in its wisdom, liked to spend Christmas at sea; ships' concerts, dances, meals prepared by other people, effortless festivities. That it was usually the last place the crew desired to be was not of the slightest significance. So Ted, back on the North Atlantic crossing, sailed for New York on the *Adriatic* on Christmas Eve 1890.

'Why don't I work in a bank?' he grumbled to Eleanor.

'Because,' she said candidly, 'you'd be no good at it. You never know where your own money goes, let alone managing other people's.'

In spite of his grumbling, Christmas Day passed very pleasantly. And it was good, a few days later, to see the familiar New York skyline as they steamed out of the Narrows and made for Ellis Island, where immigration was now carried out and from where dissembarking passengers could catch the Manhattan Ferry to the mainland.

Bruce Ismay, he discovered when he went to Broadway next day, had now become a partner in the firm, as had his younger brother James. And with the appointment had come the removal of his father-in-law's stipulation that he live in New York. Consequently, he had now removed to England with his wife and new baby.

It was the baby that gave Ted the only twinge of envy he'd ever felt for Bruce Ismay, for he knew that Eleanor would dearly love to bear a child. But so rare and rushed had been his appearances this last year, it would have been a miracle if she'd conceived.

The year 1891 should have been a good one – for in May

he was back on his beloved *Britannic* – but early in August came the news that Joseph's first grandson had given up his tenuous hold upon life in Savannah, and Joseph was inconsolable.

'He meant so much to me, Ted. My first grandson, born upon American soil, and bearing my name.'

'Will you and Anna go out there?'

'We think not, for Frank's wife is pregnant again and our presence would only serve to remind them of their loss. Besides, Frank has a new appointment now as book-keeper, and has much to do.'

For Thirza, however, the year was a good one. Ned was now an apprentice engineer and Annie had at last married her Ted, and was expected to give birth in September.

At Woodhead, Martha, following in the footsteps of Martha Hindley, was to be married.

'Mr Johnston is a most presentable young man, Ted, and they will be living at Myddleton, quite near Woodhead. Such a refined, ladylike creature she has become!' Eleanor told him.

'I'll believe it when I see it!'

Also occupying Eleanor's mind was their impending move to a larger house, The Poplars in Cow Lane, Great Sankey; a move which Eleanor's careful control of the family budget had now made possible. Thomas was also going up in the world – to Leinster Terrace, Runcorn, to be precise – so that Ada and Eleanor could happily make their plans together.

But in November '93 came the news that Ted had known must come, although he had tried not to think about it. Stout-hearted, spunky little Ma died, quite suddenly of a stroke.

'Although I think, Ted,' Thirza told him – for he'd been in New York at the time – 'that she had a premonition she was going. The night before, I went into her at bedtime, as usual, to make sure that all was well, and found her lying back on her pillows with a faraway look in her eyes. I asked her what she was thinking about.'

257

' "Oh, this and that! How things used to be. Feeling close," she said.

' "Close to whom, Ma?" I asked.

'The question seemed to surprise her. "To Edward, of course."

'I perched, then, on the edge of the bed and picked up one of her hands. Her fingers had grown a little gnarled of late, with arthritis, but they were still slender. "Do you often think about him, Ma?" I asked.

' "All the time. He's never far away. But then, none of you are. Even Ted." And then, after a moment, "You've been a good daughter to me, Thirza."

' "We've been through a lot together, Ma." I reminded her.

'She gave a little laugh then. "And Joseph! We had some happy times together, even after your pa had died."

'She seemed ready for sleep then, so I tucked her up, just as she had me when I was small. But before I could turn down the wick of her lamp, she suddenly caught my wrist. "Look after Ted for me, Thirza!" she said.

'I honestly thought she was wandering a little, in her mind. Thinking we were back in the days when I really did look after you when she was busy. But now, I think differently, I think she knew she was going to leave us that night.' Thirza dabbed her eyes. 'If only I'd stayed a little longer with her!'

'Now, don't you fret yourself, Thirza. Ma was right, you were always a good daughter to her. None better.' He waited while she mopped up her tears and blew her nose. 'And when you went up in the morning,' he prompted after a moment, not wanting to upset her, but needing desperately to know, 'she was. . . .?' He still couldn't actually frame the word. For death still seemed an impossible circumstance to overtake lively little ma.

'Well, it was obvious she'd had a stroke, but I'm sure as I can be, Ted, that she was with your Pa.'

And then he and Thirza both shed a few healing tears; as he and Joseph had, when his brother met him in

258

Liverpool and broke the news. But perhaps the most poignant moment of all came when the solicitor's letter dropped on the mat. At first, he thought there'd been some mistake.

I, Catherine Smith . . . bequeath to my son Edward John Smith . . . for his absolute use and benefit. . . . It was dated 1885.

'Yes, I knew about it, Ted,' Joseph told him. 'Ma consulted me, in fact, before she did it. Wanted me to understand there was no slight involved – neither to me nor to Thirza – but, to use her own words, "Ted's the one that never has any money!" And you hadn't met Eleanor then. But I don't suppose it's a fortune.'

It wasn't; not, at least, as the world judged such matters. 'Twenty-four pounds, fourteen shillings and one penny, Captain,' said the solicitor, almost apologetically. 'Not a great deal.'

But to Ma, who had scrimped and saved for most of her working life, it had represented the final act in a lifetime of love and devotion and, as such, was a jewel beyond price.

With the money, he bought for Joseph a print of a sailing-vessel, square-rigged on all three masts, for news had recently arrived that the *Senator Weber* was now serving as a coal hulk in the Falkland Islands, and his brother had been greatly saddened – 'even though I'm no better than a hulk myself, these days!'

For Thirza, he bought a delicate filigree brooch in the shape of a heart, and the remainder of the money he gave to Bert for his school, for 'little Bertie Brown' had always been a favourite with Ma.

259

36

'Now that Ma has gone,' Joseph said, towards the end of '94, 'we'll be off to Savannah, Ted. For a couple of years, at least.'

He had been expecting the news ever since Ma's death, so it came as no surprise. But it still caused him a great sadness; for he'd grown accustomed to meeting his brother when he could, sure of an attentive ear to whatever he had to relate. For there was always something: storms or icebergs or fog.

'Savannah's within easy travelling distance of New York on the railroad. We shall probably see more of each other over there than we do here.'

Ted doubted that. 'George will miss you,' he observed.

'As we shall miss him, but we shall be back.'

Ted doubted that, too. Once Joseph was settled in his beloved Savannah – where young Arthur Hancock had now arrived upon the scene – only a dire emergency would make him return. It was Anna who reconciled him to the move.

'The climate will be so beneficial to his health. He's become very chesty of late, as you may have noticed. It can be cold out there in the winter, I know, but nothing like these dratted Mersey mists.'

So after that, Ted raised no more objections. For some time now, he'd been considering a quick trip down to Savannah when *Britannic* was in New York for a long stay – no reason at all why his chief should not be left in charge for a few days – and Joseph's presence there would give an added impetus to his resolve. Mattie might even be persuaded to accompany him on the journey, and that would make it most pleasant.

So he did all that he could to further his brother's plans; arranging for the transportation of their possessions and booking them a passage on *Germanic*, which he was to take over for a single trip in May of '95.

'*Britannic*'s in the graving dock, having her funnels lengthened,' he explained to Joseph, 'but *Germanic*'s just as reliable.'

'As long as there's *some* canvas up top,' said Joseph. But even he became interested when Ted told him *Germanic* would be the first ship to embark passengers from Liverpool's new, floating landing-stage. He even decided, a little while before they were due to sail, to stroll down and take a closer look at her.

'I'll come with you,' Ted offered, for he'd been given some free time after bringing *Britannic* back.

He was never to forget that last stroll he took with his brother. When *Germanic* had been carefully inspected, they stood for a while watching the crowds, for it seemed to have been tacitly decided that the new landing-stage, nearly half a mile in length, was to be used as a sort of promenade. It was a fine evening and most people had come to fill their lungs with sea air after toiling in shop or office – and perhaps to pretend that the gentle movement of the stage on its pontoons was the rise and fall of a ship at sea. There were families, too, some of them bent upon catching a ferry-boat to Egremont or New Brighton. One such family caught Joseph's attention. The youngest child was perched aloft upon its father's shoulders, the remainder threatened to fall between ferry and stage, in spite of their mother's admonitions.

'Allow me, ma'am.' And he seized a child in each hand, motioning Ted to do the same.

'Why don't we stay on her,' Ted suggested after the harassed parents had expressed their gratitude. 'Just for the ride.'

'Good idea!'

'I wish,' said Joseph a few minutes later, as they stood at the rails and gazed out towards the open sea, 'that I had

261

a hundred pounds for every time I've sailed out over the bar. I'd be a rich man!'

Then he turned to gaze back at the warehouses and wharfs of the Liverpool seafront; at the miscellany of shipping at anchor — square-riggers cheek by jowl with steamers, paddle-boats soon to head for the Isle of Man or southward down the coast of Wales, cross-channel ferries getting up steam for Dublin.

'Am I mad, Ted, to be leaving all this?'

Trying to cheer him, Ted pointed to the big twin-funnelled Cunarder at anchor out in the bay — was it the *Lucania*? 'Before long, I shall be sailing you and Anna across the Atlantic in just such a vessel as that, and you'll have as comfortable a crossing as I can make it, I promise you.'

But Joseph refused to be cheered. 'I'd sooner be sailing my own ship through a squall any day of the week than wallowing in the lap of luxury on a floating gin-palace like that.'

'Right! I'll see they bed you down in the hold with bread and water and a chunk of maggoty pork!'

Joseph had the grace to grin. 'Sorry, Ted. I'm nothing but an old curmudgeon.'

'Curmudgeon or not, I shall miss you.'

'And I you. But we shall meet again, often. The world shrinks with every day that passes.'

A gull swooped by, beak already open for the piece of bread someone had thrown. 'One of these days,' Ted reflected, 'men may even fly like the birds.'

Joseph shuddered. 'I don't want to be around if that ever happens. Oh, I know I go on and on about steam power, Ted. Half the time, it's because you expect it of me. But there's something about handling a wheel, using wind and water, and sails of good, homespun flax that's natural and honest.'

For once, Ted didn't argue; didn't point out, as he wanted to, that coal was a natural product too and it was man's God-given brain that had discovered a method of turning it into steam.

'There's a great deal,' he agreed solemnly, 'in what you say.'

Dusk was falling when they got back to Liverpool. 'A noggin and a smoke?' Joseph suggested. 'I'm staying overnight with George at Seaforth, so Anna won't worry.'

And he and Eleanor were staying with Bert and Gilly, so there was no rush for him either. They chose a nearby tavern. There, wreathed in smoke, they gossiped comfortably until closing time. Their parting was brief.

'Goodnight, lad, and God keep you!'

'Goodnight, Joseph! God keep you, too!'

Just so had they said goodnight in the old days in Well Street.

They turned away from each other then, but after a few paces, Ted, as was his habit, looked back. And Joseph, who usually strode quickly away, already intent upon the next matter in hand, did the same. Hands were raised in a final salute.

It was the last time Ted saw his brother alive.

Two days later, he opened his door to a frantic knocking. It was George. White-faced, rigid with the effort of retaining his composure, he faced his uncle.

'Uncle Ted, it's Pa! He's dead!'

At first he couldn't take it in. Pa dead? But of course he was, these many years. And then he realised whom George must mean. 'Not – not Joseph?'

George nodded dumbly.

He could do nothing then, but hold open the door for George to enter. Dimly, he was aware that Eleanor was beside him. 'What happened?' he forced himself to ask. 'When? I saw him only the night before last.'

'It happened yesterday. He'd gone in to town – to see off a friend at Lime Street station. And then – in the Queen's Arcade – after the friend had gone – he – he fell down and died.'

'On his own?' Somehow, that was the worst of it – not that Joseph had died, that was still impossible to accept –

263

but that no one had been with him.

'Come and sit down, dearest,' Eleanor led him to a chair and motioned George to another.

'Yes – quite alone. But he wouldn't have known a thing, the doctor said. A massive heart attack. Passers-by were very kind, I understand. An ambulance was called. But he was – dead upon arrival at the hospital.'

'Your mother?'

'She's taken it well. Better than I. Although she's deeply shocked, of course.'

'Where is she?'

'At my house. We thought it best she stay with us, at least until after – after. . . .'

Ted turned to Eleanor. 'I must go to Anna.'

'Of course you must, my dearest.' It was typical of Eleanor, he realised later, that she did not seek to go with him, to trespass upon a grief that, instinctively, she knew should be shared only by the very closest family; those to whom Joseph Hancock had been most dear.

If Joseph had died alone, he was certainly not buried so. Wallesey churchyard, that Saturday afternoon, was thick with black-coated mourners. Andrew Gibson was there, the owner of the Company Joseph had served so long and so faithfully, and not only the old man but his son, too; and Ted Heath and James Carr, partners in the ships' stores Joseph had been involved with. These, Ted would have expected. It was the number and variety of other mourners that astounded him including at least a dozen of the master mariners he had known, coming to pay their last respects. Joseph, Ted thought wryly, could have allowed himself a morsel of pride at such a turnout.

'A great seaman,' said Andrew Gibson, Senior, shaking hands when it was all over. 'And a great man.' Sentiments that were echoed by every one of the sombre crew that filed slowly past; 'a brave man', 'an heroic man', 'a man I was proud to serve with', 'a kind man'. Between them, they seemed to say it all, yet none, Ted thought, reaching the very heart of the man.

'I think,' he tried to explain later to Anna, 'that Joseph can be best summed up in his own words: "natural and honest". He was describing a ship at the time, needless to say – any ship as long as it had sails! – but it's the way I see him, too. There was no guile about Joseph. In the true meaning of the word, he was a simple man.'

Anna nodded. 'I always knew where I stood with him.'

'Which is more than he could say about you!' And deliberately – for there was much to be said, he knew, for the healing power of memory – he reminded her of their first meeting on that sunlit hillside above Etruria, over forty years ago.

'And next day it rained, d'you remember? And he was beside himself with worry in case you wouldn't be there!'

'Come rain or shine, I would have been. But I never told him so, in as many words. More's the pity.'

'He didn't need to be told.'

And so they talked, conjuring up the past, and it was as if Joseph had never left them but was only in the next room, about to burst through the door at any moment.

'I have been so fortunate,' Anna was able to say when finally he and Eleanor left.

'I too, Anna.' And he meant it, with all his heart.

Frank met him at Savannah Railroad Station. 'It's good of you to come, Uncle Ted.'

'The least I could do, lad. And I've left *Germanic* in good hands in New York.'

'I wondered if you're not too tired after your journey, whether we could perhaps sit for a few minutes before we go home – in Pulaski, maybe – and you could tell me about Pa? And thank you, by the way, for your letter. It was good of you to write so quickly.'

So they found a bench in Pulaski Square and he gazed about him; at the gracious houses, the live oaks still draped with Spanish moss, the well-tended flower-beds, and sniffed appreciatively.

265

'I've just realised, Frank. I've never been here in the summertime before.'

'Any time of the year, it's a beautiful city.'

'No regrets, then?'

'None whatever. Except, of course, being so far away from Ma at a time like this.'

'George has been a tower of strength.' And he went on to tell Frank of the circumstances of his father's death, but dwelling particularly upon the many people who had attended his funeral. 'Everyone loved your father, Frank.'

They sat for a while in silence until Frank, swallowing hard, was in control of his emotions. 'I always remember,' he said, 'when I was a child, how wonderful it was when he came home. Suddenly, it was as if the sun shone all day and every day, and Ma went about the house singing like a bird.' He turned to Ted. 'How is she, really?'

'She's taken it very well. You see, in a way, her life has been a succession of goodbyes to your father. And though she knows this is the final farewell in this world, she's confident she'll meet him again in the next.'

But Frank had always looked at things from a practical viewpoint. 'She's well taken care of, I hope, until then?'

'Indeed yes! Your father saw to that. You'll be hearing from the solicitor in due course, for all his money is in trust for you and George, but with provision made for your mother to receive an annuity of £75 per year – to be increased if necessary.'

'That should be ample. But Annie and I are hoping she'll still come out to Savannah to live.'

'She may well do so. But for the time being, I think she feels nearer to your father in England.'

'I can understand that. Well,' slowly, he rose to his feet, 'I suppose we should be on our way, or Annie will begin to worry. By the way, Uncle, she's pregnant again.'

'Well done, lad! There must be something in this Georgian air!'

He stayed only a couple of days in Savannah but filled them

to the last minute. Rising early on his first morning, he took the well-remembered route to Factor's Walk and River Street, there to find the wharfs little changed, though with a higher proportion of steamers now. On the second morning, he visited Forsyth Park, there to sit beside the fountain and wonder that he had not noticed before the beauty of the bronze mermen, and the nymph atop the shining cascades. But then, of course, he'd had eyes only for Julia Templeton.

Visiting the wooden house, he was delighted to find the door still opened by Maria, albeit a slower, plumper Maria. Selina and Henry were there, too; Henry now a little portly and every inch the family man and Selina as devoted to him as ever. Julia and her husband, he was told, were living in Chicago and leading a busy social life. And William was carving himself a promising career in the army.

He even managed a flying visit to the lumber-yard where Frank worked, sniffing in the resinous scent of the newly cut pine and declaring it to be the best smell in the world – after the sea.

Finally, because he knew it would have been Joseph's dearest wish, he went with Frank to Bonaventure Cemetery, there to lay a posy of red roses upon the tiny grave of little Joseph Hancock – *died 8 June 1891, aged 10 months*. At least he'd have company up there, now.

Then it was the railroad depot again. 'Write soon, Uncle Ted. I shall miss Pa's letters.'

'I will, lad!'

37

His 'majestic period', was how he described those years that straddled the centuries; for right from the start, he and *Majestic* seemed to complement each other. Sister ship to the *Teutonic*, her displacement was almost twice that of the *Britannic* and she boasted twin screws to that vessel's one.

Only to Joseph could he have confided the information that *Majestic* was also an auxiliary armed cruiser and capable, if necessary, of carrying a thousand cavalry with horses, or two thousand infantry. And in view of the way the Boers in South Africa were behaving, it seemed a sensible precaution.

But he said nothing to Eleanor of all this when he took *Majestic* out for the first time, in the July following Joseph's death. But he did arrange for Thomas to escort her to the opening of the new Riverside Station, especially constructed to give America-bound passengers easier access to their ship. Lost the power of their legs, have they? Joseph would have grumbled.

Some of his passengers were now becoming familiar as they chose to cross with him again and again, especially those put at his table. Many of these were commercial giants, eager to establish branches of their empires upon both sides of the Atlantic and able to talk of little else; although some he found interesting, especially those who had penetrated beyond New York into America's vast hinterland. But generally they inhabited a world so foreign to his own, he would listen attentively and nod wisely, remaining discreetly silent, while they spoke of exports and imports, profits and losses.

Given the option, which he rarely was, he would have chosen those passengers who, like himself, provided a service for others: doctors, priests, lawyers, clergymen, writers, even soldiers or sailors. One falling into this last category was a certain Winston Churchill, a graduate of the United States Naval Academy but with literary aspirations that had led him to give up the sea and devote himself to writing novels. 'I'll let you have a copy of the first book I publish, Captain!' he promised.

Another writer he considered himself privileged to meet was William Stead, editor of the *Pall Mall Magazine*, a man who seemed to have an almost obsessive interest in the sea.

'You should have been a sailor, sir,' Ted told him.

But Stead shook his head. 'I should get us all hopelessly lost, I fear. Your ability to know in which direction to steer your ship, other than straight ahead, leaves me speechless with admiration.' This Ted doubted, somehow. 'But the sea,' Stead admitted, 'does have a strange attraction for me, as if my destiny in some extraordinary way, is bound up with it.'

Another of Ted's favourite passengers was an American, William Washington Gordon from Savannah. When Ted had first met him, years ago in the days of the *Lizzie Fennell*, he'd been a cotton factor and commission merchant on the wharfs with a gallant military career behind him, having fought for the Southern States in the Civil War; many were the stories he could, and did, tell and Ted was delighted to renew his acquaintance.

'*In truth,*' he wrote to Eleanor, '*I am a most fortunate man. Not only am I able to follow my own chosen career, but also to learn a great deal about the professions of other men. And above all, Queen of My Heart, I have you to come home to at journey's end. I would not exchange my life for anyone.*'

One of Ted's contemporaries on *Majestic* was Dr William O'Loughlin, the ship's surgeon. An Irishman from Tralee, the doctor's sense of humour could be even more outrageous than Ted's, and many an irreverent observation would be made during their daily inspection of the ship. Often, the gales of laughter coming from *his* table at dinner could cause heads to turn and eyebrows to be raised among those seated at Ted's.

'Sorry, sir,' he would say later with exaggerated deference. 'My apologies to the posh lot.'

It amused Ted to notice how the professions of first-class passengers were never entered on the lists, as if it were considered ungentlemanly to be other than a man of independent means, but it certainly didn't make his task of host any easier. If their qualifications had changed their title, if they were doctors, clergymen or professors, then he had no difficulty. Otherwise, the purser would often prime him beforehand upon the background of his 'guests'.

'But one day,' he confessed to Eleanor, 'I shall get it all wrong and ask someone about their dealings in real estate, only to discover they own a bean-canning factory!' On the whole, though, he managed to get it right.

Sometimes, he wondered what Ma would have made of them all. And yet, what basic difference was there between selling a few pounds of sugar in a front parlour and tons of it in a New York emporium? It was all a matter of providing people with what they wanted at a price they were prepared to pay. Although Ma, he reflected, often *hadn't* got the best price if she'd known someone was in need, and certainly Pa would have given the whole shop away if he'd thought it his Christian duty!

In the October of that first year on *Majestic*, Bruce Ismay crossed with him to New York. Although they'd met ashore on several previous occasions, this was the first time they'd sailed together.

'Will he tell you how to run the ship?' Eleanor wanted to know.

'Not in so many words, But no doubt he'll put in his oar wherever he can.'

And he did. Although careful never to venture on to the bridge unless specifically invited to do so, he had no compunction about stopping Ted elsewhere on the ship to discuss *Majestic*'s daily progress.

And Ted frequently overheard him boasting to other passengers, particularly the ladies, about the speed of the vessel. 'Averaged 20 knots, back in '91,' he heard him claim, 'when she took the record.'

Although as eager as anyone for *Majestic* to receive her just deserts, Ted found himself almost leaning the other way. 'I've heard rumours,' he dared to remark upon one occasion to Ismay, 'that the Company's beginning to think less about speed than about the comfort of passengers.'

Ismay shot him a quick glance. 'The ability of our ships to reach their destination at the scheduled time, Captain, will always remain one of the Company's priorities. Businessmen depend upon it.'

'Oh, indeed yes, sir!' Ted agreed smoothly. 'Punctuality is always of the greatest importance, whatever one's walk in life. But arriving *ahead* of schedule can be pointless if it means waiting to disembark.'

He was somewhat amazed to hear himself voicing such an opinion. Where was the young man who could hardly wait to try and grab back the record from Cunard? Was he growing soft as he grew older? Or had the temptation to disagree with Ismay been too much for him?

He was prudent enough to allow the official pilot – whom he was now forced by law to take on board at Sandy Hook – to take over on this particular voyage. As Joseph had guessed he would, he'd got in the way of conning *Majestic* himself into New York, now taking the bend that had grounded *Republic* without even slackening speed. He didn't know which he enjoyed more: the thrill of doing it or the gasp of consternation from any officer on the bridge who hadn't sailed with him before. The pilot usually preferred to look the other way.

'Do you realise the importance of next year, my dearest?' he asked Eleanor.

'Her Majesty's Diamond Jubilee, of course!'

'Is that all?'

She wrinkled her nose, pretending deep thought. 'I can't recall anything else of any *major* importance.'

'Anything of *minor* importance?'

'Well, let me see. Ah, yes! It will be ten years since I visited London for the first time. In January, I remember. It snowed – heavily.'

'Is that *all* you can remember of it?' he asked sternly.

'Well, I seem to remember I was there with a man. A very good-looking man with a beard and very bright blue eyes. And a habit of. . . .' She paused.

'Of. . . ?' Had he some dreadful mannerism that had annoyed her all this time?

'Of granting my every wish.'

He burst out laughing. 'What a spoiled creature you must be! Anyway, this man whose name you cannot remember has a proposition to put to you.'

She widened her eyes at him. 'Indeed?'

'He wishes to invite you to America. To New York. But not, I think, in January. Later in the year, if you are agreeable.'

'If I am agreeable! Oh, Ted, that would be wonderful!'

'That's settled then.' And he kissed her long and hard.

38

They chose the Hotel Martinique, on the corner of Broadway and 33rd Street. The Metropolitan Opera was but a few blocks away, and the shops and stores of Broadway were conveniently to hand for Eleanor to browse among when Ted's presence was required on board; although indeed, First Officer Lancaster was a most responsible officer and well able to see to things. And these days, of course, there was the telephone.

'Now,' Ted instructed as they stood at their window, gazing down upon the bustle of Broadway, 'should you venture out alone, my love, remember that the streets of New York are constructed like a chequer-board. We are on 33rd Street. Going north, you will find 34th Street and south, towards the tip of Manhattan. . .'

'. . . 32nd Street,' Eleanor chorused with him. 'Dearest, I do assure you I shall be perfectly safe. After all, I have a tongue in my head and I do speak the language. Now, am I fit to meet your Mattie at last?'

He looked at her as she stood beside him, eyes sparkling with anticipation, lips curved in a happy smile, wearing a neat grey jacket and skirt with a froth of deep pink lace at the neck. 'We should go down to the restaurant now,' he said. 'Mattie will be entranced.'

Clearly, Mattie was – and said as much within seconds of clasping Eleanor in a great hug and kissing her roundly upon both cheeks.

'I never really believed Ted when he described you, but now I can see you're even prettier and cuter than he said.'

'Ted described *you* as the quintessence of American womanhood.'

273

'Well, I don't know about that! I fear there are no worthwhile meetings or demonstrations while you are here, Eleanor, but there are many things I would like to show you.'

Hurriedly, Ted introduced Seth. 'A mere male, I'm afraid!' said that gentleman with a comic lift of an eyebrow. 'But delighted to meet you, Eleanor.'

The two women spent several hours in each others company.

'I had to soft-pedal,' Mattie confessed later to Ted when they had a moment alone together in the lounge of the Martinique. 'For it soon became clear to me that she is as tender-hearted as an overripe squash. If I hadn't stopped her, she would have bought up the entire stock of a poor woman selling buttons on Tin Pan Alley.'

'And what else did you do?'

'Well, have you heard of the Rhinelander sisters? They built an Industrial School over on East 88th, with room for three hundred children. I took Eleanor, and she talked to some of the children about England. They loved her.'

'I'm sure they did.'

'So,' Mattie added virtuously, 'she saw no bloody heads or broken limbs. No dreadful cases of malnutrition or rickets. At least, nothing to speak of! And we ended up eating in a really respectable diner.'

That evening they strolled among the fashionable throng in Madison Square Park. Eleanor must be shown every aspect of the teeming metropolis he now considered his second home.

The days passed far too quickly, but with great enjoyment as they travelled about the city, on foot, by hansom and sometimes upon the crowded streetcars. He showed Eleanor the Brooklyn Bridge, the wharfs along the East River, the uniform rows of 'brownstones' that were springing up all over New York and, because it was the latest craze, a flickering, eye-straining 'motion-picture' in the Union Square Theater. 'Most interesting!' she said as they came out from the gloom in to the bright light of day, 'but I doubt it will ever catch on.'

One particularly enjoyable excursion was with Mattie and Seth to Coney Island.

'This is considered to be one of the most democratic places in all America,' Mattie claimed as they strolled along Surf Avenue, between the sideshows and the chowder and hot-dog stands.

Eleanor jibbed at being swung a hundred feet up in the air in what appeared to be little more than a cage. Ted, on the other hand, couldn't resist the Ferris wheel, so he and Mattie were born aloft, while she and Seth drank chilled lemonade and root beer with their feet firmly upon the ground.

But they all four agreed to 'shoot the chutes', although Eleanor, once their car began its descent, deeply regretted the decision. However, at her first terrified shriek, Ted gallantly wrapped his arms around her so that the mighty splash as they hit the water became quite a pleasurable experience.

They purchased a picnic hamper and found space upon a crowded beach to sit and enjoy it.

'There are people here from every country on earth,' declared Mattie proudly, as if personally responsible for their presence; although, as Ted pointed out, *he* was probably the one who had done most to get them there.

Far too soon, it was time to stroll along the pier to catch a side-wheeler back to the city, for a visit to the opera had been planned for that evening. But as they walked, they looked back constantly to admire the strings of Mr Edison's new incandescent lights beginning to twinkle upon the skyline.

'Thank you for a truly wonderful day!' said Eleanor.

'Amen to that!' said Ted, although secretly thanking his lucky stars that First Officer Lancaster hadn't observed his Captain 'shooting the chute'. Majestic his descent had certainly *not* been!

☆

The day before Eleanor was due to leave New York, they 'did' Long Island, as Mattie put it.

Right from the start, it was a special day. They began by taking the rail-road to Sag Harbour, near the far end of the island. Protected from the Atlantic gales, it had been one of New England's largest whaling ports and although the industry had now died away, much remained to show how thriving it had once been.

'The innards of Ma's corsets probably came from here!' he informed Eleanor, as they strolled down Main Street towards the sea.

'I can think of other things,' said Eleanor frostily, 'I would rather speak of in this delightful spot than corsets!' However, she made no objection when he slid his arm around her waist, devoutly glad that it was the warmth of her body he could feel through the thin stuff of her dress and not the hardness of whalebone.

They stood for a while upon the wharf, gazing out across a calm, blue sea to the greenness of Cedar Point and the purple depths of Shelter Island, aptly named, for it kept the might of the Atlantic well in check. A two-masted schooner tacked lazily across the bay, catching what wind it could in its sails.

'The Indians used to whale-hunt long before the first white settlers appeared,' Ted explained, 'and although they were more skilled at it than the white man, it was the old story of the settlers finding more profitable ways of doing it; although Indians and whites sailed together quite amicably. But you can see that the people of Sag Harbour lived very well.' And he pointed out the big, clapboard houses among the trees. They walked up to the old whaler church, built high and with a tall steeple so whalers would see it as they safely rounded the Point.

It was an extraordinary building, half temple, half church.

'A little like St Paul's in London?' Eleanor suggested.

'Or a Japanese pagoda?'

They inspected the graveyard and discovered an ancient tombstone, with the inscription:

I bid adieu to all below
I go where Angels dwell
Since 'tis God's wish it shall be so
I bid you all farewell.

'But there is another graveyard I should like to show you,'
Ted said. 'And not just for the graves,' he added quickly,
fearing that she might think the day was becoming altogether too funereal.

And so, a little while later, they stood beside a tall stone
plinth, craning their necks to see the top of a broken mast
that rose up from it; but not so high that they could not
make out the jagged outline where the masthead had been
supposedly snapped off.

'An easy enough thing to happen in a gale,' said Ted. 'And
disastrous, especially in the North Atlantic. However, this
one will never break again for it's made of marble.'

They read the inscription upon the plinth; the mast had
been erected in memory of John E. Howell, captain of the
France, who had died while whaling in the Pacific Ocean.

'There were many encounters where the whale got the
better of man,' said Ted soberly.

Beneath the inscription, a relief showed a seaman being
pulled on to a boat – capsized, Ted noticed, presumably by
the whale that was spouting away in the background.

'But I don't feel it's there just for Captain Howell,' Ted
observed. 'It's a fitting tribute to all the men who have lost
their lives at sea while under sail. And God knows, there
were plenty of them.'

They found many other graves of men who had met the
same fate as John Howell. 'And somewhere here,' Ted
remembered, 'is a captain who was a hero of the Revolution.
His five wives are buried with him!'

But they did not search overlong for the heroic captain.
Instead, they brought out the packets of sandwiches and
fruit they'd had the foresight to bring and ate them – once
Ted had spread his jacket for Eleanor – leaning against a
mossy tombstone. 'For indeed,' Ted pointed out, 'were *I*

277

buried here, I should be very happy to accommodate us!'

As so often happens upon these occasions, they deeply regretted they could not stay longer in Westbury, where they were visiting Mattie's Quaker friend Rachel Hicks. Ted had always been interested in the Quaker movement, greatly admiring its principles of tolerance and pacifism. And the story of William Penn's arrival in America, sailing up the Delaware in 1682, had always thrilled him.

Joseph, he thought, would have greatly enjoyed meeting these friendly, modest people who took a great delight in showing off their meeting-house to the two visitors from England.

'Westbury, you know, Captain, is named after the Westbury in Wiltshire, England, and we are proud of our connections. Naturally, we were unable to take up arms upon either side during the Revolution but many of us sympathised with the English Crown.'

Although the women's apparel was simple in the extreme, its subdued colour relieved only by the shining whiteness of their caps and fichus, this did not prevent their appreciation of Eleanor's muslin gown and the daintiness of her wide-brimmed hat. And every time she spoke, they seemd to hang upon her every word; as if listening not so much to *what* she said as the inflection and timbre of her voice as she said it.

Mattie's friend Rachel they found to be a delightful person and as enthusiastic as she about the rights of women. Although very modest about her own achievements, she was also, they discovered, a painter of considerable talent and greatly interested in the art of photography.

'For it *is* an art form,' she told them over tea in the living-room of the old farmhouse, called simply the Old Place, where her family had lived since the seventeenth century. 'It's also an accurate method of recording our way of life for posterity. The camera doesn't lie.'

A typically altruistic Quaker view of life, Ted thought, to be as much concerned with the next generation as with your own.

'And now,' Rachel continued, 'I would like to record *you* – if not for posterity, certainly for myself.'

So they posed, but in the most natural manner, out in the garden with Eleanor gazing intently into the heart of a white rose – 'It was not difficult,' she told Ted later, 'for there was a most enormous spider crawling about inside!' – and Ted holding back a trailing briar from her skirts.

It seemed as if the whole community – or, at least, those not still labouring in the fields – came to wave them off at the depot.

'What lovely people!' said Eleanor, waving until they were out of sight. 'But I could not be one of them.'

They reached Rockaway as the light was fading. Their hotel room, as Ted had requested, faced out to sea, towards the dear old Neversinks clearly visible upon the horizon. 'And there'll be a moon later,' he told Eleanor.

But first they went down to the dining-room, where they were served by an Italian waiter. 'I hope all is to your liking, Capitano?' he asked, halfway through the meal.

Ted looked up, startled, for he was not in uniform. 'Thank you, it is. But how. . . ?' And he looked at the man more closely; at the olive skin, the dark eyes, dancing now with amusement, the long black hair and the thick moustache. But there was no way that he remembered him among the countless Italian immigrants he had brought in to the States over the years.

'*Britannic*, wasn't it?' he hazarded.

From the man's delighted smile, he saw that his guess had been right.

'You remember me, Capitano? That sure is wonderful! Every day, you came to inspect us. And every day, you would pat the bambinos upon the head and ask if they were happy! They always looked forward to your coming. "The kind Capitano", they called you!'

'She was a good ship, the *Britannic*. Still *is*, of course.'

There were, of course, other diners to whom he must attend, but each time he passed by their table, he would either stop for a brief word or flash them a quick smile. And these smiles, Ted noticed, were aimed expressly at Eleanor.

Indeed, he had never seen his wife look lovelier, the sun-kissed bloom of her cheeks set off to perfection by the gown she was wearing; of a heavy silk, he thought, and the colour of primroses, high to the neck but with an insert of fine lace that hinted, more than revealed, the curve of her breasts and the deep shadow between. He felt his own desire quicken. No wonder the fellow couldn't keep his eyes off her!

'We were going to watch the moon rise over the sea,' he reminded her.

'Of course!' She gathered up her bag and wrap. 'Shall we then, take a stroll along the waterfront?'

'I think,' he said swiftly, also rising, 'that our window will be the best vantage point.'

During the brief elevator ride, he stood close, his fingers caressing the soft flesh on the inner side of her wrist. Surprised, she glanced up at him and must have recognised his longing, for there came an answering gleam in her own eyes. Swiftly, he urged her along the short corridor leading from the elevator to their room and turned the key with fingers that trembled.

The door shut, he turned towards her.

'Ted – the moon! It's shining right across the bay!'

'The moon,' he said huskily, 'can wait. But I cannot!'

'Oh, my love!' Laughing softly, Eleanor put up her hands to her neck and pulled, and suddenly, miraculously, the dress was falling from her shoulders.

He groaned aloud as he began to kiss the glorious softness of her breasts, forcing her, as gently as he could, back on to the bed.

And then there was the familiar entwining of their limbs, the pressure of flesh upon flesh, the thrusting of his body and the yielding of hers, but this time he seemed to penetrate deeper than ever before.

When it was over, they lay for a long while in the moon's milky light, exhausted but deeply, richly, content.

Later, he picked up the discarded dress from the floor. 'Those were very accommodating buttons!'

Eleanor chuckled. 'Not buttons at all, dearest. Press studs, they are called.'

He didn't care what they were called; only that the fellow who'd invented them, should be knighted at least!

Helen Melville Smith was born on the second of April 1898 at 20 Alexandra Road, Waterloo, Liverpool. The move – made necessary by the Company's wish for Ted to be nearer to their offices in James Street – had been made well in advance of the birth. Maria, as sensitive as ever to the needs of others, was in attendance at what had been a difficult delivery. Briefly, as he gazed down at the tiny wrinkled face of his daughter, Ted wondered how he could have survived if her arrival into the world had caused Eleanor's departure from it but his mind immediately veered away from such a prospect.

Instead, he pondered upon her name. The choice had not been difficult. Helen, they had discovered meant 'light' – and she would surely be the light of their lives. 'Melville' was the name of the ancient house in Fife which had so enchanted them both when they had visited it, spending long hours in its beautiful grounds and wishing that the village of Monimail were just that bit nearer to Liverpool.

'And if she wishes,' Eleanor, ever practical, had pointed out, 'a hyphen can be added when she's older and she can become Miss Melville-Smith. Many people do that, nowadays.'

He knew that they did but deplored the practice; still more when a good, honest name was bastardised into 'Smythe'. What would Pa have made of that?

But did it really matter, he was to wonder a few weeks later, what names were put upon a birth certificate? For, just as Annie, the previous year, had christened her latest child Annie Norah Isabel but called her 'Queenie', so Helen Melville, within days of her arrival, became 'Babsie'.

39

The port of Liverpool was crammed with troop-ships. Hardly a day passed now without the strains of *Dolly Gray* or *Rule, Britannia* floating out across the Mersey: the words sung robustly enough by the khaki-clad 'Tommies' lining the rails but quavered feebly, with many a heart-rending sob, by their families — mostly women — crowding the wharfs.

'Men must fight and women must weep'. Sometimes, Ted thought, the men had the easier part to play. Even Eleanor, usually so brave when he bade her goodbye, had clung to him this time, her eyes wet with tears, and implored him to take care, seeming to forget that he should be back within a matter of weeks. It was sad, though, that he would miss Babsie opening her Christmas presents; miss, also, a New Year that would herald a new century.

However, compared with the poor devils he had on board, there was little for him to complain of; the Suffolks, the Somersets, the York and Lancasters, the Royal Scots, the Royal Irish Fusiliers and the Connaughts, the South Wales Borderers — from every corner of Britain they'd rallied to the colours to fight the Boers.

Now, as the band struck up *Au Revoir But Not Goodbye* and the tugs began to inch *Majestic* out towards the bar, the cheering grew to a frenzy. Caps were waved and streamers hurled into the air. Up on the bridge, Captain Edward John Smith felt a most unaccustomed lump forming in his throat. Catching the eye of Chief Officer Carter and realising that he, too, was similarly affected, he looked hastily away to where Second Officer Neill-Dibb stood to attention, his brown face impassive. How did an Indian feel about such a demonstration of patriotism? But then, Victoria was *his* Queen, also; albeit teetering, they said, upon the brink of eternity. But she still held the might of the British Empire within the palm of her hand.

Sometimes, he felt as if he was a stranger upon his own ship, although allowed to navigate and steer her and to be held responsible for such hazards as the Bay of Biscay.

'How much longer will this be kept up for, Captain?' aggrieved, sallow-cheeked officers enquired; if, that is, they were not already flat upon their backs and incapable of speech. And he was continually coming upon troopers hanging limply over the rails, unable, presumably, to reach the wash-houses in time.

Majestic was no longer the ship he knew and loved. When he and Doctor Mackenzie – a nice enough fellow, but he missed O'Loughlin – first made their daily inspection, they were continually losing their bearings.

Cargo space had been cleared to accommodate the various messes, vast, communal washhouses installed instead of private bathrooms, lounge bars stripped to become canteens for 'other ranks', deck-chair depositories converted to hammock stores. Between decks, there was now a huge armoury, holding such a collection of rifles and bayonets, shrapnel, shells and machine guns that he would, no doubt, have been shot on sight had he dared to light up a cigar in its vicinity! Certainly, no matches were allowed on board, although candles were placed at strategic intervals where smoking *was* permitted, and some resourceful Tommies, he'd noticed, used the sun's rays shining through a magnifying glass.

Only the promenade decks had been left as they were, for it was here that the daily drills were held. Now, it was bugles not bells that indicated the passage of time on board; reveille at five-thirty, sick parade, calls to meals, kit inspections, 'target firing to commence', 'target firing to cease', physical jerks, it was never ending until the last post and lights out at ten fifteen.

'Probably,' observed First Officer Carter caustically, 'they go to the lavatory by numbers!' He and Ted were standing up on the bridge, gazing down at soldiers firing at the canvas target marker towed at the stern.

And certainly, there were compensations for this standing in the wings while the play was performed by a cast of hundreds with little direction from the crew. Purser Thorpe's load was lightened considerably for there was no entertainment to be organised; the troops made their own, organising boxing and wrestling tournaments and sports for the daylight hours and impromptu sing songs in the evening.

It was only into the bowels of the ship, where the firemen, stripped to the waist, fed the perpetual hunger of the great boilers, that the troops did not penetrate.

'And they'd better not try it!' warned the Chief Engineer, John Barber.

Ted liked John Barber and looked forward to their daily meeting when Doc Mackenzie had left him. A cup of coffee in the Chief Engineer's cubby-hole, once their inspection was finished, became a regular part of his routine.

One convention that continued was placing the most prestigious passengers at the captain's table. Consequently, Ted's acquaintance with some of the senior officers blossomed as the voyage progressed. There was Major Bode from the Royal Scots, Captain de Berry from the Royal Irish Fusiliers, Major Burrows from the Special Service – who kept a most discreet silence upon the part he was to pay in the hostilities – and Captain Kilner of the Royal Artillery. For the rest, a constantly changing procession of young lieutenants took turns to sit with their seniors.

For the most part, Ted was content to sit and listen to their conversation, only occasionally asking a question. He knew already about Cecil Rhodes and his establishment of the British South Africa Company in the country that bore his name; and of his ambition to bring the Boer Republics of the Orange Free State and the Transvaal under the British rule of Cape Colony. But now he learned of the actual tactics of warfare, of the columns of British infantry that would follow their officers – mounted, of course – up into hills where the Boers, already safely ensconced, could pick them off as they came.

'But they will be so vulnerable!' he felt compelled to comment.

'But so numerous!' said Major Bode. 'Where one man falls, another will spring up to take his place.'

'And besides,' Major Burrows contributed knowledge-ably, 'our scouts will have already reconnoitred the area. *They* will know where the Boers are concealed.'

But would not the Boers have their own scouts; scouts, moreover, who knew the terrain like the backs of their hands? To Ted, it all sounded dreadfully haphazard, the optimism grievously misplaced. But he was, after all, only a humble sailor and a middle-aged one at that!

Even so, his services were in demand when the equator was reached.

'With those magnificent whiskers, Captain,' they told him, 'you'll make the perfect Neptune.'

It was, he decided, the least he could do and crossing the line, after all, was essentially a nautical ceremony. Besides, even though his half-century was coming up, he still enjoyed playing the fool.

But it was the concert on Christmas night that he enjoyed the most, even though he had the unenviable task of choosing the most entertaining turn; for all manner of hidden talents were revealed. Penny whistles, mouth organs, flutes, even a violin, were brought out and played with varying degrees of skill but enormous enthusiasm. And he'd had no idea that the human voice could be so versatile; whether imitating the first cuckoo of spring and – greatly daring – the regimental sergeant-major, or rendering *My Mother's Lock of Hair* with many an emotional throb and quaver, not to mention recitations of *Gunga Din* and *Mandalay*.

All too soon, they were sighting the Dassen Island Light and, a few hours later, engines at slow, steaming into Cape Town Harbour with the great mass of Table Mountain

285

dominating the skyline. Then all was activity with troops assembling for disembarkation, bugles making their final calls and launches coming alongside with orders for the various regiments. There was little time for prolonged farewells; which was just as well, perhaps, for he'd grown greatly attached to these young men who spoke of death so bravely; a death that some of them must surely face in the weeks that lay ahead.

It was a quiet ship – almost a sombre ship, loaded as it was with wounded – that left Cape Town for Britain a few days later. For the news they'd picked up along the wharfs had not been good; a thousand troops surrendering at Ladysmith and Baden-Powell besieged at Mafeking. But Kitchener of Khartoum, they comforted themselves, was not a man to be trifled with, any more than Redvers Buller and little Lord Roberts, the V.C. And it was clear from the other troop-ships anchored at the South Arm, that men were coming from every corner of the Empire. 'Including India!' said Neill-Dibh proudly, his white teeth flashing in a huge smile.

Ted smiled back, appreciating how he must feel. But would his compatriots be any more at home in the vast mountain ranges of Africa than Thomas Atkins? He doubted it.

There was one more voyage to Cape Town and then, in May, *Majestic* was back on the North Atlantic; the same month that Mafeking was relieved.

For the first time, Ted queried his contract. Could he not be moved to *Britannic*, which was still serving as a troop-ship? He would happily give up his command and serve in any capacity the Company chose to use him.

But they would have none of it. His wish to serve his country was greatly to be commended – eventually, no doubt, he would be given a medal for it – but both he and *Majestic* were needed back on the North Atlantic. To bring in the money, he thought cynically, but fortunately bit back the words in time.

But he felt badly about it. To leave 'his' troops in Africa

while he sailed safely for home had depressed him enough

Even Mattie – pointing out that he was well out of it and, anyway, it was not all the fault of the Boers; Cecil Rhodes was an over-ambitious, grasping individual who needed to be taught a lesson – didn't improve his spirits.

'It's like being kept in after school,' he tried to explain, 'while your friends go scrumping for apples.'

'In that case,' she told him once he'd explained 'scrumping', 'It's your pride that's hurt.' And she was probably right.

40

'Nice man!' said Babsie. Ted felt a pang of remorse. Was that all he was to his daughter – a nice man?

He'd just given her the doll with the real china face that he'd bought from Macy's, and was sprawled upon the hearthrug with her, watching her undress the doll and put it to sleep in the tiny cot he had also brought.

'You spoil her, Ted,' Eleanor said. 'But then, you spoil me, too!' and she helped herself to another of the Maillard chocolates she was so fond of.

'Nice man!' said Babsie again.

Eleanor must have seen the expression on his face for she said, quickly, 'She's young yet, my darling. She'll soon know you're her papa. I have been teaching her the word.'

It was then that Ben, their Irish wolfhound puppy, came bounding into the room.

'Papa!' Babsie immediately abandoned the doll in favour of hugging the furry little body.

'No, darling, that's Ben!' But it was too late; the point had been well and truly made.

From then on, he spent every spare moment he could with Babsie, reading to her from her book of nursery rhymes, playing with the blocks Joseph had made for him when he was a child, showing her how to count upon her abacus.

They went to watch 'Papa's ships' steaming up and down river, and he was allowed to jump her over the cracks in the pavement and swing her up on to his shoulders when she was tired. It was a proud moment when, thus adorned, he met John Barber and his wife, who also lived in Waterloo and was able to show off his loved ones.

But his greatest achievement came when he remembered Pa's horse game. 'This is the way the lady rides, trit trot, trit trot!' Forgotten for years, the words tripped off his tongue as if it were only yesterday that Pa had bounced him upon his knee in the Well Street kitchen. And Babsie loved it as much as he had done; that butcher boys now rode upon bicycles not horses worried her not at all.

As Ted had feared, not even the regiments rushed to South Africa from Australia, New Zealand and India had been equal to the cunning of the Boers, and Britain's losses that year were heavy. But the *Morning Post* was full of stories of bravery under fire, of bulldog perseverance in the face of adversity, all sent back from the scene of conflict by young Winston Spencer Churchill.

It was like news from another world to hear from Savannah of the arrival of baby James and baby John, and another on the way. Anna began to plan a 'long visit'.

Early in 1901, the old Queen finally relinquished her tenuous hold upon life and the country was plunged into mourning. As *Majestic* steamed slowly past the Isle of Wight, where she lay at Osborne House, Ted ordered the Ensign to be dipped; and again when they entered harbour in New York.

In October, Eleanor's mother passed away and was laid to rest in St Oswald's churchyard beside her husband. 'Woodhead will never be the same again,' said Eleanor.

Visiting with her and Babsie when he was next home, Ted was inclined to agree. 'We never realised,' said Maria sadly, 'that Mama was the driving force behind all that we did. John and I are now like trees at the mercy of the wind, blown hither and thither, without direction.'

Walking back with Babsie from an inspection of the well, Ted looked up at the old house, sitting four-square and solid in its bower of trees, the windows neatly set as a child would draw them, the front door precisely placed, and rememberd it as it had been; saw the Marthas rushing headlong down the hill towards him, skirts billowing in the breeze, hair streaming behind, full of some new piece of mischief; saw Maria and Eleanor, baskets over their arms, bending between the currant bushes at the side of the house; saw little Ada — long since married and gone away — shaking a rug from her third-floor window, that same window from which he and Eleanor had seen Mrs Pennington rounding the corner at Monk Farm and thought that all was lost.

It had once been a happy family home and, please God, would be so again one day. But not in this generation, he thought, for John Pennington seemed quite content with his celibate life; as was Maria.

This time, Anna crossed with him and sat at his table. Frank was to meet her in New York and take her down to Savannah. On their last evening on board, they sat for a little while in the first-class lounge, watching the sun set over a calm sea.

'This may be the last time I shall cross the North Atlantic, Ted,' said Anna, the seasoned sailor. 'Perhaps, even, the last time I shall go to sea.'

'You'll be coming back to see George in no time!'

'Perhaps. We'll see. But if only . . .' she began, then stopped abruptly and he saw that her eyes had filled with tears. Quickly, he laid his hand over hers.

'I know, my dear, I know. But we must just remember the good times.'

'I think perhaps it won't be long before I join him.'

Privately, he thought she could be right, for she had aged considerably of late. Whereas widowhood had seemed to give Ma an added strength, even to increase the resilience she had always shown towards life's adversities, Anna had grown in upon herself, lived in the past, surrounded herself with Joseph's most treasured possessions. One of her trunks, Ted knew, held his sextant and glass, both lovingly polished, his many books and pictures.

"You'll feel differently,' he told her, 'when you get to Savannah, among Frank's brood.'

'Aye, you could be right!'

He saw her off, Frank at her side, from Grand Central Station, his last view of her at the train window. The dark grey and black of her widow's weeds accentuated the stark pallor of her skin; one long, thin hand was raised in salute and her eyes glistened with tears, but upon her face was that rare, beautiful smile that had captivated Joseph for all the years of their marriage. And then her face began to blur at the edges and he realised that he, too, was crying.

The following year saw the end of the war – might, in the end, had triumphed – and Ted, along with every man, woman and child in the nation, rejoiced. Even Babsie waved her tiny flag and tied a red, white and blue ribbon around Ben's neck, which he promptly chewed into a pulp.

A spirit of change permeated the country; a younger, more easy-going monarch now sat upon the throne. And although not everyone approved of his morals, his self-indulgence where women were concerned – Ted certainly did not – there was an easy charm about him, an air of jovial bonhomie, that endeared him to his people.

'Good, old Teddy!' they cried upon the day of his coronation. Permissive he might be, but dull, never.

It was not only the monarchy whose image had altered. The winds of change were blowing through the offices and boardrooms of the White Star Line, and the private houses of its owners.

John Pierpont Morgan was an American banker of apparently unlimited resources who owned the International Mercantile Marine Company as well as several other shipping lines, and had more than a finger in the succulent pie of the American railroads. But he needed a well-known and reputable name to give weight and substance to his empire; such a name as the White Star Line.

A bargain, advantageous to both sides was struck. Although now officially under American ownership, the familiar name was kept and the Ensign, not the Stars and

Stripes was still flown from the mastheads. Bruce Ismay was the managing director, and even bigger ships, Ted heard, were being planned by the new company.

When *Majestic* went into dry dock for a lengthening of her funnels, he was given *Germanic* for a few months but could hardly wait to have *Majestic* back. Even so, he knew that if his career was to progress as he hoped, his days upon her were numbered. As, also, was his time in Liverpool, for it was becoming abundantly clear – he often discussed the matter with John Barber – that as ships became bigger and heavier, deeper harbours must be found for their increase in draught; deeper, he suspected, than Liverpool could offer.

It was a great pity, for on the home front, things could not have been better. His long-held ambition to live in Marine Crescent had at last been fulfilled and the Smiths were now comfortably ensconced at Number Seventeen. In summer, Eleanor could now sit upon the verandah, among the sweet-scented roses that climbed its elegant, wrought-iron pillars, and watch Babsie playing upon the grass; at the same time, keeping an eye open for *Majestic*'s approach up-river. Then, hand in hand, Ben beside them, they would cross the road to the shingle, there to stand and wave, with Babsie screaming, 'Papa! Papa!' at the top of her voice.

That 'Papa' could only give the briefest of salutes in return – and then only if the eyes of the other bridge officers were turned elsewhere – was a source of considerable dissatisfaction to her, but it was extraordinary how often his officers *were* looking in the other direction when they passed that excited little figure dancing up and down on the strand.

In winter, or when the weather was inclement, a large red bath towel would be waved from the front bedroom window. Quite what the neighbours thought about such goings-on, Ted never found out. 'At least,' he once overheard Eleanor telling Thomas's wife Ada, 'I am not waving my drawers!'

41

Rumours were rife; all, it was said, was not as well as had been expected with the new company, nor with the health of its American president, Clement Grisson. Bruce Ismay was now certain to replace him.

Was it, Ted wondered, that the organisation had grown too large for its own good? Just as, it sometimes crossed his mind – though he dared not voice such a suggestion except to Eleanor – its ships might also be doing? For *Baltic*, the Line's latest acquisition and the largest ship in the world, was well over twice the tonnage of *Majestic*.

It was a proud day for him when he took *Baltic* out of Liverpool on that bright June day of 1904. The schedule was maintained, if only just. Sensibly, he resisted the temptation to con her into New York himself, for her draught was much deeper than that of *Majestic*. Wiser, by far, to leave it to the experts; especially as the reporters were there in strength to welcome them.

Next day, returning from the Company offices, he decided to drop in at a drugstore for a cooling drink. A top-hatted, dark-suited man standing next to him glanced at the rings upon his sleeve and enquired politely when the captain had 'put into port'.

'Yesterday, sir, on the *Baltic*'.

'Ah! So you must be the celebrated Captain Smith I've just been reading about. Allow me to introduce myself, Captain. Horace J. Rosenbaum, at your service. I was telling my wife only yesterday that if ever I had cause to travel to England, it would be with the White Star Line.'

'We'd certainly do our best to make you comfortable, Mr Rosenbaum.'

'Unlike the unfortunate owners of the *General Slocum*. You've heard about that dreadful tragedy, I expect?'

'Only that she caught fire on the East River and there was some loss of life.'

'*Some* loss of life! My dear Captain, you have no idea! Over a thousand dead, and nearly all women and children.'

'Good God!'

'I fear He was *not* good upon this occasion, Captain.'

'How did it happen that there were so many children?'

'She'd been chartered for a combined Sunday-school outing from the Lower East Side. Every inch of space was crammed with excited kids, no doubt being held back from leaning too far over the rails by their teachers, blissfully unaware that they were soon to be victims of an even greater danger. They were near Hell Gate when the dreaded word "Fire"! was shrieked for the first time. An appropriate place to be, for within seconds it must have seemed like a raging inferno to those poor, captive children.'

Ted, leaning heavily upon the counter, wished devoutly that his new friend were less articulate. He knew Hell Gate, on the East River, so called for its dangerously narrow channel until blasting had widened it some years previously. The burning vessel with its cargo of hysterical children would have been clearly visible to parents gathered upon the shore to wave to their little ones. He thought of Babsie and felt nausea rise in his stomach. But Mr Rosenbaum, once embarked upon his tide of eloquence could not be stopped.

'The added horror was that many took what seemed the only possible course of action – to jump overboard into the water, there to quench the flames that had already taken hold of their hair and clothing. But they had forgotten the churning might of the paddle, which was still at work, carrying this. . . .' He paused, seeking for a word that could describe the horror. '. . . this pyre of human suffering into eternity.'

294

Tight-lipped, Ted straightened his shoulders and willed the blood to return to his cheeks. 'You have, indeed, a most convincing gift for narration, sir. Were you, may I ask, acquainted with any of the children who perished?'

'No, my interest is not a personal one. But the poor, unfortunate victims were from a German Lutheran neighbourhood of the Lower East side and I have the privilege of being both of German descent and a Lutheran.'

'I see. My – my condolences, sir.'

'Thank you. And if you are of a mind, Captain, your sympathy can take a more solid shape. A fund for those fortunate enough to survive but who have sustained injury, and the relatives of those who did not, will almost certainly be set up. And I, of course, shall be involved with it.'

'Indeed, yes.' Hastily he felt in his pocket and thrust a handful of bills into the other's hand. 'And now, if you'll excuse me, sir, I have business on board I must attend to. I can hardly say it has been a pleasure to talk to you, but I wish you well with your mission of mercy. Good day, sir.'

And he hurried out into the fresh air.

If only, he kept thinking as he walked back to the *Baltic*, there had not been so many children; although, in truth, it was dreadful to think of any human beings of whatever age dying in such circumstances. If only the fire precautions upon the *General Slocum* had been more rigorous, if only there had not been so many on board, if only the wheel had been stopped sooner, if only. . . .

But then he remembered Joseph's summing-up of the disaster of the *Birkenhead*, delivered upon the paddle-steamer coming from Tybee, '*Hindsight is such an easy thing to have, especially by those who were not present at the actual event*'.

He'd been right, of course, as he had been about so many things. So perhaps such a charitable summing-up might be made about the unfortunate skipper of the *General Slocum*. But please God, he himself would never be in such a situation!

☆

295

It was after the disaster of the *General Slocum* that he began the practice of mailing a letter to Babsie each time he was in New York. Sometimes, he found time to pen a few lines while still at sea, but if not, he would scrawl a hasty note as soon as they'd docked. He did not write a long letter; perhaps an anecdote or two about other children who might be crossing with him, or describing a certain concert on shipboard when a lady who clearly thought she was another Madam Clara Butt rendered *The Holy City* with such power she caused all the spoons in all the saucers of all the coffee cups to rattle an accompaniment, and a young man wielded his Indian clubs with such enthusiasm, they came sailing out into the audience – 'your Papa nearly had his ear taken off!'

Although the letters were addressed, in his neat copper-plate, to Miss Helen Melville Smith, he always enclosed a note 'for Mama', simply telling her that he missed her, that she was still the 'Queen of My Heart' and that he was counting the days before he saw her again.

As he had promised, he wrote regularly to Frank, who was now contemplating the purchase of a property in Mont-gomery, a village near Savannah, for his expanding family.

Expanding indeed! Alexander and Ann had now arrived upon the scene, with another child, inevitably, on the way.

Although not large, his own family was a tight-knit unit, complete in itself. This was largely due to Eleanor, for it was she who was the constant factor, the bridge between Babsie and himself. He did his best with his letters and little presents, the last of which had been a copy of Mr Kipling's *Just So Stories* for she was reading quite well now.

Really, the only cloud on his horizon was Bruce Ismay. Although White Star's official policy was now to offer comfort rather than speed, it hadn't stopped Ismay, when he crossed on *Baltic* at the beginning of 1906, from holding a daily inquest into her progress, although he knew as well as Ted that she was not cut out for speed. In his more cynical moments, Ted wondered why Ismay did not have a per-manent office on board every White Line Star liner and then he could spend his entire working life at sea, nagging the skipper whenever he was of a mind. But these thoughts he shared only with Eleanor. And, in fact, Ismay the family man he found a most pleasant companion, always happy to talk about his three children; even with great sadness, of the baby who had died.

'If he were just an ordinary man,' he confided in Eleanor, 'a shopkeeper or a knife-grinder or a hurdygurdy man, I would probably like him very much, As it is, I am always aware that he is my managing director and responsible for paying my salary each month.'

'I don't see,' said Eleanor reasonably, 'how it can ever be otherwise, my darling. That's the way life is. Even the King must kowtow to the Government sometimes.'

It was sheer coincidence that the next moment, a hurdygurdy man, a red scarf about his neck, a red-fezzed monkey perched upon his shoulder, should have come down the Crescent and stopped outside Number Seventeen, there to churn out Babsie's favourite tune, *If Your Lips Could Only Speak*! *That*, at least, was not coincidence for the man knew full well that she would rush out of the house the moment he had finished, with a sixpence clutched in her hand.

'She must learn to share with others less fortunate than herself,' said Eleanor as they watched from the window, 'but all the same, I do wish that monkey looked a little cleaner.' (Mothers, he reflected wryly, hadn't changed over the years!) And then she began to laugh. 'I doubt if Mr Ismay would make a good hurdy-gurdy man, my love! He's far too sleek and dapper!'

'He'd probably own a dozen of 'em in no time,' said Ted irreverently, 'and time them to the second. "Only five minutes in Marine Crescent, my man, or you won't have time for Adelaide Terrace"!'

'Ted, you are being most unfair!'

Still laughing, they went off to New Brighton for a picnic. Tomorrow, he would tell Eleanor of another conversation Ismay had had with him on *Baltic*.

☆

'As no doubt you've heard, Captain Smith, *Adriatic* will be launched later this year,' Ismay had begun. 'And if all goes well, she'll sail from Liverpool next summer, bound for New York, with yourself as commander. But she won't be returning to Liverpool, she'll be going back to Southampton. And that will be her home port from then on.'

'In other words. . . ?'

'I'm afraid it will mean a move for you and your family, Captain. But there are many advantages to Southampton. A deep and sheltered harbour and good tides. It's convenient, too, for London and the Continental ports.'

Suddenly, some imp of mischief, an urge, perhaps, to puncture Ismay's obvious complacency, had prompted Ted to say, 'From what I've heard, sir, Cunard's *Mauretania* must be nearing completion, too.' *Mauretania* would be not only the biggest ship – at 31,000 tons – in the world but also the fastest. But Ismay wouldn't need to be told that.

His face had flushed. 'You've heard correctly, Captain. However, Cunard are not claiming her to be the most *comfortable* ship in the world. We must remember our priorities, Captain.' And he had walked away.

A few weeks before he was due to take over *Adriatic*, *Baltic* ran aground just off Sandy Hook and was marooned there for several hours before floating off. And as if that wasn't enough, on her homeward trip she collided with a coal barge off New Jersey. That, he thought wryly, would teach him to try to take his managing director down a peg or two!

42

Did he want to cheer of cry? Fortunately, he had time to do neither on the June day in 1907 when he took *Adriatic* out of Liverpool on her maiden voyage, with Ismay, as he'd expected, on board. But everyone else was cheering, for it was common knowledge now that she would not be returning to Liverpool, and it was as if the entire city had turned out to bid her goodbye.

Eleanor, Babsie and Ben were already safely settled into their new home in Winn Road, Southampton. 'It will be our task to get it all ready for Papa when he comes home,' Eleanor had tried to comfort a tearful Babsie; for she had been greatly put out at having to leave her little school friends.

'It's not in the least *like* Woodhead,' Eleanor had telephoned, 'but it gives me the same feeling of homeliness.'

'Then that is what we shall call it, my love – Woodhead!'

They crossed the bar and the pilot disembarked, wishing him the best of luck, and then it was full speed ahead around the coast of Wales, before turning to Queenstown, there to embark more passengers and mail. Next time he anchored off Roche's Point, he would have reached it via Cherbourg and the English coast.

It was a good crossing; *Adriatic*, although a little larger than *Baltic*, was sufficiently like her to impose no special problems. And Ismay, perhaps because he was accompanied by one of his daughters, seemed less critical, extolling the delights of the new indoor swimming-pool and Turkish bath at least as often as he mentioned the day's performance. Also, his mother had died recently, and Ted knew that she

299

had exerted considerable influence in both family and Company affairs.

There was no grounding off Sandy Hook this time and they reached New York safely and on time; there to meet the inevitable posse of reporters. But Ted was ready for them.

'I cannot conceive of any vital disaster happening to the *Adriatic*,' he told them. 'Modern shipbuilding has gone beyond that. There will be bigger boats. The depth of harbours seems to be the great drawback at present. I cannot say, of course, just what the limit will be, but the larger boat will surely come. But speed will not develop with size, so far as merchantmen are concerned.' He paused for breath, allowing the frantically scribbling reporters to catch up.

'The travelling public,' he continued, 'prefers the large comfortable boat of average speed, and anyway that is the boat that pays. High speed eats up money mile by mile, and extreme high speed is suicidal. There will be high-speed boats for use as transports and a wise government will assist steamship companies in paying for them, as the English Government is now doing in the cases of the *Lusitania* and *Mauretania*, twenty-five knot boats; but no steamship company will put them out merely as a commercial venture.'

Not even Ismay, he thought, could have done better. He had stipulated that safety and comfort would always come before speed as far as the White Star Line was concerned and taken the wind out of their sails by pre-empting the inevitable questions about Cunard's high-speed vessels. He prepared to bid the reporters a courteous farewell.

But they hadn't finished with him yet. What about yourself, Captain? they asked. With all your experience before the mast, you must have many an exciting tale to tell.

The temptation to make up some gory tale, or even to tell them how he had once fallen from the rigging, witnessed a flogging and seen one of his mates fall victim to the crimps in San Francisco, was strong within him. But knowing full well that anything he said would be in tomorrow's papers and probably exaggerated out of all recognition, he assured them that nothing of any great consequence had ever happened to him.

But don't they realise, he thought that every time you set foot on a ship and trust yourself to the unpredictable might of the sea, you take your life in your hands? But he certainly wasn't going to say *that* with Bruce Ismay listening!

At Company offices, a letter awaited him from Frank. Dear Anna had passed away in her sleep.

'We found her in the morning,' Frank had written, *'with the most beautiful smile upon her face. And with a pile of Pa's old letters spread out across the bed. As you know, she had kept every one. So we must not be sad at her going, although we shall miss her greatly.'*

Ismay, in a mellow mood on the homeward journey, had suggested they smoke their after-dinner cigars together.

'I thought you'd lke to know, Captain, that we're very pleased with *Adriatic's* performance. And yours.'

'Thank you, sir. But with a ship like this one, she almost runs herself.'

'Your modesty does you credit, but the Company is fully aware of all that you do; and it will not go unmarked. Before you retire, and that will not be for years yet, I hope, I can promise you the most prestigious accolade the Company can give you.'

He must mean commodore. 'Thank you, sir!'

'Oh, it's not what you are thinking, Captain! Not *just*,' with an unexpected twinkle, 'commodore. How would you like to captain an even larger ship than *Adriatic*? I'll say no more at the moment. But believe me, Captain, great things are in store — for all of us!'

Somewhat bemused, Ted went to the bridge to make his routine inspection before turning in. So, there were even bigger ships in the offing. Bigger even than *Lusitania* and *Mauretania*! It was hard to imagine. But he wasn't greatly surprised; for he'd never really expected someone with Ismay's ambition to take the challenge of Cunard's magnificent vessels lying down, so to speak.

On the next Saturday he was home, he took Babsie and Ben for a walk on the nearby common. It was new ground to him.

'We are very fortunate, Babsie, to live near such a lovely expanse of open ground. And with so many beautiful trees.'

'Yes,Papa. But it doesn't smell quite as good as the sea.'

'You're right! Nothing smells as good as the sea. But there'll soon be some good scents hereabouts, once the spring sunshine has woken up the flowers.'

Just then a handsome Irish setter came bounding along the path, accompanied by a tweed-suited gentleman, sporting a brown bowler like Ted's and holding a little girl's hand, just as he was holding Babsie's.

Both girls immediately tore free and scampered towards each other.

'Babsie!'

'Rosie!' And then Babsie stopped dead in her tracks and turned back towards Ted, her arm outstretched as if to indicate some rare phenomenon.

'*This* is my Papa! You see, I *do* have one!'

Ted hurried forward, raising his hat and extending his hand. 'Edward Smith,' he introduced himself.

'Daniel Forsyth,' said the other man, clasping Ted's hand firmly. 'Our daughters attend the same school, I gather.'

Daniel Forsyth was a lawyer and lived close by, and a very pleasant hour was passed as they strolled on the common, with their daughters running ahead and their dogs maintaining a reasonably amicable relationship. After their ways had separated, Ted looked down at Babsie, his eyes troubled.

'I'm sorry, my dear, that I cannot be here every day, as other fathers are.'

'Oh, do not fret yourself, Papa! I much prefer it like this. For you are never cross with me and bring me back such lovely presents from New York. I am the envy of all the other girls in my class. For no one else,' she added proudly, 'has a father who is captain of a big ship.' She seemed cheerful enough and they walked a little way in silence until a small hand was suddenly thrust into his. 'But I do miss you, Papa, when you go away. So does Mama. We always have a little cry together when you've gone.'

He felt his throat tighten and, with a sudden flash of inspiration, remembered the words Ma had first used when she was trying to console him about Joseph's departure and had spoken ever afterwards as a sort of talisman to bring him safely home. He cleared his throat. 'It's like this, my dear one. If I didn't go away, I wouldn't have the delight of coming back to you. Nor you, I hope, the pleasure of seeing me again.'

She looked up at him, her eyes wide. 'I think that's what Mama must mean when she wipes my eyes and says we must be sad sometimes, or we wouldn't know how to be happy.'

'That's it, exactly, Babsie! What a clever pair you are!'

Babsie gave an excited little skip. 'Mind you, Papa, I soon cheer up for we always have muffins for tea the day you go, with strawberry jam.'

In June, he sailed from Test Quay for the first time, bound for Cherbourg, thus inaugurating the new weekly service. And Babsie and Rosie, as a special treat, were given leave of absence from school to see him off; travelling on the electric tramway all the way to the docks.

'I'm not sure which was the greater treat,' Eleanor admitted when he was home next. 'Waving goodbye to you or travelling on the tram! But the hoots were definitely the climax of the day. That was very clever of you, dearest.' For Ted had told the little girls that as *Adriatic* moved away from the quayside, three hoots would be sounded from the ship's siren. 'One for Babsie, one for Rosie and one for Mama.' No need to mention that three hoots was the traditional indication of departure!

In February of the following year, Bruce Ismay travelled as a passenger on board the *Mauretania* and Ted smiled to himself when he heard. Taking points, no doubt!

The keel of the giant *Olympic* was laid down in Belfast — on a berth especially extended for her. As was her sister ship, *Titanic*, three months later.

43

On the night before he took *Olympic* out on her maiden voyage, Eleanor and Ted sat for a while by the open window, talking quietly, breathing in the midsummer scents of roses, mignonette and stocks. Babsie had long since gone to bed, hugging Ted hard as she kissed him goodnight.

'Goodnight, Papa! Don't forget to write to us. Goodnight, Mama!'

Now, a couple of hours later, he glanced at his watch, 'Time for bed, dearest. I'll just let Ben out.'

And, as they stood at the door, waiting for Ben to go through his nightly ritual of gazing up at the stars – 'getting his bearings!' said Ted – sniffing along the wall for signs of next door's cat and generally behaving as if he were out there merely for a breath of fresh air before retiring, Eleanor reminded him, as Babsie had, 'Don't forget to write, my love.'

'You enjoy my scrawls, then?'

'Oh, yes! Immensely. And besides, when they arrive, I know you'll soon be with me again.'

As always on the night before he sailed, they made love; gently now, with little of the passion of the honeymoon years, but satisfying each other simultaneously, and leaving them relaxed and content.

'I love you, dearest!'

'And I you, my darling!'

Perhaps, after all, there was something to be said for his regular absences.

If Ismay had been relaxed during *Adriatic*'s maiden voyage, he was certainly not so during *Olympic*'s. He was like a mother hen, Ted thought, with only one chick, but that the biggest and best in the farmyard. At least, Thomas Andrews, managing director of the shipbuilders Harland and Wolff, was there to listen to him, when he wasn't pouring over construction charts in his cabin or wandering around the ship with that absorbed look upon his face which meant he was planning ways of improving even upon this magnificent product of his yard. Until recently, Andrews had been head of the firm's designing department, and had been involved in the construction of *Adriatic*. Not only did he have a reputation for brilliant design but also for the more prosaic virtues of hard work and precise attention to detail. However, both men seemed pleased with Olympic's average performance of just over twenty-one knots. And he must be grateful, too, that Ismay's wife was with him; for Florence would only stand for a certain amount of 'ship talk' at table.

Unfortunately, the voyage was not without incident. Steaming across the Upper Bay of New York, towards the crowds waiting at the White Star Line pier, was rather like a royal progress as other, smaller craft hooted or whistled a welcome and even *Lusitania*, outward bound for Britain, had sounded her siren. But, when docking was nearly completed, disaster struck.

The huge ship had needed twelve tugs to complete the intricate manoeuvre and one of them, the *O.L. Halenbeck*, came too near to the backwash from one of *Olympic*'s propellers. Washed perilously close to the liner's great stern, she took the full force of the surge and was driven into an underwater cable, almost sinking. Fortunately, she managed to clear herself in time and the crowd on the quayside let out its breath in an audible gasp of relief. So, too, did Captain Edward J. Smith up on the bridge, although rather less audibly. Now, there would have to be a visit to the notary next morning to lodge a protest, but at least the smaller vessel was still afloat and, most important of all, no lives had been lost. The damage to *Olympic*, he guessed, would be negligible but the incident had underlined the problems facing a ship of this size when close to other vessels. It was only in the open sea, it seemed, that she could be given her head without fear of calamity.

Once again, Ismay was in an expansive mood. 'There'll be *Titanic* to take out next year, Captain,' he said on the homeward journey. 'In March, probably, before the ice starts breaking up. And then. . . .' he paused significantly and Ted thought, now what? Are the rumours true and there is to be another, even larger, ship? '. . . there will be *Gigantic*!'

'I shall be honoured, indeed, to take out *Titanic*, sir. But as for — for *Gigantic*. . .' He fell silent. The very word was difficult for him to take seriously, for to him it was a child's word. Had not Babsie used it at an early age to describe the big teddy bear that Mattie had sent her?

He had thought *Olympic* presumptuous enough and *Titanic* almost dangerous, tempting Providence; his dictionary's definition of 'Titan' as 'a strong nature battling with Fate'. What Joseph would have made of such a name, he daren't imagine!

'Thinking of retirement, are you?' Ismay asked, putting his own interpretation upon Ted's continuing silence. 'Well, you could be right. I, too, am contemplating it.'

'*You*, sir!' His surprise was genuine for Ismay could be no more than fifty, if that.

'Well, let us say retirement from the White Star Line. Of course, I shall have other plans. Well,' he smiled expansively, 'let us keep this to ourselves for the moment, Captain. Let us just say that, for both of us, *Titanic* may be our final voyage together.'

Nodding his agreement, Ted wondered if Ismay knew of the invitation that had been awaiting him in New York — to a dinner to be held in his honour at the Metropolitan Club towards the end of the year, if that fitted in with his sailing schedules. He could still hardly believe it. The so-called Milionaires' Club giving a dinner especially for *him*! John

Pierpont Morgan, a founder member of the club, would have been responsible for the invitation. What would Eleanor say to that?

But there was to be another disturbing incident before his dinner at the Metropolitan.

On the twentieth of September, he bade goodbye as usual to Eleanor and Babsie and drove off in his customary cab to Canute Road. The following afternoon, he was back. Eleanor, alerted by the sound of the cab drawing up outside and by Ben's welcoming bark, met him at the door. 'Dearest, what's wrong? What has happened? Are you ill?'

He bent to kiss her. 'No, my love, I am well. But very, very cross! Although I am certainly calmer now than I was.'

She took his arm and led him into the sitting-room. 'Sit down, dearest. I'll see about some tea.'

He drank three cups of it. Then Eleanor passed him his cigar box. He lit up, inhaled deeply and let out the smoke in a long, relaxing sigh.

'George Bowyer was our pilot as usual,' he said at last. 'A good, experienced man, if ever there was one. As we neared the Isle of Wight, he said, "Port as usual, I suppose, Captain?" for he knows I always prefer to take the Spithead route around the Bramble.'

" 'Port as usual, please",' I said.

'Accordingly, speed was reduced from seventeen knots to twelve, ready for the turn. So far, so good! Then everything seemed to happen at once. The usual instructions were given from the bridge, plus a couple of loud whistle blasts to indicate our imminent turn to port. This we managed perfectly and began to increase speed. While this was going on, young Hune – he's my second – who was up in the crow's nest had spotted another ship rounding Egypt Point and closing fast. She was identified as His Majesty's cruiser *Hawke*, and going considerably faster than ourselves, in fact overtaking us. And then – quite unexpectedly as far as Bowyer and I were concerned – she began to drop back. At this point, *Hawke* suddenly turned to port – and came straight for us.'

Eleanor drew in her breath sharply and Ted smiled at her reassuringly. 'Perhaps I should have begun my story by telling you that no lives were lost! Anyway, I realised that a collision was unavoidable. Bower immediately ordered the helm hard to port but, although *Olympic* responded like the great lady that she is, it was too late. *Hawke* rammed us below the mainmast.' He paused again, obviously reliving the moment.

'Even on a ship that size, the noise of the impact was something I shall never forget. But it could have been a great deal worse. Although she now has a very large hole in her side, it is above the water-line. There is some damage below but the water was held in check by the closure of the watertight doors.'

'And HMS *Hawke*?'

'In a far worse state than us, I fear. Her bow was torn apart and her plates torn.' He managed a wry smile. 'It was as well, perhaps, that her commander and I were still some distance apart!'

'So what happened next?'

'Well, we couldn't put back into Southampton until high tide so we anchored in Osborne Bay for the night and the passengers were taken off by tender. And poor *Hawke* limped off in the direction of Portsmouth with her pumps going full blast.'

'But what an extraordinary thing to do,' said Eleanor, 'to come straight at you like that.'

'Well, the enquiry may explain why it happened. But I have the feeling that *Hawke*'s commander may have been just as astonished as Bowyer and I. It's possible that suction might have had something to do with it. From a ship the size of *Olympic*, it must be enormous.' He glanced at his wife, saw that she was biting her lip and leaned over to touch her cheek. 'Don't worry, my love. I'm back, safe and sound!'

For a while, he wondered if *Olympic*'s command would now be given to another skipper, but there was no fear of that, he was told; he would be back with *Olympic* just as soon as she was repaired, probably at the end of November.

'So all should be well,' he tried to reassure Eleanor. 'It's the crew I feel sorry for. They've come out of it with only three days' pay instead of the round trip they'd expected. Cheer up, sweetheart!' he added, for Eleanor still seemed distinctly unhappy.

'There's a part of me that almost wishes they *had* retired you. It's so wonderful to have you at home all day and every day. But it's not just the delight of your company.' She paused, chafing one hand inside the other. 'Well, I know I've said it already, Ted, but I just don't like these big ships.'

He held her close, stroking her hair while he murmured reassurances. 'Teething troubles, sweetheart, that's all they are.'

But in his heart of hearts, he agreed with her. Not that he thought these great leviathans of the sea had no future. People like Andrews would soon sort it all out and he had no doubt of his own ability to master the problems, once they were fully known – he had certainly learned something from this last episode. No, *his* disquiet lay in the fear that man was getting above himself and trying to ape the Almighty. And he was too much the son of his father – for Pa had always preached that God would grow extremely wrathful if man tried to emulate Him – not to feel it.

'Listen, sweetheart,' he said, 'I'm committed to taking out *Titanic*. I've told Ismay I will and it's the least I can do now that they're letting me keep *Olympic*. But after her maiden voyage, I promise you I'll give it all up and retire.'

Her smile was like sunshine breaking through a rack of storm clouds. 'Dearest Ted, will you really? You wouldn't mind?'

He shook his head. 'I can promise you I shall have no regrets.' Nor would he, if he could make her happy.

To many, their routine in those days before the enquiry, might have seemed dull in the extreme; but to both of them it was precious beyond words. Each morning, he and Ben would accompany Babsie to school, where she would embrace him fondly – for all to see! – and then he and Ben would turn on to the common; while Ben careered ecstatically through the bushes, he would stride just as happily through the gold and reds and tawny orange of the fallen leaves. Was he, after all, a countryman at heart?

Then it was back to a welcome cup of coffee while he scanned the *Daily Echo* or *Southampton Times* and Eleanor completed her household tasks. There might be shopping then and his initiation into a whole new world.

Sometimes, they would stroll down to the Old Town below Bargate, perhaps to visit St Michael's Church, whose tall spire he would always look for as he sailed up Southampton Water; just as countless sailors had done before him. Or take a turn along the Royal pier, or stand, with other passers-by outside the South Western Hotel to watch the dropping of the Time Ball at eleven o'clock. Occasionally, he would persuade Eleanor inside to take lunch.

And then it was back to Woodhead, to take Ben to meet Babsie from school, followed by ludo, or card games like snap and rummy, while tea was prepared. But perhaps the evenings, after Babsie had gone to bed, were the most precious times of all, with the two of them on either side of the hearth and Ben sprawled between.

Even when *Olympic* was passed fit for duty at the end of November, and their idyll drew to a close, Fate was on their side. For fog delayed her departure for a whole day. Never had it been so welcome!

On Thursday the twenty-seventh of December 1911, a little piece of history was made on board *Olympic*; General and Mrs Steward L. Woodford arranged a dinner party at the Waldorf-Astoria for that same night. They did it by using the Marconi operator to telegraph their requirements to their friend George C. Boldt, the proprietor of the hotel, and, to show their appreciation of the service, they invited *Olympic*'s captain. It was a grand occasion and Ted enjoyed it enormously – but not as much as the even grander occasion on the following evening.

311

☆

The interior of the Metropolitan Club was even more impressive than he'd expected. After being signed in, he was taken through the foyer into the gilded magnificence of the lounge that ran the whole length of the building and which, in daylight, must give a magnificent view of Fifth Avenue.

'The building, as you may know, is designed in the Italian Renaissance Palazzo style, Captain,' he was informed as he was led further, along sumptuously carpeted corridors.

'Indeed!'

'Indeed' was a word he found extremely useful when faced with a subject about which he knew very little.

'Similar in many ways to your Reform Club, I understand, Captain.'

'So I've heard.' Not that he frequented that bastion of the élite!

He was taken first into the Strangers' Room where guests were received, and offered a glass of excellent sherry. 'And you smoke, Captain, I understand, so we'll move in to the Smokers' Room, if you don't mind.'

Soon after he'd lit up, John Pierpont Morgan arrived, and Ted relaxed. From now on, the conversation would surely be of ships and shipping. And it was.

'You've heard the result of the *Hawke* enquiry, I take it?' Pierpont Morgan enquired after he'd welcomed his guest.

'Yes, sir. I heard over the wireless that we'd lost the case. I'm very sorry, sir.'

'Not your fault, Captain. In fact, none of it was your fault according to my reckoning. I don't know what those fellows at your Admiralty were thinking about, if you don't mind my saying.'

'I don't mind in the least, sir! I was most indignant. Particularly since they appeared to blame Bowyer. I should have done exactly the same, had I been in total command. I hope we shall continue to use him.'

'I've no doubt we shall. Anyway, enough about the *Hawke*. I can't tell you how much my wife and I are looking

312

forward to crossing with you on *Titanic's* maiden voyage.'

'It will be a pleasure to have you both on board, sir.'

Soon afterwards, they went into dinner; it was, he discovered, to be served in one of the many smaller rooms built especially for these comparatively intimate occasions, for there were no more than twenty-five people present.

He was given the place of honour next to Pierpont Morgan. The president of the club, Mr Levi P. Morton, he was told, was unfortunately unable to attend; but Ted remembered a sufficient number of those seated around the circular table to feel quite at home. John Jacob Astor, for instance, and Charles Hays from the Grand Trunk Railway, and James Harding and Philip Dodge, and Henry Frick, the steel magnate, who must have come up from Pittsburgh. No Vanderbilt? he wondered, but then spotted George.

After they had eaten a most delicious roast saddle of lamb followed by numerous desserts came the part he least relished. Pierpont Morgan rose to make a speech in his honour.

He didn't take in – and certainly couldn't remember – all that was said about him, although he knew it was distinctly complimentary and the phrase 'the Millionaires' Captain' stayed in his mind. And then they all rose and raised their glasses to him. 'Captain Edward John Smith, Commodore of the White Star Line! Long may he sail with us!'

That night, lying in bed he remembered others who had also sat at his table, sometimes more than once; William Stead, the magazine editor, for instance, Winston Churchill, the old Civil War general, William Washington Gordon, still alive down in Savannah, and Dr Perrin, now the Bishop of Willesden, as happy to talk about dogs and horses as about God.

Drowsily now, he remembered then that dear couple, Mr and Mrs John Thalton, who had first sailed with him on *Baltic* and then popped up with the most flattering frequency on every ship he'd skippered since.

Almost asleep, he thought of the countless thousands he

must have transported in steerage across the Atlantic. Some party if they could be gathered together! Dockers, lumberjacks, millers, farriers, shoemakers, farmers, tailors, nursemaids. . . .

The wrath of God? Pa would have had no doubt whatsoever that was what was let loose upon them on that mid-January crossing to New York. And even the most hardened atheist would surely have wondered.

There was one moment when he found himself wondering if a ship the size of *Olympic* could actually be pooped, for her bow was lifted high into the air by a wave of terrifying proportions. Up, up they went, with eveyone on the bridge hanging on for dear life to whatever they could find – *he* happened to be in the chart room, bent over the compass table – and then the wave broke and, like an old grampus, they wallowed in the trough. But that was not all; another great wave broke over them and for a moment it seemed as if they were sailing *under* the sea. Fleetingly, he thanked the Almighty that they were at least under cover. God help the crew of any sailing-ship that was out in this blinding snow!

It was no surprise to find that a forward hatch cover had been wrenched loose, even though it weighed all of five tons. Other fittings had also been torn away, including the forward portside rail.

'Bit breezy, was it?' asked Mattie, tongue in cheek, when he met her at their customary soda fountain. She was just back from a trip home to see her parents.

'Just a little! Now, tell me, how was everyone in Savannah?'

'My parents are reasonably well, I'm pleased to say, although Mama now has to walk with a stick and Papa finds walking anywhere very difficult. And poor Maria, they fear, is not long for this world. She nearly died of pneumonia in the fall, and now breathes with difficulty, although she is as cheerful as ever.

'But your lot, Ted, are flourishing. They all lined up to receive your presents – all nine of them, stretching from Clara. now twenty-two, down to those adorable little twins, Richy and Robby – it was like embracing a baseball team!'

314

'And Frank and Annie?'

'Surprisingly well, considering. Although I think Annie has now said enough is enough. Fortunately, Frank is doing very well in the lumber business and Arthur has now joined him. They all send their love and are hopeful that one day you will get down to see them.'

'I would have managed it, I think, if *Olympic* hadn't been laid up. But I will be writing, of course. And to your parents. Thanks, Mattie, I'm sorry I must rush away.'

'You're still leaving on schedule?'

'Oh, yes − *Olympic* will soon be as good as new!'

But her chapter of accidents was not yet over; seven hundred miles out into the Atlantic, homeward bound, in the middle of an icy February, a propeller fouled some object beneath the surface and lost a blade.

'What was that?' Ted rushed from his cabin to the bridge, for the shock had reverberated through the ship.

But Wilde, his chief officer, was as perplexed as he. 'A submerged wreck, Captain? That's all I can imagine. There was no warning. Just bad luck, I suppose.'

Bad luck? Or something more sinister? Once again, he felt unease. And this last occurrence, he reflected grimly, would probably mean *Olympic* returning yet again to Belfast for repairs; and a further delay for *Titanic*.

He was right in that forecast; there was only one more crossing on *Olympic* for him. And unusually, he felt no regret when he came off her at the end of March. A wonderful ship, there was no doubt of that, but one on which he had never felt completely at ease; not as he had on his dear old *Majestic*. Nor, he supposed, going back even further in time, on the *Lizzie Fennell*. But what a comparison to make when he was about to take out the largest ship in the world! Unsinkable, they said. Well, *that* was tempting Providence and no mistake!

But he hadn't time to think about it now. He was off to Belfast in the morning for *Titanic*'s trials. Time enough to see how he felt about her, when they were over.

44

'These are your quarters, Captain.'

Sixth Officer Moody stood back respectfully to allow him passage and he glanced swiftly around.

'Thank you, Mr Moody. I trust your quarters are as comfortable?'

'They'll do very nicely, sir. Thank you.'

Ted turned from his inspection to look directly at his most junior officer. 'Your last berth was *Oceanic*, I understand?'

'Yes, sir.' The young officer gazed back with something like reverence in his eyes. Ted extended his hand.

'Good to have you on board *Titanic*, Mr Moody.'

'Thank you sir.' James Moody clasped the hand briefly but firmly, saluted smartly, then turned on his heel and left.

Ted unpacked the small bag Moody had carried in for him. If *Titanic*'s trials went well, he'd be in Belfast for only a couple of days before sailing her to Southampton for her band-playing, flag-wagging departure to the States. He would welcome a few more days with Eleanor and Babsie but he was glad, even so, to have this time of comparative peace to come to terms, as it were, with the enormous vessel.

Standing just now, on the edge of the Abercorn Basin, gazing up at the enormity of her hull, he'd felt an absurd sense of inadequacy and, for a moment sensed how ants must feel beside the immensity of the garden spade that had disturbed them. And then he'd squared his shoulders. He would be sailing with sane, sensible William Murdoch as first officer and he was bringing Wilde over from the *Olympic* as chief. They considered it their good fortune to be part of

Titanic's crew, to be able to tell their grandchildren, 'I sailed on her maiden voyage' – as *he* would tell Babsie's children, God willing.

Titanic's sea trials were scheduled for the morning of Monday the first of April, and, as if to cock a snook at authority for selecting a day traditionally dedicated to fools, a fresh north-westerly wind set the white caps dancing in Belfast Lough and caused the water in the narrow confines of the Victoria Channel to slap smartly against its sides. To reach the Lough and then the open sea, *Titanic* had to negotiate the Channel. With *Olympic*'s escapade with *Hawke* still very much on everyone's mind, no one, least of all Ted, wanted to risk the possibility of *Titanic* scraping her sides against the walls of the Channel. At nine o'clock, with the tugs already fussing alongside, it was decided to abandon the trials for that day.

Ted knew it was the right decision. Outwardly, he accepted it with his customary philosophic calm. But it was a nuisance. With an inward sigh, he handed over the bridge to Murdoch and went to his cabin. Then, a mere five minutes later, emerged to sniff the breeze and pace the decks until it occurred to him that his presence might be a distraction to the workmen still scurrying about, putting countless finishing touches to various parts of the great ship. So he went back to his cabin but still paced restlessly, wishing he were back in Southampton, where he would have known just what to do with this extra time.

'Let me show you around *Titanic*, Captain!'

He'd eaten lunch with O'Loughlin, a hilarious meal, and was now drinking a cup of coffee with Andrews, who had just made the extraordinary suggestion. 'Oh, I know you've walked around a bit,' Andrews continued, 'and no doubt said, "how wonderful!" and "how marvellous!" and "whatever next!" And I admit that you will know all about her tonnage and her draught and her engine power etcetera, but I doubt if you're aware that fifteen thousand bottles of beer will be taken on board at Southampton?'

317

Ted chuckled. 'As a matter of fact, I do! O'Loughlin has just told me so. He also mentioned a thousand pounds of tea!'

'He has his priorities right, has the Doc! Now, how about it? There must be lots of places on board you haven't visited yet.'

'Won't I put the workmen off, wandering around in my uniform? They're used to seeing you.'

'Well, how about if I lend you a spare overall? That way, no one will notice you. Can't do much about your whiskers, I'm afraid, but I'll give you a bag of tools. That should be disguise enough.'

Chuckling like a couple of schoolboys, they rigged him out, Andrews even unearthing an old cloth cap from among his kit and an ancient muffler. 'You'd make a lovely plumber's mate'

They set off. Andrews, Ted soon discovered, was a superb guide. 'Just look at the colours of that stained glass!' he said in the first-class smoking-room. 'And feel the quality of the armchairs. All leather, of course. I tell you, Captain, there'll be as many deals made here in the middle of the ocean, as in the Exchanges of London and Liverpool.'

Ted nodded. With people like John Jacob Astor and Benjamin Guggenheim on board, it was to be expected, especially with the Marconi wireless service at their disposal.

The next stop was the Café Parisien; light and airy but more British, he would have thought, than French, with its uncompromising wickerwork chairs and tables,; but no doubt the food and the music would be suitably Continental.

They inspected the gymnasium, the squash court, the Turkish baths, the reading and writing-rooms and the sumptuous staterooms, each with its own bathroom.

Gazing at one of them, there flashed into his mind, the memory of the back kitchen in Well Street on a Saturday night, with the old tin bath in front of the fire and himself having 'first splash', as Pa had put it. 'But not too much of the splash!' Ma would caution. What would she have made of all this? he wondered.

'Penny for them?' Andrews offered as he led him away towards the children's play area.

'Oh, nothing important! Just wondering what my dear mother would have made of all this grandeur.'

'Sometimes I wonder what I make of it myself,' said Andrews unexpectedly.

Ted glanced at him in surprise. 'But surely, as managing director of Harland and Wolff, you're one hundred percent in favour?'

'Well, yes, in a way. And like you, no doubt, I'm honoured to be associated with such a wonderful creation. But we only carry out the instructions of our clients, you know. And now and then, I ask myself if we're not becoming a shade too ambitious for our own good.'

'I feel rather that way myself.' Secretly pleased that Andrews seemd to share his views, he decided to test him further. 'According to my brother Joseph, steam power was an invention of the devil.'

'Oh, I think God is on our side, all right,' said Andrews easily. 'God and the watertight bulkheads! Tell me,' he paused upon the threshold of the nursery suite, 'how do you feel about the eleventh commandment – thou shalt not desert thy ship, but founder with her? Surely it doesn't still hold good in this modern age?'

'Well, it would depend, of course. But if anything were to happen to the *Titanic*, well. . . .' He shrugged expressively. Andrews must know as well as he that the lifeboats on board, while meeting Board of Trade regulations, would be hopelessly inadequate; the reasoning of the Board being that if the vessel was divided into efficient watertight compartments and had the means of communication with the shore or with other vessels, they would never be needed. '. . . I certainly shouldn't want to survive.'

'Nor I,' said Andrews simply, pushing open the door to the nursery.

They were both much taken with it and stood for several moments, admiring the dappled splendour of an enormous rocking horse. 'There'll be a fight for that,' said Ted, remembering how he'd coveted one as a child, although Pa's knees had certainly done their best.

Although naturally not so luxurious, the second and third-class accommodation he thought of an excellent standard; and would be greatly appreciated by the many Irish emigrants that *Titanic* would take on board at Queenstown.

By now, they were well down into the bowels of the vessel and Andrews was showing him the great larders and cold rooms, the ice-making machine, the enormous storage areas for the coal that would be needed to get them across the Atlantic at a reasonable speed.

'Coal strike still on, I suppose?' he asked Andrews.

'Afraid so, but the last I heard, it was looking more hopeful. Anyway, *we* should be all right. Your other Company ships won't like it but they'll have to hand over their reserves.'

Ted nodded, glad that he didn't have that particular headache to worry over.

'We'll leave out the engine and boiler rooms, if you don't mind,' Andrews said. 'They've got enough to think about at the moment, without me fussing around.'

He didn't mind at all; in fact he was feeling more than grateful that he wasn't a steward having to dash along these miles of corridors at everyone's beck and call.

'Anyway,' Andrews added with a grin, 'they might try to give you a job down there! We've been lucky so far.'

They were mounting the crew's staircase on their way back to Andrews' quarters when the luck ran out.

'Mr Andrews, can you spare a moment, sir?' It was one of the electricians, hung about with coils of wire and wearing a harassed expression.

Andrews turned to Ted. 'Right, Smith,' he said briskly, and the eye furthest away from the workman dropped its lid. 'I'll see you in my cabin.'

And Ted, now feeling as vulnerable as a newborn child, could do nothing else but carry on his way. However, he did remember to touch the peak of his cap. 'Very good, sir.'

He was torn between increasing his stride or shortening it. In the end, he compromised with a sort of shamble, head sunk upon his chest.

'Here, you!' He could be forgiven for not at first realising that the command – from a burly individual wearing a similar overall to his own – was addressed to himself; particularly since *he* would never have dreamed of using such a phrase to a subordinate.

'You! Rip Van Winkle, with the beard! Come over here and lend a hand with these shelves!'

Not since he and Bert had been caught scrumping apples in Cobridge had he felt such panic. On that occasion, they'd taken to their heels and run for their lives, and it took all his willpower not to do so now. But to feign deafness, he decided quickly, was the wisest course. 'Rip Van Winkle', after all, was entitled to be a little hard of hearing! But he could feel the sweat pouring down the back of his neck, and the hand holding the bag of tools was gripping the handle like a vice – then a firm hand fell upon his shoulder.

'It's all right,' Andrews hissed in his ear. 'I'm back!'

Once in Andrews' cabin, their laughter was uncontrollable. And his relief enormous. He took off the overall, cap and muffler and shrugged himself back into his jacket. 'Thank you. That was a memorable experience! Now, I sincerely hope you're going to be able to stay with us when we're in Southampton.'

'I'm already booked into the South Western and anyway, want to be as near as possible to the ship. But thank you.'

It was strange, and yet perhaps not so strange, that his tour of inspection with Andrews seemed to have reassured him that he and *Titanic* would eventually achieve the harmony, the integration of personality almost, that he had felt with his other ships, bar *Oympic*. That the trials next day were an unqualified success no doubt added to this conviction.

From the moment when the tug *Hercules* had thrown the first line overboard, followed by those from *Huskisson* and *Herculaneum*, *Hornby* and *Herald* – 'No *Hell* and *High Water*?'

Ted had wanted to murmur to Murdoch but, of course, hadn't – to conduct her down the Victoria Channel and out into Belfast Lough, *Titanic* had behaved with the impeccable manners of a great lady, allowing the steam from her newly fired boilers to set her great heart pulsing with life.

It was a grand feeling to be up on her bridge, Murdoch beside him, Moody and Lightoller fore and aft, as her speed rose and he began to put her through her paces; turns to port and starboard using the rudder by itself, then with the aid of the propellers; stops and starts; a magnificent, full-circle turn when her bow cut across her wake in a flurry of foam. And then, her grand finale when, running full speed ahead, he put her suddenly to full astern. Shuddering violently, for it must, indeed, have been a cruel shock to her nervous system, *Titanic* took a little less than half a mile to come to a complete stop.

It didn't need the excited murmurs from the bigwigs on board to tell him that her performance had been exemplary.

It only remained, then, to run her out into the Irish Sea for a couple of hours, then turn back to Belfast – all at an average speed of eighteen knots but reaching twenty-one for a short while. Ted felt both exhilaration and relief.

And now, all formalities completed; the Board of Trade Certificate – *Good for one year from today* – duly signed and the ship officially handed over from the builders to the Company, she was free to proceed to her home port of Southampton. A great pity there would be no time to look in at Liverpool en route, as *Olympic* had done after her trials – he would have given much to catch even a glimpse of Bert and Thomas and George – but there was nothing to be done about it. Her schedule had been delayed quite enough already.

The days passed far too quickly. On Good Friday, they strolled, like everyone else in Southampton it seemed, along the dockside with Ted in discreet mufti, and admired the beauty of the ship; and spotted Andrews from afar still busy about some task or other. On Easter Sunday, with

Eleanor and Babsie sporting the latest millinery creations – Eleanor's an intricate ruching of multicoloured ribbons and Babsie's a youthful arrangement of marguerites – they attended morning service.

'Good luck, Captain,' said the Reverend Mitchell as they left. 'We shall be thinking of you!'

For the rest of the time, when he was not concerned with the preliminaries of *Titanic's* sailing day, he walked with Ben upon a common bright with daffodils – how he loved those golden harbingers of spring! – or sat, weather permitting, in the garden with Eleanor.

'Bright and early, Papa!' said Babsie when she kissed him goodnight on the day before he was to sail.

'Bright and early, it is, my precious!'

That night, as Eleanor slept peacefully beside him, one arm thrown across his body, he awoke and made out the shape of his uniform hanging behind the door, as it always did on the eve of his departure, once Eleanor had brushed and pressed it. Nostalgia swept over him as he remembered the night in Well Street, prior to his first departure on the *Senator Weber*, when the uniform of a 'boy' had hung behind the door and a mixture of anticipation and regret had kept him awake; regret at leaving Ma mingling with the excitement of going to sea. Now, his life had come full circle; regret at leaving the sea mingling with the anticipation of being at home with his loved ones.

As always, they said their real goodbye in the privacy of their bedroom.

'Goodbye, my precious girl! Take care of yourself!'

'Goodbye, my dearest dear! God speed!'

Then it was down to the hall to stroke Ben, who knew quite well what was happening and clearly deplored it from the bottom of his faithful heart, licking his master's hand in a frenzy of affection. And then came the familiar rush on the stairs, as Babsie, still in her nightgown, still flushed from sleep, came skimming down, to crash into his outstretched arms and hug him fiercely.

'Goodbye, dear, *dear* Papa!'

'Goodbye, my pretty one! Take care of Mama.'

And then, from inside the cab, the final wave and the picture of the three of them that would stay with him until he saw them again. Eleanor and Babsie with their arms around each other, Ben downcast, but managing a feeble wag of his tail.

Several hours later, steaming across the Channel towards Cherbourg, where lights were already beginning to prick the April dusk, he was still counting himself lucky. But only just! Thank heaven that, this time, he and Bowyer had been prepared. Even so, it had been a close thing.

Titanic had moved out – against the tide – into the River Test, heading for Southampton Water. To reach it, she had to pass *Oceanic* and the American liner, *New York*, moored further downstream. As she gathered speed, the force of her bow wave on the port side caused the stern of the *New York* to lift in the water and her mooring ropes to slacken. Inevitably, as *Titanic* proceeded and the pressure lifted, *New York*'s hull descended and the ropes tightened once again, but to such an extent that they broke. Suddenly, *New York* was let loose upon the tide with her stern heading straight for *Titanic*'s side.

With *Olympic*'s collision with the *Hawke* still fresh in their minds, both Ted and George Bowyer had almost seen it coming. *Titanic* was immediately halted and her anchor poised – to drop if needed. But it wasn't needed. The captain of the tug *Vulcan*, standing by after helping *Titanic* away from her berth, and acting with most commendable speed and initiative, had put a wire cable over the port quarter of *New York*'s stern. Although it fell away, another quickly followed and then another and her haphazard progress was halted. *Titanic* was free to proceed.

Up on the bridge, Ted and Bowyer exchanged eloquent glances but did not speak. Not yet. For there was still the Bramble bank to negotiate. But this time, there was no mishap.

'Well done, George!'

Bowyer grinned. 'We live and learn, eh?'

'I think we're getting there.'

When Bowyer was dropped off at the Nab Light Vessel, they shook hands with the firm grip of men who had faced disaster together, and seen it averted.

'Good luck, Captain. See you in a fortnight!'

'Thank you, George. Look after yourself!'

That night, as *Titanic* steamed steadily back across the Channel from Cherbourg, Ted, needing to relax, wrote to Eleanor:-

Well, my love, we're under way and all is now going smoothly. A few hiccups to begin with which, no doubt, you will have already read about in the newspapers, but these are safely behind us and we are now heading for Queenstown, which we should reach shortly before midday tomorrow, there to take on the 'Irish contingent' as O'Loughlin calls them. The 'French contingent' came on board peaceably enough – in spite of several Gallic tempers being frayed by our delay, slight though it was – and thus added a few more millionaires to my already sizeable collection; Benjamin Guggenheim and, of course, the Duff-Gordons – actually travelling under the name of 'Morgan'.

Now, I know, my dear, that Lady Duff-Gordon is also 'Lucile', the dress designer, but you will just have to bear with me for the time being – for I did *not* notice what she was wearing when she came aboard! But I do know that they made a very handsome couple.

The George Vanderbilts had already cancelled – I know not why – but John Jacob Astor and his new wife are aboard. Ismay is here too, of course, but sadly, not John Pierpont Morgan, who had to cancel because of business commitments. I was sorry to hear this as, besides enjoying his company, I had thought he might 'cushion' me against Ismay! As it is, I shall just have to try and maintain my calm; at least he is always punctilious about not coming on to the bridge. I know the routine quite well enough without him reminding me of it: we shall hope to maintain a steady speed of nineteen to twenty knots and increase it, conditions permitting, to the ship's maximum of twenty-two – perhaps a little over – before we reach New York. I owe this to the chief engineer and dear Mr Andrews, as much as to Ismay, as they will want to test the vessel to her utmost capacity.

Sadly, the Thaltons – my 'regulars' – are not with me, having decided to take a holiday in Italy, but I was overjoyed to see that my old friend William Stead is on board – on his way to some rally or other in New York (no doubt Mattie will know all about it).

There are many others I recognise, but I feel I have already burdened your eyes sufficiently for one day and, in any case, it is time that I had some rest, although I am, indeed, very happy with my officers: Wilde, Murdoch, Lightoller, Pitman, Boxall, Lowe and Moody – in that order – all trusted men and true. And McElroy is my purser: a kind and thoughtful man, very popular with the passengers and experienced at dealing with the strange and unpredictable ways of men and – dare I say it? – women. One in particular, I could mention, is always surprising me with her perfection!

They stayed off Queenstown for only a couple of hours; long enough to take on over a hundred more passengers and over a thousand sacks of mail.

The Irish must have been writing for weeks, (he wrote to Babsie) but then, I suppose it will be something, in years to come, to have a letter that was carried on *Titanic*'s maiden voyage. Sometimes, I have thought that people may forget that we carry mail as well as people – that we are the Royal Mail Steamship *Titanic* not just the *Titanic* – and a letter can mean so much, as I hope this one will!

We must definitely try to arrange for you and Mama to

sail upon this beautiful ship sometime. You would enjoy it greatly, particularly the swimming-pool. Not that we would be allowed to use it together, for ladies have their set times of day and gentlemen theirs. I shudder to think what they would make of Coney Island beach at week-ends!

The gymnasium you would only be allowed to use for a couple of hours after luncheon, as for the rest of the day it is reserved for your elders and betters! But the library you could read in to your heart's content, provided that you were quiet. The smoking-room, of course, you would not wish to enter; just imagine all those irascible old gentlemen, each beneath his separate little cloud of smoke and each threatening you with all manner of dreadful fates if you disturbed it by a single centimetre – just like your Papa!

You would find the Marconi wireless cabin most interesting of all, perhaps, staffed as it is by two most presentable young men; although you would not be allowed in to see them, as they are kept constantly busy with all the messages people are sending to wherever they are going or wherever they have come from. It is costing them twelve shillings and sixpence for this privilege; for which sum they may have only ten words.

Many entertainments, however, are free; as when your Papa, resplendent in his uniform, his 'ironmongery' pinned to his chest, parades through the ship, followed at a respectful distance by the chief engineer, the purser, the assistant purser, the surgeon and the chief steward. Nothing escapes his eagle eye, although, just between you and me, he lives in constant fear of one day falling flat upon his face in front of the passengers he is supposed to be looking after!

Goodnight, my precious child, I will add more as the voyage progresses.

Well, he thought, locking the sheets away as usual, in his desk, with luck that will give Babsie a laugh or two.

In fact, at one point, *Titanic's* Marconi equipment gave up the ghost and Phillips and Bride, the operators, had to work through the night to mend it. They had managed it by the early morning but were then faced with an enormous backlog of messages.

On Saturday, as he'd expected, the occasional ice warning began to come through: 'Field ice, some growlers, some bergs'.

Ismay dismissed them as normal for the time of year. Which, indeed, they were; although he knew as well as Ted that if there was poor visibility when they entered the ice region, speed would *have* to be decreased, inconvenient to passengers or not.

'But you'll let me know, at once, Captain, the moment you receive anything that might cause us concern?' It was phrased as a question, but Ted knew it to be an order – or as much of a one as a captain could be given upon his own ship. Briefly, he remembered that fine skipper Ben Gleadell telling him on the *Republic* that if a captain's performance 'does not equal Company expectations; if he does not, as it were, bring home the goods, then he's for it'.

Meanwhile, he was amused and sometimes, he had to admit, a little annoyed when he heard Ismay chatting away to other passengers about *Titanic's* achievements to date and how they would be bettered before the ship arrived in New York. He had also spotted him in earnest conversation with the chief engineer, not that he had anything but the greatest trust in that gentleman; Joseph Bell would listen courteously but do nothing except at Ted's request.

But he curbed his annoyance; for it had been definitely confirmed that Ismay would be retiring, if not in December of this year, then in June of next. And no doubt the man wanted to go out, so to speak, upon the crest of the wave.

On Sunday morning, soon after nine, he was handed an ice warning from the eastbound *Caronia*. More growlers, bergs and field ice had been sighted on the previous day, at 42 degrees North from 49 to 51 degrees West. This one could be important for *Titanic*, for she should be reaching the ice area that night. He took the message in to the chartroom, marked the chart with a large cross at the correct point and wrote in *ice*, then posted the message for everyone to see. He'd tell Ismay about it later.

There was no ship inspection on Sundays, but a church service which he took himself. He always enjoyed this, for it was the only occasion on board when second and third-class passengers were allowed in to the first-class dining-area, and all classes mingled. Other denominations would be holding their own smaller services at appropriate places in the ship but certainly the largest gathering was here. 'O God, our help in ages past', was roared out as from a pride of lions. He thought of Eleanor and Babsie in Christ Church, although their time would now be several hours behind *Titanic*'s.

Sunday morning was also, traditionally, the time for lifeboat drill but he decided to forgo it. Why spoil what seemed a perfect day with the embarrassment of underlining the hopeless inadequacy of the lifeboats? The important drill, he always felt, was the daily six o'clock run-through of the launching of the emergency boat, in case a man went overboard. Unlikely, perhaps, on *Titanic* – but it was a routine that he always insisted upon. A legacy, perhaps, from his sailing days, when the fear of men falling overboard had always been there.

The ship's telegraphs and whistles were tested at noon, when even the most seasoned travellers jumped out of their skins, unless they were standing there, watches open, to check the hour. It was the time, too, for 'shooting the sun' and calculating their position, so that Ismay and his cronies could study the previous day's mileage. Well, they should certainly be pleased with the last twenty-four hours; 546 was better than the previous one by 27 miles.

Just before going in to lunch, he had a chat with Lightoller on the bridge and pointed out *Caronia*'s ice warning. Not that Lightoller wouldn't have already seen it for himself, but it was as well to mention it, especially as he would be the officer of the watch when they neared the ice region.

Coming out from lunch, he bumped into Ismay. Ted took the initiative. 'Yesterday's progress was excellent, sir – 546 miles!' He tried to make it sound as if it was entirely Ismay's doing.

'But it would be even better, Captain, as I mentioned yesterday, if we could beat *Olympic's* maiden and arrive in New York on Tuesday night.'

Would he never be satisfied? But he was spared the repetition of his reply – that they would then have to bide their time out at sea, for there was no way that he was going to try and berth *Titanic* in anything but daylight – by the arrival of a second ice warning. Most opportune!

This one was from the *Baltic*, reporting 'icebergs and large quantities of field ice' 41 degrees North from 49 degrees West.'

'We're getting nearer to it, sir. We also had a signal from the *Caronia* this morning.'

'Yes, well, to be expected, I suppose. May I see the signal? There appears to be more on it than the ice warning.'

In fact, there was: a report of a drifting German oil-tanker that was asking for a tow. He could imagine Ismay's face if he were to suggest going to her aid! Fortunately, there would be other vessels much nearer.

Ismay scanned the report, slipped it into his pocket and turned away with a muttered, 'I'll let you have it back later.'

He'd better! But as long as he was able to post it in the chartroom that evening, all would be well. On his way to arrange an acknowledgement to *Baltic*, he thought that if there were no more warnings, he'd have nothing too much to worry about. In the signals cabin, he noticed that Phillips and Bride were still hard at it and with a pile of messages still to send. Poor chaps; not much sleep for *them* tonight!

Just before six o'clock, *Titanic* changed direction to bring her on a westerly course for New York. Normally, Ted would have ordered the change half an hour earlier, but by delaying, the ship would be sufficiently far south to avoid the icebergs he'd been warned of but still well within the accepted shipping lane for the time of year.

That evening, he had been invited to a small dinner party, but before going, he went in search of Ismay.

'That ice warning from the *Baltic*, sir. May I have it?'

Ismay took it out of his pocket. 'I would have returned it earlier, Captain, but did not like to trespass on to the bridge.'

Ted made no comment and returned to the chartroom, and posted the warning with the other, after he had marked it upon the chart. He also made an entry in the Night Order Book to keep a sharp look-out for ice. While doing so, he heard Murdoch – there, presumably, to relieve Lightoller for his meal – ordering Samuel Hemming, the lamp trimmer, to secure the for'ard fo'castle hatch. 'Otherwise, we shall have the light from it interfering with the vision of the look-outs. I want everything dark.'

It was a sensible precaution to take early on. A good man, Murdoch, Ted thought as he made his way towards the à la carte restaurant; he had a reputation for resource and initiative. It was his prompt action, when only a second officer, that had averted a collision between the White Star liner *Arabic* and a large sailing-ship. It had caused quite a stir at the time, he remembered, for not only had he countermanded the order of the first officer, he'd actually pushed the quartermaster from the helm and steered the ship away from danger himself – and in the nick of time. Murdoch would be relieving Lightoller at ten for the critical ice watch, and he couldn't think of a better man to take it. Not that they weren't all a magnificent bunch and shaking down well together; they would soon be given their own commands, if he had anything to do with it.

It was a very pleasant little dinner party and he would have stayed longer had it not been for the proximity of the danger area. He never liked to be far away from the bridge at such times. He excused himself just before nine o'clock, stopped to collect his greatcoat, for the air was growing cold, and went to see Lightoller. He found him gazing fixedly ahead.

'Not much wind tonight, Mr Lightoller.'

'No, sir, a flat calm.'

They both knew that this was one of the few occasions when a light wind would have been desirable, for it would have set the water dancing around the base of any bergs and made them clearly visible from a considerable distance away.

'But of course,' said Lightoller, knowing what he was thinking, 'there would be a certain amount of reflected light anyway.'

'That's right. Even if the dark side were turned towards us, we'd still see the white outline. The main thing is that visibility is so good.' For, although there was no moon, he could almost have seen to read under the massed brilliance of the stars. He thought that he had never seen them so bright.

'And the sea flat as a table top,' Lightoller observed.

'Best warn the look-outs to stay on their toes, although I've no doubt they're doing that already.'

'Will do, sir.'

'Well, I'll leave you to it, Mr Lightoller. Call me if there is the slightest change, especially if it becomes the least bit hazy. For then we should have to reduce the speed.' And be damned to Ismay, he thought. 'I shall be just inside,' he said as he walked the few paces to his sea cabin behind the chartroom.

'Inside' but not undressed or asleeep. For some reason – perhaps because, as Eleanor had put it, *Titanic* was 'rather special' – he found himself taking the unusual step of running a check-list through his mind that all possible precautions had been taken; a responsible officer was in charge and would shortly be relieved by another equally responsible, the look-outs would soon be changed in the crow's nest and had been warned that there could be ice ahead, there was an entry in the Night Order Book to that effect, which would be seen and signed by Murdoch when he came on duty, the for'ard fo'castle hatch had been closed, the position of the icebergs they had been warned of had been clearly marked upon the charts and, in any case, he'd altered course to avoid them. There was nothing else. Although his speed was high it was no more so than usual in the area, for it was better to get out of danger as quickly as possible, provided you could see clearly where you were going.

Fleetingly, he considered actually going out to stand upon the bridge but decided against it. Delegation, after all, was the essence of a good commander, and his cabin was virtually part of the bridge, anyway. Yes, he assured himself, all that could be done *had* been done; he could rest easy. And yet he found that he could not; that something was nagging at the corners of his mind. Something that he couldn't put a finger upon but wouldn't, even so, go away. Perhaps he *would* stroll out on to the bridge in an hour or two, just to reassure himself. Around midnight, maybe.

He was sitting there, completely relaxed as long practice had taught him to be; one half of his mind thinking ahead to the following day, the other half aware of the sounds around him — the steady throb of the engines, the occasional murmur of voices as Murdoch spoke to Boxall or Moody, the sound of bells as the watch progressed.

It was soon after eleven thirty when he decided that now was the time to show himself on the bridge. And then, fastening himself into his greatcoat, he heard, quite distinctly, the sound of three bells; the warning from the crow's nest that meant 'object directly ahead'. At the same moment, the bridge telephone rang, to be followed immediately by shouted commands. Then he felt the ship begin to turn, and somewhere ahead, to starboard he thought, there came a steady, crunching sound — almost like that of a heavy boot descending upon the crispness of freshly fallen snow. It lasted for what seemed an eternity but could only have been a few seconds. By then, he was out on the bridge and facing Murdoch.

'What have we struck?'

'An iceberg, sir. I hard-a-starboarded and reversed the engines and was going to hard-a-port around it but she was too close. I could do no more. I have closed the watertight doors.'

'And the warning bell?'

'Rung, sir.'

Even as he spoke, they were crossing to the starboard wing of the bridge to peer downward. What they saw was, at first, reassuring: a berg certainly, but not a high one. Please God, the damage was minimal.

'Mr Boxall, would you please check what damage has been done.'

'Yes, sir.'

As Boxall turned to leave the bridge, Ted added, 'As discreetly as possible, if you please, Mr Boxall. We don't want to alarm the passengers unnecessarily.'

'Very good, sir.'

Boxall despatched, Ted crossed to the engine-room telegraph and signalled half-ahead. Then turned to the standby quartermaster.

'Tell the chief engineer that I'm stopping the engines altogether, and would he step up to the bridge as soon as he can.'

'Aye, aye, sir!'

The time before Boxall returned seemd interminable. Ted spent it in the wheelhouse, gazing fixedly at the commutator, the small, clock-like instrument in front of the compass which would tell him if the ship was listing. It was, by five degrees. Crossing again to the starboard wing, he stared out. He had never seen so much field ice, so many bergs. There must have been an unusually warm spring up in the Arctic regions. So why, then, had there been no further warnings?

'I could see no damage myself, sir,' Boxall reported. 'But a postal clerk told me that there was water seeping into the sorting office.'

'Thank you. Would you now please find the carpenter and ask him to sound the ship.'

'Yes, sir.'

Boxall hadn't far to go; the carpenter was already on his way – to report that water was flooding the holds.

There was only one course of action to take now. 'I'm going to find Mr Andrews, Murdoch.'

He found Andrews in his cabin and, for a moment, in spite of the gravity of the situation, could not help smiling. For Andrews, pencil in hand, was completely immersed in the charts spread across his desk. He looked up, surprised, when Ted knocked and entered.

'Hello, Captain! I was just working out –'

'Andrews, my dear fellow, I am so sorry to disturb you at such an hour, but I'm afraid we have struck an iceberg.' Even as he spoke, he thought how ridiculously casual the statement sounded.

'Indeed?' said Andrews, quite unperturbed. 'Well, it could not have been a very large one or I would surely have felt it.'

'Large enough, I fear, to cause flooding in the holds. Would you come with me to assess the damage?'

Ted thought that he had never seen a man's face change so suddenly. Without a word, Andrews put down his pencil and strode to the door.

A brief inspection was enough to show that their worst fears had been realised. The iceberg had made a three-hundred-foot gash in the *Titanic's* starboard side, about ten feet above the level of the keel. Water was flooding in to the forepeak, numbers one, two and three holds and two of the boiler-rooms. Ted could only hope that no lives had been lost – yet.

Without delay, he and Andrews returned to Andrews' cabin by the crew's staircase. Once inside, Andrews made some hasty calculations.

'The ship is doomed, I fear, Captain. She cannot remain afloat with the four forward compartments flooded *and* the forward boiler-room.'

'How long have we got?'

Andrews glanced at his watch. 'Just over a couple of hours, I should say.'

They spoke no more, but at the door they stopped briefly and silently gripped each other's hand. Neither had any illusions about what the future held for them.

☆

When he reached the bridge, he found his officers assembled. First thanking them for their prompt appearance, he gave them a brief account of what had happened and told them Andrews' estimated life-span for the ship. However, he told them, they must not despair; distress calls would be sent out once their position had been established, and he felt confident that other vessels would soon be coming to their assistance. Meanwhile the boats were to be uncovered although not, for the moment, swung out. Murdoch would take control of those on the starboard side and Wilde on the portside with Lightoller. Lowe, Moody and Pitman would first alert McElroy and the stewards – who would then alert the rest of the ship – and then go themselves to the lifeboats. Boxall would work out the *Titanic*'s position for the distress signal to be sent by the Marconi operators.

'Good luck, gentlemen! Try to combine speed with confidence; confidence that, with God's help, we shall survive.'

As the officers scattered about their tasks, he caught Murdoch by the arm. 'A moment, if you please, Mr Murdoch.' He knew his first officer well; conscientious officer that he was, beneath that impassive exterior he would have been feeling a deep remorse, for *he* had been the one in charge when the berg struck.

'You did all that you could, my friend. In your place, I should have done exactly the same. And,' he added soberly, 'it was *I* who should have been there. It was *my* responsibility.' It was an unprecedented admission to make to a subordinate. But he owed it to the man; Murdoch must not be allowed either to go to a watery grave or to survive, if others did not, with such a burden of guilt upon his conscience.

He saw the flicker of gratitude in Murdoch's eyes, but, indeed, he had only spoken the truth. He was confident that he would have taken the same course of action as Murdoch, even though he now knew that a head-on collision with the berg would have been infinitely preferable; for then only one, possibly two, of the watertight compartments would have been holed. But, please God, Murdoch would never know that.

And then, on his way to the wireless cabin to acquaint Phillips and Bride with what was happening, he realised what it was that had nagged at his mind earlier that night. Suddenly, he was back again upon that Savannah paddle-boat with Joseph and Mattie, all those years ago, and speaking of the loss of the *Birkenhead*.

'*We grow accustomed,*' Joseph had said, '*to not knowing what is ahead, what trick the elements may suddenly play upon us.*' And again, '*We are the victims of our own knowledge and experience and of those who have gone before us. We think we know all there is to know about a certain situation.*'

The parallels between the *Birkenhead* and the *Titanic* could not have been more similar. Like the unfortunate Captain Salmond, he had taken everything known to him into account; if he had been entering the ice region for the *first time*, with no personal experience or knowledge gathered from his predecessors, then he would have proceeded with the utmost caution, perhaps even stopped *Titanic* altogether. But bolstered up by the experience of years, he had steamed ahead – like a madman! For a moment, he closed his eyes; his guilt – far greater than any Murdoch might have felt – bitter as aloes in his mouth.

But then, straightening his shoulders, he carried on to the wireless cabin. Recrimination would not help. Now, he must do all in his power to aid those whose trust he had so terribly betrayed.

To his astonishment, he found Phillips still dealing with a pile of messages. Bride seemed to be taking a well-earned respite. Quickly, he explained the situation. 'Prepare to send out a distress call, I will let you have our position in a few minutes.'

As he turned to go back to the bridge, he reflected that perhaps he had now discovered the reason why no more ice warnings had been received – had *Titanic*, in her efforts to please her passengers, unknowingly sounded her own death knell? But there was no point now, in holding an inquest. Phillips and Bride, he had no doubt, would continue to do their duty like the loyal servants they were.

He glanced at his watch. Already well past midnight and still so much to be done. On the bridge, he found that Boxall had now worked out their position – Latitude 41.46 degrees North. Longitude 50.14 degrees West. He went back to the Marconi operators. It was time to send out the distress signal CQD, the regulation international call for help.

'Why not send out the new SOS signal instead of CQD?' Phillips suggested.

'Yes – it may be the last opportunity you have!' said Bride with a chuckle.

Ted forced himself to join in their laughter. Anything that would lighten the darkness of this nightmare was welcome. 'Well, whatever you send, let me know what response you get.'

By now, the sound of steam escaping from the boilers was deafening, and could not be helping the stewards in their efforts to alert the passengers; but at least the sound should help convince them that this was no false alarm. He hoped his order to swing out the boats would be even more convincing. He watched as Murdoch and Pitman swung out Number 7. It went smoothly, and in two minutes it was over the side, level with the deck. All it needed now were its occupants. But they, incredibly, were in short supply. For the first time, he cursed the complacency of the Line in assuring the world that the *Titanic* was virtually unsinkable. Even now, with the decks already listing and the sound of the steam so great that Murdoch was having to cup his hands to his mouth to make himself heard, they clearly felt they were safe; that this was a sort of charade that the crew felt obliged to enact for appearance's sake.

And yet the opposite – panic and terror as places in the boats were fought over by those who had already worked out their inadequacy – was not to be contemplated. Grimly, he went to draw the pistols that were a little-publicised part of the ship's inventory and had them distributed, unobtrusively, to his officers; none of them seemed surprised to receive them.

It was soon afterwards that Boxall sighted the lights of another vessel on the port bow and Ted felt a wave of hope. 'Use the Morse lamp,' he told Boxall. 'How far away would you say she is? Five miles?'

'Five or six, sir. She could be a passenger steamer or just a cod-banker with her nets.'

'Even a fishing-vessel would be of help!'

But the ship, whatever she was, gave no sign of having seen Boxall's signals.

'Rockets, sir?' Boxall suggested.

'Yes – no point in keeping them any longer.'

Soon the white stars of the rockets were exploding into the sky. But the other ship still gave no sign that she had seen them. 'Keep trying!' he told Boxall.

Surreptitiously, he glanced at his watch. It was now almost an hour since the *Titanic* had struck; one precious hour of the 'just over two' that Andrews had forecast. At least Murdoch had now launched Number 7 boat, although well short of its capacity.

He went back to the wireless cabin; and was told that the Cunard liner *Carpathia* had altered course and was steaming towards them.

'How long before they reach us?'

'They thought about three hours, sir.' Instinctively, Ted glanced up at the clock. If Andrews' calculations were right – and he was confident they were – *Titanic* would have foundered long before.

'Any other vessels responded?' he asked.

'*Frankfurt*, sir, but she's well over a hundred miles away. And *Olympic*, a good five hundred miles off.'

Olympic! He could imagine the consternation on her bridge when Captain Haddock heard that *Titanic* was sinking.

The noise of escaping steam had abated a little, and as he turned away he became aware of the sound of music: cheerful, rhythmic music with a strong beat – 'ragtime', he thought they called it – coming from somewhere close, the first-class lounge perhaps. William Hartley and his band!

What a magnificent gesture! There was nothing like cheerful music to raise a man's spirits. But was it, perhaps, also helping to lull people into a false sense of security? The news of the *Carpathia*'s approach seemed to have already permeated among the passengers and he heard one woman remark that *she* had no intention of leaving the ship, for was not *Titanic* unsinkable?

'Even so, madam,' he cautioned her, 'I should put on your life-jacket. It will at least keep you warm. And I think it advisable that you *do* step into a lifeboat. After all, you can always return to the ship later, if circumstances permit.' He knew what a hollow hope that was, but habit died hard and for so long he had sought to reassure and calm his passengers. 'Nothing dreadful can happen to you on board a White Star vessel,' he had said, like a good Company man. May God forgive him now!

Although he could hardly believe his ears, he actually heard one woman asking a passing steward for coffee. And was relieved to hear the man reply that it would be far more sensible for her to go back to her cabin and collect a warm topcoat, for she might be needing it.

Andrews and McLoughlin were moving among the passengers, lingering here and there to help a woman or a child into their life-jackets, although, Ted noticed, wearing none themselves.

He also saw Ismay in his nightclothes, doing what he could to urge women into the lifeboats but, as always with Ismay, going too far and trying to take command. He wasn't surprised when Pitman came to him and asked for confirmation of an order that Ismay had given.

'Yes, Pitman, go ahead! Women and children first!'

It said much for Ismay, he though, that he was not trying to use his position to get away himself, although he doubted if Pitman would have permitted it, anyway.

The first lifeboat had been launched a little before one o'clock on the starboard side, but many passengers were still lining the railings on the port side, staring out at the lights of that other vessel; which seemed now to be receding. Or was it that they were becoming more difficult to see as *Titanic* listed?

He saw Lightoller loading up Number 6 boat, but having as little success as Murdoch.

'Women and children first!' he was shouting, but so many women, almost hysterical in their protest, were refusing to leave their menfolk that precious minutes were being lost. He wasn't surprised when Lightoller, growing impatient, ordered the lowering of the boat while it was only half full, but at least he also ordered Quartermaster Hichens, who was in charge, to pull to the unidentified ship standing off in the darkness and then return for a second load. Unfortunately, in his haste he had forgotten that Hichens would need help to row and the boat was already two decks below when Hichens called out in alarm. Lowering was immediately stopped while Lightoller sought another crewman. But it was a passenger who stepped forward, a Major Peuchen, Ted thought. But how to get him in to the boat?

'Get below to B deck,' he shouted from the bridge. 'Break a port if need be and get in that way.'

But the major, showing great courage for he was not young, had already swung himself out on to one of the fall ropes by which the boat was suspended and was climbing down it as nimbly as any seasoned sailor.

It was after that incident that Ted sent a couple of men to open the gangway doors in the side of the ship. Several women, he had noticed, seemed to be terrified of stepping out, even with assistance, over that sickening drop. From the gangway doors descent could easily be made by means of ladders. Trusting that the seamen would be able to fight their way through the ever-increasing press of bewildered humanity, he told Murdoch and Lightoller what he had done, so that any other boats lowered without their complement could stay near to pick up from the lower decks. And using the bridge megaphone, he also bellowed out an order to that effect to those boats already launched. And yet, he realised, they must not stay too near for too long or they would risk being sucked under when the ship finally went.

341

He saw many acts of heroism that night; by Ida Strauss, who steadfastly refused to leave her husband, Isidor. 'I will not be separated from my husband,' she said quietly but firmly. 'As we have lived, so will we die – together!''; by John Jacob Astor, who handed his pregnant wife into a boat and asked Lightoller if he might join her 'as she is in a delicate condition', but, when told that he could not, kissed her fondly and stepped meekly back; by George Widener, John B. Thayer and Charles Hayes, all of whom did the same with their wives. He was proud of his millionaires!

Benjamin Guggenheim and his manservant actually went below and changed from the warm garments they had put on after the impact into full evening dress. 'We shall go down like gentlemen!' they said.

But there were acts of cowardice as well as bravery; men who tried to enter the boats disguised as women; men who jumped into boats as they were being lowered so that it was impossible to remove them; men who pushed women roughly aside so anxious were they for their own safety. He was glad, then, that he had issued the firearms, for only when Lightoller fired a couple of shots into the air did they desist.

There were many harrowing sights; when weeping women had to be forcibly separated from their husbands, and children from their fathers; when children, inadvertently separated from their mothers, were put into different boats and cried out in terror to find themselves alone in such frightening circumstances.

Initiative, too, played its part; in one instance, when Boat 14 was being lowered with Fifth Officer Lowe in charge and almost its full complement, one of the fall ropes became entangled so that the boat tilted dangerously, threatening to tumble its terrified occupants into the water. Quickly, a seaman whipped out a knife from his pocket and severed the rope, thus releasing the boat but causing it to drop like a stone. However, the shrieks of alarm that rose from some of the women when it hit the water with an almighty smack, were as nothing, Ted reflected grimly, to those that would rend the air when the *Titanic* finally disappeared beneath the waves, taking their loved ones with it.

And that time was fast approaching, although he was astonished to see that some women were still standing in line outside the purser's office to claim their valuables, in spite of the repeated urgings of the stewards that they step into the boats without delay. Several stewardesses, he was pleased to notice, had been persuaded to climb in. This was no time for class distinction.

Even so, the odds, he knew, were heavily weighted in favour of the first-class passengers, because of their position in the vicinity of the boats. Second-class had a considerable way to come and third even further. And when they did come, many of them were foreigners who clearly did not understand what they were being told to do. He was relieved to see the crew manhandling reluctant women into the boats, and children being literally thrown from the deck into the open arms of their mothers. For *Titanic*'s bows were now lapped by the waves and her list noticeable to everyone. Her enormous propellers, Ted estimated, would be out of the water and clearly visible to the occupants of the lifeboats. It was now after two o'clock and all boats had been launched. Only three of the collapsibles remained.

It was then that he saw Ismay for the last time. Wilde, seeing to the launching of one of the collapsibles, called repeatedly for more women and children to come forward, but when none did, Ismay stepped, almost furtively, into the boat just before it was lowered.

For a moment, Ted had an absurd desire to rush forward and detain him; to point out that, as managing director of the Company, he too had an obligation to stay with the ship. But of course he did no such thing; simply watched him disappear from sight, a pathetic figure at the last.

The time came when he had to fulfil his final duty: to release the crew from their obligations. He went first to the wireless cabin. 'It's every man for himself now, boys. You have done your duty.'

They looked up and actually smiled at him. And not for

the first time that night, he thought how incredible it was that no one had accused him of dereliction of duty; although he could imagine what would be said at the enquiry. The collision between *Olympic* and *Hawke* would be as nothing, compared with this one! But some good must come of it, he thought as he returned to the bridge; the lifeboat complement, for a start. And some more efficient way of keeping masters informed of the immediate hazards of moving ice.

Back on the bridge, he took up his megaphone to tell his faithful crew – those, at least, who had not already gone – that their duty was done. And then, seeing Lightoller and Moody even now trying to launch another collapsible from the roof of the officers' quarters and being impeded by men struggling to get into it, he called out – to his own astonishment – the phrase first uttered by old Smithy and used ever afterwards by himself and Bert as a sort of private joke: 'Be British, men! Be British!'

Was it an outmoded sentiment these days? But then he thought of the gallant behaviour of William Hartley and his band, now assembled upon the deck and still playing vigorously. Certainly, *they* merited the description. Ragtime had given way to hymns and, as the familiar tune of *Nearer my God to Thee* rang out and was taken up by the men and women now crowding towards the stern, he felt a lump rise in his throat.

For the first time, he regretted the Company ruling that no official clergyman was carried on the short North Atlantic route. And yet, what good would one man of the cloth have been among this multitude?

He had no way of knowing how many were left. All he could be sure of was that *Titanic* had carried 2,201 souls when she had left Cherbourg, of which 885 had been crew and the remainder passengers. Please God, some at least would be rescued by the lifeboats or by the *Carpathia*. He had met Rostron, her captain, and knew him to be a man of great bravery and resource. What that ship to starboard was about, he could only imagine.

Looking back – or rather, *up* – along the length of the

boat-deck, he was amazed at the calmness of the remaining passengers. Mostly, the men stood about in groups, chatting quietly among themselves as if, indeed, they fully expected to 'join the ladies' in a little while. He thought for a moment of going to seek out Andrews, to exchange a last poignant farewell, but then thought better of it. Andrews, he guessed, would wish to spend the time left to him alone, thinking of his family, making his peace with his Maker.

Except for Mrs Strauss, and one or two sitting calmly with their husbands, he could see no women on the boat-deck, although up on the stern, now tilted at an alarming angle and where people were massing like a swarm of bees, the situation was probably very different. They would be mostly third class up there, and many of them would be women. But he hoped – Oh God, how he hoped! – there would be no children. For how could he bear the sound of their cries as the water rose towards them? And if *he* could not bear it, with his own child safely in bed thousands of miles away, how much worse for the mothers who held them in their arms?

And then he saw that someone had had the forethought and compassion to release the dogs from their kennels, for they were now racing along the deck, barking wildly as they sought their owners. Few would find them, he feared, although he did witness John Jacob Astor embracing a magnificent Airedale, burying his face for a moment in its wiry coat as the dog licked his face in a frantic reunion. And Ted was reminded, almost unbearably, of Ben's joyful greeting each time he came home.

There was nothing more he could do now, he decided sadly, other than remember his loved ones and wait for the end. When it came, he hoped that he would not instinctively fight against the water; the mind and spirit willing but the body, at the end, resisting.

He thought of his officers: Pitman, Lowe and Boxall had gone with the boats, but Lightoller, Wilde and Murdoch were still on board. Wilde, he suspected, would not try to save himself for he had never been the same man since his wife had died; but Murdoch, he hoped, would survive – and that cheerful sprig Lightoller, who had worked like a Trojan that night. He breathed a silent prayer for Joseph Bell and his men who, against all the odds, had kept the *Titanic* brilliant with light. He doubted if any of *them* would be rescued.

For the first time since disaster had struck, he allowed himself to think of Eleanor and Babsie. With all his heart, he wished he could spare them the grief and pain they would soon be called upon to bear. Especially Eleanor, for Babsie was young and resilient.

And then he remembered Eleanor once saying that it was better for a man to go first because a woman could survive her deprivation more easily, and felt some small comfort; and Thomas and Bert and other good friends would support her as best they could. But for a few, heart-warming moments, he allowed himself to think back over their life together, and thanked God that it had been so happy, even though he had had to leave her so often. Perhaps, indeed, that had been the key to it! Even so, he knew that the life they had planned together after *Titanic* would have been a time of blissful contentment. And now she must face it alone. For the first time that night, alone upon the bridge, he wept.

And then he pulled himself together and turned his mind to Thirza, his staunch ally since childhood; and Mattie, such a good friend over the years.

And finally, he thought again of his faithful Ben, to whom the circumstances of his going could never be explained, but who would spend the rest of his life waiting patiently for his master to come home.

For himself, he had no fear; for he knew, as surely as he knew that the *Titanic* would shortly sink for ever beneath the waves, that he would soon be with his loved ones; Ma and Pa, Joseph and Anna.

His body now relaxing, he became aware of an urgent desire to pass water, and made his way, mocking himself for his modesty, towards the officers' lavatory. For what would it matter now if he were simply to walk to the side!

But he was not alone in clinging to convention. He found another man there – an Irish steward. As they relieved themselves, Ted said gently, 'It would be better, if you can bring yourself to do so, to jump into the water and make for a lifeboat, rather than wait for the ship to sink beneath you.'

The Irishman looked at him. 'Is that what you're going to do, sir?'

'Well, no. But in my case, it's rather different. And besides, you are still a young man, your life is ahead of you.'

As they left the lavatory, the steward said, 'Thank you, your honour. It's been a privilege to talk to you.'

Ted drew in his breath sharply. Although the man was younger by far than Kennedy, and the circumstances could not have been more different, he was back at Woodhead, and Kennedy and young John were taking Midnight from him and Eleanor was running out of the house in a white dress – and suddenly, life was unbearably sweet and he did not want to die.

But he pulled himself together, shook the steward by the hand, not trusting himself to speak, and turned back towards the bridge. This was not the moment for self-pity.

But his task was not yet finished. On the bridge, he found another man and a woman – an Italian, he thought – who held a baby to her breast and had two other tiny children clinging to her skirts.

'I've been trying to persuade the lady to jump for it, sir,' the man said.

Ted turned to the woman. 'He's right, you know. Let me take one of the children.' And to the man, 'If you take the other child, I think we may have a chance of reaching a boat.' For several were clearly visible at the edge of the light that still blazed from the portholes. He doubted if the woman knew what he had said and feared that she would refuse, but when the man and Ted each took a child, she was persuaded. All three prepared to jump.

Even through his thick clothing, the shock of the water was numbing. But at least he could still swim. He turned on his back, clutched the screaming child to his chest, and made for the nearest boat. Willing hands reached out and took the child from him.

'And now yourself, sir.' He did not recognise the woman who spoke, and she, he thought, did not recognise him.

'Not I, thank you, madam. But good luck to you all!' He thought he saw the man and woman with the other children being pulled into another boat but could not be sure. As vigorously as he could, he turned and swam back towards his doomed ship, now poised, like some huge and fiery sword – Excalibur, indeed! – above the waves. For a second, he was tempted to give up then; to simply abandon himself to the water, but then, unbidden, there came into his mind the words of Ma's prayer:

O Lord, on whom I shall depend, keep me safely till my end. I trust in thy redeeming power for comfort in my final hour.

Not just the Lord, but Ma, he felt confident, would sustain him now. With luck – although why should he expect luck on a night like this? – he would reach the ship before she foundered, and go down, as tradition demanded, upon the bridge. But then he saw the forward funnel suddenly collapse towards the bows like a child's bricks tumbled by an unseen hand; and the lights were extinguished. Only a deluge of sparks and the lights of the lifeboats remained to illuminate the last dying moments of the great liner.

Silhouetted against the starry sky, she was now almost vertical; those in the stern must be sliding off like flies into the icy water. Now, indeed, there were screams and cries as loved ones were torn apart; and mingling with them, the deafening crash of thousands of objects inside the ship, from massive boilers to tiny teaspoons, hurtling down towards the bows.

But not all of them. Some – the deck-chairs that people, even now, were throwing into the sea as makeshift rafts, and doors wrenched from their hinges – rained down around Ted's shoulders as he trod water, desperately trying to stay afloat in the massive swell, so that he could go down, if not upon her, at least with her. A chair hit his shoulder, another his arm, and another. . . . It was only a glancing blow to the head, but it was sufficient. He drifted into unconsciousness.

Far away in Southampton, Ben raised his muzzle and gave a long-drawn-out, quivering howl. And Eleanor, as she listened to him, felt a terrible, draining deprivation; as if her very soul had suddenly been torn from her.

Ted, her dearest dear!

EPILOGUE

Since his calling was considered more appropriate to a boy than to a girl, the photograph of 'Uncle Edward', the handsome, bearded sailor in the uniform of the White Star Line, always hung upon the wall of my brother's bedroom. I was given the slim volume of verse inscribed in a clear precise hand, *To Edward J. Smith from his mother, on his 10th birthday*. That, at least, is how I remember it, since I was foolish enough to lend out the book and not to ensure its return – an oversight that I was later to regret deeply.

My mother (Queenie) never met 'Uncle Edward' nor 'Uncle Joseph' but recalls being told by her mother (Annie), among other anecdotes, that Edward was more like a friendly brother to her than an uncle, and that both he and Joseph were happy, laughing men. 'Aunt Anna' was remembered as a strong-minded lady who was seldom without her umbrella! She sailed around the world with Joseph at least twice.

'Grandpa and Grandma Harrington' (William and Thirza), my mother remembered with affection – but also with a healthy respect, since visits to Hanley were occasions when children had to behave themselves, to be 'seen and not heard'; for Grandpa Harrington didn't like noise!

Shortly after *Titanic*'s sinking, Eleanor went back to Liverpool to stay with a friend, David Cook, at Adelaide Terrace and later with Thomas at The Nook. *Titanic* archives have a letter she wrote from The Nook in June 1915, to the Trustees for the Titanic Relief Fund, asking them to reconsider the allowance in respect of First Officer Wilde's four children.

For Babsie, now called Mel, life continued to be tragic.

It was she who unveiled the statue of her father in Beacon Park, Lichfield, in 1914. In the same year, she and Eleanor moved to London to live, and there, at St Marks, Mayfair, in 1922, she married Sidney Russell-Cooke, a stockbroker whose family home was Bellcroft, near Newport on the Isle of Wight. It was at Bellcroft that the twins, Simon and Priscilla, were born in June, 1923. Only seven years later, Sidney was killed as the result of a shooting accident, about which little is known.

A year later, while out with Mel, Eleanor was run over in a street accident and killed. At least, Mel must have thought, she still had her children. Perhaps wanting to bring them up in a more tranquil atmosphere than London offered, in 1934 she moved to Leafield, near Witney in Oxfordshire; to a house called Pratts. Gardening and embroidery now occupied her leisure time and she also entered wholeheartedly into village life. Then came the war and Simon enlisted in the Royal Air Force as a pilot. In 1944, off the Norwegian coast, he was shot down. Like the grandfather he had never known, the sea was his grave.

Now, only Priscilla remained, but her marriage a few months after the war ended must have given Mel renewed hope that the family would continue. But Fate had other ideas; two years after her marriage, Priscilla contracted polio and died in Scotland.

Mel's life, it was always thought, was a tragic affair from start to finish but now, thanks to an article by John Pladdys in the August 1993 issue of *The Titanic Commutator* – the journal of the Titanic Historical Society, Inc. – this view can, in part at least, now be amended. For clearly she lived life to the full.

From a letter written by Eleanor to Frank Hancock in Savannah soon after the sinking of the *Titanic*, it is clear that she had inherited her father's happy disposition; but to this can now be added his qualities of courage and fortitude and the charisma of his personality. She acquired a pilot's licence and flew to many parts of the world; she had a fast car; and, during the war, drove a local ambulance.

Many parties were given at Pratts, attended by many well-known people of the day – Bomber Harris was a frequent weekend visitor – and soon after she went to live there, David Rhode, the artist, moved in, subsequently painting portraits of Mel and the twins.

Like her father, she died suddenly; in August 1973 at Pratts. Her ashes were taken to Brookwood Cemetery in Surrey and are buried in her husband's grave, near to that of her mother.

As for Frank and Annie out in Savannah, they did indeed have sufficient children for a baseball team (at least three other children having died) so that the number of Hancocks who must now live in America would warm the cockles of Joseph's heart.

Of the *Titanic's* officers, Boxall, Lightoller, Lowe and Pitman survived. Of the two Wireless Operators, Bride survived but Phillips did not. Bruce Ismay was picked up by the Cunarder *Carpathia*, along with seven hundred and ten other survivors. As planned, he retired in 1913 and spent his remaining years between his homes in London and Ireland. However, surviving the disaster of the *Titanic* did not enhance his reputation with the public. He died in 1937.

Courtesy of the archives of the Memorial University of St John's Newfoundland and the Greenwich Maritime Museum in London, details of Joseph's and Ted's voyages under sail and the crews that signed up with them are correct. AB Edward Smith was flogged by Joseph in Hong Kong after the monsoon, Thomas Forster and James Grieve jumped ship in San Francisco, along with many others, and three Scandinavian seamen were drowned in the South Pacific Ocean off the *Lizzie Fennell*. And Ted was promoted from 'boy' to third mate in San Francisco. However, I think it can be safely assumed that a promotion so rapid would never have occurred had Joseph not been his captain. In Victorian times, nepotism was rife, even, I understand, in the Merchant Service; it came as no surprise to discover James Harrington of Hanley on the crew list of the *Lizzie Fennell* on her last voyage under Ted's command, although it is unlikely that *he* was ever promoted to third mate.

As far as family details are concerned, I have stuck to them as closely as possible, but the movements of master mariners under sail are extremely difficult to follow when they are ashore. As one might expect, they lived either in temporary lodgings or rented houses, which made it difficult to pinpoint Joseph's exact whereabouts at the times of the ten-yearly Census Returns. However, he does appear in the Liverpool Street Directories towards the latter part of his life.

Anecdotes about the *Titanic* are still surfacing; only recently, when Steve Rigby, of the British Titanic Society, was giving a talk to a senior citizens' association in Warrington, he discovered that Ted's picture hung in the Winwick schoolhouse at least until the 1930s, and that on Armistice Day, when the minute's silence was observed in memory of those who had fallen in the Great War, the pupils would turn in the direction of the photograph and remember the *Titanic*, also.

A more lasting memorial – and perhaps the most poignant of all – is the banding of purple that, ever since the disaster, has laced the gold braid around the cuffs of all Merchant Navy engineers, in memory of Joseph Bell and his shipmates who, knowing full well that they had no chance of survival, still kept the pumps working and the lights blazing until the very end. No men could have shown greater courage; except, perhaps, those gallant musicians under the direction of Wallace H. Hartley.

Fortunately, many acts of heroism performed upon that fateful April night have been recorded in the several excellent books that have been written about the disaster, but who knows how many others went unnoticed? The older women who stood back to let young mothers go, the wives who remained with their husbands, the young lads who suddenly became men. . . . It was a night of great tragedy but also of sublime sacrifice. And it will never be forgotten.

Pat Lacey
July 1994

ACKNOWLEDGEMENTS

My thanks to:

Brian Ticehurst, Steve Rigby and Geoff Whitfield, officers of the British Titanic Society without whose invaluable help this book could never have got off the ground; Philip Croucher of Rembrandt Commemorative Cover Specialists, Milford-on-Sea who gave not only information but support.

My cousins: Bunny Lang in Australia, Robin Tubbs in New Zealand and Inez Bishop in Devon, for allowing me to pick their brains.

Descendants of Ted: Neville Stanier, Don Smith, Herbert Smith, Chris Eastwood, Mrs Cocker.

Researchers: Marjorie Whitby of Liverpool, Peter Simmons of New York, Kay Kohl of Savannah and Diane Backhouse of Chester; all of whom went that little bit further and thereby uncovered unsuspected nuggets of information.

My technical advisers: Richard Hills, Ray Lister, Christopher and Nick Perkins, Colin Horton, Zillah and Hugh Dovey, Captain Tom Wilson (Merchant Navy, ret.) and George Trenfield, none of whom seemed to mind what inane questions I fired at them.

Audrey Dudson, Historian of the Dudson Pottery, Hanley, Staffs, who gave me invaluable technical advice.

Captain R.J. Campbell of the Ministry of Defence Hydrographic Office, who was kind enough to give me details of the New York pilotage laws at the end of the nineteenth century and to explain how it was possible for Ted to negotiate Sandy Hook – or not, as the case might be!

Bill Evans of Salt Lake City, for much helpful advice and information; Walter Lord, for his time and courtesy in replying so promptly to my letter; Don Lynch, Historian of the Titanic Historical Society of America, for putting me in touch with various American organisations.

Mr and Mrs Cooper of Woodhead Farm, for kindly allowing me access to their home and for much useful local information. Also the Reverend Pankhurst, Vicar of Winwick, and his wife.

Mrs Sylvia Lloyd of Warrington, Stoke-on-Trent, for providing information that enabled me to 'find' Thirza and William again, after I had 'lost' them in the 1870s.

John Abberley of the *Staffordshire Evening Sentinel*, for publishing my request for local knowledge; and Mr Brock, Mrs Cocker, Mr Herbert Smith and Mr Neil Egginton, who were kind enough to contact me, as a result. Also Mr Arthur Slight with his views about the *Titanic* disaster.

Tommy Rowe of Swansea, who showed enormous initiative – and enormous patience! – in tracking down the lad to whom, many years ago, I thought I had lent Ted's poetry book; the fact that *he* remembered nothing at all about it in no way detracted from Tommy's achievement.

Mr Fisher, antiquarian bookseller of Hanley, Anne Derrick of Peebles, Kathleen Stinson of New York, Paul Duck, late of Winslow; all of whom helped in various extremely useful ways; Ruth Hall of Winslow Public Library, who could always find the answers!

My two scribes, Hilary and Peter Thornton, for their hard work, encouragement and cheerful patience over the last few years.

And finally, my long-suffering husband, who doubled as messenger boy upon many occasions.

BIBLIOGRAPHY

BARNES, Jim, *Southampton Reflections*, Hampshire County Library, 1989.

BEVAN, David, *Drums of the Birkenhead*, Larson Publications Ltd, 1972.

BISSETT, James, *Tramps and Ladies*, Angus & Robertson (UK) Ltd, 1959. Reprint Patrick Stephens, 1988.

BULLOCK, Shan F., *A Titanic Hero, Thomas Andrews, Shipbuilder*, 1912. Reprint Riverside Connecticut 7Cs Press Inc, 1973.

BYRON, Joseph & BARAGWANATH, Albert K., *New York Life at the Turn of the Century in Photographs*, Dover Publications Inc., New York, 1985, in co-operation with the Museum of the City of New York.

BYRON, Joseph & LANCASTER, Clay, *New York Interiors at the Turn of the Century*, Dover Publications Inc., New York, 1976.

EATON, John P. & MASS, Charles A., *A Falling Star – Misadventures of White Star Ships*, Patrick Stephens, 1989.

EATON, John P. & MASS, Charles A., *Titanic – Triumph & Tragedy. A Chronicle in Words and Pictures* , Patrick Stephens, 1989.

EATON, John P., 'Edward J. Smith, A captain's career', *Voyage*, magazine of the Titanic International, USA, July 1989.

GALLAGHER, Matthew, 'Murdoch of the Titanic', *The Scots Magazine* Vol.137 No.1, April 1992.

GRAFTON, John, *New York in the 19th Century*, Dover Publications Inc., New York, 1977/80.

GRAY, Christopher, *Changing New York, The Architectural Scene*, Dover Publications Inc., New York, 1992.

HAWS, Duncan, *Merchant Fleets, White Star Line (Ocean Steam Navigation Company)*, ICL Publications, 1990.

HUTCHINGS, David, *RMS Titanic, 75 Years of Legend*, Kingfisher Publications, 1987.

JOHNSON, Harry & LIGHTFOOT, Frederick S., *Maritime New York in 19th Century Photographs*, Dover Publications Inc., New York, 1980.

JENNINGS, Philip S. & BOSEK, Dany, *Shipwrecks*, Bison Books, 1992.

LIGHTOLLER, C. H.,*Titanic and Other Ships*, Ivor Nicholson & Watson, 1935.

LORD, Walter, *A Night to Remember*, Henry Holt & Co., New York, 1955.

LYNCH, Don & MARSCHALL, Ken, *Titanic. An Illustrated History*, Hodder & Stoughton Madison Press, 1992.

McLEAN, W. & SHACKLETON, E. H., *O.H.M.S.*, Simpkin Marshall, 1900.

OLDFIELD, Pamela, *Turn of the Tide*, Century, 1988.

OLDHAM, Wilton J., *The Ismay Line*, Charles Birchall & Sons, 1961.

PLADDYS, John, 'The captain's daughter, Helen Melville Russell-Cooke "Mel" 1898-1973', *The Titanic Commutator*, August-October 1993.

PRICE, Eugenia, *The Savannah Quartet*, Collins, circa 1980s.

ROSEBROCK, Ellen Fletcher & GILLON, Jnr., Edmund V., *South Street*, Dover Publications Inc., New York, 1977.

STENSON, Patric, *Lights. The Odyssey of C. H. Lightoller*, The Bodley Head, 1984.

STEWARD, D. M., *Through the Suez Canal*, Beale, 1926.

WALKER, Brian & HINCHLIFFE, Ann, *In Our Liverpool Home*, Blackstaff Press, 1978.

WARRILOW, E. D. D., *History of Etruria*, Etruscan publications, 1953.

WEDGWOOD, Barbara & Hensleigh, *The Wedgwood Circle 1730-1897*, Studio Vista, 1980.

WEIDMAN, Bette S. & MARTIN, Linda B., *Nassau County Long Island in Early Photographs 1869-1940*, Dover Publications Inc., New York, 1981.

WHITE STAR LINE OFFICIAL GUIDE, 1877, Sea Breezes Publication, 1989.

YOUNG, Gavin, 'The quest for Queequeg', *Observer*, 17.1.1993.

Loss of the Steamship Titanic, HMSO., July 1912.

'Titanic Disaster. Report of the Committee on Commerce', US Senate, Washington, Government Printing Office, May 1912.

Excerpts from various New York newspapers including the *New York Times* and the *New York Herald*.

Excerpts from various Staffordshire and Cheshire Journals and newspapers, including the *Staffordshire Magazine* and the *Staffordshire Sentinel*, the *Earlestown Guardian* and the *Warrington Examiner*.

Excerpts from *Evergreen* magazines.

The Atlantic Daily Bulletin, Brian Ticehurst, Ed., journal of the British Titanic Society, 1 Mardon Close, Swaythling, Southampton SO18 2HP, England.

The Titanic Commutator, Edward S. Kamuda, Ed., journal of the Titanic Historical Society, Inc. Post Office Box 51053, Indian Orchard, Massachusetts 01151-0053, USA.

INSTITUTIONS

Aylesbury Reference Library
G. W. Blunt White Library, Mystic Seaport Museum, Massachusets,
    (Curator: Douglas L. Stein)
Charlie Chester Sunday evening radio programme
Cheshire Record Office, Chester
District Registrar, Hanley (Mrs D. R. Gould)
Etruscan Bone & Flint Mill, Hanley (Archie Johnson and Hedley Perry)
Georgia Historical Society (for Gordon Family Papers)
Greenwich Maritime Museum (particularly Elizabeth Wiggins and Brian
    Thynne)
Hanley Reference Library
Heritage Services, Wigan (Nicholas Webb)
Illustrated London News archives
The Ironbridge Gorge Museum and Library
Keele University Library
Lancashire Record Office, Preston
Liverpool Record Office
Memorial University of Newfoundland (Roberta Thomas and Mary Bridson)
Museum of the City of New York
National Army Museum, Chelsea
Paris, Smith & Randall (Public Notary), Southampton
Public Record Offices at Kew, St Catherine's House and Chancery Lane
The Savannah Historical Society
The Savannah Area Convention & Visitors' Bureau
South Wales Evening Post, Swansea
Southampton Reference Library
Southampton Maritime Museum (Alastair Forsyth)
The Staffordshire Sentinel, Stoke-on-Trent
The Wedgwood Museum, Wedgwood, Staffs (Gaye Blake Roberts and Lynn
    Miller)